W9-DHY-678

HARRY KEOGH

NECROSCOPE

AND OTHER

WEIRD HEROES!

TOR BOOKS BY BRIAN LUMLEY

Brian Lumley Companion

THE NECROSCOPE SERIES

Necroscope
Necroscope II: Vamphyri!
Necroscope III: The Source
Necroscope IV: Deadspeak
Necroscope V: Deadspawn
Blood Brothers
The Last Aerie
Bloodwars
Necroscope: The Lost Years
Necroscope: Resurgence
Necroscope: Invaders
Necroscope: Defilers
Necroscope: Avengers
Harry Keogh: Necroscope and Other Weird Heroes!

THE TITUS CROW SERIES

Titus Crow, Volume One: The Burrowers Beneath & Transition
Titus Crow, Volume Two: The Clock of Dreams & Spawn of the Winds
Titus Crow, Volume Three: In the Moons of Borea & Elysia

THE PSYCHOMECH TRILOGY

Psychomech
Psychosphere
Psychamok

OTHER NOVELS

Demogorgon
The House of Doors
Maze of Worlds

SHORT STORY COLLECTIONS

Beneath the Moors and Darker Places
Fruiting Bodies and Other Fungi
The Whisperer and Other Voices

THE DREAMLAND SERIES

Hero of Dreams
Ship of Dreams
Mad Moon of Dreams
Iced on Aran

HARRY KEOGH

NECROSCOPE

AND *OTHER*

WEIRD HEROES!

BRIAN LUMLEY

 A TOM DOHERTY ASSOCIATES BOOK

TOR® NEW YORK

HARRY KEOGH: NECROSCOPE AND OTHER WEIRD HEROES!

This collection and introduction, copyright © Brian Lumley, 2003. "Inception" and "Lord of
the Worms," copyright © Brian Lumley, 1987, first published in *The Compleat Crow* by W.
Paul Ganley 1987. "Name and Number," copyright © Brian Lumley, 1982, first published in
Kadath, July 1982, edited/published by Francesco Cova. "The Weird Wines of Naxas Niss" and
"The Stealer of Dreams," copyright © Brian Lumley, 1991 and 1992 respectively, first published in *Weirdbook Magazine*, numbers 26 and 27, edited/published by W. Paul Ganely. The
three Necroscope stories "Dead Eddy," "Dinosaur Dreams," and "Resurrection" are new to this
volume, copyright © Brian Lumley, 2003.

This book is printed on acid-free paper.

A Tor Book
Published by Tom Doherty Associates, LLC
175 Fifth Avenue
New York, NY 10010

www.tor.com

Tor® is a registered trademark of Tom Doherty Associates, LLC.

Library of Congress Cataloging-in-Publication Data

Lumley, Brian.
    Harry Keogh : necroscope and other weird heroes! / Brian Lumley.—1st ed.
        p.   cm.
    "A Tom Doherty Associates book."
    ISBN 0-765-30847-9 (alk. paper)
    1. Keogh, Harry (Fictitious character)—Fiction.   2. Crow, Titus (Fictitious
character)—Fiction.   3. Fantasy fiction, English.   4. Horror tales, English.
5. Vampires—Fiction.   I. Title.

PR6062.U45H37   2003
823'.914—dc21

2003042619

First Edition: July 2003

Printed in the United States of America

0   9   8   7   6   5   4   3   2   1

FOR TOM DOHERTY,
WHO WOULDN'T LET IT REST

CONTENTS

INTRODUCTION

Over the years I've written quite a few more than just three or four weird heroes into my horror, fantasy, and science fiction. Let's face it, most stories or novels in the triple genres have at least one such. Robert E. Howard created an entire galaxy of them, mostly eclipsed by Conan; Jack Vance's *Dying Earth* novels had perhaps the weirdest, best loved of all weird heroes, Cugel the Clever; even H. P. Lovecraft—the Old Gent of Providence, Rhode Island, who wasn't especially known for tales of derring-do—had his main man, despite that Randolph Carter came close to fainting on more than one occasion. However:

It isn't that the heroes presented here are necessarily my favorites from my own books (they're *all* pretty much my favorites . . . how does one separate out a favorite child?). But it is that these stories are either brand-new, or they've not hitherto seen mass market publication in America. The Dreamland tales weren't included in the *Hero of Dreams* series because they were relatively new when that quartet was published and wouldn't fit into the collection of short stories and novelettes titled *Iced on Aran.* But they fit perfectly well here. The Titus Crow stories—including his origin and his first encounter with satanic forces—were only available in a handsome small-press book and in a paperback collection in the United Kingdom. There are several more Titus Crow tales, but the ones presented here *are* my favorites, at least of this weird hero's exploits.

Then we get to Harry Keogh, the eponymous Necroscope.

Not so long ago, during a transatlantic telephone conversation with my American friend and publisher, Tom Doherty, the subject of the Necroscope surfaced when Tom mentioned *The Lost Years,* a pair of prequels I had written to cover what seemed a protracted period of inactivity in Harry Keogh's life. But Tom had noticed, like a good many others before him, a gaping hole in the chronology. There was plenty of time which I hadn't yet accounted for. Hadn't the Necroscope done anything during that period between *The Lost Years* and *The Source?*

Well, that set the wheels turning. I still had a few notes lying about from years ago, when I'd been working on the books in the series: this or that paragraph, hand-written on a scrap of paper, literally a few, mainly undecipherable words; eleven typed but coffee-stained, creased-up pages; a short incomplete Keogh episode or adventure that hadn't wanted to fit in at the time . . . that sort of thing. And I remembered all of the short stories I'd worked into the longer novels. Like Wratha's story in *Blood Brothers,* and poor little Cynthia's tale, in *The Last Aerie.* And I saw that indeed there was no reason why the Necroscope had to be written large; Harry could as well put in appearances in short stories and novelettes as in inch-and-a-half-thick blockbuster novels. And Tom Doherty was right: there was indeed this gap in the chronology.

So let's cut a long story short. The bits and pieces came together in two novelettes, *Dead Eddy* and *Dinosaur Dreams,* and the eleven coffee-stained pages were rewritten, expanded, and typed up into the short episode set on Starside in the vampire world. (The reason why *Resurrection* didn't appear in *Deadspawn,* which was to have been its original destination, is that at the time, thirteen years ago, I thought it was too like a dark episode toward the end of *The Source.* I can't think why I thought that, because now I see that the two tales are entirely different.)

One last thing. Harry Keogh, like many another weird hero whose exploits we've followed, was a hell of a vampire fighter. As the stories in this volume attest, however, the Necroscope's battles weren't restricted to the undead; he frequently had to deal with the alive and viciously kicking, too.

Whatever your tastes—alive, dead, or undead—the people and creatures in the stories that you'll read here are all fictitious. Of course they are, but let's not forget: there really are monsters out there, very real, very terrible monsters, and the ones we need to be most concerned about are those who apparently *don't care* if they're alive or dead!

And oddly enough—or perhaps not, considering what happened in New York—neither do I. . . .

—Brian Lumley
Torquay, Devon, England
MARCH 2002

TITUS CROW

INCEPTION

December 1916. One week before Christmas.

London, in the vicinity of Wapping, an hour before dawn . . .

Mist-shrouded facades of warehouses formed square, stony faces, bleakly foreboding with their blind eyes of boarded windows; Dickensian still, the cobbled riverside streets rang to the frantic clatter of madly racing footsteps. Except for the figure of a man, flying, his coat flapping like broken wings, nothing stirred. Just him . . . and his *pursuer*: a second male figure, tall, utterly silent, flowing like a fog-spawned wraith not one hundred yards behind.

As to who these two were: their names do not matter. Suffice to say that they were of completely opposite poles, and that the one who feared and ran so noisily was a good man and entirely human, because of which he'd been foolish . . .

And so he fled, that merely human being, clamorously, with pounding heart, tearing the mist like cobwebs in a tunnel and leaving a yawning hole behind; and his inexorable pursuer flowing forward through that hole, with never the sound of a footfall, made more terrible *because* of his soundlessness.

London, and the fugitive had thought he would be safe here. Panting, he skidded to a halt where a shaft of light lanced smokily down from a high window and made the cobbles shiny bright. In a black doorway a broken derelict sprawled like a fallen scarecrow, moaned about the night's chill and clutched his empty bottle. Coarse laughter came from above, the chink of glasses and a low-muttered, lewd suggestion. Again the laughter, a woman's, thick with lust.

No refuge here, where the air itself seemed steeped in decay and in-grown vice—but at least there was the light, and humanity too, albeit dregs.

The fugitive hugged the wall, fused with it and became one with the shadows, gratefully gulped at the sodden, reeking river air and looked back the way he had come. And there at the other end of the street, silhouetted against a rolling bank of mist from the river, motionless now and yet full of an awesome kinetic energy, like the still waters of a dam before the gates are opened—

The guttural laughter came again from above, causing the fleeing man to start. Shadow figures moved ganglingly, apishly together in the beam of light falling on the street, began tearing at each other's clothing. Abruptly the light was switched off, the window slammed shut, and the night and the mist closed in. And along the street the silent pursuer once more took up the chase.

With his strength renewed a little but knowing he was tiring rapidly now, the fugitive pushed himself free of the wall and began to run again, forcing his legs to pump and his lungs to suck and his heart to pound as desperately as before. But he was almost home, almost safe. Sanctuary lay just around the next corner.

"London" . . . "Home" . . . "Sanctuary." Words once full of meaning, but in his present situation almost meaningless. Could anywhere be safe ever again? Cairo should have been, but instead, with the European war spilling over into the Middle East, it had been fraught. Paris had been worse: a seething cauldron on the boil and about to explode shatteringly. And in Tunisia . . . In Tunisia the troubles had seemed endless, where the French fought a guerrilla war on all sides, not least with the Sahara's Sanusi.

The Sanusi, yes—and it was from the secret desert temple of an ancient Sanusi sect that the fugitive had stolen the Elixir. That had been his folly—it was *why* he was a fugitive.

Halfway round the world and back their Priest of the Undying Dead had chased him, drawing ever closer, and here in London it seemed that at last the chase was at an end. He could run no further. It was finished. His only chance was the sanctuary, that secret place remembered from the penniless, friendless childhood of a waif. It had been more than thirty years ago, true, but still he remembered it clearly. And if a long-forsaken God had not turned from him entirely . . .

Wrapped in mist he rounded the corner, came out of the mazy streets and onto the river's shoulder. The Thames with all its stenches, its poisons, its teeming rats and endless sewage—and its sanctuary. Nothing had changed, all was exactly as he remembered it. Even the mist was his friend now, for it cloaked him and turned him an anonymous gray, and he knew that from here on he could find his way blindfolded. Indeed he might as well be blind, the way the milky mist rolled up and swallowed him.

With hope renewed he plunged on across the last deserted street lying parallel to the river, found the high stone wall he knew would be there, followed it north for fifty yards to where spiked iron palings guarded its topmost tier against unwary climbers. For immediately beyond that wall at this spot the river flowed sluggish and deep and the wall was sheer, so that a man might easily drown if he should slip and fall. But the fugitive did not intend to fall; he was still as agile as the boy he'd once been, except that now he also had a grown man's strength.

Without pause he jumped, easily caught the top of the wall, at once transferred his grip to the ironwork. He drew himself up, in a moment straddled the treacherous spikes, swung over and slid down the palings on the other side. And now—now, dear God—only keep the pursuer at bay; only let him stay back there in the mist, out of sight, and not come surging forward with his rotten eyes aglow and his crumbling nose sniffing like that of some great dead nightmare hound!

And now too let memory stay sharp and serve the fugitive well, let it not fail him for a single moment, and let everything continue to be as it had been. For if anything had changed beyond that ancient, slimy wall . . .

. . . But it had not!

For here, remembered of old, was his marker—the base of a lone paling, bent to one side, like a single idle soldier in a perfect rank—where if he swung his feet a little to the left, in empty space above the darkly gurgling river—

—His left foot made contact with a stone sill, at which he couldn't suppress the smallest cry of relief. Then, clinging to the railings with one hand, he tremblingly reached down the other to find and grip an arch of stone; and releasing his grip on the railings entirely, he drew himself down and into the hidden embrasure in the river's wall. For this was the entrance to his sanctuary.

But no time to pause and thank whichever lucky stars still shone on him; no, for back there in the roiling mist the pursuer was following still, unerringly tracking him, he was sure. Or tracking the Elixir?

Today, for the first time, that idea had dawned on him. It had come as he walked the chill December streets, when patting his overcoat's inside pocket, for a moment he had thought the vial lost. Oh, and how he'd panicked then! But in a shop doorway where his hands trembled violently, finally he'd found the tiny glass bottle where it had fallen through a hole into the lining of his coat, and then in the gray light of wintry, war-depleted London streets, he had gazed at it—and at its contents.

The Elixir—which might as well be water! A few drops of crystal-clear water, yes, that was how it appeared. But if you held it up to the light in a certain way . . .

The fugitive started, held his breath, stilled his thoughts and brought his fleeting mind back to the present, the Now. Was that a sound from the street above? The faintest echo of a footfall on the cobbles three or four feet overhead?

He crouched there in the dark embrasure, waited, listened with terror-sensitized ears—heard only the pounding of his own heart, his own blood singing in his ears. He had paused here too long, had ignored the Doom hanging over his immortal soul to favor the entirely mortal fatigue of bone and muscle. But now, once more, he forced himself to move. Some rubble blocked the way—blocks of stone, fallen from the low ceiling, perhaps—but he crawled over it, his back brushing the damp stonework overhead. Small furry rodents squealed and fled past him toward the faint light of the entrance, tumbling into the river with tiny splashes. The ceiling dripped with moisture, where nitre stained the walls in faintly luminous patches.

And when at last the fugitive had groped his way well back along the throat of the passage, only then dared he fumble out a match and strike it to flame.

The shadows fled at once; he crouched and peered all about, then sighed and breathed easier; all was unchanged, the years flown between then and now had altered nothing. This was "his" place, his secret place, where he'd come as a boy to escape the drunken wrath of a brutish stepfather. Well, that old swine was dead now, pickled in cheap liquor and undeservingly buried in the grounds of a nearby church. Good luck to him! But the sanctuary remained.

The match burned down, its flame touching the fugitive's fingers. He dropped it, swiftly struck another, pushed on along the subterranean passage.

Under a ceiling less than five feet high and arched with ancient stone, he must keep his back bowed; at his elbows the walls gave him six inches to spare on both sides. But while he could go faster now, still he must go quietly for a while yet. The follower had tracked him halfway round the world, tracked him supernaturally. And who could say but that he might track him here too?

Again he paused, scratched at the stubble on his chin, wondered about the Elixir. Oh, that was what his pursuer wanted, sure enough—but it was not *all* he wanted. No, for his chief objective was the life of the thief! A thief, yes, which was what he had been all of his miserable life. At first a petty thief, then a burglar of some skill and daring (and eventually of some renown, which in the end had forced him abroad), finally a looter of foreign tombs and temples.

Tombs and temples . . .

Again he thought of the Elixir, that tiny vial in his pocket. If only he had known then . . . but he had not known. He had thought those damned black Sanusi wizards kept treasure in that dune-hidden place, the tribal treasures of their ancestors; or at least, so he'd been informed by Erik Kuphnas in Tunis. Kuphnas, the dog, himself one of the world's foremost experts in the occult. "Ah!" he had said, "but they also keep the Elixir there—which is all that interests me. Go there, enter, steal! Keep what you will, but only bring me the Elixir. And never work again, my friend, for that's how well I'll pay you . . ."

And he had done it! All of his skill went into it, and a deal of luck, too—and for what? No treasure at all, and only the tiny vial in his pocket to show for his trouble. And *what* trouble! Even now he shuddered, thinking back on those corpse-laden catacombs under the desert.

Straight back to Tunis he'd taken the vial, to Erik Kuphnas where he waited. And: "Do you have it?" The black magician had been frantically eager.

"I might have it." The fugitive had been tantalizingly noncommittal. "I might even sell it—if only I knew what it was. But the truth this time, Erik, for I've had it with lies and tales of priceless treasure."

And Kuphnas had at once answered:

"No use, that vial, to you. No use to anyone who is not utterly pure and completely innocent."

"Oh? And are you those things?"

How Kuphnas had glared at him then. "No," he had answered slowly. "I am not—but neither am I a fool. I would use it carefully, sparingly, and so dilute as to be almost totally leached of its power. At first, anyway—until I knew what I was dealing with. As to what it is: no man knows that, except perhaps a certain Sanusi wizard. The legends have it that he was a chief three hundred years ago—and that now he's high priest of the cult of the Undying Dead!"

"What?" the fugitive had snorted and laughed. "*What?* And you believe such mumbo-jumbo, such utter rubbish?" Then his voice had hardened. "Now for the last time, tell me: *What is it?*"

At that Kuphnas had jumped up, strode to and fro across the fine rugs of his study. "Fool!" he'd snarled, glaring as before. "How may any mere man of the twentieth century 'know' what it is? It's the essence of mandrake, the sweat on the upper lip of a three-day corpse, six gray grains of Ibn Ghazi's powder. It's the humor of a zombie's iris, the mist rising up from the Pool of All Knowledge, the pollen-laden breath of a black lotus. Man, I don't 'know' what it is! But I know something of what it can do . . ."

"I'm still listening," the fugitive had pressed.

"To one who is pure, innocent, unblemished, the Elixir is a crystal ball, a shewstone, an oracle. A single drop will make such a man—how shall we say?—AWARE!"

"Aware?"

"Yes, but when you say it, say and think it in capitals—AWARE!"

"Ah! It's a drug—it will heighten a man's senses."

"Rather, his perceptions—if you will admit the difference. And it is *not* a drug. It is the Elixir."

"Would you recognize it?"

"Instantly!"

"And what will you pay for it?"

"If it's the real thing—fifty thousand of your pounds!"

"Cash?" (Suddenly the fugitive's throat had become very dry.)

"Ten thousand now, the rest tomorrow morning."

And then the fugitive had held out his hand and opened it. There in his palm had lain the vial, a tiny stopper firmly in its neck.

Kuphnas had taken it from him into hands that shook, held it up eagerly to the light from his window. And the vial had lit up at once in a golden glow, as if the occultist had captured a small part of the sun itself! And: "Yes!" he had hissed then. "Yes, this is the Elixir!"

At that the fugitive had snatched it back, held out his hand again. "My ten thousand—on account," he'd said. "Also, we'll need an eyedropper."

Kuphnas had fetched the money, asked: "And what is this about an eyedropper?"

"But isn't it obvious? You have given me one-fifth of my money, and I will give you one-fifth of the Elixir. Three drops, as I reckon it. And the rest tomorrow, when I'm paid."

Kuphnas had protested, but the fugitive would not be swayed. He gave him three drops, no more. And five minutes later when he left him, already the occultist had been calculating the degree of dilution required for his first experiment. His first, and very likely *only*, experiment. Certainly his last.

For when, with the dawn the fugitive had returned and passed into Kuphnas' high-walled courtyard and up the fig-shaded marble steps to his apartments, he had found the exterior louvre doors open; likewise the Moorishly ornate iron lattice beyond them; and in Kuphnas' study itself—

There on the table, effulgent in the first bright beams of day, a bowl of what appeared to be simple water—and the empty eyedropper beside it. But of Erik Kuphnas and the fugitive's forty thousand pounds, no sign at all. And then, in the corner of the occultist's study, tossed down there and crumpled in upon itself, he had spied what seemed to be a piece of old leather or perhaps a large canvas sack; except it was the general *shape* of the thing that attracted the fugitive's attention. That and the question of what it was doing here in these sumptuous apartments. Only when he moved closer had he seen what it really was: that it had hair and dead, glassy, staring orblike eyes—Kuphnas' eyes—still glaring a strange composite glare of shock, horror, and permanently frozen malignance!

Innocence and purity, indeed!

That had been enough for the fugitive: he had fled at once, with nightmares gibbering on his heels, and with something else there, too. For to his knowledge that was when he had first become the fugitive, since then he had always been on the move, always running.

Nor could he scoff any longer at the idea of an undead guardian of that Sanusi temple he'd robbed; for indeed the thing which had followed him, drawing closer every day, and certainly closer with each passing night, was not alive as men understood that word. Oh, he'd seen it often enough—its burning eyes and crumbling features—in various corners of the world, and now here in London finally it had tracked him down, forced him to earth . . .

His eyes had grown accustomed to the tunnel's darkness now, where the nitrous walls with their foxfire luminosity sufficed however faintly to light his way, so that matches were no longer required. A good thing, too, for his box was severely depleted. But he had come perhaps, oh, 150 yards along this ancient passage from the river, and knew that it would soon open out into a series of high-vaulted cellars. There would be stone steps leading up, and at their top a dark oak door standing open. Beyond that a high-walled, echoing room—five-sided, containing round its walls five wooden benches, and at its center a pedestal bearing a stone bowl—would wait within a greater hall which, for all that it remained unseen, the fugitive had always known must be vast. And here a second oaken door would be locked, permitting no further exploration. Or at least, the door had always been locked when he was a boy.

As to what the place was: he had never known for sure, but had often guessed. A library, perhaps, long disused; or some forgotten factory once powered by the river? And the tunnel would have served as an exit route for refuse, with the tidal Thames as the agent of dispersal. Whichever, to him it had always been a refuge, a sanctuary. And now it must play that role again, at least until the dawn. His pursuer was least active in daylight, so that with luck he should make a clean getaway for parts further afield. Meanwhile—

He was into the vaults now, where ribbed stone ceilings rose to massy keystone centers; and there, beyond this junction of bare subterrene rooms, he recognized at once the old stone steps rising into gloom. Crossing echoing flags to climb those steps, at last he arrived at the door and shouldered it open on hinges which had not known oil for many a year. And as the squealing reverberations died away, so he gazed again into that dusty, cobwebbed pentagon of carved stonework, whose walls partitioned it off from the unseen, but definitely *sensed*, far greater hall of which it must be the merest niche.

The light was better here, still faint and confused by dust and ropes of gray cobwebs, but oh so gradually gathering strength as night crept toward day. And there were the benches where often the fugitive had lain through long, lonely nights; and there, too, central in the room, the pedestal and its bowl, but draped now with a white cloth; and over there, set in the farthest of the five walls, the second oaken door . . . *ajar*!

Hands shaking so badly he could scarce control them, the fugitive struck another match and held it high, driving back the shadows. And there on the stone flags of the floor—footprints other than his own! Fresh prints in the dust of—how many years? The clean sheet, too, draped across the stone basin . . . what did these things mean?

The fugitive crossed to the basin, turned back a corner of the sheet. Fresh water in the bowl, its surface softly gleaming. He scooped up a little in his hand, sniffed at it, finally drank and slaked his burning thirst.

And as he turned from the pedestal, he almost collided with a slender, polished wooden pole set in a circular base, whose top branched over the basin. Shaped like a narrow gallows, still the thing was in no way sinister; depending from its bar on a chain of bronze, a burnished hook hung overhead.

The fugitive began to understand where he was, and knew now how to prove his location beyond any further doubt. Quickly he went to the door where it stood ajar, eased it open and stepped through. And then he knew that he was right, knew what this place was and wondered if he really had any right being here. Probably not.

But in any case he could not stay; the dawn would soon be breaking, when once more he would be safe; he had far, far to go before night fell again. He reentered the five-sided room, crossed its floor, paused at the pedestal and bowl to adjust the sheet where he'd disturbed it. And that was when the idea came to him and fixed itself in his mind.

He took out the vial and held it up in the gloom, and feeble though the light was, still the Elixir gathered to itself a faintly roseate glow. Was this really what the follower sought? Was this truly the purpose of the pursuit? Yes, it must be so. And *which* was that worm-ravaged ghoul compelled to track: flesh-and-blood thief, or the object of his thievery? Could the creature be thrown off the trail? And in any case, what good to anyone was the Elixir now?

A good many questions, and the fugitive knew the answers to none of them, not for certain. But there might be a way to find out.

Again, quickly, he turned back the corner of the sheet, unstoppered the tiny bottle, held his face well away and poured the contents out into the stone bowl. Glancing from the corner of his eye, he saw a faint glimmer of gold passing like a stray beam of sunlight over the surface of the water, watched it fade as those smallest of ripples grew still.

There, it was done. He sighed, stoppered the vial, replaced it in his pocket and moved on.

Back through the door at the top of the steps he went, and down those steps to the vault, and so once more to the claustrophobic passage under the earth. Dawn must be mere minutes away; surely by now the pursuer had given up the chase, hidden himself away for the day to come. With his footsteps ringing in his ears, so the fugitive retraced his steps, clambered over the fallen debris close to the entrance, finally stuck his head out of the embrasure in the wall and gazed out over the river.

Not quite dawn yet, no, but there on a distant horizon, on gray roofs, a pinkish stain which heralded the rising sun; and already the mist settling back to the river, where it curled like a thick topping of ethereal cream. There was a riming of frost on the stonework now, perhaps the first of winter, but the fugitive ignored the cold as he put up a groping hand to blindly discover and clutch an iron paling. Then, without pause, he swung himself out of the embrasure and began to climb—

—Only to freeze in that position as irresistible fingers grasped his wrists and drew him effortlessly up!

The pursuer! There beyond the palings, clinging like a great black leech to the wall! And when their faces were level, when only the iron palings separated them—how the fugitive would have screamed then. But he could not; for transferring both of his trapped wrists to one black and leathery and impossibly powerful claw, the pursuer had shoved his free hand between the bars and *into* his forehead!

The fugitive knew what was happening. He could feel this monstrous undead creature's fingers groping in his brain, fumbling among all his secrets. Also, he knew he was a dead man. The black zombie's fingers had gone into his head effortlessly, flowing into flesh and bone and painlessly mingling—but they need not necessarily come out the same way. And it could be just as slow as the monster wished it. What was that for a way to die?

Hope does not always spring eternal—not when you gaze into eyes like coals under a bellows, worn by a creature spawned in hell.

The fugitive filled his mouth and spat straight into those blazing eyes.

The fingers at once shifted their position in his head, solidified, were withdrawn through his eyes, taking the eyeballs with them. Blood and brains spouted in twin jets. Still clinging to the palings like a leech, the thing jerked the fugitive's head up and quickly back down, impaling it on one of the spikes. His arms and legs flew outward, jerked spastically, fell back loosely. And he twitched. Not life but death.

The cursed thing sniffed his corpse with tattered nostrils, found nothing. It plucked him from the palings and tossed him down. The mist parted for a moment as he struck the water, then rolled back and eddied as before . . .

Dawn was only a minute or two away and the dead thing knew it. He also knew where the fugitive had been, or at least where he had come from. Like treacle his body dissolved and flowed through the bars on top of the wall, and down into the embrasure where he quickly reassembled.

And following the fugitive's old route, the monster flowed forward in darkness, along the passage to the vaults, through them to the upward-leading steps.

Here the thing paused as it felt the first waves of some unknown force, the presence of a Power. But dawn was coming, and the Elixir remained to be found. It flowed forward up the steps, flowed like smoke through the open door and into the five-sided room—and paused again.

Yes, the Elixir was here. Somewhere. *Here!* But something else was here too. The Power was stronger, unbearably strong . . .

Moora Dunda Sanusi crossed the floor to the second door, leaving no footprints. But at the door he paused a third time before something which angered him to a frenzy of hate, something he could not see, something in the air and in the stone and filling the very ether. And in that same instant the sun's first rays struck on high dusty windows and penetrated them, falling in splintered beams within—beams with all the colors of the rainbow!

Dawn and the light it brought increased the unseen Power tenfold. Moora Dunda Sanusi's magic began to fail him. Unwanted solidity returned and gave him weight, and faint prints began to show in the dust where he staggered backward, driven back into the five-sided room and across its stone paving. He reeled against the pedestal and displaced the bowl's sheet, and a flailing hand fell for a moment into the gleaming water.

Agony! Impossible agony! The thing which Dunda was should feel no pain for it had no life as such—and yet there was pain. And Moora Dunda Sanusi knew that pain at once, and knew its source—the Elixir. The Elixir, yes, but no longer contained, no longer safe.

The thing snatched its mummied claw from the water, reeled toward the steps which led down into darkness and safety. But the place was sanctuary no longer. Not for such as Moora Dunda Sanusi, dead for more than 270 years. Striking from above through many high-arched, stained-glass windows, the sun's rays formed a fiery lattice of lances, stabbing down into the five-sided room and converging on the undead thing, consuming it even as the Elixir consumed its arm.

Clutching that melting member to him, the zombie crumpled in reeking silence to the flags, foul smoke billowing outward and bearing his substance away. In a moment the fires in his eyes flickered low, and in the next blinked out, extinguished. The final, solitary sound he made was a sigh of great peace long overdue, and then he was gone.

A breeze, blowing in under the doors of the ancient church, scattered what was left and blended it with the dust of decades.

THE SUN CAME UP and London's mists dispersed. Dawn grew into a bright December day.

A local vicar, hurrying along the riverside streets, paused to glance at his watch: 10:00 A.M.—they would be waiting. He made his legs go faster, clucked his tongue against his teeth in annoyance. It was all so irregular. *Very* irregular, but hardly improper. And of course the family were well-known church benefactors. And maybe it wasn't so irregular after all; for all of the line's children *had* been christened in the old church for several centuries now. A matter of tradition, really . . .

Turning a corner away from the river, the vicar came in view of the church, saw its steeple rising against the sky, where many slates were loose or missing altogether; its beautiful windows, some broken, but all doomed now to demolition, along with the rest of the fine old structure. And they called this progress! But it was still consecrated, still holy, still a proper house of God. For a few weeks more, anyway.

He saw, too, his verger, sneaking along the street with his collar up, coming away from the church, and the vicar nodded grimly to himself. *Oh, yes?* But he'd told him to see to the old place a full week ago, and not leave it until the last minute.

Approaching, finally the verger saw him, saw too that he was identified. His frown turned to a smile in a moment; he came directly forward, beaming at the vicar. "Ah, Vicar! All's prepared; I've spent the better part of two whole hours in there! But the dust and cobwebs—incredible! I *did* come round earlier in the week, but such a lot to do that—"

"All is understood." The vicar nodded, holding up his hand. And: "Are they waiting?"

"Indeed they are—just arrived. I told them you'd be along directly."

"I'm sure you did." The vicar nodded again. "Well, I'd best be seeing to it, then."

A moment later the churchyard was in view, and there up the path between old headstones, just inside the arched, impressive entrance, where the massive doors stood open, the couple themselves and a handful of friends. They saw the vicar hurrying, came to greet him; the normal pleasantries were exchanged; the party entered the towering old building. The vicar had brought the books with him and all preliminaries and signatures and countersignatures were quickly completed; the little ceremony commenced without a hitch.

Finally the vicar took the crucifix from around his neck and hung it from the hook over the font, held out his arms for the child. He'd done it all a thousand times before, so that it was difficult these days to get any real meaning into the words; but of course they had meaning anyway, and in any case he tried.

And at last all was done. The vicar dipped his hand into the water, sprinkled droplets, made the sign—and the church seemed to hold its breath...

But only for an instant.

Then the five-sided room came alive in a glow like burnished gold (the sun, of course, moving out from behind a cloud, burning on the old windows), and smiling, the vicar passed the child in his christening gown to his father.

"So there we have you," said the proud, handsome man, his voice deep and strong; and he showed the child to his mother.

A rose of a woman, she gazed with love on the infant, kissed his brow. "Those eyes," she said, "with so much still to see. And that little mind, with so much still to fill it. Look at his face—see how it glows!"

"It's the light in here," said the vicar. "It turns the skin to roses! Ah, but indeed a beautiful child."

"Oh, he *is*!" said the mother, taking him and holding him up. "He is! So pure, so innocent. Our little Titus. Our little Titus Crow..."

LORD OF
THE WORMS

Twenty-two is the Number of the **Master**! A 22 may only be described in glowing terms, for he is the Great Man. Respected, admired by all who know him, he has the Intellect and the Power and he has the Magic! Aye, he is the Master Magician. But a word of warning: just as there are Day and Night, so are there two sorts of Magic—White, and Black!

—*Grossmann's* Numerology
VIENNA, 1776

I

The war was well over. Christmas 1945 had gone by and the New Year festivities were still simmering, and Titus Crow was out of a job. A young man whose bent for the dark and mysterious side of life had early steeped him in obscure occult and esoteric matters, his work for the War Department had moved in two seemingly unconnected, highly secretive directions. On the one hand he had advised the ministry in respect of certain of *Der Führer's* supernatural interests, and on the other he had used the skills of the numerologist and cryptographer to crack the codes of his goosestepping war machine. In both endeavors there had been a deal of success, but now the thing was finished and Titus Crow's talents were superfluous.

Now he was at a loss how best to employ himself. Not yet known as one of the world's foremost occultists, nor even suspecting the brilliance he was yet to achieve in many diverse fields of study and learning—and yet fully conscious of the fact that there was much to be done and a course to be run—for the moment he felt without a purpose, a feeling not much to his liking. And this after living and working in bomb-ravaged London through the war years, with the fever and stress of that conflict still bottled inside him.

For these reasons he was delighted when Julian Carstairs—the so-called Modern Magus, or Lord of the Worms, an eccentric cult or coven leader—accepted his agreeable response to an advertisement for a young man to undertake a course of secretarial duties at Carstairs' country home, the tenure of the position not to exceed three months. The money seemed good (though that was not of prime importance), and part of the work would consist of cataloging Carstairs' enviable occult library. Other than this the advertisement had not been very specific; but Titus Crow had little doubt but that he would find much of interest in the work and eagerly awaited the day of his first meeting with Carstairs, a man he assumed to be more eccentric than necromantic.

Wednesday, 9 January 1946, was that day, and Crow found the address, The Barrows—a name which immediately conjured mental pictures of tumuli and cromlechs—at the end of a wooded, winding private road not far from the quaint and picturesque town of Haslemere in Surrey. A large, two-story house surrounded by a high stone wall and expansive gardens of dark shrubbery, overgrown paths and gaunt-limbed oaks weighed down with festoons of unchecked ivy, the place stood quite apart from any comparable habitation.

That the house had at one time been a residence of great beauty seemed indisputable; but equally obvious was the fact that recently, possibly due to the hostilities, it had been greatly neglected. And quite apart from this air of neglect and the generally drear appearance of any country property in England during the first few weeks of the year, there was also a gloominess about The Barrows. Something inherent in its grimy upper windows, in the oak-shaded brickwork and shrouding shrubbery, so that Crow's pace grew measured and just a trifle hesitant as he entered the grounds through a creaking iron gate and followed first the drive, then a briar-tangled path to the front door.

And then, seeming to come too close on the heels of Crow's ringing of the bell, there was the sudden opening of the great door and the almost spectral face and figure of Julian Carstairs himself, whose appearance the young applicant saw from the start was not in accordance with his preconceptions. Indeed, such were Carstairs' looks that what little remained of Crow's restrained but ever-present exuberance was immediately extinguished. The man's aspect was positively dismal.

Without introduction, without even offering his hand, Carstairs led him through the gloomy interior to the living room, a room somber with shadows which seemed almost painted into the dark oak paneling. There, switching on lighting so subdued that it did absolutely nothing to dispel the drabness of the place or its fungal taint of dry rot, finally Carstairs introduced himself and bade his visitor be seated. But still he did not offer his hand.

Now, despite the poor light, Crow was able to take in something of the aspect of this man who was to be, however temporarily, his employer; and what he saw was not especially reassuring. Extremely tall and thin almost to the point of emaciation, with a broad forehead, thick dark hair and bushy eyebrows, Carstairs' pallor was one with the house. With sunken cheeks and slightly stooped shoulders, he could have been any age between seventy and eighty-five, perhaps even older. Indeed, there was that aura about him, hinting of a delayed or altered process of aging, which one usually associates with mummies in their museum alcoves.

Looking yet more closely at his face (but guardedly and as unobtrusively as possible), Crow discovered the pocks, cracks and wrinkles of years without number; as if Carstairs had either lived well beyond his time, or had packed far too much into a single lifespan. And again the younger man found himself comparing his host to a sere and dusty mummy.

And yet there was also a wisdom in those dark eyes, which at least redeemed for the moment an otherwise chill and almost alien visage. While Crow could in no wise appreciate the outer shell of the man, he believed that he might yet find virtue in his knowledge, the occult erudition with which it was alleged Carstairs had become endowed through a life of remote travels and obscure delvings. And certainly there was that of the scholar about him, or at least of the passionate devotee.

There was a hidden strength there, too, which seemed to belie the supposed age lines graven in his face and bony hands; and as soon as he commenced to speak, in a voice at once liquid and sonorous, Crow was aware that he was up against a man of great power. After a brief period of apparently haphazard questioning and trivial discourse, Carstairs abruptly asked him the date of his birth. Having spoken he grew silent, his eyes sharp as he watched Crow's reaction and waited for his answer.

Caught off guard for a moment, Crow felt a chill strike him from nowhere, as if a door had suddenly opened on a cold and hostile place; and some sixth sense warned him against all logic that Carstairs' question was fraught with danger, like the muzzle of a loaded pistol placed to his temple. And again illogically, almost without thinking, he supplied a fictitious answer which added four whole years to his actual age:

"Why, second December 1912," he answered with a half-nervous smile. "Why do you ask?"

For a moment Carstairs' eyes were hooded, but then they opened in a beaming if cadaverous smile. He issued a sigh, almost of relief, saying: "I was merely confirming my suspicion, astrologically speaking, that perhaps you were a Saggitarian—which of course you are. You see, the sidereal science is a consuming hobby of mine, as are a great many of the so-called 'abstruse arts.' I take it you are aware of my reputation? That my name is linked with all manner of unspeakable rites and dark practices? That according to at least one daily newspaper I am, or believe myself to be, the very Antichrist?" And he nodded and mockingly smiled. "Of course you are. Well, the truth is far less damning, I assure you. I dabble a little, certainly—mainly to entertain my friends with certain trivial talents, one of which happens to be astrology—but as for necromancy and the like . . . I ask you, Mr. Crow—in this day and age?" And again he offered his skull-like smile.

Before the younger man could make any sort of comment to fill the silence that had fallen over the room, his host spoke again, asking, "And what are your interests, Mr. Crow?"

"My interests? Why, I——" But at the last moment, even as Crow teetered on the point of revealing that he, too, was a student of the esoteric and occult—though a white as opposed to a black magician—so he once more felt that chill as of outer immensities and, shaking himself from a curious lethargy, noticed how large and bright the other's eyes had grown. And at that moment Crow knew how close he had come to falling under Carstairs' spell, which must be a sort of hypnosis. He quickly gathered his wits and feigned a yawn.

"You really must excuse me, sir," he said then, "for my unpardonable boorishness. I don't know what's come over me that I should feel so tired. I fear I was almost asleep just then."

Then, fearing that Carstairs' smile had grown more than a little forced—thwarted, almost—and that his nod was just a fraction too curt, he quickly continued: "My interests are common enough. A little archaeology, paleontology . . ."

"Common, indeed!" answered Carstairs with a snort. "Not so, for such interests show an inquiring nature, albeit for things long passed away. No, no, those are admirable pastimes for such a young man." And he pursed his thin lips and fingered his chin a little before asking:

"But surely, what with the war and all, archaeological work has suffered greatly. Not much of recent interest there?"

"On the contrary," Crow answered at once, "1939 was an exceptional year. The rock art of Hoggar and the excavations at Brek in Syria; the Nigerian Ife bronzes; Bleger's discoveries at Pylos and Wace's at Mycenae; Sir Leonard Woolley and the Hittites . . . myself, I was greatly interested in the Oriental Institute's work at Megiddo in Palestine. That was in '37. Only a bout of ill health held me back from accompanying my father out to the site."

"Ah! Your interest is inherited, then? Well, do not concern yourself that you missed the trip. Megiddo was not especially productive. Our inscrutable Oriental friends might have found more success to the northeast, a mere twenty-five or thirty miles."

"On the shores of Galilee?" Crow was mildly amused at the other's assumed knowledge of one of his pet subjects.

"Indeed," answered Carstairs, his tone bone dry. "The sands of time have buried many interesting towns and cities on the shores of Galilee. But tell me: what are your thoughts on the Lascaux cave paintings, discovered in, er, '38?"

"No, in 1940." Crow's smile disappeared as he suddenly realized he was being tested, that Carstairs' knowledge of archaeology—certainly recent digs and discoveries—was at least the equal of his own. "September 1940. They are without question the work of Cro-Magnon man, some twenty to twenty-five thousand years old."

"Good!" Carstairs beamed again, and Crow suspected that he had passed the test.

Now his gaunt host stood up to tower abnormally tall even over his tall visitor. "Very well, I think you will do nicely, Mr. Crow. Come then, and I'll show you my library. It's there you will spend most of your time, after all, and you'll doubtless be pleased to note that the room has a deal more natural light than the rest of the house. Plenty of windows. Barred windows, for of course many of my books are quite priceless."

Leading the way through gloomy and mazy corridors, he mused: "Of course, the absence of light suits me admirably. I am hemeralopic. You may have noticed how large and dark my eyes are in the gloom? Yes, and that is why there are so few strong electric lights in the house. I hope that does not bother you?"

"Not at all," Crow answered, while in reality he felt utterly hemmed in, taken prisoner by the mustiness of dry rot and endless, stifling corridors.

And you're a rock hound, too, are you?" Carstairs continued. "That is interesting. Did you know that fossil lampshells, of the sort common here in the South, were once believed to be the devil's cast-off toenails?" He laughed a mirthless, baying laugh. "Ah, what it is to live in an age enlightened by science, eh?"

II

Using a key to unlock the library door, he ushered Crow into a large room, then stooped slightly to enter beneath a lintel uncomfortably shallow for a man of his height. "And here we are," he unnecessarily stated, staggering slightly and holding up a hand to ward off the weak light from barred windows. "My eyes," he offered by way of an explanation. "I'm sure you will understand . . ."

Quickly crossing the carpeted floor, he drew shades until the room stood in somber shadows. "The lights are here," he said, pointing to switches on the wall. "You are welcome to use them when I am not present. Very well, Mr. Crow, this is where you are to work. Oh, and by the way: I agree to your request as stated in your letter of introduction, that you be allowed your freedom at weekends. That suits me perfectly well, since weekends are really the only suitable time for our get-togethers—that is to say, when I entertain a few friends.

"During the week, however, you would oblige me by staying here. Behind the curtains in the far wall is a lighted alcove, which I have made comfortable with a bed, a small table and a chair. I assure you that you will not be disturbed. I will respect your privacy—on the understanding, of course, that you will respect mine; with regard to which there are certain house rules, as it were. You are not to have guests or visitors up to the house under any circumstances—The Barrows is forbidden to all outsiders. And the cellar is quite out of bounds. As for the rest of the house: with the sole exception of my study, it is yours to wander or explore as you will—though I suspect you'll have little enough time for that. In any case, the place is quite empty. And that is how I like it.

"You do understand that I can only employ you for three months? Good. You shall be paid monthly, in advance, and to ensure fair play and goodwill on both sides I shall require you to sign a legally binding contract. I do not want you walking out on me with the job only half completed.

"As for the work: that should be simple enough for anyone with the patience of the archaeologist, and I will leave the system entirely up to you. Basically, I require that all my books should be put in order, first by category, then by author, and alphabetically in the various categories. Again, the breakdown will be entirely your concern. All of the work must, however, be cross-referenced; and finally I shall require a complete listing of books by title, and once again alphabetically. Now, are you up to it?"

Crow glanced around the room, at its high shelves and dusty, book-littered tables. Books seemed to be piled everywhere. There must be close to seven or eight thousand volumes here! Three months no longer seemed such a great length of time. On the other hand, from what little he had seen of the titles of some of these tomes . . .

"I am sure," he finally answered, "that my work will be to your complete satisfaction."

"Good!" Carstairs nodded. "Then today being three-quarters done, I suggest we now retire to the dining room for our evening meal, following which you may return here if you so desire and begin to acquaint yourself with my books. Tomorrow, Thursday, you begin your work proper, and I shall only disturb you on those rare occasions when I myself visit the library, or perhaps periodically to see how well or ill you are progressing. Agreed?"

"Agreed," answered Crow, and he once more followed his host and employer out into the house's airless passages.

On their way Carstairs handed him the key to the library door, saying: "You shall need this, I think." And seeing Crow's frown he explained, "The house has attracted several burglars in recent years, hence the bars at most of the windows. If such a thief did get in, you would be perfectly safe locked in the library."

"I can well look after myself, Mr. Carstairs," said Crow.

"I do not doubt it," answered the other, "but my concern is not entirely altruistic. If you remain safe, Mr. Crow, then so do my books." And once again his face cracked open in that hideous smile . . .

THEY ATE AT OPPOSITE ENDS of a long table in a dimly lighted dining room whose gloom was one with the rest of the house. Titus Crow's meal consisted of cold cuts of meat and red wine, and it was very much to his liking; but he did note that Carstairs' plate held different fare, reddish and of a less solid consistency, though the distance between forbade any closer inspection. They ate in silence and when finished Carstairs led the way to the kitchen, a well-equipped if dingy room with a large, well-stocked larder.

"From now on," Carstairs explained in his sepulchral voice, "you are to prepare your own meals. Eat what you will, everything here is for you. My own needs are slight and I usually eat alone; and of course there are no servants here. I did note, however, that you enjoy wine. Good, so do I. Drink what you will, for there is more than sufficient and my cellar is amply stocked."

"Thank you," Crow answered. "And now, if I may, there are one or two points..."

"By all means."

"I came by car, and—"

"Ah! Your motorcar, yes. Turn left on the drive as you enter through the gate. There you will find a small garage. Its door is open. Better that you leave your car there during the week, or else as winter lengthens the battery is sure to suffer. Now then, is there anything else?"

"Will I need a key?" Crow asked after a moment's thought. "A key to the house, I mean, for use when I go away at weekends?"

"No requirement," Carstairs shook his head. "I shall be here to see you off on Fridays, and to welcome you when you return on Monday mornings."

"Then all would appear to be very satisfactory. I do like fresh air, however, and would appreciate the occasional opportunity to walk in your gardens."

"In my wilderness, do you mean?" and Carstairs gave a throaty chuckle. "The place is so overgrown I should fear to lose you. But have no fear—the door of the house will not be locked during the day. All I would ask is that when I am not here you are careful not to lock yourself out."

"Then that appears to be that," said Crow. "It only remains for me to thank you for the meal—and of course to offer to wash the dishes."

"Not necessary." Again Carstairs shook his head. "On this occasion I shall do it; in future we shall do our own. Now I suggest you garage your car."

He led Crow from the kitchen through gloomy passages to the outer door, and as they went the younger man remembered a sign he had seen affixed to the ivy-grown garden wall. When he mentioned it, Carstairs once more gave his throaty chuckle. "Ah, yes—Beware of the Dog! There is no dog, Mr. Crow. The sign is merely to ensure that my privacy is not disturbed. In fact I hate dogs, and dogs hate me!"

On that note Crow left the house, parked his car in the garage provided, and finally returned to Carstairs' library. By this time his host had gone back to the study or elsewhere and Crow was left quite alone. Entering the library he could not help but lick his lips in anticipation. If only one or two of the titles he had seen were the actual books they purported to be . . . then Carstairs' library was a veritable gold mine of occult lore! He went directly to the nearest bookshelves and almost immediately spotted half a dozen titles so rare as to make them half-fabulous. Here was an amazingly pristine copy of du Nord's *Liber Ivonie*, and another of Prinn's *De Vermis Mysteriis*. And these marvelous finds were simply inserted willy-nilly in the shelves, between such mundane or common treatises as Miss Margaret Murray's *Witch-Cult* and the much more doubtful works of such as Mme. Blavatsky and Scott-Elliot.

A second shelf supported d'Erlette's *Cultes des Goules,* Gauthier de Metz's *Image du Mond,* and Artephous' *The Key of Wisdom.* A third was filled with an incredible set of volumes concerning the theme of oceanic mysteries and horrors, with such sinister-sounding titles as Gantley's *Hydrophinnae,* the *Cthaat Aquadingen,* the German *Unter Zee Kulten,* le Fe's *Dwellers in the Depths,* and Konrad von Gerner's *Fischbuch,* circa 1598.

Moving along the shelved wall, Crow felt his body break out in a sort of cold sweat at the mere thought of the *value* of these books, let alone their contents, and such was the list of recognizably "priceless" volumes that he soon began to lose all track of the titles. Here were the *Pnakotic Manuscripts,* and here *The Seven Cryptical Books of Hsan;* until finally, on coming across the *R'lyeh Text* and, at the very last, an ancient, ebony-bound, gold-and-silver-arabesqued tome which purported to be none other than the *Al Azif* itself! . . . He was obliged to sit down at one of the dusty tables and take stock of his senses.

It was only then, as he unsteadily seated himself and put a hand up to his fevered brow, that he realized all was not well with him. He felt clammy from the sweat which had broken out on him while looking at the titles of the books, and his mouth and throat had been strangely dry ever since he sampled (too liberally, perhaps?) Carstairs' wine. But this dizziness clinched it. He did not think that he had taken overmuch wine, but then again he had not recognized the stuff and so had not realized its potency. Very well, in future he would take only a single glass. He did not give thought, not at this point, to the possibility that the wine might have been drugged.

Without more ado, still very unsteady on his feet, he got up, put on the light in the alcove where his bed lay freshly made, turned off the library lights proper, and stumblingly retired. Almost before his head hit the pillow he was fast asleep.

HE DREAMED.

The alcove was in darkness but dim moonlight entered the library through the barred windows in beams which moved with the stirring of trees in the garden. The curtains were open and four dark-robed, hooded strangers stood about his bed, their half-luminous eyes fixed upon him. Then one of them bent forward and Crow sensed that it was Carstairs.

"Is he sleeping, Master?" an unknown voice asked in a reedy whisper.

"Yes, like a baby," Carstairs answered. "The open, staring eyes are a sure sign of the drug's efficacy. What do you think of him?"

A third voice, deep and gruff, chuckled obscenely. "Oh, he'll do well enough, Master. Another forty or fifty years for you here."

"Be quiet!" Carstairs immediately snarled, his dark eyes bulging in anger. "You are never to mention that again, neither here nor anywhere else!"

"Master," the man's voice was now a gasp. "I'm sorry! I didn't realize—"

Carstairs snorted his contempt. "None of you ever realize," he said.

"What of his sign, Master?" asked the fourth and final figure, in a voice as thickly glutinous as mud. "Is it auspicious?"

"Indeed it is. He is a Saggitarian, as am I. And his numbers are . . . most propitious." Carstairs' voice was now a purr. "Not only does his name have nine letters, but in the orthodox system his birth number is twenty-seven—a triple nine. Totaled individually, however, his date gives an even better result, for the sum is eighteen!"

"The triple six!" The other's gasp was involuntary.

"Indeed," said Carstairs.

"Well, he seems tall and strong enough, Master," said the voice of the one already chastised. "A fitting receptacle, it would seem."

"Damn you!" Carstairs rounded on him at once. "Fool! How many times must I repeat—" and for a moment, consumed with rage, his hissing voice broke. Then, "Out! Out! There's work for you fools, and for the others. But hear me now: He is The One, I assure you—and he came of his own free will, which is as it must always be."

Three of the figures melted away into darkness but Carstairs stayed. He looked down at Crow one last time, and in a low, even whisper said, "It was a dream. Anything you may remember of this was only a dream. It is not worth remembering, Mr. Crow. Not worth it at all. Only a dream ... a dream ... a dream ..." Then he stepped back and closed the curtains, shutting out the moonbeams and leaving the alcove in darkness. But for a long time it seemed to the sleeping man in the bed that Carstairs' eyes hung over him in the night like the smile of the Cheshire Cat in Alice.

Except that they were malign beyond mortal measure. . . .

III

In the morning, with weak, grime-filtered January sunlight giving the library a dull, time-worn appearance more in keeping with late afternoon than morning, Crow awakened, stretched and yawned. He had not slept well and had a splitting headache, which itself caused him to remember his vow of the previous night: to treat his employer's wine with more respect in future. He remembered, too, something of his dream—something vaguely frightening—but it had been only a dream and not worth remembering. Not worth it at all ...

Nevertheless, still lying abed, he struggled for a little while to force memories to the surface of his mind. They were there, he was sure, deep down in his subconscious. But they would not come. That the dream had concerned Carstairs and a number of other, unknown men, he was sure, but its details ... (he shrugged the thing from his mind) were not worth remembering.

Yet still he could not rid himself of the feeling that he should remember, if only for his own peace of mind. There was that frustrating feeling of having a word on the tip of one's tongue, only to find it slipping away before it can be voiced. After the dream there had been something else—a continuation, perhaps—but this was far less vague and shadowy. It had seemed to Crow that he had heard droning chants or liturgies of some sort or other echoing up from the very bowels of the house. From the cellars? Well, possibly that had been a mental hangover from Carstairs' statement that the cellars were out of bounds. Perhaps, subconsciously, he had read something overly sinister into the man's warning in that respect.

But talking—or rather thinking—of hangovers, the one he had was developing into something of a beauty! Carstairs' wine? Potent? ... Indeed!

He got up, put on his dressing gown, went in search of the bathroom and from there, ten minutes later and greatly refreshed, to the dining room. There he found a brief note, signed by Carstairs, telling him that his employer would be away all day and urging an early start on his work. Crow shrugged, breakfasted, cleared up after himself and prepared to return to the library. But as he was putting away his dishes he came upon a packet of Aspros, placed conspicuously to hand. And now he had to smile at Carstairs' perception. Why, the man had known he would suffer from last night's overindulgence, and these pills were to ensure Crow's clearheadedness as he commenced his work!

His amusement quickly evaporated, however, as he moved from kitchen to library and paused to ponder the best way to set about the job. For the more he looked at and handled these old books, the more the feeling grew within him that Carstairs' passion lay not in the ownership of such volumes but in their use. And if that were the case, then yesterday's caution—however instinctive, involuntary—might yet prove to have stood him in good stead. He thought back to Carstairs' question about his date of birth, and of the man's alleged interest—his "consuming" interest—in astrology. Strange, then, that there was hardly a single volume on that subject to be found among all of these books.

Not so strange, though, that in answer to Carstairs' question he had lied. For as a numerologist Crow had learned something of the importance of names, numbers, and dates—especially to an occultist! No magician in all the long, macabre history of mankind would ever have let the date of his birth be known to an enemy, nor even his name, if that were at all avoidable. For who could tell what use the other might make of such knowledge, these principal factors affecting a man's destiny?

In just such recesses of the strange and mystical mind were born such phrases of common, everyday modern usage as: "That bullet had his number on it," and "His number is up!" And where names were concerned, from Man's primal beginnings the name was the identity, the very spirit, and any wizard who knew a man's name might use it against him. The Holy Bible was full of references to the secrecy and sanctity of names, such as the third and "secret" name of the rider of the Horse of Revelations, or that of the angel visiting Samson's father, who asked: "Why asketh thou then after my name, seeing it is secret?" And the Bible was modern fare compared with certain Egyptian legends concerning the use of names in inimical magic. Well, too late to worry about that now; but in any case, while Carstairs had Crow's name, at least he did not have his number.

And what had been that feeling, Crow wondered, come over him when the occultist had asked about his interests, his hobbies? At that moment he would have been willing to swear that the man had almost succeeded in hypnotizing him. And again, for some reason he had been prompted to lie; or if not to lie, to tell only half the truth. Had that, too, been some mainly subconscious desire to protect his identity? If so, why? What possible harm could Carstairs wish to work upon him? The idea was quite preposterous.

As for archaeology and paleontology: Crow's interest was quite genuine and his knowledge extensive, but so too (apparently) was Carstairs'. What had the man meant by suggesting that the Oriental Institute's expedition might have had more success digging in Galilee?

On impulse Crow took down a huge, dusty atlas of the world—by no means a recent edition—and turned its thick, well-thumbed pages to the Middle East, Palestine and the Sea of Galilee. Here, in the margin, some-one had long ago written in reddish, faded ink the date 1602; and on the map itself, in the same sepia, three tiny crosses had been marked along the north shore of Galilee. Beside the center cross was the word *Chorazin*.

Now, this was a name Crow recognized at once. He went back to the shelves and after some searching found a good copy of John Kitto's *Illustrated Family Bible* in two volumes, carrying the bulky second volume back to his table. In Matthew and in Luke he quickly located the verses he sought, going from them to the notes at the end of Chapter 10 of Luke. There, in respect of Verse 13, he found the following note:

> Chorazin—This place is nowhere mentioned but in this and the parallel texts, and in these only by way of reference. It would seem to have been a town of some note, on the shores of the Lake of Galilee, and near Capernaum, along with which and Bethsaide its name occurs. The answer of the natives to Dr. Richardson, when he inquired concerning Capernaum (see the note on iv, 31) connected Chorazin in the same manner with that city....

Crow checked the specified note and found a further reference to Chorazin, called by present-day natives Chorasi and lying in extensive and ancient ruins. Pursing his lips, Crow now returned to the atlas and frowned again at the map of Galilee with its three crosses. If the central one was Chorazin, or the place now occupied by its ruins, then the other two probably identified Bethsaide and Capernaum, all cursed and their destruction foretold by Jesus. As Carstairs had observed: the sands of time had indeed buried many interesting towns and cities on the shores of Galilee.

And so much for John Kitto, D.D., F.S.A. A massive and scholarly work to be sure, his great Bible—but he might have looked a little deeper into the question of Chorazin. For to Crow's knowledge this was one of the birthplaces of "the Antichrist"—whose birth, in its most recent manifestation, had supposedly taken place about the year 1602...

TITUS CROW would have dearly loved to research Carstairs' background, discover his origins and fathom the man's nature and occult directions; so much so that he had to forcefully remind himself that he was not here as a spy but an employee, and that as such he had work to do. Nor was he loath to employ himself on Carstairs' books, for the occultist's collection was in a word, marvelous.

With all of his own esoteric interest, Crow had never come across so fantastic an assemblage of books in his life, not even in the less public archives of such authoritative establishments as the British Museum and the Bibliothèque Nationale. In fact, had anyone previously suggested that such a private collection existed, Crow might well have laughed. Quite apart from the expense necessarily incurred in building such a collection, where could a man possibly find the time required and the dedication in a single lifetime? But it was another, and to Crow far more astonishing, aspect of the library which gave him his greatest cause to ponder: namely the incredible carelessness or sheer ignorance of anyone who could allow such a collection to fall into such disorder, disuse, and decay.

For certainly decay was beginning to show; there were signs of it all about, some of them of the worst sort. Even as midday arrived and he put aside his first rough notes and left the library for the kitchen, just such a sign made itself apparent. It was a worm—a bookworm, Crow supposed, though he had no previous experience of them—which he spotted crawling on the carpeted floor just within the library door. Picking the thing up, he discovered it to be fat, pinkish, vaguely morbid in its smell and cold to the touch. He would have expected a bookworm to be smaller, drier, more insectlike. This thing was more like a maggot! Quickly he turned back into the room, crossed the floor, opened a small window through the vertical bars and dropped the offensive creature into the dark shrubbery. And before making himself a light lunch he very scrupulously washed and dried his hands.

THE REST OF THE DAY passed quickly and without incident, and Crow forswore dinner until around 9:00 P.M. when he began to feel hungry and not a little weary. In the interim he had made his preliminary notes, decided upon categories, and toward the last he had begun to move books around and clear a shelf upon which to commence the massive job of work before him.

For a meal this time he heated the contents of a small flat tin of excellent sliced beef, boiled a few potatoes and brewed up a jug of coffee; and last but not least, he placed upon the great and otherwise empty table a single glass and one of Carstairs' obscure but potent bottles. On this occasion, however, he drank only one glass, and then not filled to the brim. And later, retiring to his alcove with a book—E.-L. de Marigny's entertaining *The Tarot: A Treatise*—he congratulated himself upon his restraint. He felt warm and pleasantly drowsy, but in no way as intoxicated as he had felt on the previous night. About 10:30, when he caught himself nodding, he went to bed and slept soundly and dreamlessly all through the night.

FRIDAY WENT BY VERY QUIETLY, without Crow once meeting, seeing or hearing Carstairs, so that he could not even be sure that the man was at home. This suited him perfectly well, for he still entertained certain misgivings with regard to the occultist's motives. As Carstairs had promised, however, he was there to see Crow off that evening, standing thin and gaunt on the drive, with a wraith of ground mist about his ankles as the younger man drove away.

AT HIS FLAT IN LONDON Crow quickly became bored. He did not sleep well that Friday night, nor on Saturday night, and Sunday was one long misery of boredom and depression, sensations he was seldom if ever given to experience. On two occasions he found himself feeling unaccountably dry and licking his lips, and more than once he wished he had brought a bottle of Carstairs' wine home with him. Almost without conscious volition, about 7:30 on Sunday evening, he began to pack a few things ready for the return journey. It had completely escaped his usually pinpoint but now strangely confused memory that he was not supposed to return until Monday morning.

About 10:00 P.M. he parked his car in the small garage in the grounds of The Barrows, and walked with his suitcase past three other cars parked on the drive. Now, approaching the house, he began to feel a little foolish; for Carstairs was obviously entertaining friends, and of course he would not be expecting him. If the door should prove to be unlocked, however, he might just be able to enter without being heard and without disturbing his employer.

The door was unlocked; Crow entered and went quietly to the library, and there, on a table beside his open notebook, he discovered a bottle of wine and this note:

Dear Mr. Crow,

I have perused your notes and they seem very thorough. I am well pleased with your work so far. I shall be away most of Monday, but expect to see you before I depart. In the event that you should return early, I leave you a small welcome.

Sleep well.

J. C.

All of which was very curious. The note almost made it seem that Carstairs had *known* he would return early! But at any rate, the man seemed in a good humor; and it would be boorish of Crow not to thank him for the gift of the bottle. He could at least try, and then perhaps he would not feel so bad about sneaking into the house like a common criminal. The hour was not, after all, unreasonable.

So thinking, Crow took a small glass of wine to fortify himself, then went quietly into the gloomy passages and corridors and made his unlighted way to Carstairs' study. Seeing a crack of feeble electric light from beneath the occultist's door and hearing voices, he paused, reconsidered his action and was on the point of retracing his steps when he heard his name mentioned. Now he froze and all his attention concentrated itself upon the conversation being carried on in Carstairs' study. He could not catch every word, but—

"The date ordained . . . Candlemas Eve," Carstairs was saying. "Meanwhile, I . . . my will on him. He *works* for me—do you understand?—and so was partly . . . power from the start. My will, aided . . . wine, will do the rest. Now, I . . . decided upon it, and will . . . no argument. I have said it before and now . . . again: he *is* the one. Garbett, what has he in the way of vices?"

A thick, guttural voice answered—a voice which Crow was almost certain he knew from somewhere—saying: "None at all, that I . . . discover. Neither women—not as a vice—nor drugs, though . . . very occasionally likes a cigarette. He . . . not gamble . . . no spendthrift, he—"

"Is pure!" Carstairs' voice again. "But you . . . worked for the War Department? In . . . capacity?"

"That is a stone wall, Master . . . as well try . . . into . . . Bank of England! And it . . . dangerous to press too far."

"Agreed," answered Carstairs. "I want as little as possible to link him with us and this place. Afterward, he will seem to return . . . old haunts, friends, interests. Then the gradual breaking away—and nothing . . . connect him and me. Except . . . shall be one!"

"And yet, Master," said another voice, which again Crow thought he knew, a voice like a windblown reed, "you seem less . . . completely satisfied . . ."

After a pause Carstairs' voice came yet again. "He is not, as yet, a subject . . . hypnotism. On our first . . . resisted strongly. But that is not necessarily a bad sign. There is one . . . need to check. I shall attend to that tomorrow, by letter. It is possible, just possible . . . lied . . . birthdate. In which case . . . time to find another."

"But . . . *little* time!" a fourth voice said. "They mass within you, Master, ravenous and eager to migrate—and Candlemas . . . so close." This voice was thickly glutinous, as Crow had somehow suspected it would be; but Carstairs' voice when it came again had risen a note or two. While it still had that sonorous quality, it also seemed to ring—as in a sort of triumph?

"Aye, they mass, the Charnel Horde—for they know it nears their time! Then—that which remains shall be theirs, and they shall have a new host!" His voice came down a fraction, but still rang clear. "If Crow has lied, I shall deal with him. Then—" and his tone took on a sudden, demonic bite, a sort of crazed amusement, "perhaps *you* would volunteer, Durrell, for the feasting of the worm? Here, *see how taken they are with you!*"

At that there came a scuffle of feet and the scraping sound of table and chairs sharply moved. A gurgling, glutinous cry rang out, and Crow had barely sufficient time to draw back into a shallow, arched alcove before the study door flew open and a frantic figure staggered out into the corridor, almost toppling a small occasional table which stood there. White-faced, with bulging eyes, a man of medium build hurried past Crow and toward the main door of the house. He stumbled as he went and uttered a low moan, then threw something down which plopped on the fretted carpet.

When the house door slammed after him, Crow made his way breathlessly and on tiptoe back to the library. He noted, in passing, that something small and leprous-white crawled on the floor where Durrell had thrown it. And all the while the house rang with Carstairs' baying laughter . . .

IV

It might now reasonably be assumed that Titus Crow, without more ado, would swiftly take his leave of The Barrows and Carstairs forever; that he would go home to London or even farther afield, return the month's wages that Carstairs had paid him in advance, revoke the contract he had signed and so put an end to the . . . whatever it was that his employer planned for him. And perhaps he would have done just that; but already the wine was working in him, that terribly potent and rapidly addictive wine which, along with Carstairs' sorcerous will, was binding him to this house of nameless evil.

And even sensing his growing dependence on the stuff, having heard it with his own ears from Carstairs' own lips, still he found himself reaching with trembling hand for that terrible bottle, and pouring another glass for himself in the suddenly morbid and prisonlike library. All sorts of nightmare visions now raced through Crow's mind as he sat there atremble—chaotic visions of immemorial madness, damnable conclusions totalled from a mass of vague and fragmentary evidences and suspicions—but even as his thoughts whirled, so he sipped, until his senses became totally confounded and he slipped into sleep slumped at the table, his head cushioned upon his arm.

And once more he seemed to dream....

THIS TIME THERE WERE ONLY THREE OF THEM. They had come silently, creeping in the night, and as they entered so one of them, probably Carstairs, had switched off the library lights. Now, in wan moonlight, they stood about him and the hour was midnight.

"See," said Carstairs, "my will and the wine combined have sufficed to call him back, as I said they would. He is now bound to The Barrows as by chains. In a way I am disappointed. His will is not what I thought it. Or perhaps I have made the wine too potent."

"Master," said the one called Garbett, his voice thickly glutinous as ever, "it may be my eyes in this poor light, but—"

"Yes?"

"I think he is trembling! And why is he not in his bed?"

Crow felt Garbett's hand, cold and clammy, upon his fevered brow. "See, he trembles!" said the man. "As if in fear of something..."

"Ah!" came the occultist's voice. "Yes, your powers of observation do you credit, friend Garbett, and you are a worthy member of the coven. Yes, even though the wine holds him fast in its grip, still he trembles. Perhaps he has heard something of which it were better he remained in ignorance. Well, that can be arranged. Now help me with him. To leave him here like this would not be a kindness, and prone upon his bed he will offer less resistance."

Crow felt himself lifted up by three pairs of hands, steadied and guided across the floor, undressed, put to bed. He could see dimly, could feel faintly, could hear quite sharply. The last thing he heard was Carstairs' hypnotic voice, telling him to forget...forget. Forget anything he might have overheard this night. For it was all a dream and unimportant, utterly unimportant...

ON MONDAY MORNING Crow was awakened by Carstairs' voice. The weak January sun was up and the hands on his wristwatch stood at 9:00 A.M. "You have slept late, Mr. Crow. Still, no matter...Doubtless you need the rest after a hectic weekend, eh? I am going out and shall not be back before nightfall. Is there anything you wish me to bring back for you? Something to assist you in your work, perhaps?"

"No," Crow answered, "nothing that I can think of. But thanks anyway." He blinked sleep from his eyes and felt the first throb of a dull ache developing in the front of his skull. "This is unpardonable—my sleeping to this hour. Not that I slept very well . . ."

"Ah?" Carstairs tut-tutted. "Well, do not concern yourself—nothing is amiss. I am sure that after breakfast you will feel much better. Now you must excuse me. Until tonight, then." And he turned and strode from the room.

Crow watched him go and lay for a moment thinking, trying to ignore the fuzziness inside his head. There had been another dream, he was sure, but very little of it was clear, and fine details utterly escaped him. He remembered coming back to The Barrows early . . . after that nothing. Finally he got up, and as soon as he saw the half-empty bottle on the table he understood—or believed he understood—what had happened. That damned wine!

Angry with himself, at his own stupidity, he went through the morning's routine and returned to his work on Carstairs' books. But now, despite the fact that the sun was up and shining with a wintry brightness, it seemed to Crow that the shadows were that much darker in the house and the gloom that much deeper.

THE FOLLOWING DAY, with Carstairs again absent, he explored The Barrows from attic to cellar, but not the cellar itself. He did try the door beneath the stairs, however, but found it locked. Upstairs the house had many rooms, all thick with dust and sparsely furnished, with spots of mold on some of the walls and woodworm in much of the furniture. The place seemed as disused and decayed above as it was below, and Crow's inspection was mainly perfunctory. Outside Carstairs' study he paused, however, as a strange and shuddery feeling took momentary possession of him.

Suddenly he found himself trembling and breaking out in a cold sweat; and it seemed to him that half-remembered voices echoed sepulchrally and ominously in his mind. The feeling lasted for a moment only, but it left

Crow weak and full of a vague nausea. Again angry with himself and not a little worried, he tried the study door and found it to be open. Inside the place was different from the rest of the house.

Here there was no dust or disorder but a comparatively well-kept room of fair size, where table and chairs stood upon an Eastern-style carpet, with a great desk square and squat beneath a wall hung with six oil paintings in matching gilt frames. These paintings attracted Crow's eyes and he moved forward the better to see them. Proceeding from right to left, the pictures bore small metallic plaques which gave dates but no names.

The first was of a dark, hawk-faced, turbaned man in desert garb, an Arab by his looks. The dates were 1602–68. The second was also of a Middle Eastern type, this time in the rich dress of a sheik or prince, and his dates were 1668–1734. The third was dated 1734–90 and was the picture of a statuesque, high-browed Negro of forceful features and probably Ethiopian descent; while the fourth was of a stern-faced young man in periwig and smallclothes, dated 1790–1839. The fifth was of a bearded, dark-eyed man in a waistcoat and wearing a monocle—a man of unnatural pallor— dated 1839–88; and the sixth—

The sixth was a picture of Carstairs himself, looking almost exactly as he looked now, dated 1888–1946!

Crow stared at the dates again, wondering what they meant and why they were so perfectly consecutive. Could these men have been the previous leaders of Carstairs' esoteric cult, each with dates which corresponded to the length of his reign? But 1888 ... yes, it made sense; for that could certainly *not* be Carstairs' birth date. Why, he would be only fifty-seven years of age! He looked at least fifteen or twenty years older than that; certainly he gave the impression of advanced age, despite his peculiar vitality. And what of that final date, 1946? Was the man projecting his own death?—or was this to be the year of the next investiture?

Then, sweeping his eyes back across the wall to the first picture, that of the hawk-faced Arab, something suddenly clicked into place in Crow's mind. It had to do with the date 1602 ... and in another moment he remembered that this was the date scrawled in reddish ink in the margin of the old atlas. The date of birth of the supposed Antichrist, 1602, in a place once known as Chorazin the Damned!

Still, it made very little sense—or did it? There was a vague fuzziness in Crow's mind, a void desperately trying to fill itself, like a mental jigsaw puzzle with so many missing pieces that the picture could not come together. Crow knew that somewhere deep inside he had the answers—and yet they refused to surface.

As he left Carstairs' study he cast one more half-fearful glance at the man's sardonic picture. A white crawling thing, previously unnoticed, dropped from the ledge of the frame and fell with a plop to the Boukhara rug . . .

LEFT ALMOST ENTIRELY ON HIS OWN NOW, Crow worked steadily through the rest of Tuesday, through Wednesday and Thursday morning; but after a light lunch on Thursday he decided he needed some fresh air. This coincided with his discovering another worm or maggot in the library, and he made a mental note that sooner or later he must speak to Carstairs about the possibility of a health hazard.

Since the day outside was bright, he let himself out of the house and into the gardens, choosing one of the many overgrown paths rather than the wide, gravelly drive. In a very little while all dullness of the mind was dissipated and he found himself drinking gladly and deeply of the cold air. This was something he must do more often, for all work and no play was beginning to make Titus Crow a very dull boy indeed.

He was not sure whether his employer was at home or away; but upon reaching the main gate by a circuitous route he decided that the latter case must apply. Either that or the man had not yet been down to collect the mail. There were several letters in the box, two of which were holding the metal flap partly open. Beginning to feel the chill, Crow carried the letters with him on a winding route back to the house. Out of sheer curiosity he scanned them as he went, noting that the address on one of them was all wrong. It was addressed to a Mr. Castaigne, Solicitor, at The Burrows. Alongside the postage stamps the envelope had been faintly franked with the name and crest of Somerset House in London.

Somerset House, the central registry for births and deaths? Now, what business could Carstairs have with—

And again there swept over Titus Crow that feeling of nausea and faintness. All the cheeriness went out of him in a moment and his hand trembled where it held the suspect envelope. Suddenly his mind was in motion, desperately fighting to remember something, battling with itself against an invisible inner voice which insisted that it did not matter. But he now knew that it did.

Hidden by a clump of bushes which stood between himself and the house, Crow removed the crested envelope from the bundle of letters and slipped it into his inside jacket pocket. Then, sweating profusely if coldly, he delivered the bulk of the letters to the occasional table outside the door of Carstairs' study. On his way back to the library he saw that the cellar door stood open under the stairs, and he heard someone moving about down below. Pausing, he called down:

"Mr. Carstairs, there's mail for you. I've left the letters outside your study."

The sounds of activity ceased and finally Carstairs' voice replied: "Thank you, Mr. Crow. I shall be up immediately."

Not waiting, Crow hurried to the library and sat for a while at the table where he worked, wondering what to do and half-astonished at the impulse which had prompted him to steal the other's mail; or rather, to take this one letter. He had previously installed an electric kettle in the library with which to make himself coffee, and as his eyes alighted upon the kettle, an idea dawned. For it was far too late now for anything else but to let his suspicions carry him all the way. He must now follow his instincts.

Against the possibility of Carstairs' sudden, unannounced entry, he prepared the makings of a jug of instant coffee, an invention of the war years which found a certain favor with him; but having filled the jug to its brim with boiling water, he used the kettle's surplus steam to saturate the envelope's gummed flap until it came cleanly open. With trembling fingers he extracted the letter and placed the envelope carefully back in his pocket. Now he opened the letter in the pages of his notebook, so that to all intents and purposes he would seem to be working as he read it.

The device was unnecessary, since he was not disturbed; but this, written in a neat hand upon the headed stationery of Somerset House, was what he read:

Dear Mr. Castaigne,

In respect of your inquiry on behalf of your client, we never answer such by telephone. Nor do we normally divulge information of this nature except to proven relatives or, occasionally, the police. We expect that now that hostilities are at an end, these restrictions may soon be lifted. However, since you have stressed that this is a matter of some urgency, and since, as you say, the person you seek could prove to be beneficiary of a large sum of money, we have made the necessary inquiries.

There were several Thomas Crows born in London in 1912 and one Trevor Crow; but there was no Titus. A Timeus Crow was born in Edinburgh, and a Titus Crew in Devon.

The name Titus Crow is, in fact, quite rare, and the closest we can come to your specifications is the date 1916, when a Titus Crow was indeed born in the city on the 2nd December. We are sorry if this seems inconclusive.

If you wish any further investigations made, however, we will require some form of evidence, such as testimonials, of the validity of your credentials and motive.

Until then, we remain,

etc . . .

Feeling a sort of numbness spreading through all his limbs, his entire body and mind, Crow read the letter again and yet again. Evidence of Carstairs' credentials and motive, indeed!

Very well, whatever it was that was going on, Titus Crow had now received all the warnings he needed. Forewarned is forearmed, they say, and Crow must now properly arm himself—or at least protect himself—as best he could. One thing he would not do was run, not from an as-yet-undefined fear, an unidentified threat. His interest in the esoteric, the occult, had brought him to The Barrows, and those same interests must now sustain him.

And so, in his way, he declared war. But what were the enemy's weapons, and what was his objective? For the rest of the afternoon Crow did very little of work but sat in thoughtful silence and made his plans...

V

At 4:45 P.M. he went and knocked on Carstairs' door. Carstairs answered but did not invite him in. Instead he came out into the corridor. There, towering cadaverously over Crow and blocking out even more of the gloomy light of the place, he said, "Yes, Mr. Crow? What can I do for you?"

"Sir," Crow answered, "I'm well up to schedule on my work and see little problem finishing it in the time allowed. Which prompts me to ask a favor of you. Certain friends of mine are in London tonight, and so—"

"You would like a long weekend, is that it? Well, I see no real problem, Mr. Crow . . ." But while Carstairs' attitude seemed genuine enough, Crow suspected that he had in fact presented the man with a problem. His request had caught the occultist off guard—surprised and puzzled him—as if Carstairs had never for a moment considered the possibility of Crow's wishing to take extra time off. He tried his best not to show it, however, as he said: "By all means, yes, do go off and see your friends. And perhaps you would do me the honor of accepting a little gift to take with you? A bottle of my wine, perhaps? Good! When will you be going?"

"As soon as possible," Crow answered at once. "If I leave now I'll have all of tomorrow and Saturday to spend with my friends. I may even be able to return early on Sunday, and so make up for lost time."

"No, I wouldn't hear of it." Carstairs held up long, tapering hands. "Besides, I have friends of my own coming to stay this weekend—and this time I really do not wish to be disturbed." And he looked at Crow pointedly. "Very well, I shall expect to see you Monday morning. Do enjoy your weekend and I do urge you to take a bottle of my wine with you." He smiled his ghastly smile.

Crow said, "Thank you," and automatically stuck out his hand—which Carstairs ignored or pretended not to see as he turned and passed back into his study . . .

AT 5:20 P.M. CROW PULLED UP at a large hotel on the approaches to Guildford and found a telephone booth. On his first day at The Barrows Carstairs had given him his ex-directory number, in case he should ever need to contact him at short notice. Now he took out the letter from Somerset House, draped his handkerchief over the mouthpiece of the telephone and called Carstairs' number.

The unmistakable voice of his employer answered almost at once. "Carstairs here. Who is speaking?"

"Ah, Mr. Castaigne," Crow intoned. "Er—you did say Castaigne, didn't you?"

There was a moment's silence, then: "Yes, Mr. Castaigne, that's correct. Is that Somerset House?"

"Indeed, sir, I am calling in respect of your inquiry about a Mr. Crow?"

"Of course, yes. Titus Crow," Carstairs answered. "I was expecting a communication of one sort or another."

"Quite," said Crow. "Well, the name Titus Crow is in fact quite rare, and so was not difficult to trace. We do indeed have one such birth on record, dated second December 1912."

"Excellent!" said Carstairs, his delight clearly in evidence.

"However," Crow hastened on, "I must point out that we do not normally react to unsolicited inquiries of this nature and advise you that in future—"

"I quite understand," Carstairs cut him off. "Do not concern yourself, sir, for I doubt that I shall ever trouble you again." And he replaced his telephone, breaking the connection.

And that, thought Crow as he breathed a sigh of relief and put down his own handset, is that. His credentials were now authenticated, his first line of defense properly deployed.

Now there were other things to do...

BACK IN LONDON, Crow's first thought was to visit a chemist friend he had known and studied with in Edinburgh. Taylor Ainsworth was the man, whose interests in the more obscure aspects of chemistry had alienated him from both tutors and students alike. Even now, famous and a power in his field, still there were those who considered him more alchemist than chemist proper. Recently returned to London, Ainsworth was delighted to renew an old acquaintance and accepted Crow's invitation to drinks at his flat that night, with one reservation: he must be away early on a matter of business.

Next Crow telephoned Harry Townley, his family doctor. Townley was older than Crow by at least twenty years and was on the point of giving up his practice to take the cloth, but he had always been a friend and confidant; and he, too, in his way was considered unorthodox in his chosen field. Often referred to as a charlatan, Townley held steadfastly to his belief in hypnotism, homeopathy, herbalism and such as tremendous aids to more orthodox treatments. Later it would be seen that there was merit in much of this, but for now he was considered a crank.

The talents of these two men, as opposed to those of more mundane practitioners, were precisely what Crow needed. They arrived at his flat within minutes of each other, were introduced and then invited to sample—in very small doses—Carstairs' wine. Crow, too, partook, but only the same minute amount as his friends, sufficient to wet the palate but no more. Oh, he felt the need to fill his glass, certainly, but he now had more than enough of incentives to make him refrain.

"Excellent!" was Harry Townley's view.

"Fine stuff," commented Taylor Ainsworth. "Where on earth did you find it, Titus?" He picked up the bottle and peered closely at the label. "Arabic, isn't it?"

"The label is, yes," Crow answered. "It says simply, 'table wine,' that much at least I know. So you both believe it to be of good quality, eh?"

They nodded in unison and Townley admitted, "I wouldn't mind a bottle or two in my cellar, young Crow. Can you get any more?"

Crow shook his head. "I really don't think I want to," he said. "It seems I'm already partly addicted to the stuff—and it leaves me with a filthy headache! Oh, and you certainly shouldn't take it if you're driving. No, Harry, I've other stuff here you can drink while we talk. Less potent by far. This bottle is for Taylor."

"For me?" Ainsworth seemed pleasantly surprised. "A gift, do you mean? That's very decent of you . . ." Then he saw Crow's cocked eyebrow. "Or is there a catch in it?"

Crow grinned. "There's a catch in it, yes. I want an analysis. I want to know if there's anything in it. Any drugs or such like."

"I should be able to arrange that okay," said the other. "But I'll need a sample."

"Take the bottle," said Crow at once, "and do what you like with it afterward—only get me that analysis. I'll be in touch next weekend, if that's all right with you?"

Now Crow pulled the cork from a commoner brand and topped up their glasses. To Townley he said, "Harry, I think I'm in need of a checkup. That's why I asked you to bring your tools."

"What, you?" The doctor looked surprised. "Why, you're fit as a fiddle—you always have been."

"Yes," said Crow. "Well, to my knowledge the best fiddles are two hundred years old and stringy! And that's just how I feel," and he went on to describe in full his symptoms of sudden nausea, headaches, bouts of dizziness and apparent loss of memory. "Oh, yes," he finished, "and it might just have something to do with that wine which both of you find so excellent!"

While Townley prepared to examine him, Ainsworth excused himself and went off to keep his business appointment. Crow let him go but made him promise not to breathe a word of the wine or his request for an analysis to another soul. When he left, Carstairs' bottle was safely hidden from view in a large inside pocket of his overcoat.

Townley now sounded Crow's chest and checked his heart, then examined his eyes—the latter at some length—following which he frowned and put down his instruments. Then he seated himself facing Crow and tapped with his fingers on the arms of his chair. The frown stayed on his face as he sipped his wine.

"Well?" Crow finally asked.

"You may well say 'well,' young Crow," Townley answered. "Come on, now, what have you been up to?"

Crow arched his eyebrows. "Up to? Is something wrong with me, then?"

Townley sighed and looked a little annoyed. "Have it your own way, then," he said. "Yes, there is something wrong with you. Not a great deal, but enough to cause me some concern. One: there is some sort of drug in your system. Your pulse is far too slow, your blood pressure too high— oh, and there are other symptoms I recognize, including those you told me about. Two: your eyes. Now, eyes are rather a specialty of mine, and yours tell me a great deal. At a guess—I would say you've been playing around with hypnosis."

"I most certainly have not!" Crow denied, but his voice faltered on the last word. Suddenly he remembered thinking that Carstairs had a hypnotic personality.

"Then perhaps you've been hypnotized," Townley suggested, "without your knowing it?"

"Is that possible?"

"Certainly." Again the doctor frowned. "What sort of company have you been keeping just lately, Titus?"

"Fishy company indeed, Harry," the other answered. "But you've interested me. Hypnosis and loss of memory, eh? Well, now," and he rubbed his chin thoughtfully. "Listen, could you possibly dehypnotize me? Trace the trouble back to its source, as it were?"

"I can try. If you've been under once—well, it's usually far easier the second time. Are you game?"

"Just try me," Crow grimly answered. "There's something I have to get to the bottom of, and if hypnosis is the way—why, I'll try anything once!"

An hour later, having had Crow in and out of trance half a dozen times, the good doctor finally shook his head and admitted defeat. "You *have* been hypnotized, I'm sure of it," he said. "But by someone who knows his business far better than I. Do you remember any of the questions I asked you when you were under?"

Crow shook his head.

"That's normal enough," the other told him. "What's extraordinary is the fact that I can get nothing out of you concerning the events of the last couple of weeks!"

"Oh?" Crow was surprised. "But I'll gladly tell you all about the last few weeks if you like—without hypnosis."

"*All* about them?"

"Of course."

"I doubt it." Townley smiled. "For that's the seat of the trouble. You don't *know* all about them. What you remember isn't the whole story."

"I see," Crow slowly answered, and his thoughts went back again to those dim, shadowy dreams of his and to his strange pseudomemories of vague snatches of echoing conversation. "Well, thank you, Harry," he finally said. "You're a good friend and I appreciate your help greatly."

"Now, listen, Titus." The other's concern was unfeigned. "If there's anything else I can do—anything at all—just let me know, and—"

"No, no, there's nothing." Crow forced himself to smile into the doctor's anxious face. "It's just that I'm into something beyond the normal scope of things, something I have to see through to the end."

"Oh? Well, it must be a damned funny business that you can't tell me about. Anyway, I'm not the prying type—but I do urge you to be careful."

"It *is* a funny business, Harry," Crow nodded, "and I'm only just beginning to see a glimmer of light at the end of the tunnel. As for my being careful—you may rely upon that!"

Seeing Townley to the door, he had second thoughts. "Harry, do I remember your having a gun, a six-shooter?"

"A forty-five revolver, yes. It was my father's. I have ammunition, too."

"Would you mind if I borrowed it for a few weeks?"

Townley looked at him very hard, but finally gave a broad grin. "Of course you can," he said. "I'll drop it round tomorrow. But there is such a thing as being too careful, you know!"

VI

Following a very poor night's sleep, the morning of Friday, 18 January, found Titus Crow coming awake with a start, his throat dry and rough and his eyes gritty and bloodshot. His first thought as he got out of bed was of Carstairs' wine—and his second was to remember that he had given it to Taylor Ainsworth for analysis. Stumbling into his bathroom and taking a shower, he cursed himself roundly. He should have let the man take only a sample. But then, as sleep receded and reason took over, he finished showering in a more thoughtful if still sullen mood.

No amount of coffee seemed able to improve the inflamed condition of Crow's throat, and though it was ridiculously early he got out the remainder of last night's bottle of his own wine. A glass or two eased the problem a little, but within the hour it was back, raw and painful as ever. That was when Harry Townley turned up with his revolver, and seeing Crow's distress he examined him and immediately declared the trouble to be psychosomatic.

"What?" said Crow hoarsely. "You mean I'm imagining it? Well, that would take a pretty vivid imagination!"

"No," said Townley, "I didn't say you were imagining it. I said it isn't a physical thing. And therefore there's no physical cure."

"Oh, I think there is," Crow answered. "But last night I gave the bottle away!"

"Indeed?" And Townley's eyebrows went up. "Withdrawal symptoms, eh?"

"Not of the usual sort, no," answered Crow. "Harry, have you the time to put me into trance just once more? There's a certain precaution I'd like to take before I resume the funny business we were talking about last night."

"Not a bad idea," said the doctor, "at least where this supposed sore throat of yours is concerned. If it is psychosomatic, I might be able to do something about it. I've had a measure of success with cigarette smokers."

"Fine," said Crow, "but I want you to do more than just that. If I give you a man's name, can you order me never to allow myself to fall under his influence—never to be hypnotized by him—again?"

"Well, it's a tall order," the good doctor admitted, "but I can try."

Half an hour later when Townley snapped his fingers and Crow came out of trance, his throat was already feeling much better, and by the time he and Townley left his flat the trouble had disappeared altogether. Nor was he ever bothered with it again. He dined with the doctor in the city, then caught a taxi and went on alone to the British Museum.

Through his many previous visits to that august building and establishment he was well-acquainted with the curator of the Rare Books Department, a lean, learned gentleman thirty-five years his senior, sharp-eyed and with a dry and wicked wit. Sedgewick was the man's name, but Crow invariably called him sir.

"What, you again?" Sedgewick greeted him when Crow sought him out. "Did no one tell you the war was over? And what code-cracking business are you on this time, eh?"

Crow was surprised. "I hadn't suspected you knew about that," he said.

"Ah, but I did! Your superiors saw to it that I received orders to assist you in every possible way. You didn't suppose I just went running all over the place for any old body, did you?"

"This time," Crow admitted, "I'm here on my own behalf. Does that change things, sir?"

The other smiled. "Not a bit, old chap. Just tell me what you're after and I'll see what I can do for you. Are we back to cyphers, codes, and cryptograms again?"

"Nothing so common, I'm afraid," Crow answered. "Look, this might seem a bit queer, but I'm looking for something on worm worship."

The other frowned. "Worm worship? Man or beast?"

"I'm sorry?" Crow looked puzzled.

"Worship of the annelid—family, *Lumbricidae*—or of the man, Worm?"

"The man-worm?"

"Worm with a capital *W*." Sedgewick grinned. "He was a Danish physician, an anatomist. Olaus Worm. Around the turn of the sixteenth century, I believe. Had a number of followers. Hence the word *Wormian,* relating to his discoveries."

"You get more like a dictionary every day!" Crow jokingly complained. But his smile quickly turned to a frown. "Olaus Worm, eh? Could a Latinized version of that be Olaus Wormius, I wonder?"

"What, old Wormius who translated the Greek *Necronomicon?* No, not possible, for he was thirteenth century."

Crow sighed and rubbed his brow. "Sir," he said, "you've thrown me right off the rails. No, I meant worship of the beast—the annelid, if you like—worship of the maggot."

Now it was Sedgewick's turn to frown. "The maggot!" he repeated. "Ah, but now you're talking about a different kettle of worms entirely. A maggot is a grave worm. Now, if that's the sort of worm you mean . . . have you tried *The Mysteries of the Worm?*"

Crow gasped. *The Mysteries of the Worm!* He had seen a copy in Carstairs' library, had even handled it. Old Ludwig Prinn's *De Vermis Mysteriis!*

Seeing his look, Sedgewick said: "Oh? Have I said something right?"

"Prinn." Crow's agitation was obvious. "He was Flemish, wasn't he?"

"Correct! A sorcerer, alchemist and necromancer. He was burned in Brussels. He wrote his book in prison shortly before his execution, and the manuscript found its way to Cologne where it was posthumously published."

"Do you have a copy in English?"

Sedgewick smiled and shook his head. "I believe there is such a copy— circa 1820, the work of one Charles Leggett, who translated it from the German black-letter—but we don't have it. I can let you see a black-letter, if you like."

Crow shook his head. "No, it gives me a headache just thinking of it. My knowledge of antique German simply wouldn't run to it. What about the Latin?"

"We have half of it. Very fragile. You can see but you can't touch."

"Can't touch? Sir—I want to borrow it!"

"Out of the question, old chap. Worth my job."

"The black-letter, then." Crow was desperate. "Can I have a good long look at it? Here? Privately?"

The other pursed his lips and thought it over for a moment or two, and finally smiled. "Oh, I daresay so. And I suppose you'd like some paper and a pen, too, eh? Come on, then."

A few minutes later, seated at a table in a tiny private room, Crow opened the black-letter—and from the start he knew he was in for a bad time, that the task was near hopeless. Nonetheless he struggled on, and two hours later Sedgewick looked in to find him deep in concentration, poring over the decorative but difficult pages. Hearing the master librarian enter, Crow looked up.

"This could be exactly what I'm looking for," he said. "I think it's here—in the chapter called 'Saracenic Rituals.' "

"Ah, the Dark Rites of the Saracens, eh?" said Sedgewick. "Well, why didn't you say so? We have the 'Rituals' in a translation!"

"In English?" Crow jumped to his feet.

Sedgewick nodded. "The work is anonymous, I'm afraid—by Clergyman X, or some such, and of course I can't guarantee its reliability—but if you want it—"

"I do!" said Crow.

Sedgewick's face grew serious. "Listen, we're closing up shop soon. If I get it for you—that is if I let you take it with you—I must have your word that you'll take infinite care of it. I mean, my heart will quite literally be in my mouth until it's returned."

"You know you have my word," Crow answered at once.

Ten minutes later Sedgewick saw him out of the building. Along the way Crow asked him, "Now how do you suppose Prinn, a native of Brussels, knew so much about the practice of black magic among the Syria-Arabian nomads?"

Sedgewick opened his encyclopedic mind. "I've read something about that somewhere," he said. "He was a much-traveled man, Prinn, and lived for many years among an order of Syrian wizards in the Jebel el Ansariye. That's where he would have learned his stuff. Disguised as beggars or holy men, he and others of the order would make pilgrimages to the world's most evil places, which were said to be conducive to the study of demonology. I remember one such focal point of evil struck me as singularly unusual, being as it was situated on the shore of Galilee! Old Prinn lived in the ruins there for some time. Indeed, he names it somewhere in his book." Sedgewick frowned. "Now, what was the place called . . . ?"

"Chorazin!" said Crow flatly, cold fingers clutching at his heart.

"Yes, that's right," answered the other, favoring Crow with an appraising glance. "You know, sometimes I think you're after my job! Now, do look after that pamphlet, won't you?"

THAT NIGHT, through Saturday and all of Sunday, Crow spent his time engrossed in the "Saracenic Rituals" reduced to the early nineteenth-century English of Clergyman X, and though he studied the pamphlet minutely still it remained a disappointment. Indeed, it seemed that he might learn more from the lengthy preface than from the text itself. Clergyman X (whoever he had been) had obviously spent a good deal of time researching Ludwig Prinn, but not so very much on the actual translation.

In the preface the author went into various dissertations on Prinn's origins, his lifestyle, travels, sources and sorceries—referring often and tantalizingly to other chapters in *De Vermis Mysteriis,* such as those on familiars, on the demons of the Cthulhu Myth Cycle, on divination, necromancy, elementals and vampires—but when it came to actually getting a few of Prinn's blasphemies down on paper, here he seemed at a loss. Or perhaps his religious background had deterred him.

Again and again Crow would find himself led on by the writer, on the verge of some horrific revelation, only to be let down by the reluctance of X to divulge Prinn's actual words. As an example, there was the following passage with its interesting extract from Alhazred's *Al Azif,* which in turn gave credit to an even older work by Ibn Schacabao:

And great Wisdom was in Alhazred, who had seen the Work of the Worm and knew it well. His Words were ever cryptic, but never less than here, where he discusses the Crypts of the Worm-Wizards of olden Irem, and something of their Sorceries:

"The nethermost Caverns," (said he) "are not for the fathoming of Eyes that see; for their Marvels are strange and terrific. Cursed the Ground where dead Thoughts live new and oddly bodied, and evil the Mind that is held by no Head. Wisely did Ibn Schacabao say, that happy is the Town whose Wizards are all Ashes. For it is of old Rumor that the Soul of the Devil-bought hastes not from his charnel Clay, but fats and instructs *the very Worm that gnaws,* till out of corruption horrid Life springs, and the dull Scavengers of Earth wax crafty to vex it and swell monstrous to plague it. Great Holes secretly are digged where Earth's Pores ought to suffice, and Things have learned to walk that ought to crawl . . ."

In Syria, with my own Eyes, I Ludwig Prinn saw one Wizard of Years without Number transfer himself to the Person of a younger man, whose Number he had divined; when at the appointed Hour he spoke the Words of the Worm. And this is what I saw . . ." [Editor's note: Prinn's description of the dissolution of the wizard and the investment of himself into his host is considered too horrific and monstrous to permit of any merely casual or unacquainted perusal—X]

Crow's frustration upon reading such as this was enormous; but in the end it was this very passage which lent him his first real clue to the mystery, and to Carstairs' motive; though at the time, even had he guessed the whole truth, still he could not have believed it. The clue lay in the references to the wizard knowing the younger man's number—and on rereading that particular line Crow's mind went back to his first meeting with Carstairs, when the man had so abruptly inquired about his date of birth. Crow had lied, adding four whole years to his span and setting the date at 2 December 1912. Now, for the first time, he considered that date from the numerologists' point of view, in which he was expert.

According to the orthodox system, the date 2 December 1912 would add up thus:

$$
\begin{array}{r}
2 \\
12 \\
1 \\
9 \\
1 \\
\underline{2} \\
= 27 \text{ and } 2 + 7 = 9 \\
\text{Or: } 27 = \text{Triple } 9
\end{array}
$$

Nine could be considered as being either the Death Number or the number of great spiritual and mental achievement. And of course the finding would be reinforced by the fact that there were nine letters in Crow's name—*if* that were the true date of his birth, which it was not.

To use a different system, the fictional date's numbers would add up thus:

$$2$$
$$1$$
$$2$$
$$1$$
$$9$$
$$1$$
$$\underline{2}$$

$= 18$ and $1 + 8 = 9$

Or: $18 =$ Triple 6

Triple six! The number of the Beast in Revelations! Crow's head suddenly reeled. Dimly, out of some forgotten corner of his mind, he heard an echoing voice say, "*His numbers are most propitious . . . propitious . . . propitious . . .*" And when he tried to tie that voice down it wriggled free, saying, "*Not worth it . . . just a dream . . . unimportant . . . utterly unimportant . . .*"

He shook himself, threw down his pen—then snatched it back up. Now Crow glared at the familiar room about him as a man suddenly roused from nightmare. "It *is* important!" he cried. "Damned important!"

But of course there was no one to hear him.

LATER, FORTIFIED WITH COFFEE and determined to carry on, he used the Hebrew system to discover his number, in which the letters of the alphabet stand for numbers and a name's total equals the total of the man. Since this system made no use of the 9, he might reasonably expect a different sort of answer. But this was his result:

1	2	3	4	5	6	7	8
A	B	C	D	E	U	O	F
I	K	G	M	H	V	Z	P
Q	R	L	T	N	W		
J		S			X		
Y							

Titus Crow equals T,4 I,1 T,4 U,6 S,3 C,3 R,2 O,7 W,6. Which is 4+1+4+6+3+3+2+7+6 = 36. And 3+6 = 9. Or 36, a double 18. The Beast redoubled!

Propitious? In what way? For whom? Certainly not for himself!

For Carstairs?

Slowly, carefully, Titus Crow put down his pen . . .

VII

To Carstairs, waiting in the shadow of his doorway, it seemed that Crow took an inordinately long time to park his car in the garage, and when he came into view there were several things about him which in other circumstances might cause concern. A semidisheveled look to his clothes; a general tiredness in his bearing; an unaccustomed hang to his leonine head and a gritty redness of eye. Carstairs, however, was not at all concerned; on the contrary, he had expected no less.

As for Crow: despite his outward appearance, he was all awareness! The inflammation of his eyes had been induced by a hard rubbing with a mildly irritating but harmless ointment; the disheveled condition of his dress and apparent lack of will were deliberately affected. In short, he was acting, and he was a good actor.

"Mr. Crow," said Carstairs as Crow entered the house. "Delighted to have you back." And the other sensed a genuine relief in the occultist's greeting. Yes, he *was* glad to have him back. "Have you breakfasted?"

"Thank you, yes—on my way here." Crow's voice was strained, hoarse, but this too was affected.

Carstairs smiled, leading the way to the library. At the door he said, "Ah, these long weekends! How they take it out of one, eh? Well, no doubt you enjoyed the break."

As Crow passed into the library, Carstairs remained in the corridor. "I shall look in later," he said, "when perhaps you'll tell me something of the system you've devised for your work—and something of the progress you are making. Until then . . ." And he quietly closed the door on Crow.

Now the younger man straightened up. He went directly to his worktable and smiled sardonically at the bottle of wine, its cork half-pulled, which stood there waiting for him. He pulled the cork, poured a glass, took the bottle to the barred windows and opened one a crack, then stuck the neck of the bottle through the bars and poured the filthy stuff away into the garden. The empty bottle he placed in his alcove bedroom, out of sight.

Then, seating himself and beginning to work, he forced himself to concentrate on the task in hand—the cataloging of Carstairs' books, as if that were the real reason he was here—and so without a break worked steadily through the morning. About midday, when he was sure that he had done enough to satisfy his employer's supposed curiosity, should that really be necessary, he made himself coffee. Later he would eat, but not for an hour or so yet.

The morning had not been easy. His eyes had kept straying to the library shelf where he knew an edition of Prinn's book stood waiting for his eager attention. But he dared not open the thing while there was a chance that Carstairs might find him with it. He must be careful not to arouse the occultist's suspicions. Also, there was the glass of red wine close to hand, and Crow had found himself tempted. But in removing the symptoms of his supposed addiction, Harry Townley had also gone a good deal of the way toward curbing the need itself; so that Crow half suspected it was his own perverse nature that tempted him once more to taste the stuff, as if in contempt of Carstairs' attempted seduction of his senses.

And the glass was still there, untouched, when half an hour later Carstairs quietly knocked and strode into the room. His first act on entering was to go directly to the windows and draw the shades, before moving to the table and picking up Crow's notes. Saying nothing, he studied them for a moment, and Crow could see that he was mildly surprised. He had not expected Crow to get on quite so well, that much was obvious. Very well, in future he would do less. It made little difference, really, for by now he was certain that the "work" was very much secondary to Carstairs' real purpose in having him here. If only he could discover what that purpose really was . . .

"I am very pleased, Mr. Crow," said Carstairs presently. "Extremely so. Even in adverse conditions you appear to function remarkably well."

"Adverse conditions?"

"Come, now! It is dim here—drab, lonely and less than comfortable. Surely these are adverse conditions?"

"I work better when left alone," Crow answered. "And my eyes seem to have grown accustomed to meager light."

Carstairs had meanwhile spotted the glass of wine, and turning his head to scan the room he casually searched for the bottle. He did not seem displeased by Crow's apparent capacity for the stuff.

"Ah . . . ," Crow mumbled. "Your wine. I'm afraid I—"

"Now, no apologies, young man," Carstairs held up a hand. "I have more than plenty of wine. Indeed, it gives me pleasure that you seem to enjoy it so. And perhaps it makes up for the otherwise inhospitable conditions, which I am sure are not in accordance with your usual mode of existence. Very well, I leave you to it. I shall be here for the rest of today—I have work in my study—but tomorrow I expect to be away. I shall perhaps see you on Wednesday morning?" And with that he left the library.

Satisfied that he was not going to be disturbed any further, without bothering to open the window shades, Crow took down *De Vermis Mysteriis* from its shelf and was at once dismayed to discover the dark, cracked leather bindings of the German black-letter, almost the duplicate of the book he had looked into in the British Museum. His dismay turned to delight, however, on turning back the heavy cover and finding, pasted into the old outer shell a comparatively recent work whose title page declared it to be:

THE MYSTERIES OF THE WORM
being
THE COMPLETE BOOK
in sixteen chapters
With many dozens wood engravings;
representing
THE ORIGINAL WORK
of
LUDWIG PRINN,
after translation
By Charles Leggett,
and including his notes;
this being Number Seven of
a very Limited Edition,
LONDON
1821

Crow immediately took the book through into his alcove room and placed it under his pillow. It would keep until tonight. Then he unpacked a few things, hiding Townley's gun under his mattress near the foot of the bed. Finally, surprised to find he had developed something of an appetite, he decided upon lunch.

But then, as he drew the curtains on the alcove and crossed the room toward the library door, something caught his eye. It was an obscene, white wriggling shape on the faded carpet where Carstairs had stood. He took it to the window but there, even as he made to toss it into the garden, discovered a second worm crawling on the wainscotting. Now he was filled with revulsion. These were two worms too many!

He disposed of the things, poured the still-untouched glass of wine after them and went straight to Carstairs' study. Knocking, he heard dull movements within, and finally the occultist's voice:

"Come in, Mr. Crow."

This surprised him, for until now the room had supposedly been forbidden to him. Nevertheless he opened the door and went in. The gloom inside made shadows of everything, particularly the dark figure seated at the great desk. A thick curtain had been drawn across the single window and only the dim light of a desk lamp, making a pool of feeble yellow atop the desk, gave any illumination at all. And now, here in these close quarters, the musty smell of the old house had taken to itself an almost charnel taint which was so heavy as to be overpowering.

"I was resting my eyes, Mr. Crow," came Carstairs' sepulchral rumble. "Resting this weary old body of mine. Ah, what it must be to be young! Is there something?"

"Yes," said Crow firmly. "A peculiar and very morbid thing. I just thought I should report it."

"A peculiar thing? Morbid? To what do you refer?" Carstairs sat up straighter behind his desk.

Crow could not see the man's face, which was in shadow, but he saw him start as he answered, "Worms! A good many of them. I've been finding them all over the house."

The figure in the chair trembled, half stood, sat down again. "Worms?" There was a badly feigned tone of surprise in his voice, followed by a short silence in which Crow guessed the other sought for an answer to this riddle. He decided to prompt him.

"I really think you should have it seen to. They must be eating out the very heart of the house."

Now Carstairs sat back and appeared to relax. His chuckle was throaty when he answered. "Ah, no, Mr. Crow—for they are not of the house-eating species. I rather fancy they prefer richer fare. Yes, I too have seen them. They are maggots!"

"Maggots?" Crow could not keep the disgusted note out of his voice, even though he had half suspected it. "But . . . is there something dead here?"

"There was," Carstairs answered. "Shortly after you arrived here I found a decomposing rabbit in the cellar. The poor creature had been injured on the road or in a trap and had found a way into my cellar to die. Its remains were full of maggots. I got rid of the carcass and put down chemicals to destroy the maggots. That is why you were forbidden to go into the cellar; the fumes are harmful."

"I see . . ."

"As for those few maggots you have seen, doubtless some escaped and have found their way through the cracks and crevices of this old house. There is nothing for them here, however, and so they will soon cease to be a problem."

Crow nodded.

"So do not concern yourself."

"No, indeed." And that was that.

CROW DID NOT EAT AFTER ALL. Instead, feeling queasy, he went out into the garden for fresh air. But even out there the atmosphere now seemed tainted. It was as if a pall of gloom hovered over the house and grounds, and that with every passing minute the shadows deepened and the air grew heavy with sinister presences.

Some sixth, psychic sense informed Crow that he walked the strands of an incredibly evil web, and that a great bloated spider waited, half hidden from view, until the time was just right—or until he took just one wrong step. Now a longing sprang up in him to be out of here and gone from the place, but there was that obstinate streak in his nature which would not permit flight. It was a strange hand that Fate had dealt, where at the moment Carstairs seemed to hold more than his fair share of the aces and Titus Crow held only one trump card.

Even now he did not realize how much depended upon that card, but he felt sure that he would very soon find out.

VIII

Crow did little or no work that afternoon but, affected by a growing feeling of menace—of hidden eyes watching him—searched the library wall to wall and over every square inch of carpeting, wainscotting, curtains and alcove, particularly his bed, for maggots. He did not for one moment believe Carstairs' explanation for the presence of the things, even though logic told him it might just be plausible. But for all that his search was very thorough and time-consuming; he found nothing.

That night, seated uneasily in the alcove behind drawn curtains, he took out *De Vermis Mysteriis* and opened it to the "Saracenic Rituals," only to discover that the greater part of that chapter was missing, the pages cleanly removed with a razor-sharp knife. The opening to the chapter was there, however, and something of its middle. Reading what little remained, Crow picked out three items which he found particularly interesting. One of these fragments concerned that numerology in which he was expert, and it was an item of occult knowledge written down in terms no one could fail to understand:

> The Names of a Man, along with his Number, are all-important. Knowing the First, a Magician knows something of the Man; knowing the Second, he knows his Past, Present, and Future; and he may control the Latter by means of his Sorceries, even unto the Grave and beyond!

Another offered a warning against wizardly generosity:

> Never accept a Gift from a Necromancer, or any Wizard or Familiar. Steal which may be stolen, buy which may be bought, earn it if that be at all possible and if it must be had—but do *not* accept it, neither as a Gift nor as a Legacy ...

Both of these seemed to Crow to have a bearing on his relationship with Carstairs; but the last of the three interested and troubled him the most, for he could read in it an even stronger and far more sinister parallel:

> A Wizard will not offer the Hand of Friendship to one he would seduce. When a Worm-Wizard refuses his Hand, that is an especially bad Omen. And having once refused his Hand, if he then offers it, that is even worse!

Finally, weary and worried but determined in the end to get to the root of the thing, Crow went to bed. He lay in darkness and tossed and turned for a long time before sleep finally found him; and this was the first time, before sleeping, that he had ever felt the need to turn his key in the lock of the library door.

ON TUESDAY MORNING Crow was awakened by the sound of a motorcar's engine. Peeping through half-closed window shades he saw Carstairs leave the house and get into a car which waited on the winding drive. As soon as the car turned about and bore the occultist away, Crow quickly dressed and went to the cellar door under the stairs in the gloomy hall. The door was locked, as he had expected.

Very well, perhaps there was another way in. Carstairs had said that a rabbit had found its way in; and even if that were untrue, still it suggested that there *might* be such an entry from the grounds of the house. Going into the garden, Crow first of all ensured that he was quite alone, then followed the wall of the house until, at the back, he found overgrown steps leading down to a basement landing. At the bottom a door had been heavily boarded over, and Crow could see at a glance that it would take a great deal of work to get into the cellar by that route. Nor would it be possible to disguise such a forced entry. To one side of the door, completely opaque with grime, a casement window next offered itself for inspection. This had not been boarded up, but many successive layers of old paint had firmly welded frame and sashes into one. Using a penknife, Crow worked for a little while to gouge the paint free from the joint; but then, thinking he heard an unaccustomed sound, he stopped and hastily returned to the garden. No one was there, but his nerves had suffered and he did not return to his task. That would have to wait upon another day.

Instead he went back indoors, washed, shaved and breakfasted (though really he did not have much of an appetite) and finally climbed the stairs to scan the countryside all around through bleary windows. Seeing nothing out of the ordinary, he returned to the ground floor and once more ventured along the corridor to Carstairs' study. That door, too, was locked; and now Crow's frustration and jumpiness began to tell on him. Also he suspected that he was missing the bolstering—or deadening—effect of the occultist's wine. And Carstairs had not been remiss in leaving him a fresh bottle of the stuff upon the breakfast table.

Now, fearing that he might weaken, he rushed back to the kitchen and picked up the bottle on the way. Only when he had poured it down the sink, every last drop, did he begin to relax; and only then did he realize how tired he was. He had not slept well; his nerves seemed frayed; at this rate he would never have the strength to solve the mystery, let alone see it through to the end.

At noon, on the point of preparing himself a light meal, he found yet another maggot—this time in the kitchen itself. That was enough. He could not eat here. Not now.

He left the house, drove into Haslemere and dined at a hotel, consumed far too many brandies and returned to The Barrows cheerfully drunk. All the rest of the day he spent sleeping it off—for which sheer waste of time he later cursed himself—and awakened late in the evening with a nagging hangover.

Determined now to get as much rest as possible, he made himself a jug of coffee and finally retired for the night. The coffee did not keep him awake; and once again he locked the library door.

WEDNESDAY PASSED QUICKLY and Crow saw Carstairs only twice. He did a minimum of "work" but searched the library shelves for other titles which might hint at his awful employer's purpose. He found nothing, but such was his fascination with these old books—the pleasure of reading and handling them—that his spirits soon rose to something approaching their previous vitality. And throughout the day he kept up the pretense of increasing dependence on Carstairs' wine, and he continued to effect a hoarse voice and to redden his eyes by use of the irritating ointment.

On Thursday Carstairs once again left the house, but this time he forgot to lock his study door. By now Crow felt almost entirely returned to his old self, and his nerves were steady as he entered that normally forbidden room. And seeing Carstairs' almost antique telephone standing on an occasional table close to the desk, he decided upon a little contact with the outside world.

He quickly rang Taylor Ainsworth's number in London. Ainsworth answered, and Crow said: "Taylor, Titus here. Any luck yet with that wine?"

"Ah!" said the other, his voice scratchy with distance. "So you couldn't wait until the weekend, eh? Well, funny stuff, that wine, with a couple of really weird ingredients. I don't know what they are or how they work, but they do. They work on human beings like aniseed works on dogs! Damned addictive!"

"Poisonous?"

"Eh? Dear me, no! I shouldn't think so, not in small amounts. You wouldn't be talking to me now if they were! Listen, Titus, I'd be willing to pay a decent price if you could—"

"Forget it!" Crow snapped. Then he softened. "Listen, Taylor, you're damned *lucky* there's no more of that stuff, believe me. I think it's a recipe that goes back to the very blackest days of Man's history—and I'm pretty sure that if you knew those secret ingredients you'd find them pretty ghastly! Thanks anyway, for what you've done." And despite the other's distant protests he put down the telephone.

Now, gazing once more about that dim and malodorous room, Crow's eyes fell upon a desk calendar. Each day, including today, had been scored through with a thick black line. The 1st, February, however, Candlemas Eve, had been ringed with a double circle.

Candlemas Eve, still eight days away . . .

Crow frowned. There was something he should remember about that date, something quite apart from its religious connections. Dim memories stirred sluggishly. *Candlemas Eve, the date ordained.*

Crow started violently. The date ordained? Ordained for what? Where had that idea come from? But the thought had fled, had sunk itself down again into his subconscious mind.

Now he tried the desk drawers. All were locked and there was no sign of a key. Suddenly, coming from nowhere, Crow had the feeling that there were eyes upon him! He whirled, heart beating faster—and came face-to-face with Carstairs' picture where it hung with the others on the wall. In the dimness of that oppressive room, the eyes in the picture seemed to glare at him piercingly . . .

AFTER THAT THE DAY passed uneventfully and fairly quickly. Crow visited the sunken casement window again at the rear of the house and did a little more work on it, scraping away at the old, thick layers of paint, seeming to make very little impression. As for the rest of the time; he rested a good deal and spent an hour or so on Carstairs' books, busying himself with the "task" he had been set, but no more than that.

About 4:30 P.M. Crow heard a car pull up outside and going to the half-shaded windows he saw Carstairs walking up the drive as the car pulled away. Then, giving his eyes a quick rub and settling himself at his worktable, he assumed a harassed pose. Carstairs came immediately to the library, knocked and walked in.

"Ah, Mr. Crow. Hard at it as usual, I see?"

"Not really," Crow hoarsely answered, glancing up from his notebook. "I can't seem to find the energy for it. Or maybe I've gone a bit stale. It will pass."

Carstairs seemed jovial. "Oh, I'm sure it will. Come, Mr. Crow, let's eat. I have an appetite. Will you join me?" Seeing no way to excuse himself, Crow followed Carstairs to the dining room. Once there, however, he remembered the maggot he had found in the kitchen and could no longer contemplate food under any circumstances.

"I'm really not very hungry," he mumbled.

"Oh?" Carstairs raised an eyebrow. "Then I shall eat later. But I'm sure you wouldn't refuse a glass or two of wine, eh?"

Crow was on the point of doing just that—until he remembered that he could not refuse. He was not supposed to be able to refuse! Carstairs fetched a bottle from the larder, pulled its cork and poured two liberal glasses. "Here's to you, Mr. Crow," he said. "No—to us!"

And seeing no way out, Crow was obliged to lift his glass and drink . . .

IX

Nor had Carstairs been satisfied to leave it at that. After the first glass there had been a second, and a third, until Titus Crow's head was very quickly spinning. Only then was he able to excuse himself, and then not before Carstairs had pressed the remainder of the bottle into his hand, softly telling him to take it with him, to enjoy it before he retired for the night.

He did no such thing but poured it into the garden; and then, reeling as he went, made his way to the bathroom where he drank water in such amounts and so quickly as to make himself violently ill. Then, keeping everything as quiet as possible, he staggered back to the library and locked himself in.

He did not think that a great deal of wine remained in his stomach— precious little of anything else, either—but his personal remedy for any sort of excess had always been coffee. He made and drank an entire jug of it, black, then returned to the bathroom and bathed, afterward thoroughly dousing himself with cold water. Only then did he feel satisfied that he had done all he could to counteract the effects of Carstairs' wine.

All of this had taken it out of him, however, so that by 8:00 P.M. he was once again listless and tired. He decided to make an early night of it, retiring to his alcove with *De Vermis Mysteriis*. Within twenty minutes he was nodding over the book and feeling numb and confused in his mind. The unvomited wine was working on him, however gradually, and his only hope now was that he might sleep it out of his system.

Dazedly returning the heavy book to its shelf, he stumbled back to his bed and collapsed onto it. In that same position, spread-eagled and face-down, he fell asleep; and that was how he stayed for the next four hours.

CROW CAME AWAKE slowly, gradually growing aware that he was being addressed, aware too of an unaccustomed feeling of cold. Then he remembered what had gone before and his mind began to work a little faster. In the darkness of the alcove he opened his eyes a fraction, peered into the gloom and made out two dim figures standing to one side of his bed. Some instinct told him that there would be more of them on the other side, and only by the greatest effort of will was he able to restrain himself from leaping to his feet.

Now the voice came again, Carstairs' voice, not talking to him this time but to those who stood around his bed. "I was afraid that the wine's effect was weakening, but apparently I was wrong. Well, my friends, you are here tonight to witness an example of my will over the mind and body of Titus Crow. He cannot be allowed to go away this weekend, of course, for the time is too near. I would hate anything to happen to him."

"So would we all, Master," came a voice Crow recognized. "For—"

"For then I would need to make a second choice, eh, Durrell? Indeed, I *know* why you wish nothing to go amiss. But you *presume*, Durrell! You are no fit habitation."

"Master, I merely—" the other began to protest.

"Be quiet!" Carstairs snarled. "And watch." Now his words were once more directed at Crow, and his voice grew deep and sonorous.

"Titus Crow, you are dreaming, only dreaming. There is nothing to fear, nothing at all. It is only a dream. Turn over onto your back, Titus Crow."

Crow, wide awake now—his mind suddenly clear and realizing that Harry Townley's counterhypnotic device was working perfectly—forced himself to slow, languid movement. With eyes half-shuttered, he turned over, relaxed and rested his head on his pillow.

"Good!" Carstairs said. "That was good. Now sleep, Titus Crow, sleep and dream."

Now Garbett's voice said: "Apparently all is well, Master."

"Yes, all is well. His Number is confirmed, and he comes more fully under my spell as the time approaches. Now we shall see if we can do a little more than merely command dumb movement. Let us see if we can make him talk. Mr. Crow, can you hear me?"

Crow, mind racing, opened parched lips and gurgled, "Yes, I hear you."

"Good! Now, I want you to remember something. Tomorrow you will come to me and tell me that you have decided to stay here at The Barrows over the weekend. Is that clear?"

Crow nodded.

"You do want to stay, don't you?"

Again he nodded.

"Tell me you wish it."

"I want to stay here," Crow mumbled, "over the weekend."

"Excellent!" said Carstairs. "There'll be plenty of wine for you here, Titus Crow, to ease your throat and draw the sting from your eyes."

Crow lay still, forcing himself to breathe deeply.

"Now I want you to get up, turn back your covers and get into bed," said Carstairs. "The night air is cold and we do not wish you to catch a chill, do we?"

Crow shook his head, shakily stood up, turned back his blankets and sheets and lay down again, covering himself.

"Completely under your control!" Garbett chuckled, rubbing his hands together. "Master, you are amazing!"

"I have been amazing, as you say, for almost three and a half centuries," Carstairs replied with some pride. "Study my works well, friend Garbett, and one day you too may aspire to the Priesthood of the Worm!"

On hearing these words so abruptly spoken, Crow could not help but give a start—but so too did the man Durrell, a fraction of a second earlier, so that Crow's movement went unnoticed. And even as the man on the bed sensed Durrell's frantic leaping, so he heard him cry out: "*Ugh!* On the floor! I trod on one! The maggots!"

"Fool!" Carstairs snarled. "Idiot!" And to the others, "Get him out of here. Then come back and help me collect them up."

After that there was a lot of hurried movement and some scrambling about on the floor, but finally Crow was left alone with Carstairs; and then the man administered that curious droning caution which Crow was certain he had heard before.

"It was all a dream, Mr. Crow. Only a dream. There is nothing really you should remember about it, nothing of any importance whatsoever. But you will come to me tomorrow, won't you, and tell me that you plan to spend the weekend here? Of course you will!"

And with that Carstairs left, silently striding from the alcove like some animated corpse into the dark old house. But this time he left Crow wide awake, drenched in a cold sweat of terror and with little doubt in his mind but that this had been another attempt of Carstairs' to subvert him to his will—at which he had obviously had no little success in the recent past!

Eyes staring in the darkness, Crow waited until he heard engines start up and motorcars draw away from the house—waited again until the old place settled down—and when far away a church clock struck one, only then did he get out of bed, putting on lights and slippers, trembling in a chill which had nothing at all to do with that of the house. Then he set about to check the floor of the alcove, the library, to strip and check and reassemble his bed blanket by blanket and sheet by sheet; until at last he was perfectly satisfied that there was no crawling thing in this area he had falsely come to think of as his own place, safe and secure. For the library door was still locked, which meant either that Carstairs had a second key, or—

Now, with Harry Townley's .45 tucked in his dressing-gown pocket, he examined the library again, and this time noticed that which very nearly stood his hair on end. It had to do with a central section of heavy shelving set against an internal wall. For in merely looking at this mighty bookcase, no one would ever suspect that it had a hidden pivot—and yet such must be the case. Certain lesser books where he had left them stacked on the carpet along the frontage of the bookshelves had been moved, swept aside in an arc; and now indeed he could see that a small gap existed between the bottom of this central part and the carpeted floor proper.

Not without a good deal of effort, Crow finally found the trick of it and caused the bookcase to move, revealing a blackness and descending steps which spiraled steeply down into the bowels of the house. At last he had discovered a way into the cellar; but for now he was satisfied simply to close that secret door and make for himself a large jug of coffee, which he drank to its last drop before making another.

And so he sat through the remaining hours of the night, sipping coffee, occasionally trembling in a preternatural chill, and promising himself that above all else, come what may, he would somehow sabotage whatever black plans Carstairs had drawn up for his future . . .

THE WEEKEND WAS NIGHTMARISH.

Crow reported to Carstairs Saturday morning and begged to be allowed to stay at The Barrows over the weekend (which, it later occurred to him in the fullness of his senses, whether *he himself* willed it or not, was exactly what he had been instructed to do) to which suggestion, of course, the master of the house readily agreed. And after that things rapidly degenerated.

Carstairs was there for every meal, and whether Crow ate or not his host invariably plied him with wine; and invariably, following a routine which now became a hideous and debilitating ritual, he would hurry from dining room to bathroom there to empty his stomach disgustingly of its stultifying contents. And all of this time he must keep up the pretense of falling more and more willingly under Carstairs' spell, though in all truth this was the least of it. For by Sunday night his eyes were inflamed through no device of his own, his throat sore with the wine and bathroom ritual, and his voice correspondingly hoarse.

He did none of Carstairs' "work" during those hellish days, but at every opportunity pored over the man's books in the frustrated hope that he might yet find something to throw more light on the occultist's current activities. And all through the nights he lay abed, desperately fighting the drugs which dulled his mind and movements, listening to cellar-spawned chantings and howlings until with everything else he could very easily imagine himself the inhabitant of bedlam.

Monday, Tuesday, and Wednesday passed in like fashion—though he did manage to get some food into his system, and to avoid excessive contact with Carstairs' wine—until, on Wednesday evening over dinner, the occultist offered him the break he so desperately longed for. Mercifully, on this occasion, the customary bottle of wine had been more than half-empty at the beginning of the meal; and Crow, seizing the opportunity to pour, had given Carstairs the lion's share, leaving very little for himself; and this without attracting the attention of the gaunt master of the house, whose thoughts seemed elsewhere. Crow felt relieved in the knowledge that he would not have to concern himself yet again with the morbid bathroom ritual.

At length, gathering his thoughts, Carstairs said: "Mr. Crow, I shall be away tomorrow morning, probably before you are up and about. I will return about midafternoon. I hesitate to leave you alone here, however, for to be perfectly frank you do not seem at all well."

"Oh?" Crow hoarsely mumbled. "I feel well enough."

"You do not look it. Perhaps you are tasking yourself too hard." His eyes bored into Crow's along the length of the great table, and his voice assumed its resonant, hypnotic timber. "I think you should rest tomorrow, Mr. Crow. Rest and recuperate. Lie late abed. Sleep and grow strong."

At this Crow deliberately affected a fluttering of his eyelids, nodding and starting where he sat, like an old man who has difficulty staying awake. Carstairs laughed.

"Why!" he exclaimed, his voice assuming a more casual tone. "Do you see how right I am? You were almost asleep at the table! Yes, that's what you require, young man: a little holiday from work tomorrow. And Friday should see you back to normal, eh?"

Crow dully nodded, affecting disinterest—but his mind raced. Whatever was coming was close now. He could feel it like a hot wind blowing from hell, could almost smell the sulfur from the fires that burned behind Carstairs' eyes . . .

AMAZINGLY, CROW SLEPT WELL and was awake early. He remained in bed until he heard a car pull up to the house, but even then some instinct kept him under his covers. Seconds later Carstairs parted the alcove's curtains and silently entered; and at the last moment hearing his tread, with no second to spare, Crow fell back upon his pillow and feigned sleep.

"That's right, Titus Crow, sleep," Carstairs softly intoned. "Sleep deep and dreamlessly—for soon your head shall know no dreams, no thoughts but mine! Sleep, Titus Crow, sleep . . ." A moment later the rustling of the curtains signaled his leaving; but still Crow waited until he heard the receding crunch of the car's tires on the gravel of the drive.

After that he was up in a moment and quickly dressed. Then: out of the house and around the grounds, and upstairs to spy out the land all around. Finally, satisfied that he was truly alone, he returned to the library, opened the secret bookcase door and descended to the Stygian cellar. The narrow stone steps turned one full circle to leave him on a landing set into an arched alcove in the cellar wall, from which two more paces sufficed to carry him into the cellar proper. Finding a switch, he put on subdued lighting—and at last saw what sort of wizard's lair the place really was!

Now something of Crow's own extensive occult knowledge came to the fore as he moved carefully about the cellar and examined its contents; something of that, and of his more recent readings in Carstairs' library. There were devices here from the very blackest days of Man's mystical origins, and Titus Crow shuddered as he read meaning into many of the things he saw.

The floor of the cellar had been cleared toward its center, and there he found the double interlocking circles of the Persian Mages, freshly daubed in red paint. In one circle he saw a white-painted ascending node, while in the other a black node descended. A cryptographic script, immediately known to him as the blasphemous Nyhargo Code, patterned the brick wall in green and blue chalks, its huge Arabic symbols seeming to leer where they writhed in obscene dedication. The three remaining walls were draped with tapestries so worn as to be threadbare—due to their being centuries-old—depicting the rites of immemorial necromancers and wizards long passed into the dark pages of history; wizards robed, Crow noted, in the forbidden pagan cassocks of ancient *deserta Arabia,* lending them an almost holy aspect.

In a cobwebbed corner he found scrawled pentacles and zodiacal signs; and hanging upon hooks robes similar to those in the tapestries, embroidered with symbols from the *Lemegeton,* such as the Double Seal of Solomon. Small jars contained hemlock, henbane, mandrake, Indian hemp and a substance Crow took to be opium—and again he was given to shudder and to wonder at the constituents of Carstairs' wine . . .

Finally, having seen enough, he retraced his steps to the library and from there went straight to Carstairs' study. Twice before he had found this door unlocked, and now for the third time he discovered his luck to be holding. This was hardly unexpected, however: knowing Crow would sleep the morning through, the magician had simply omitted to take his customary precautions. And inside the room . . . another piece of luck! The keys to the desk dangled from a drawer keyhole.

With trembling hands Crow opened the drawers, hardly daring to disturb their contents; but in the desk's bottom left-hand drawer at last he was rewarded to find that which he most desired to see. There could be no mistaking it: the cleanly sliced margins, the woodcut illustrations, the precise early nineteenth-century prose of one Charles Leggett, translator of Ludwig Prinn. This was the missing section from Leggett's book: these were the "Saracenic Rituals," the Mysteries of the Worm!

Closing the single window's shades, Crow switched on the desk lamp and proceeded to read, and as he read so time seemed to suspend itself in the terrible lore which was now revealed. Disbelievingly, with eyes that opened wider and wider, Crow read on; and as he turned the pages, so the words seemed to leap from them to his astonished eyes. An hour sped by, two, and Crow would periodically come out of his trance long enough to glance at his watch, or perhaps pass tongue over parched lips, before continuing. For it was all here, all of it—and finally everything began to click into place.

Then . . . it was as if a floodgate had opened, releasing pent-up, forbidden memories to swirl in the maelstrom of Crow's mind. He suddenly *remembered* those hypnotically erased night visits of Carstairs', the conversations he had been willed to forget; and rapidly these pieces of the puzzle slotted themselves together, forming a picture of centuries-old nightmare and horror out of time. He *understood* the mystery of the paintings with their consecutive dates, and he *knew* Carstairs' meaning when the man had spoken of a longevity dating back almost three and a half centuries. And at last, in blinding clarity, he could see the part that the wizard had planned for him in his lust for sorcerous survival.

For Crow was to be the receptacle, the host body, youthful haven of flesh for an ancient black phoenix risen again from necromantic ashes! As for Crow himself, the *Identity*, Titus Crow: that was to be cast out—exorcised and sent to hell—*replaced by the mind and will of Carstairs, a monster born of the blackest magicks in midnight ruins by the shore of Galilee in the year 1602! . . .*

Moreover, he knew when the deed was to be done. It was there, staring at him, ringed in ink on Carstairs' desk calendar: the first day of February, 1946.

Candlemas Eve, "the day ordained."
Tomorrow night!

X

That night, though he had never been much of a believer, Titus Crow said his prayers. He did manage to sleep—however fitfully and with countless startings awake, at every tiniest groan and creak of the old place—and in the morning looked just as haggard as this last week had determined he should look. Which was just as well, for as the time approached Carstairs would hardly let him out of his sight.

On four separate occasions that morning, the man came to visit him in the library, eyeing him avidly, like a great and grotesque praying mantis. And even knowing Carstairs' purpose with him—*because* he knew that purpose—Crow must keep up his pretense of going to the slaughter like a lamb, and not the young lion his looks normally suggested.

Lunch came and went, and Crow—mainly by deft sleight of hand— once more cut his wine intake to a minimum; and at 6:00 P.M. he negotiated the evening repast with similar skill and success. And through all of this it was plain to him that a morbid excitement was building in Carstairs, an agitation of spirit the man could barely contain.

At 7:30 P.M.—not long after Crow had finished off an entire jug of coffee and as he sat in silence by the light of one dim lamp, memorizing tonight's monstrous rite from what he had read of it in the "Saracenic Rituals"—Carstairs came and knocked upon the library door, walking in as usual before Crow could issue the customary invitation. No need now for Crow to feign haggardness or the weary slump of his shoulders, for the agonizingly slow buildup to the night's play had itself taken care of these particulars.

"Mr. Crow," said Carstairs in unusually unctuous tones, "I may require a little assistance tonight..."

"Assistance?" Crow peered at the other through red-rimmed eyes. "My assistance?"

"If you have no objection. I have some work to do in the cellar, which may well keep me until the middle of the night. I do not like to keep you from your bed, of course, but in the event I should call for you"—his voice stepped slyly down the register—"you will answer, won't you?"

"Of course," Crow hoarsely answered, his eyes now fixed on the burning orbs of the occultist.

"You will come when I call?" Carstairs now droned, driving the message home. "No matter how late the hour? You will awaken and follow me? You will come to me in the night, when I call?"

"Yes," Crow mumbled.

"Say it, Titus Crow. Tell me what you will do, when I call."

"I shall come to you," Crow obediently answered. "I will come to you when you call me."

"Good!" said Carstairs, his face ghastly as a skull. "Now rest, Titus Crow. Sit here and rest—and wait for my call. Wait for my call . . ." Silently he turned and strode from the room, quietly closing the door behind him.

Crow got up, waited a moment, switched off the one bulb he had allowed to burn. In his alcove bedroom he drew the curtains and put on the light, then quickly changed into his dressing gown. He took Harry Townley's .45 revolver out from under his mattress, loaded it and tucked it out of sight in the large pocket of his robe. Now he opened the curtains some twelve inches and brushed through them into the library proper, pacing the floor along the pale path of light from the alcove.

To and fro he paced, tension mounting, and more than once he considered flight; even now, close as he was to those dark mysteries which at once attracted and repelled him. The very grit of his makeup would not permit it, however, for his emotions now were running more to anger than the terror he had expected. He was to be, to *have been*, this monster Carstairs' victim! How now, knowing what the outcome would be—praying that it *would be* as he foresaw it—could he possibly turn away? No, flight was out of the question; Carstairs would find a substitute: the terror would continue. Even if Crow were to go, who could say what revenge might or might not fly hot on his heels?

At 9:30 P.M. cars pulled up at the house, quiet as hearses and more of them than at any other time, and through a crack in his shades Crow watched shadowy figures enter the house. For a little while then there were faint, subdued murmurings and creakings; all of which Crow heard with ears which strained in the library's darkness, fine-tuned to catch the merest whisper. A little later, when it seemed to him that the noises had descended beneath the house, he put out the alcove light and sat in un-mitigated darkness in the chair where Carstairs had left him. And all about him the night grew heavy, until it weighed like lead upon his head and shoulders.

As the minutes passed he found his hand returning again and again to the pocket where Townley's revolver lay comfortably heavy upon his thigh, and every so often he would be obliged to still the nervous trembling of his limbs. Somewhere in the distance a great clock chimed the hour of eleven, and as at a signal Crow heard the first susurrations of a low chant-ing from beneath his feet. A cold sweat immediately stood out upon his brow, which he dabbed away with a trembling handkerchief.

The Ritual of the Worm had commenced!

Angrily Crow fought for control of himself . . . for he knew what was coming. He cursed himself for a fool—for several fools—as the minutes ticked by and the unholy chanting took on rhythm and volume. He stood up, sat down, dabbed at his chill brow, fingered his revolver . . . and started at the sudden chiming of the half hour.

Now, in an instant, the house seemed full of icy air, the temperature fell to zero! Crow breathed the black, frigid atmosphere of the place and felt the tiny hairs crackling in his nostrils. He smelled sharp fumes— the unmistakable reek of burning henbane and opium—and sat rigid in his chair as the chanting from the cellar rose yet again, in a sort of frenzy now, throbbing and echoing as with the acoustics of some great cathedral.

The time must surely approach midnight, but Crow no longer dared glance at his watch.

Whatever it had been, in another moment his terror passed; he was his own man once more. He sighed raggedly and forced himself to relax, knowing that if he did not, that the emotional exhaustion must soon sap his strength. Surely the time—

—Had come!

The chanting told him: the way it swelled, receded and took on a new meter. For now it was his own name he heard called in the night, just as he had been told he would hear it.

Seated bolt upright in his chair, Crow saw the bookshelf door swing open, saw Carstairs framed in the faintly luminous portal, a loose-fitting cassock belted about his narrow middle. Tall and gaunt, more cadaverous than ever, the occultist beckoned.

"Come, Titus Crow, for the hour is at hand. Rise up and come with me, and learn the great and terrible mysteries of the worm!"

Crow rose and followed him, down the winding steps, through reek of henbane and opium and into the now luridly illumined cellar. Braziers stood at the four corners, glowing red where heated metal trays sent aloft spirals of burned incense, herbs, and opiates; and round the central space a dozen robed and hooded acolytes stood, their heads bowed and facing inward, toward the painted, interlocking circles. Twelve of them, thirteen including Carstairs, a full coven.

Carstairs led Crow through the coven's ring and pointed to the circle with the white-painted ascending node. "Stand there, Titus Crow," he commanded. "And have no fear."

Doing as he was instructed, Crow was glad for the cellar's flickering lighting and its fume-heavy atmosphere, which made faces ruddy and mobile and his trembling barely noticeable. And now he stood there, his feet in the mouth of the ascending node, as Carstairs took up his own position in the adjoining circle. Between them, in the "eye" where the circles interlocked, a large hourglass trickled black sand from one almost empty globe into another which was very nearly full.

Watching the hourglass and seeing that the sands had nearly run out, now Carstairs threw back his cowl and commanded: "Look at me, Titus Crow, and heed the Wisdom of the Worm!" Crow stared at the man's eyes, at his face and cassocked body.

The chanting of the acolytes grew loud once more, but their massed voice no longer formed Crow's name. Now they called on the Eater of Men himself, the loathsome master of this loathsome ritual:

"Wamas, Wormius, Vermi, WORM!"

"Wamas, Wormius, Vermi, WORM!"

"Wamas, Wormius, Vermi—"

And the sand in the hourglass ran out!

"Worm!" Carstairs cried as the others fell silent. "Worm, I command thee—come out!"

Unable, not daring to turn his eyes away from the man, Crow's lips drew back in a snarl of sheer horror at the transition which now began to take place. For as Carstairs convulsed in a dreadful agony, and while his eyes stood out in his head as if he were splashed with molten metal, still the man's mouth fell open to issue a great baying laugh.

And out of that mouth—out from his ears, his nostrils, even the hair of his head—there now appeared a writhing white flood of maggots, grave worms erupting from his every orifice as he writhed and jerked in his hellish ecstasy!

"Now, Titus Crow, now!" cried Carstairs, his voice a glutinous gabble as he continued to spew maggots. "Take my hand!" And he held out a trembling, quaking mass of crawling horror.

"No!" said Titus Crow. "No, I will not!"

Carstairs gurgled, gasped, cried, "What?" His cassock billowed with hideous movement. "Give me your hand—I command it!"

"Do your worst, wizard," Crow yelled back through gritted teeth.

"But . . . I have your Number! You must obey!"

"Not my Number, wizard," said Crow, shaking his head, and at once the acolyte circle began to cower back, their sudden gasps of terror filling the cellar.

"You lied!" Carstairs gurgled, seeming to shrink into himself. "You . . . cheated! No matter—a small thing." In the air he shaped a figure with a forefinger. "Worm, he is yours. I command you—take him!"

Now he pointed at Crow, and now the tomb horde at his feet rolled like a flood across the floor—and drew back from Crow's circle as from a ring of fire. "Go on!" Carstairs shrieked, crumbling into himself, his head wobbling madly, his cheeks in tatters from internal fretting. "Who is *he*? What does he know? I command you!"

"I know many things," said Crow. "They do not want me—they dare not touch me. And I will tell you why: I was born not in 1912 but in 1916—on second December of that year. Your ritual was based on the wrong date, Mr. Carstairs!"

The 2nd December 1916! A concerted gasp went up from the wavering acolytes. "*A Master!*" Crow heard the whisper. "*A twenty-two!*"

"No!" Carstairs fell to his knees. "*No!*"

He crumpled, crawled to the rim of his circle, beckoned with a half-skeletal hand. "Durrell, to me!" His voice was the rasp and rustle of blown leaves.

"Not me!" shrieked Durrell, flinging off his cassock and rushing for the cellar steps. "Not me!" Wildly he clambered from sight—and eleven like him hot on his heels.

"*No!*" Carstairs gurgled once more.

Crow stared at him, still unable to avert his eyes. He saw his features melt and flow, changing through a series of identities and firming in the final—the first!—dark, Arab visage of his origin. Then he fell on his side, turned that ravaged, sorcerer's face up to Crow. His eyes fell in and maggots seethed in the red orbits. The horde turned back, washed over him. In a moment nothing remained but bone and shreds of gristle, tossed and eddied on a ravenous tide.

Crow reeled from the cellar, his flesh crawling, his mind tottering on the brink. Only his Number saved him, the 22 of the Master Magician. And as he fumbled up the stone steps and through that empty, gibbering house, so he whispered words half forgotten, which seemed to come to him from nowhere:

"For it is of old renown that the soul of the devil-bought hastes not from his charnel clay, but fats and instructs *the very worm that gnaws*; till out of corruption horrid life springs . . ."

LATER, IN HIS RIGHT MIND but changed forever, Titus Crow drove away from The Barrows into the frosty night. No longer purposeless, he knew the course his life must now take. Along the gravel drive to the gates, a pinkish horde lay rimed in white death, frozen where they crawled. Crow barely noticed them.

The tires of his car paid them no heed whatever.

NAME AND NUMBER

I

Of course, nothing now remains of Blowne House, the sprawling bunga-low retreat of my dear friend and mentor Titus Crow, destroyed by tem-pestuous winds in a freak storm on the night of 4 October 1968, but . . .

Knowing all I know, or knew, of Titus Crow, perhaps it has been too easy for me to pass off the disastrous events of that night simply as a vindictive attack of dark forces; and while that is exactly what they were, I am now given to wonder if perhaps there was not a lot more to it than met the eye.

Provoked by Crow's and my own involvement with the Wilmarth Foundation (that vast, august and amazingly covert body, dedicated to the detection and the destruction of Earth's elder evil, within and outside of Man himself, and working in the sure knowledge that Man is but a small and comparatively recent phenomenon in a cosmos which has known sen-tience, good and evil, through vast and immeasurable cycles of time), dark forces did indeed destroy Blowne House. In so doing they effectively re-moved Titus Crow from the scene, and as for myself . . . I am but recently returned to it.

But since visiting the ruins of Crow's old place all these later years (perhaps because the time flown in between means so very little to me?), I have come to wonder more and more about the *nature* of that so well-remembered attack, the nature of the very winds themselves—those twist-ing, rending, tearing winds—which fell with such intent and purpose upon the house and bore it to the ground. In considering them I find myself casting my mind back to a time even more remote, when Crow first outlined for me the facts in the strange case of Mr. Sturm Magruser V.

CROW'S LETTER—a single hand-written sheet in a blank, sealed envelope, delivered by a taxi driver and the ink not quite dry—was at once terse and cryptic, which was not unusual and did not at all surprise me. When Titus Crow was idling, then all who wished anything to do with him must also bide their time, but when he was in a hurry—

> Henri,
>   Come as soon as you can, midnight would be fine. I expect you will stay the night. If you have not eaten, don't—there is food here. I have something of a story to tell you, and in the morning we are to visit a cemetery!
>
>   Until I see you—
>   Titus

The trouble with such invitations was this: I had never been able to refuse them! For Crow being what he was, one of London's foremost occultists, and my own interest in such matters amounting almost to obsession—why, for all its brevity, indeed by the very virtue of that brevity—Crow's summons was more a royal command!

And so I refrained from eating, wrote a number of letters which could not wait, enveloped and stamped them, and left a note for my housekeeper, Mrs. Adams, telling her to post them. She was to expect me when she saw me, but in any matter of urgency I might be contacted at Blowne House. Doubtless the dear lady, when she read that address, would complain bitterly to herself about the influence of "that dreadful Crow person," for in her eyes Titus had always been to blame for my own deep interest in darkling matters. In all truth, however, my obsession was probably inherited, sealed into my personality as a permanent stamp of my father, the great New Orleans mystic Etienne-Laurent de Marigny.

Then, since the hour already approached twelve and I would be late for my "appointment," I phoned for a taxi and double-checked that my one or two antique treasures were safely locked away; and finally I donned my overcoat. Half an hour or so later, at perhaps a quarter to one, I stood on Crow's doorstep and banged upon his heavy oak door; and having heard the arrival of my taxi, he was there at once to greet me. This he did with his customary grin (or enigmatic smile?), his head cocked slightly to one side in an almost inquiring posture. And once again I was ushered into the marvelous Aladdin's cave which was Blowne House.

Now, Crow had been my friend ever since my father sent me out of America as a child in the late '30s, and no man knew him better than I; and yet his personality was such that whenever I met him—however short the intervening time—I would always be impressed anew by his stature, his leonine good looks, and the sheer weight of intellect which seemed invariably to shine out from behind those searching, dark eyes of his. In his flame-red, wide-sleeved dressing gown, he might easily be some wizard from the pages of myth or fantasy.

In his study he took my overcoat, bade me sit in an easy chair beside a glowing fire, tossed a small log onto ruddy embers and poured me a customary brandy before seating himself close by. And while he was thus engaged I took my chance to gaze with fascination and unfeigned envy all about that marvelous room.

Crow himself had designed and furnished that large room to contain most of what he considered important to his world, and certainly I could have spent ten full years there in constant study of the contents without absorbing or even understanding a fifth part of what I read or examined. However, to give a brief and essentially fleshless account of what I could see from my chair:

His "library," consisting of one entire wall of shelves, contained such works as the abhorrent *Cthaat Aquadingen* (in a binding of human skin!), Feery's *Original Notes on the Necronomicon* (the complete book, as opposed to my own abridged copy), Wendy-Smith's translation of the *G'harne Fragments,* a possibly faked but still priceless copy of the *Pnakotic Manuscripts,* Justin Geoffrey's *People of the Monolith*, a literally fabulous *Cultes des Goules* (which, on my next birthday, having derived all he could from it, he would present to me), the *Geph Transcriptions,* Wardle's *Notes on Nitocris,* Urbicus' *Frontier Garrison,* circa A.D. 183, Plato's *Atlantis,* a rare, illustrated, pirated and privately printed *Complete Works of Poe* in three sumptuous volumes, the far more ancient works of such as Josephus, Magnus, Levi and Erdschluss, and a connected set of volumes on oceanic lore and legend which included such works as Gantley's *Hydrophinnae* and Konrad von Gerner's *Fischbuch* of 1598. And I have merely skimmed the surface...

In one dim corner stood an object which had been a source of fascination for me, and no less for Crow himself: a great hieroglyphed, coffin-shaped monstrosity of a grandfather clock, whose tick was quite irregular and abnormal, and whose four hands moved independently and without recourse to any time system with which I was remotely familiar. Crow had bought the thing in auction some years previously, at which time he had mentioned his belief that it had once belonged to my father—of which I had known nothing, not at that time.

As for the general decor and feel of the place:

Silk curtains were drawn across wide windows; costly Boukhara rugs were spread on a floor already covered in fine Axminister; a good many Aubrey Beardsley originals—some of them most erotic—hung on the walls in equally valuable antique rosewood frames; and all in all the room seemed to exude a curiously mixed atmosphere of rich, warm, Olde World gentility on the one hand, a strange and alien chill of outer spheres on the other.

And thus I hope I have managed to convey something of the nature of Titus Crow and of his study—and of his *studies*—in that bungalow dwelling on Leonard's Heath known as Blowne House... As to why I was there—

"I suppose you're wondering," Crow said after a while, "just why I asked you to come? And at such an hour on such a chilly night, when doubtless you've a good many other things you should be doing? Well, I'll not keep you in suspense—but first of all I would greatly appreciate your opinion of something." He got up, crossed to his desk and returned with a thick book of newspaper cuttings, opening it to a previously marked page. Most of the cuttings were browned and faded, but the one Crow pointed out to me was only a few weeks old. It was a photograph of the head and shoulders of a man, accompanied by the following legend:

Mr. Sturm Magruser, head of Magruser Systems UK, the weapons manufacturing company of world repute, is on the point of winning for his company a £2,000,000 order from the Ministry of Defense in respect of an at-present "secret" national defense system. Mr. Magruser, who himself devised and is developing the new system, would not comment when he was snapped by our reporter leaving the country home of a senior Ministry of Defense official, but it has been rumored for some time that his company is close to a breakthrough on a defense system which will effectively make the atomic bomb entirely obsolete. Tests are said to be scheduled for the near future, following which the Ministry of Defense is expected to make its final decision . . .

"Well?" Crow asked as I read the column again.

I shrugged. "What are you getting at?"

"It makes no impression?"

"I've heard of him and his company, of course," I answered, "though I believe this is the first time I've actually seen a picture of him—but apart from—"

"Ah!" Crow cut in. "Good! This is the first time you've seen his picture: and him a prominent figure and his firm constantly in the news and so on. Me too."

"Oh?" I was still puzzled.

"Yes, it's important, Henri, what you just said. In fact, I would hazard a guess that Mr. Magruser is one of the world's least photographed men."

"So? Perhaps he's camera shy."

"Oh, he is, he is—and for a very good reason. We'll get to it—eventually. Meanwhile, let's eat!"

Now, this is a facet of Crow's personality which did annoy me: his penchant for leaping from one subject to another, willy-nilly, with never a word of explanation, leaving one constantly stumbling in the dark. He could only do it, of course, when he knew that his audience was properly hooked. But in my case I do not expect he intended any torment; he merely offered me the opportunity to use my mind. This I seized upon, while he busied himself bringing out cold fried chicken from his kitchen.

II

Sturm Magruser . . . A strange name, really. Foreign, of course. Hungarian, perhaps? As the "Mag" in "Magyar?" I doubted it, even though his features were decidedly Eastern or Middle Eastern; for they were rather pale, too. And what of his first name, Sturm? If only I were a little more proficient in tongues, I might make something of it. And what of the man's reticence, and of Crow's comment that he stood among the least photographed of men?

We finished eating. "What do you make of the *V* after his name?" Crow asked.

"Hmm? Oh, it's a common enough vogue nowadays," I answered, "particularly in America. It denotes that he's the fifth of his line, the fifth Sturm Magruser."

Crow nodded and frowned. "You'd think so, wouldn't you? But in this case it can't possibly be. No, for he changed his name by deed poll after his parents died." He had grown suddenly intense, but before I could ask him why, he was off again. "And what would you give him for nationality, or rather origin?"

I took a stab at it. "Romanian?"

He shook his head. "Persian."

I smiled. "I was way off, wasn't I?"

"What about his face?" Crow pressed.

I picked up the book of cuttings and looked at the photograph again. "It's a strange face, really. Pale somehow . . ."

"He's an albino."

"Ah!" I said. "Yes, pale and startled—at least in this picture—displeased at being snapped, I suppose."

Again he nodded. "You suppose correctly . . . All right, Henri, enough of that for the moment. Now I'll tell you what I made of this cutting— Magruser's picture and the story when first I saw it. Now, as you know I collect all sorts of cuttings from one source or another, tidbits of fact and fragments of information which interest me or strike me as unusual. Most occultists, I'm told, are extensive collectors of all sorts of things. You yourself are fond of antiques, old books and outré bric-a-brac, much as I am, but as yet without my dedication. And yet if you examine all of my scrapbooks you'll probably discover that this would appear to be the most mundane cutting of them all. At least on the surface. For myself, I found it the most frightening and disturbing."

He paused to pour more brandy and I leaned closer to him, fascinated to find out exactly what he was getting at. "Now," he finally continued, "I'm an odd sort of chap, as you'll appreciate, but I'm not eccentric—not in the popular sense of the word. Or if I am," he hurried on, "it's of my choosing. That is to say, I believe I'm mentally stable."

"You are the sanest man I ever met," I told him.

"I wouldn't go that far," he answered, "and you may soon have reason for reevaluation, but for the moment I *am* sane. How then might I explain the loathing, the morbid repulsion, the absolute shock of horror which struck me almost physically upon opening the pages of my morning newspaper and coming upon that picture of Magruser? I could not explain it—not immediately . . ." He paused again.

"Presentiment?" I asked. "A forewarning?"

"Certainly!" he answered. "But of what, and from where? And the more I looked at that damned picture, the more sure I became that I was onto something monstrous! Seeing him—that face, startled, angered, trapped by the camera—and despite the fact that I could not possibly know him, I *recognized* him."

"Ah!" I said. "You mean that you've known him before, under his former name?"

Crow smiled, a trifle wearily I thought. "The world has known him before under several names," he answered. Then the smile slipped from his face. "Talking of names, what do you make of his forename?"

"Sturm? I've already considered it. German, perhaps?"

"Good! Yes, German. His mother was German, his father Persian, both nationalized Americans in the early 1900s. They left America to come here during McCarthy's UnAmerican Activities witch-hunts. Sturm Magruser, incidentally, was born on first April 1921. An important date, Henri, and not just because it was April Fool's Day."

"A fairly young man," I answered, "to have reached so powerful a position."

"Indeed." Crow nodded. "He would have been forty-three in a month's time."

"Would have been?" I was surprised by Crow's tone of finality. "Is he dead then?"

"Mercifully, yes," he answered, "Magruser and his project with him! He died the day before yesterday, on fourth March 1964, also an important date. It was in yesterday's news, but I'm not surprised you missed it. He wasn't given a lot of space, and he leaves no mourners that I know of. As to his 'secret weapon' "—and here Crow gave an involuntary little shudder—"the secret has gone with him. For that, too, we may be thankful."

"Then the cemetery you mentioned in your note is where he's to be interred?" I guessed.

"Where he's to be cremated," he corrected me. "Where his ashes are to be scattered to the winds."

"Winds!" I snapped my fingers. "Now I have it! *Sturm* means 'storm'—it's the German word for storm!"

Crow nodded. "Again correct," he said. "But let's not start adding things up too quickly."

"Add things up?" I snorted. "My friend, I'm completely lost!"

"Not completely," he denied. "What you have is a jigsaw puzzle without a picture to work from. Difficult, but once you have completed the frame the rest will slowly piece itself together. Now, then, I was telling you about the time three weeks ago when I saw Magruser's picture.

"I remember I was just up, still in my dressing gown, and I had just brought the paper in here to read. The curtains were open and I could see out into the garden. It was quite cold but relatively mild for the time of the year. The morning was dry and the heath seemed to beckon me, so that I made up my mind to take a walk. After reading the day's news and after breakfast, I would dress and take a stroll outdoors. Then I opened my newspaper—and Sturm Magruser's face greeted me!

"Henri, I dropped the paper as if it were a hot iron! So shaken was I that I had to sit down or risk falling. Now, I'm a fairly sturdy chap, and you can well imagine the sort of shock my system would require to disturb it. Then as I sat down in my chair and stooped to recover the newspaper—the other thing.

"Out in the garden, a sudden stirring of wind. The hedgerow trembling and last year's leaves blowing across my drive. And birds startled to flight, as if by the sudden presence of some one or thing I could not see. And the sudden gathering and rushing of spiraling winds, dust devils that sucked up leaves and grit and other bits of debris and shot them aloft. Dust devils, Henri, in March—in England—half a dozen of them that paraded all about Blowne House for the best part of thirty minutes! In any other circumstance, a marvelous, fascinating phenomenon."

"But not for you?"

"No." He shook his head. "Not then. I'll tell you what they signified for me, Henri. They told me that just as I had recognized *something*, so I had been recognized! Do you understand?"

"Frankly, no," and it was my turn to shake my head.

"Let it pass," he said after a moment. "Suffice it to say that there were these strange spiraling winds, and that I took them as a sign that indeed my psychic sense had detected something unutterably dangerous and obscene in this man Sturm Magruser. And I was so frightened by my discovery that I at once set about to discover all I could of him, so that I should know what the threat was and how best to deal with it."

"Can I stop you for a moment?" I requested.

"Eh? Oh, certainly."

"Those dates you mentioned as being important, Magruser's birth and death dates. In what way important?"

"Ah! We shall get to that, Henri." He smiled. "You may or may not know it, but I'm also something of a numerologist."

Now it was my turn to smile. "You mean like those fellows who measure the Great Pyramid and read in their findings the secrets of the universe?"

"Do not be flippant, de Marigny!" he answered at once, his smile disappearing in an instant. "I meant no such thing. And in any case, don't be in too great a hurry to discredit the pyramidologists. Who are you to say what may or may not be? Until you have studied a thing for yourself, treat it with respect."

"Oh!" was all I could say.

"As for birth and death dates, try these: 1889, 1945."

I frowned, shrugged, said: "They mean nothing to me. Are they, too, important?"

"They belong to Adolf Hitler," he told me, "and if you add the individual numbers together you'll discover that they make five sets of nine. Nine is an important number in occultism, signifying death. Hitler's number, 99999, shows him to have been a veritable Angel of Death, and no one could deny that! Incidentally, if you multiply five and nine you get forty-five, which are the last two numbers in 1945—the year he died. This is merely one example of an ancient science. Now, please, Henri, no more scoffing at numerology . . ."

Deflated, still I was beginning to see a glimmer of light in Crow's reasoning. "Ah!" I said. "And Sturm Magruser, like Hitler, has dates which add up to forty-five? Am I right? Let me see: the 1st of the 4th 1921—that's eighteen—and the 4th of the 3rd 1964. That's forty-five!"

Crow nodded, smiling again. "You're a clever man, Henri, yes—but you've missed the most important aspect of the thing. But never mind that for now, let me get back to my story . . .

"I have said that I set about to discover all I could of this fellow with the strange name, the camera-shy manner, the weight of a vast international concern behind him—and the power to frighten the living daylights out of me, which no other man ever had before. And don't ask me how, but I knew I had to work fast. There wasn't a great deal of time left before . . . before whatever was coming came.

"First, however, I contacted a friend of mine at the British Museum, the curator of the Rare Books Department, and asked him to search something out for me in the *Necronomicon*. I must introduce you one day, Henri. He's a marvelous chap. Not quite all there, I fancy—he can't be, to work in that place—but so free of vice and sin, so blindly naive and innocent, that the greatest possible evils would bounce right off him, I'm sure. Which is just as well, I suppose. Certainly I would never ask an inquiring or susceptible mind to lay itself open to the perils of Alhazred's book.

"And at last I was able to concentrate on Magruser. This was about midday and my mind had been working frantically for several hours, so that already I was beginning to feel tired—mentally if not physically. I was also experiencing a singular emotion, a sort of morbid suspicion that I was being watched, and that the observer lurked somewhere in my garden!

"Putting this to the back of my mind, I began to make discreet telephone inquiries about Magruser, but no sooner had I voiced his name than the feeling came over me again, more strongly than before. It was as if a cloud of unutterable malignity, heavy with evil, had settled suddenly over the entire house. And starting back from the telephone, I saw once again the shadow of a nodding dust devil where it played with leaves and twigs in the center of my drive."

III

"Now my fear turned to anger. Very well, if it was war . . . then I must now employ weapons of my own. Or if not weapons, defenses, certainly.

"I won't go into details, Henri, but you know the sort of thing I mean. I have long possessed the necessary knowledge to create barriers of a sort against evil influences; no occultist or student of such things worth his salt would ever be without them. But it had recently been my good fortune to obtain a certain—shall we call it 'charm?'—allegedly efficacious above all others.

"As to how this 'charm' happened my way:

"In December Thelred Gustau had arrived in London from Iceland, where he had been studying Surtsey's volcanic eruption. During that eruption, Gustau had fished from the sea an item of extreme antiquity—indeed, a veritable time capsule from an age undreamed-of. When he contacted me in mid-December, he was still in a high fever of excitement. He needed my skills, he said, to help him unravel a mystery 'predating the very dinosaurs.' His words.

"I worked with him until mid-January, when he suddenly received an offer from America in respect of a lecture tour there. It was an offer he could not refuse—one which would finance his researches for several years to come—and so, off he went. By that time I had become so engrossed with the work I almost went with him. Fortunately I did not." And here he paused to refill our glasses.

"Of course," I took the opportunity to say, "I knew you were extremely busy with something. You were so hard to contact, and then always at Gustau's Woolwich address. But what exactly were you working on?"

"Ah!" he answered. "That is something which Thelred Gustau himself will have to reveal—which I expect he'll do shortly. Though who'll take him seriously, heaven only knows. As to what I may tell you of it—I'll have to have your word that it will be kept in the utmost secrecy."

"You know you have it," I answered.

"Very well . . . During the course of the eruption, Surtsey ejected a . . . a *container*, Henri, the 'time capsule' I have mentioned. Inside—fantastic!

"It was a record from a prehistoric world, Theem'hdra, a continent at the dawn of time, and it had been sent to us down all the ages by one of that continent's greatest magicians, the wizard Teh Atht, descendant of the mighty Mylakhrion. Alas, it was in the unknown language of that primal land, in Teh Atht's own hand, and Gustau had accidentally lost the means of its translation. But he did have a key, and he had his own great genius, and—"

"And he had you." I smiled. "One of the country's greatest paleographers."

"Yes," said Crow, matter-of-factly and without pride. "Second only to Professor Gordon Walmsley of Goole. Anyway, I helped Gustau where I could, and during the work I came across a powerful spell against injurious magic and other supernatural menaces. Gustau allowed me to make a copy for myself, which is how I came to be in possession of a fragment of elder magic from an age undreamed-of. From what I could make of it, Theem'hdra had existed in an age of wizards, and Teh Atht himself had used this very charm or spell to ward off evil.

"Well, I had the thing, and now I decided to employ it. I set up the necessary paraphernalia and induced within myself the required mental state. This took until well into the afternoon, and with each passing minute the sensation of impending doom deepened about the house, until I was almost prepared to flee the place and let well alone. And, if I had not by now been certain that such flight would be a colossal dereliction of duty, I admit I would have done so.

"As it was—when I had willed myself to the correct mental condition, and upon the utterance of certain words—the effect was instantaneous!

"Daylight seemed to flood the whole house; the gloom fled in a moment; my spirits soared, and outside in the garden a certain ethereal watchdog collapsed in a tiny heap of rubbish and dusty leaves. Teh Atht's rune had proved itself effective indeed . . ."

"And then you turned your attention to Sturm Magruser?" I prompted him after a moment or two.

"Not that night, no. I was exhausted, Henri. The day had taken so much out of me. No, I could do no more that night. Instead I slept, deeply and dreamlessly, right through the evening and night until the jangling of my telephone awakened me at nine o'clock on the following morning."

"Your friend at the Rare Books Department?" I guessed.

"Yes, enlisting my aid in narrowing down his field of research. As you'll appreciate, the *Necronomicon* is a large volume—compared to which Feery's *Notes* is a pamphlet—and many of its sections appear to be almost repetitious in their content. The trouble was, I wasn't even certain that it contained what I sought; only that I believed I had read it there. If not"— and he waved an expansive hand in the direction of his own more than appreciable occult library—"then the answer must be here somewhere— whose searching out would form an equally frustrating if not utterly im- possible task. At least in the time allowed."

"You keep hinting at this urgency." I frowned. "What do you mean, 'the time allowed?'"

"Why," he answered, "the time in which Magruser must be disposed of, of course!"

"Disposed of?" I could hardly believe my ears.

Crow sighed and brought it right out in the open: "The time in which I must kill him!" he said.

I tried to remain calm, tried not to seem too flippant when I said, "So, you had resolved to do away with him. This was necessary?"

"Very. And once my inquiries began to produce results, why, then his death became more urgent by the minute! For over the next few days I turned up some very interesting and very frightening facts about our Mr. Magruser, not the least of them concerning his phenomenal rise from obscurity and the amount of power he controlled here and abroad. His company extended to no less than seven different countries, with a total of ten plants or factories engaged in the manufacture of weapons of war. Most of them conventional weapons—for the moment. Ah, yes! And those numbers too, Henri, are important.

"As for his current project—the completion of this 'secret' weapon or 'defense system'—in this I was to discover the very root and nature of the evil, after which I was convinced in my decision that indeed Magruser must go!"

The time was now just after three in the morning and the fire had burned very low. While Crow took a break from talking and went to the kitchen to prepare a light snack, I threw logs on the fire and shivered, not merely because of the chill the night had brought. Such was Crow's story and his method of delivery that I myself was now caught up in its cryptic strangeness, the slowly strangling threads of its skein. Thus I paced the floor and pondered all he had told me, not least his stated intention to— murder?—Sturm Magruser, who now apparently was dead.

Passing Crow's desk I noticed an antique family Bible in two great volumes, the New Testament lying open, but I did not check book or chapter. Also littering his desk were several books on cryptology, numerology, even one on astrology, in which "science" Crow had never to my knowledge displayed a great deal of faith or interest. Much in evidence was a well-thumbed copy of Walmsley's *Notes on Deciphering Codes, Cryptograms and Ancient Inscriptions,* also an open notebook of obscure jottings and diagrams. My friend had indeed been busy.

Over cheese and crackers we carried on, and Crow took up his tale once more by hinting of the awesome power of Magruser's "secret" weapon.

"Henri," he began, "there is a tiny island off the Orkneys which, until mid-1961, was green, lovely, and a sanctuary for seabirds. Too small and isolated to settle, and far too cold and open to the elements in winter, the place was never inhabited and only rarely visited. Magruser bought it, worked there, and by February '62—"

"Yes?"

"A dustbowl!"

"A dustbowl?" I repeated him. "Chemicals, you mean?"

Crow shrugged. "I don't know how his weapon works exactly, only what it produces. Also that it needs vast amounts of energy to trigger it. From what I've been able to discover, he used the forces of nature to fuel his experiment in the Orkneys, the enormous energies of an electrical storm. Oh, yes, and one other thing: the weapon was *not* a defense system!"

"And of course you also know," I took a stab at it, "what he intended to do with this weapon?"

"That too, yes." He nodded. "He intended to destroy the world, reduce us to savagery, return us to the Dark Ages. In short, to deliver a blow from which the human race would never recover."

"But—"

"No, let me go on. Magruser intended to turn the world into a desert, start a chain reaction that couldn't be stopped. It may even have been worse than I suspected. He may have aimed at total destruction—no survivors at all!"

"You had proof?"

"I had evidence. As for proof: he's dead, isn't he?"

"You did kill him, then?"

"Yes."

After a little while I asked, "What evidence did you have?"

"Three types of evidence, really," he answered, relaxing again in his chair. "One: the evidence of my own five senses—and possibly that sixth sense by which I had known him from the start. Two: the fact that he had carried out his experiments in other places, several of them, always with the same result. And three—

"Yes?"

"That too, was information I received through government channels. I worked for MOD as a very young man, Henri. Did you know that? It was the War Department in those days. During the war I cracked codes for them, and I advised them on Hitler's occult interests."

"No," I said, "I never knew that."

"Of course not," he replied. "No man has *my* number, Henri," and he smiled. "Did you know that there's supposed to be a copy of the *Necronomicon* buried in a filled-in bunker just across the East German border in Berlin? And did you know that in his last hour Hitler was approached in his own bunker by a Jew—can you imagine that?—a Jew who whispered something to him before he took his life? I believe I know what that man whispered, Henri. I think he said these words: 'I know you, Adolf Hitler!'"

"Titus," I said, "there are so many loose ends here that I'm trying to tie together. You've given me so many clues, and yet—"

"It will all fit, Henri." He calmed me. "It will fit. Let me go on . . .

"When I discovered that Magruser's two-million-pound 'order' from the MOD was not an order at all but merely the use of two million pounds' worth of equipment—and as soon as I knew what that equipment was— then I guessed what he was up to. To clinch matters there finally came that call from the British Museum, and at last I had all the information I needed. But that was not until after I had actually met the man face-to-face.

"First, the government 'equipment' Magruser had managed to lay his hands on: two million pounds' worth of atomic bombs!"

IV

"*What?*" I was utterly astonished. "You're joking!"

"No," he answered, "I am not joking. They were to provide the power he needed to trigger his doomsday weapon, to start the chain reaction. A persuasive man, Magruser, and you may believe that there's hell to pay right now in certain government circles. I have let it be known—

anonymously, of course—just exactly what he was about and the holocaust the world so narrowly escaped. Seven countries, Henri, and seven atomic bombs. Seven simultaneous detonations powering his own far more dreadful weapon, forging the links in a chain reaction which would spread right across the world!"

"But . . . how . . . when was this to happen?" I stammered.

"Today," he answered, "at ten o'clock in the morning, a little more than five hours from now. The bombs were already in position in his plants, waiting for the appointed time. By now of course they have been removed and the plants destroyed. And now too, Britain will have to answer to the heads of six foreign powers; and certain lesser heads will roll, you may be sure. But very quietly, and the world as a whole shall never know."

"But what was his purpose?" I asked. "Was he a madman?"

He shook his head. "A madman? No. Though he was born of human flesh, he was not even a man, not completely. Or perhaps he was more than a man. A force? A power . . .

"A week ago I attended a party at the home of my friend in the MOD. Magruser was to be there, which was why I *had* to be there—and I may tell you that took a bit of arranging. And all very discreetly, mind you, for I could not let any other person know of my suspicions. Who would have believed me anyway?

"At the party, eventually I cornered Magruser—as strange a specimen as ever you saw—and to come face-to-face with him was to confirm my quarry's identity. I now knew beyond any question of doubt that indeed he was the greatest peril the world has ever faced! If I sound melodramatic, Henri, it can't be helped.

"And yet to look at him . . . any other man might have felt pity. As I have said, he was an albino, with hair white as snow and flesh to match, so that his only high points seemed to lie in pallid pulses beating in his throat and forehead. He was tall and spindly, and his head was large but not overly so; though his cranium did display a height and width which at one and the same time hinted of imbecility and genius. His eyes were large, close together, pink, and their pupils were scarlet. I have known women—a perverse group at best—who would call him attractive, and certain men who might envy him his money, power, and position. As for myself, I found him repulsive! But of course my prejudice was born of knowing the truth.

"He did not wish to be there, that much was plain, for he had that same trapped look about him which came through so strongly in his photograph. He was afraid, Henri, afraid of being stopped. For of course he knew that someone, somewhere, had recognized him. What he did not yet know was that I was that someone.

"Oh, he was nervous, this Magruser. Only the fact that he was to receive his answer that night, the go-ahead from the ministry, had brought him out of hiding. And he did receive that go-ahead, following which I cornered him, as I have said."

"Wait," I begged him. "You said he knew that someone had recognized him. How did he know?"

"He knew at the same moment I knew, Henri, at the very instant when those spinning winds of his sprang up in my garden! But I had destroyed them, and fortunately before he could discover my identity. Oh, you may be sure he had tried to trace me, but I had been protected by the barriers I had placed about Blowne House. Now, however, I too was out in the open . . ."

"But I still can't see how the British government could be tricked into giving him a handful of atomic bombs!" I pressed. "Are we all in the hands of lunatics?"

Crow shook his head. "You should know by now," he said, "that the British give nothing for nothing. What the government stood to gain was far greater than a measly two million pounds. Magruser had promised to deliver a power screen, Henri, a dome of force covering the entire land, to be switched on and off at will, making the British Isles totally invulnerable!"

"And we believed him?"

"Oh, there had been demonstrations, all faked, and it had been known for a long time that he was experimenting with a 'national defense system.' And remember, my friend, that Magruser had never once stepped out of line. He was the very model of a citizen, a man totally above suspicion who supported every welfare and charity you could name. Why, I believe that on occasion he had even funded the government itself; but for all this he had not the means of powering his damnable weapons. And now you begin to see something of the brilliance of the man, something of his fiendishness.

"But to get back to what I was saying: I finally cornered him, we were about to be introduced, I even stuck out my hand for him to shake, and—

"At that very moment a window blew in and the storm which had been blowing up for over an hour rushed into the room. Rushing winds, Henri, and fifty ladies and gentlemen spilling their drinks and hanging on to their hats—and a whirling dervish of a thing that sucked up invitation cards and flowers from vases and paper napkins and flew *between* Magruser and myself like . . . like one of hell's own devils!

"How his pink eyes narrowed and glared at me then, and in another moment he had stepped quickly out of my reach. By the time order was restored Magruser was gone. He had rushed out of the house to be driven away, probably back to his plant outside Oxford.

"Well, I too left in something of a hurry, but not before my friend had promised not to tell Magruser who I was. Later, Magruser did indeed call him, only to be fobbed off with the answer that I must have been a gate-crasher. And so I was safe from him—for the moment.

"When I arrived home my telephone was ringing, and at first I was of a mind not to pick it up—but . . . it was the information I had been waiting for, a quotation from the Mad Arab himself, Abdul Alhazred." Here Crow paused to get up, go to his desk, rummage about for a second or two and return with a scrap of paper. He seated himself once more and said: "Listen to this, Henri:

'Many and multiform are ye dim horrors of Earth, infesting her ways from ye very prime. They sleep beneath ye unturned stone; they rise with ye tree from its root; they move beneath ye sea, and in subterranean places they dwell in ye inmost adyta. Some there are long known to man, and others as yet unknown, abiding ye terrible latter days of their revealing. One such is an evil born of a curse, for ye Greatest Old One, before He went Him down into His place to be sealed therein and sunken under ye sea, uttered a cry which rang out to ye very corners of ye All; and He cursed this world then and forever. And His curse was this: that whosoever inhabit this world which was become his prison, there should breed among them and of their flesh great traitors who would ever seek to destroy them and so leave ye world cleared off for ye day of His return. And when they heard this great curse, them that held Him thrust Him down where He could do no more harm. And because they were good, they sought to eradicate ye harm He had willed, but could not do so. Thus they worked a counterspell, which was this: that there would always be ones to know the evil ones when they arose and waxed strong, thus protecting ye innocents from His great curse. And this also did they arrange: that in their fashion ye evil ones would reveal themselves, and that any man with understanding might readily dispose of such a one by seizing him and saying unto him, "I know you," and by revealing his number . . .'

"And in the end it was as simple as that, Henri . . .

"Late as the evening had grown, still I set about to strengthen those psychic or magical protections I had built about Blowne House. Also, I placed about my own person certain charms for self-protection when I was abroad and outside the safety of these stout walls; all of which took me until the early hours of the morning. That day—that very day—Sturm Magruser would be collecting his deadly detonators, the triggers for his devilish device; and in my mind's eye I pictured a vehicle pulling up at some innocuous-seeming but well-guarded and lethally supplied establishment, and the driver showing a pass, and documents being signed in triplicate and the subsequent very careful loading of seven heavy crates.

"There would be a pair of executive jets waiting on the private runway inside Magruser's Oxford plant, and these would take six of the atomic bombs off to their various destinations around the globe. And so it can be seen that my time was running down. Tired as I was, worn down by worry and work, still I had to press on and find the solution to the threat."

"But surely you had the solution?" I cut in. "It was right there in that passage from Alhazred."

"I had the means to destroy him, Henri, yes—but I did not have the means of delivery! The only thing I could be sure of was that he was still in this country, at his center of operations. But how to get near him, now that he knew me?"

"He knew you?"

Crow sighed. "My face, certainly, for we had now met. Or almost. And if I knew my quarry, by now he might also have discovered my name and particulars. Oh, yes, Henri. For just as I have my means, be sure Magruser had his. Well, obviously I could not stay at Blowne House, not after I realized how desperate the man must be to find me. I must go elsewhere, and quickly.

"And I did go, that very night. I drove up to Oxford."

"To Oxford?"

"Yes, into the very lion's den, as it were. In the morning I found a suitable hotel and garaged my car, and a little later I telephoned Magruser."

"Just like that?" Again I was astonished. "You telephoned him?"

"No, not just like that at all," he answered. "First I ordered and waited for the arrival of a taxi. I dared not use my Mercedes for fear that by now he knew both the car and its number." He smiled tiredly at me. "You are beginning to see just how important numbers really are, eh, Henri?"

I nodded. "But please go on. You said you phoned him?"

"I tried the plant first and got the switchboard, and was told that Mr. Magruser was at home and could not be disturbed. I said that it was important, that I had tried his home number and was unable to obtain him, and that I must be put through to him at once."

"And they fell for that? Had you really tried his home number?"

"No, it's not listed. And to physically go near his estate would be sheer lunacy, for surely the place would be heavily guarded."

"But then they *must* have seen through your ruse," I argued. "If his number was ex-directory, how could you possibly tell them that you knew it?"

Again Crow smiled. "If I was the fellow I pretended to be, I would know it," he answered.

I gasped. "Your friend from the ministry! You used his name."

"Of course," said Crow. "And now we see again the importance of names, eh, my friend? Well, I was put through and eventually Magruser spoke to me, but I knew that it was him before ever he said a word. The very sound of his breathing came to me like exhalations from a tomb! 'This is Magruser,' he said, his voice full of suspicion. 'Who is speaking?'

" 'Oh, I think you know me, Sturm Magruser,' I answered. 'Even as I know you!' "

V

"There was a sharp intake of breath. Then: 'Mr. Titus Crow,' he said. 'You are a most resourceful man. Where are you?'

" 'On my way to see you, Magruser,' I answered.

" 'And when may I expect you?'

" 'Sooner than you think. I have your number!'

"At that he gasped again and slammed the phone down; and now I would discover whether or not my preliminary investigation stood me in good stead. Now, too, I faced the most danger-fraught moments of the entire business.

"Henri, if you had been Magruser, what would you do?"

"Me? Why, I'd stay put, surrounded by guards—and they'd have orders to shoot you on sight as a dangerous intruder."

"And what if I should come with more armed men than you? And would your guards, if they were ordinary chaps, obey that sort of order in the first place? How could you be *sure* to avoid any encounter with me?"

I frowned and considered it. "I'd put distance between us, get out of the country, and—"

"Exactly!" Crow said. "Get out of the country."

I saw his meaning. "The private airstrip inside his plant?"

"Of course," Crow nodded. "Except I had ensured that I was closer to the plant than he was. It would take me fifteen to twenty minutes to get there by taxi. Magruser would need between five and ten minutes more than that . . .

"As for the plant itself—proudly displaying its sign, Magruser Systems, UK—it was large, set in expansive grounds and surrounded by a high, patrolled wire fence. The only entrance was from the main road and boasted an electrically operated barrier and a small guardroom sort of building to house the security man. All this I saw as I paid my taxi fare and approached the barrier.

"As I suspected, the guard came out to meet me, demanding to know my name and business. He was not armed that I could see, but he was big and heavy. I told him I was MOD and that I had to see Mr. Magruser.

" 'Sorry, sir,' he answered. 'There must be a bit of a flap on. I've just had orders to let no one in, not even pass-holders. Anyway, Mr. Magruser's at home.'

" 'No, he's not,' I told him. 'He's on his way here right now, and I'm to meet him at the gate.'

" 'I suppose that'll be all right then, sir,' he answered. 'Just as long as you don't want to go in.'

"I walked over to the guardroom with him. While we were talking, I kept covert watch on the open doors of a hangar spied between buildings and installations. Even as I watched, a light aircraft taxied into the open and mechanics began running to and fro, readying it for flight. I was also watching the road, plainly visible from the guardroom window, and at last was rewarded by the sight of Magruser's car speeding into view a quarter mile away.

"Then I produced my handgun."

"What?" I cried. "If all else failed you planned to shoot him?"

"Not at all. Oh, I might have tried it, I suppose, but I doubt if a bullet could have killed him. No, the gun had another purpose to serve, namely the control of any merely human adversary."

"Such as the security man?"

"Correct. I quickly relieved him of his uniform jacket and hat, gagged him and locked him in a small back room. Then, to make absolutely certain, I drove the butt of my weapon through the barrier's control panel, effectively ruining it. By this time Magruser's car was turning off the road into the entrance, and of course it stopped at the lowered barrier. There was Magruser, sitting on my side and in the front passenger seat, and in the back a pair of large young men who were plainly bodyguards.

"I pulled my hat down over my eyes, went out of the guardroom and up to the car, and as I had prayed Magruser himself wound down his window. He stuck out his hand, made imperative, flapping motions, and said, 'Fool! I wish to be in. Get the barrier—'

"But at that moment I grabbed and held on to his arm, lowered my face to his, and said, 'Sturm Magruser, I know you—and I know your number!'

"'What? What?' he whispered—and his eyes went wide in terror as he recognized me.

"Then I told him his number, and as his bodyguards leaped from the car and dragged me away from him, he waved them back. 'Leave him be,' he said, 'for it's too late now.' And he favored me with such a look as I shall never forget. Slowly he got out of the car, leaning heavily upon the door, facing me. 'That is only half my number,' he said, 'but sufficient to destroy me. Do you know the rest of it?'

"And I told him the rest of it.

"What little color he had drained completely from him and it was as if a light had gone out behind his eyes. He would have collapsed if his men hadn't caught and supported him, seating him back in the car. And all the time his eyes were on my face, his pink and scarlet eyes which had started to bleed.

"'A very resourceful man,' he croaked then, and, 'So little time.' To his driver he said, 'Take me home . . .'

"Even as they drove away I saw him slump down in his seat, saw his head fall on one side. He did not recover."

After a long moment I asked, "And you got away from that place?" I could think of nothing else to say, and my mouth had gone very dry.

"Who was to stop me?" Crow replied. "Yes, I got away, and returned here. Now you know it all."

"I know it," I answered, wetting my lips, "but I still don't understand it. Not yet. You must tell me how you—"

"No, Henri." He stretched and yawned mightily. "The rest is for you to find out. You know his name and you have the means to discover his number. The rest should be fairly simple. As for me: I shall sleep for two hours, then we shall take a drive in my car for one hour; following which we shall pay, as it were, our last respects to Sturm Magruser V."

CROW WAS GOOD as his word. He slept, awakened, breakfasted and drove—while I did nothing but rack my brains and pore over the problem he had set me. And by the time we approached our destination I believed I had most of the answers.

Standing on the pavement outside the gardens of a quiet country crematorium between London and Oxford, we gazed in through spiked iron railings across plots and headstones at the pleasant-seeming, tall-chimneyed building which was the House of Repose, and I for one wondered what words had been spoken over Magruser. As we had arrived, Magruser's cortege, a single hearse, had left. So far as we were aware, none had remained to join us in paying "our last respect."

Now, while we waited, I told Crow, "I think I have the answers."

Tilting his head on one side in that old-fashioned way of his, he said, "Go on."

"First his name," I began. "Sturm Magruser V. The name Sturm reveals something of the nature of his familiar winds, the dust devils you've mentioned as watching over his interests. Am I right?"

Crow nodded. "I have already allowed you that, yes," he said.

"His full name stumped me for a little while, however," I admitted, "for it has only thirteen letters. Then I remembered the V, symbolic for the figure five. That makes eighteen, a double nine. Now, you said Hitler had been a veritable Angel of Death with his 99999 . . . which would seem to make Magruser the very Essence of Death itself!"

"Oh? How so?"

"His birth and death dates," I reminded. "The 1st April 1921, and 4th March 1964. They, too, add up to forty-five, which, if you include the number of his name, gives Magruser 9999999. Seven nines!" And I gave myself a mental pat on the back.

After a little while Crow said, "Are you finished?" And from the tone of his voice I knew there was a great deal I had overlooked.

VI

I sighed and admitted: "I can't see what else there could be."

"Look!" Crow said, causing me to start.

I followed his pointing finger to where a black-robed figure had stepped out onto the patio of the House of Repose. The bright wintry sun caught his white collar and made it a burning band about his neck. At chest height he carried a bowl, and began to march out through the garden with measured tread. I fancied I could hear the quiet murmur of his voice carrying on the still air, his words a chant or prayer.

"Magruser's mortal remains," said Crow, and he automatically doffed his hat. Bareheaded, I simply stood and watched.

"Well," I said after a moment or two, "where did my calculations go astray?"

Crow shrugged. "You missed several important points, that's all. Magruser was a 'black magician' of sorts, wouldn't you say? With his demonic purpose on Earth and his 'familiar winds,' as you call them? We may rightly suppose so; indeed the Persian word *magu* or *magus* means magician. Now, then, if you remove Magus from his name, what are you left with?"

"Why," I quickly worked it out, "with *R, E, R*. Oh, yes and with *V*."

"Let us rearrange them and say we are left with *R, E, V* and *R*," said Crow. And he repeated, "*R, E, V* and *R*. Now, then, as you yourself pointed out, there are thirteen letters in the man's name. Very well, let us look at—"

"Rev. 13!" I cut him off. "And the family Bible you had on your desk. But wait! You've ignored the other *R*."

Crow stared at me in silence for a moment. "Not at all," he finally said. "For R is the *eighteenth* letter of the alphabet. And thus Magruser, when he changed his name by deed poll, revealed himself!"

Now I understood, and I gasped in awe at this man I presumed to call friend, the vast intellect which was Titus Crow. For clear in my mind I could read it all in the eighteenth verse of the thirteenth chapter of the Book of Revelations.

Crow saw knowledge written in my dumbfounded face and nodded. "His birthdate, Henri, adds up to eighteen—666, the Number of the Beast!"

"And his ten factories in seven countries," I gasped. "The ten horns upon his seven heads! And the Beast in Revelations rose up *out of the sea*!"

"Those things, too." Crow grimly nodded.

"And his death date, 999!"

Again, his nod and, when he saw that I was finished: "But most monstrous and frightening of all, my friend, his very name—which, if you read it in reverse order—"

"Wh-what?" I stammered. But in another moment my mind reeled and my mouth fell open.

"*Resurgam*!"

"Indeed," and he gave his curt nod. "I shall rise again!"

Beyond the spiked iron railings the priest gave a sharp little cry and dropped the bowl, which shattered and spilled its contents. Spiraling winds, coming from nowhere, took up the ashes and bore them away . . .

HERO AND
ELDIN

THE WEIRD WINES
OF NAXAS NISS

"You pays your money and you takes your chance!" the barker cried. "For the price of admission only, drink as many measures of my priceless magical wines as you can. The measures may be small, but the results can be totally un-be-*lievable*! Just step inside and a variety of choices are yours. Admission is just one tond—which may seem expensive, until you realize that you're drinking *priceless* wines! And for a mere tond you enter, imbibe my measures one at a time but as many as you can, then exit, and you're back where you started—maybe! But one thing's certain: you'll never be the same man again! You pays your money and you takes your chance! One at a time, gents, if you please ..."

David Hero and Eldin the Wanderer looked at each other with raised eyebrows, then turned their gaze back to the barker. He was a dapper if somewhat eccentric little specimen of Homo ephemerens, (which is to say, a dreamlander) dressed in a red velvet jacket, green pants which came only halfway down his chubby calves, bright blue socks with their tops thonged to the bottoms of his trousers, like reversed suspenders, and tiny black high-heeled clogs. Tubby enough to be termed rotund, he had a voice to match his girth, but in height came up only so tall as somewhere short of the questers' shoulders. This meant that while he was a little shorter than most full-grown denizens of dream, it was likely that he'd also be a good deal heavier; one of those rare exceptions where Eldin's cognomen (it was the Wanderer who'd first coined Homo ephemerens) scarce fitted the subject. No one could be less ephemeral than this one!

But a dreamlander he was, a showman, too, and a barker of no mean prowess to boot—as Eldin's suddenly dry tongue in his clammy cave of a mouth might readily attest. "What with all his pattering on about his damned wines," the Wanderer said, as he and Hero elbowed closer to the tent, "and the sun being so hot today and all, I do believe I'm developing a thirst."

"So what else is new?" Hero grunted, continuing to observe the little showman and his doings.

Beneath his velvet jacket—whose lapels merely flanked the barker's chest, like the wings of a great plump rooster—he wore a gray silk shirt blazoned with the gold-glowing legend: "Naxas Niss, Exotic Wines!" Niss' hair was black as coal, grown from a single tuft in the middle of his head, plastered down in a fringe which was cropped uniformly and equidistant from its center at a point just above his bushy black eyebrows and right round to the back of his skull. If he were slimmer, he'd be like the clothes-peg men that the children of Celephais painted to look like soldiers, but being fat he looked more like a toy lead-bottomed clown who won't fall over, because when you knock him down he wobbles upright again. As for his origin: there was that in his accent which said he was probably a Dylath-Leener, but being so radically different he could in fact be from just about anywhere. Indeed, outlandish anonymity might well be his principal disguise!

All in all, a more harmless-seeming, amusing, and amiable little man the questers had never seen, which was just about the last thing they'd expected; for the fact of the matter was that they were here to "bring him in." Naxas Niss was a criminal; so said King Kuranes, and being king, Kuranes was the boss around here. What's more, Hero and Eldin were his agents, and very well-paid for it, too.

It was Fair Day in Celephais; which meant nothing very much, for you could find a fair somewhere in the Timeless City almost every other day of the week all year round. A surfeit of fairs, in fact. Not hard to explain, really: Fairs require that people are giving, and at the same time nothing kills them off faster than inclement weather. The people of Celephais were good and giving, the climate invariably kind, and rain extremely rare. So Celephais and fairs went hand in hand. As long as Mount Aran had had its snowy crest, and palms and ginkgos at its foot, and rocky spurs reaching out and sinking into the incredible blue of the Southern Sea, just *precisely* so long had there been fairs in Celephaïs; which is to say a very long time indeed.

However, (and as any addict will readily attest) not all fairs are fair fairs, and some are downright unfair. For every fair with shies where coconuts may be won, there's at least one where they can't, with more glue in the cups than coconuts! And if the shies are fixed, then it may generally be reckoned that the rest of the fair will follow suit. Word soon gets about, though, and *un*fairs quickly lose their customers, move on, or go broke. *Fairs* may therefore be recognized by their great crowds of laughing, jostling, bright-eyed people, while *unfairs* have surly men out cropping the grass between the various stalls and sideshows. This is nothing new, merely a reminder.

"And yet," said Hero, out of the corner of his mouth, for he and Eldin were close now to the barker, "this bloke seems to be getting all the customers he can handle."

"So I've noticed," Eldin answered. "And a good many of 'em go back for more. There's one old lad I've seen go in the front of that tent and out the back three times already. At a tond a time he'll soon be broke! So it can't be a confidence trick 'cos no one gets caught on the same hook twice, and certainly not three times! On the other hand, if Niss's a thief, then what's he stealing? We've been here an hour at least and I haven't heard a single cry for help, nor yet seen a sign of distress or even discomfort on a single face."

They thought back on this morning's message from Kuranes, delivered to them by runner at the tiny garret where they lodged overlooking the wharves. Normally the king would have called them to his ivy-clad Cornish manor house on the city's outskirts, where a bit of Cornwall went down from the walls to the shore and became a jumble of granite and seaweed called Fang Rocks; but the note explained why on this occasion he had not done so:

Hero, Eldin—

I've matters to attend to in Serannian, else I'd speak to you personally. Here's the problem: nakedness, imprudence bordering on madness, possible fraud and probable theft, and a lot of aimless running about! It's like a plague, which by the various embarrassments of its nature remains hidden. It has been brought to my attention not by its victims but their wives. The one common factor (malefactor, I suspect) is a man called Naxas Niss in his tent at the fair. Niss works whichever fair suits him, only an hour or two at a time, and pays a fat percentage to the organizers for the privilege. But he never works the same fair on consecutive days, which means he'll need tracking down. So that's your job: find him, get the goods on him, and bring him to book in front of Leewas Nith. And let me know how it worked out when I get back. And stay out of trouble!

Yours, Kuranes

Which in a nutshell explains the presence and purpose of the adventurers here, outside Naxas Niss' tiny, tassled yellow tent.

Hero was the rangy one, quite young, all blond, fond, and smiling, and dressed in russet brown; while Eldin was some years older, thicker-set, long-armed, dark to match his attire and scarred a bit around the face, which made him threatening even when he wasn't. Late of the waking world, they made a living now as questers in Earth's dreamlands. They loved each other like brothers (though like most brothers they'd never admit it); loved booze and a good fight, too, and girls even more; if they weren't such rogues then by now they'd be legends. Rogues they were, however, or rogu*ish*, anyway . . . but in any case they wouldn't want anyone apologizing for them. Kuranes thought they were good 'uns, which just about says it all.

"Something's wrong, though." Hero smiled, nodded, and chuckled, as if he engaged the other in light and trivial conversation. "For I've been taking note of the people going in—one at a time, you've doubtless observed, and each accompanied personally by Niss—not all of whom come out again."

"Eh?" The Wanderer smiled in his turn. "No, I hadn't noticed that. But if it's so, why, then the rest are still inside!" It seemed obvious.

"What, twenty-five in the front and only nineteen out the back?" said Hero, chortling and slapping his thigh. "But there's hardly room in there for two or three, let alone six. Not and Naxas Niss to boot!"

"What I *have* just noticed, however," said Eldin, "is this: that of those who do come out, a third dash off in unseemly haste, in all directions, and all wearing queer expressions. Gone to puke, d'you think?"

Most of the crowd had melted away by now, leaving the pair right up front and quite conspicuous. "How about you, young sir?" said Niss to Hero, pointing his black, gold-tipped cane at him. "Can't I interest you in my wines? I'll not be here all day—an hour more at most—so if you've a mind to try a tipple, now's the time, young sir, now's the time!"

"And my father?" said Hero, who liked to make a lot of the difference in his and Eldin's ages. "Can he come in, too? See, he's just this morning in receipt of his pension, and—"

With a low growl, Eldin elbowed him none too gently aside. And to Naxas Niss: "I'm sorry, sir, but the village, er, pumpkin here is in my care." Stepping back a pace, he made twirling motions alongside Hero's ear. "Can't let him out of my sight, if you see what I mean. He, er—he *does* things, you know."

"Does things?" Niss looked up at Hero a little warily, considered his peculiar grin, and backed off a pace.

"Too true!" Eldin replied, completely carried away. "Put bats up spinsters' knickers, piddles in the reservoir, generally annoys his elders and betters." And tone hardening, and tweaking Hero's ear: "Indeed, he *especially* annoys his—"

"We'd gladly come in, by all means." Hero cut him short, wriggling free of his ear-tweaking, bowing low and with a flourish to Naxas Niss. "And please excuse our horseplay; it was harmless, I assure you, much like my oafish companion here. But you see, we do everything—*almost* everything, anyway—together. Aye, and we'd dearly love to try out your wines, but not if you can only accommodate us one at a time." He then went on to explain about fair fairs and unfair fairs, finishing with: "And who's to say we'd not get nobbled as we stepped inside, eh? Not that I'd hint for one moment that you're such a blackguard yourself, Naxas Niss, but one can't be too careful these days. Best to be cautious, that's what I always say. And so, if my friend and I mayn't tipple together, why, then we'll simply take our thirsts to the marquee yonder, where they sell those excellent dark brown ales!"

He and Eldin made as if to move along, but Niss grabbed their elbows. Looking guardedly this way and that, finally he said: "What? I should let you ruin your throats and burn your innards on slop like that? And never know the delights of my exotiques? Unthinkable!"

"Exotiques?" Eldin lifted an eyebrow.

"Antique and exotic both," Niss explained. "Exotique! Very well, since the crowd's thinned out a bit, I'll take the two of you together. But let's have an understanding, gentlemen. You've explained your fear of thuggery, so I'll explain mine. The reason I normally insist upon only one customer at a time is for fear of just such felons. Not that I would ever believe it of you two, you understand; but in any case. I must insist that once inside you follow my instructions to the letter. Are we agreed?"

Hero and Eldin shrugged, nodded.

"Very well, then it's this way, gentlemen, please." And leading them inside, he reversed his Open sign to read Closed—for Now!

What the pair had expected would be hard to say, but it was not what they found. Inside the tent was . . . the inside of a tent; with a grass floor, a small folding table, and a large locked trunk in one corner. In front of the table stood a folding chair, and another behind it, while upon the table itself:

"Naxas Niss' weird wines!" said Niss, beaming.

Hero and Eldin stared fixedly at the five bottles on the table, and at the five tiny (oh so tiny) glasses which stood beside them. The bottles were chunky, of clear crystal, and each contained a wine of a different color. There were red, green, white, and golden wines all in a row, and a black one, which stood a little apart. "Mine, that one," Niss explained. "A potion, a remedy for stomach cramps, purely medicinal, you understand."

"Right," said Eldin, approaching the table and rubbing his huge hands. "So what'll we try first, eh?"

Naxas Niss stepped nimbly between. "Caution, my large and eager friend," he said. "First your tond, if you please, and then an explanation."

"I have nothing to explain," Eldin frowned, forking out.

"But I have," said Naxas Niss.

"I see no point." The Wanderer was bemused. "Here's the wine, openly displayed, and here a bone-dry receptacle." And he pointed to his bobbing

Adam's apple. "Will you explain how I must tilt the glass into my mouth? I've taken wine before, sir, I assure you."

"But there are wines and there are wines," purred Naxas Niss. "Except be sure that *these* wines require something of an explanation."

Now Hero spoke up, handing over his tond in turn, saying: "Very well, so explain."

While the pair looked on astonished, Naxas Niss commenced a very nimble jig for a creature his shape while singing:

> "It's a ritual,' said the little man, 'now listen and you'll see,
>   One wine sends you where you were before you were
>   here,
> And one transports you blushing where you most desire
>   to be!
> I can guarantee that one wine will guarantee your return,
> And the last wine tells which color fits which—
> Ah, and turns you color blind in turn!"

He quit dancing, beamed at the would-be bibbers, took a seat behind his table and poured wine from each bottle into its own tiny glass, a thimbleful to each. "Take your pick, my lads," he said expansively. "For you've paid your money, and now you takes your chances."

"Now hold!" snapped Eldin at once, scowling a little. "That riddle you've just riddled seems a strange and sinister thing to me. Are you hinting there's danger in these wines?"

"Danger?" Naxas Niss drew back his head, tucked in his chin, looked pained. "How so? They change perspectives, that's all—but all very quickly reverts, I promise you. Sinister? But if my intentions were dishonest, would I warn you in the words of my song? No, of course not! Or perhaps there *is* an element of danger—to the faint of heart. But to the adventurer born . . . ? However"—and he shrugged, perhaps disappointedly—"no one can force you to drink. And so, since you no longer desire to avail your-selves of—"

"Hold!" Now it was Hero's turn to bark, as Niss made as if to pour the wines back into their bottles. He reached out and stayed the little man's hands. "We've paid our money, Naxas, after all."

"So choose your poison!" said Niss, and at once burst out laughing—and just as quickly sobered. "Why, what *is* all this? Do you really suppose I'd harm you?"

"Not if you know what's good for you!" growled Eldin.

"Ah!" said Niss, eyes narrowing, hand straying just a little toward the black bottle. "So you're a pair of bullyboys after all, eh?"

"No such thing," said Hero. "We're cautious, that's all, as I've avowed."

"Now, look," said Niss, sighing, as he picked up one of the glasses—with red wine in it—which he at once tossed back! An expression of extreme delight crossed his face, and before it could fade he tilted the red wine bottle and topped up the tiny glass again. "Now, tell me," he was all innocence, "would I poison myself?"

The questers studied his face for several long moments but he seemed entirely unharmed. "Red it is," said Eldin then, reaching for the same glass.

"And I'll go for gold," said Hero. "For if aught peculiar happens to me, why you'll still be around to settle the score."

"Good!" cried Naxas Niss. "We're getting somewhere at last."

They drank.

The wine was good, indeed exotique! Niss watched the tipplers with an expression like an Ulthar cat, some of which retire there from the waking world when they've spent their nine lives, notably from a place called Cheshire.

Hero said: "Excellent!" And a strange dazed look came into his eyes. "Truly excellent!" he said again, and before Eldin could stop him promptly walked out through the flap in the back wall of the tent. The Wanderer gaped, then dashed after him.

Outside he grabbed Hero, turned him about. "And where, pray, do you think you're going?"

Hero licked his lips and the vacant look receded. His eyes gradually focused. "Going?" he finally said. "Why, for another drink, of course!"

"Are you all right?" Eldin stared deep into Hero's eyes.

"Entirely," Hero nodded. "And you?"

"My eyes sting a bit," Eldin blinked, "but otherwise—"

"Thank you for your custom, sirs!" cried Naxas Niss, closing the rear flap of his tent on them.

They glanced at each other, gawped, galloped back round to the front just as Niss came out and reversed his sign to read Open. Hero grabbed him by a red velvet shoulder. "Whoa!" he said, dangerously low. " 'Drink as many of my measures as you can,' you said. And as yet we've tried but one."

Naxas Niss looked astonished. "But . . . did I ask you to leave? I did not. You walked out of your own free will, and that one ran after you. Now lads, the rules are simple: enter my tent and a tond gets you all you can drink, but once you exit the contract's broken. Or . . . p'raps you'd care to try again?"

"Too damned *true!*" cried Eldin, dragging Hero by the collar back into the tent right on Niss' heels. And yet again the latter reversed his sign to read Closed—for Now!

"Now sit!" said Eldin, thumping Hero down in the chair in front of the table. "Sit right there, where I can keep an eye on you." And he stood behind him.

"I can't think why I left like that." Hero seemed genuinely astonished. "I certainly didn't want to. Indeed, I wanted nothing so much as another glass of wine!"

"No problem there," said Niss, rubbing his hands. "Your tonds, gentlemen, please." They paid up, however grumblingly. And again Niss went into his song and dance routine:

> "Now listen and you'll see,
> You'll go where you have been,
> Or arrive in all innocence where you'd really like to be;
> Or you'll lick your lips and feel the thirst—
> And come right on back to me!"

"You missed out the color-blind bit," said Eldin.

Niss shrugged. "I was in haste," he explained. "And anyway, I couldn't make it rhyme."

Hero looked up at Eldin, and they both looked down at the wines, which Niss had topped up again. "Now, then," said Eldin to Hero, "you had gold, and apart from acting daft—which isn't really unusual—you're okay. So—" And he reached for the *red* glass again!

Hero put his hand over the glass, stopping him. "That's red," he said.

"Eh?" Eldin peered close. "No, no—it's plainly gold!"

"What, are you color-blind?" Hero cried . . . and they stared at each other in amaze.

"Or . . . are you?" said Eldin.

And Naxas Niss grinned.

"What color are my clothes?" Hero demanded.

Eldin glanced at them, cried, "Blue, of course!"—and his mouth at once fell open. "But they should be brown. Which means—I *am* colorblind!"

"But only temporarily," said Naxas Niss.

Eldin snapped his fingers. *"Hah!* But that also means I should know which color's which. And I do! Green transports you blushing where you most desire to be, and white sends you where you were before you were here. Except, because I'm color-blind, I don't know which bottle's which!"

"But I do," Hero reminded.

"Good!" said Eldin. "So which one's gold?"

"I don't see much point in trying gold again," said Hero, "for I've already tried it and ended up back here. It guaranteed my return, d'you see?"

"True," said Eldin, "but at least we know it's harmless."

"Well, if the point of the exercise is not to be harmed," said Hero, "why drink any of the bloody stuff?"

Eldin, thoroughly confused by now, said, "Eh? Why . . . because we've paid for it, that's why! Now, then, which one's gold?"

"That one," Hero pointed at the green bottle, the while winking at Naxas Niss, who grinned on unabated. For it had dawned on Hero that there was an easy way round the problem, except he needed a guinea pig. Or a not-quite-so-expensive tond pig, as the case was.

Eldin picked up the green glass and stared at it suspiciously. "Gold?"

"Indeed," said Hero.

"You're sure you feel okay?"

"Positive," said Hero. "Me, I'll try the white." And white it was.

"Hold!" said Eldin. "That's green."

Hero shook his head. "You're color-blind, remember? It's white."

"White?" said Eldin. "But if you drink that you'll end up where you were before you were here. Like...outside the tent again?"

"That's how I figure it, yes," said Hero. "Nothing harmful in that, and all the time we're narrowing down the field."

Eldin nodded and they raised the glasses to their lips. And: "Go!" said Eldin. They quickly drank the measures down.

Now, this was Hero's plan:

They'd tried red and gold. Red made you color-blind and gold sent you staggering about, with a great desire to return. That left green and white. Eldin had swallowed green. He would now be transported (blushing?) where he most desired to be (which with this old pervert might be just about anywhere; Hero dreaded to think!). Hero on the other hand had swallowed white, so he'd likely end up outside the tent again as Eldin had surmised—but nowhere and nothing dangerous, anyway.

The beauty of it was this: that they'd now sampled all of Naxas Niss' exotiques—except his black medicine, of course. They could probably do him for fraud (forcing folks to come back for more) and possibly even for theft (the way he snapped up tonds must be *some* kind of theft, Hero felt sure). They might get him for technical aggravated assault, too (making people color-blind and all); but for the life of Hero, he couldn't see how they could make those other charges of Kuranes' stick. What, nakedness? Gross imprudence? Aimless running about? He could only hope that all would come to light now that they'd sampled of green and white.

And of course all did come to light, and almost immediately.

Standing behind Hero, Eldin felt suddenly all aflutter. "B'God!" he gasped, and commenced staggering about a little. Hero leaped to his feet—and started running on the spot!

"What? What?" he cried. But he was unable to stop his feet, which went stamp, stamp, stamp, stamp, like a squad of Baharna's regulators on muster parade.

Then Eldin uttered a very small "Eek!" and fizzled out—quite literally—leaving his good black leather clothes floating on air. Unsupported, they flopped to the floor, loose tonds clinking in their pockets.

"Now, what's all this, Niss?" Hero snarled, but his feet gave Niss no time to answer. They marched him right out the back door of the tent, and hurried him out of the fairground, and ran him wildly across a dusty road, and raced him frantically down an alley toward the harbor. All the way home, they took him, those rebellious feet, and all the time accelerating; until finally they hurled him upstairs to his and Eldin's garret room, where at last they came to a halt, smoking and blistered inside his quaking boots. Hero would never know it, but he had done the three-and-a-half-minute mile . . .

AFTER BATHING HIS FEET in cold water for half an hour, and changing his boots for moccasins, Hero returned limping to the fairground. Eldin arrived a little later, dressed in a white sheet which he'd converted into a passable replica of desert raiment.

"If I thought I might attack you here and now," said The Wanderer out the side of his mouth and almost conversationally, "without losing my sheet and what's left of my dignity, you'd be dead in a trice. Or if not exactly dead, badly beaten. Unable to walk, at very least. Likewise, when I find him, Naxas Niss, purveyor of exotiques." And he gloomed down on the square of flattened grass where recently had stood the yellow tent of that last mentioned.

Hero pointed to his feet, which he could swear steamed visibly through the lace holes of his soft shoes. "As for crippling me," he growled, "why, I'm already unable to walk! Indeed, I have feet like puddings! So as you can see—and while I admit my behavior left something wanting—I really do consider myself punished quite enough. No major harm done, however, and all wines tasted and effects observed at extremely close quarters. And so—"

They swapped experiences.

Hero's tale was quickly told, as above, but Eldin's proved far more interesting. "I drank what I *thought* was gold," The Wanderer growled, "but which I now know to have been green, and in the next moment— *zzzip!*—there I was all naked, and maybe even blushing, in the bed of the young and buxom widow Misha Oosh, owner of the Yellow Yak, where nightly she displays her generous jigglers all bundled up in their blue silk blouse behind the bar."

Hero nodded knowingly. "So that's why we've been drinking in the Yellow Yak every night for the past week, eh? I fancied you fancied her."

"And there was Misha herself," Eldin continued, "taking her afternoon nap, right there in that very bed with me! Except . . . my arrival woke her up."

Hero couldn't suppress a grin. "When do you go up?" he inquired. "Before Leewas Nith, I mean."

"Eh?" said Eldin. "You think she gave a shriek and kicked me out? Well, and I thought she might, too—at first. But you say you fancied I fancied her? And so I did—except I didn't know that she fancied me in turn! Throw me out? No, she did not. Oh, she was somewhat agog and all atremble at first, but when she saw who it was . . ."

"God help the poor woman." Hero sighed, turning his face away and shaking his head. "She must be desperate!"

"Pup!" Eldin snarled. "Why, I've seen *you* making eyes at her!"

"Anyway," Hero changed the subject, "what then?"

"Well, we spent a very pleasant hour or so together, and then she said she must be up and preparing her place for evening opening. She loaned me this sheet, and helped me tuck it in a bit here and there, and here I am."

"She didn't find your being without your clothes a bit odd? Didn't she even want to know how come?"

"She did, and I explained all, which she accepted at once. It's handy being a quester for Kuranes. The king's much loved, you know. And likewise those who look after him. And after all, her bed *was* the single place in all the dreamlands where I most desired to be."

"So why are you so miffed?" Hero asked, acting innocent. "I mean, it seems to me I did you a favor!"

"And if I'd been unwelcome in Misha's bed?"

"But you weren't."

"Huh!"

"Huh, indeed!" said Hero. "And how about me when this case is cracked, eh? Oh, *you'll* be okay: free booze and all, and when the Yellow Yak turns out, all comfy and warm in the loving arms of Misha Oosh. But what of poor Hero?"

"You've girls aplenty," Eldin snorted, which was true enough. "You'll not go short."

"The fact is," said Hero, "that I really have done you a powerful favor. And it's to be hoped you won't forget it. So let's have no more of these threats on my life and limbs, if you please."

"What angers me," said Eldin, curling his lip a bit, "is this: that there are lots of other places I might have ended up, not all of them in Celephais, and *none* of 'em so comfy! I mean, can you imagine floating naked in a large vat of Lippy Unth's muth? Or finding yourself propped up, everything adangle, at a bar somewhere in downtown Dylath-Leen? Or in some harem in Kled, with a dozen little black eunuchs after your bits with their curved, razor-sharp knives?"

"God!" said Hero. "It says a lot for your desires!"

"Never mind that!" Eldin snapped. "What about my clothes, eh? You've cost me a fine suit, shirt, shoes, and my purse to boot, which contained a hundred tonds!"

"Liar," said Hero, but without emphasis. "Kuranes' runner brought us a hundred tonds for expenses, fifty each, two of which you'd spent on Niss' wines."

"Well, half a hundred, then," Eldin grumbled. "But I'll have it back again, b'God I will, when I catch up with that wretch! Except . . . where is he, eh?" And again he gloomed on the vacant patch of grass.

"Where indeed?" Hero nodded thoughtfully, chewing his lip. "Where indeed?"

HERO LOANED ELDIN EIGHT TONDS with which to buy himself new if less satisfying togs, and they then split up and went their own ways, combing the city's markets and thoroughfares for sign or word of Naxas Niss. They paid for and sent out a pair of extra eyes, too, in the shape of the urchin Kimp Lootis, a waif late of the waking world like themselves. Kimp, long-haired as a girl and bright as a fresh-minted tond, however ragged, came to them that night with his report, catching them just before they could enter the Yellow Yak, in the cobbled mews which led to that estimable alehouse.

"Hero, Eldin!" The waif stepped out of the shadows, came between the two and grasped their great hands in his own small ones. "I know where he is, or where he was, or where he most likely will be, anyway."

"Eh?" Eldin gazed down on a moon-silvered elfin face. "Where he is, was, or will be? You're sure you've not been drinking his wines, Kimp?"

The urchin grinned. "It's worth a tond or two, I'm sure."

Hero gave a mock groan, flipped the child a triangular tond that glinted gold, silver, gold and silver again before being snatched unerringly from the smoky evening air. He knew Kimp could use the money, having neither home nor family to call his own. But: "Lord," he said, "I don't know who's the bigger crook: you or Naxas Niss! One tond's all you'll get. And now that you've been paid twice, less of your riddles and a little more information, if you please."

Kimp stepped back into shadows. "A caravan passed by, on its way to Nir and Ulthar," he whispered. "Naxas Niss joined it at a watering hole just outside the city. He paid a pouchful of tonds for passage and protection en route to Nir, which was his destination, and was last seen dragging his large trunk into the back of a covered cart."

"When was this?" Hero hissed.

"Three hours gone. By now they're halfway there."

"Good work!" said Hero, and went to pat what he guessed was a head, which was only a shadow. Soft footfalls fell like a patter of gentle rain in the courtyard, and Kimp Lootis was gone.

"It can wait till morning," said Eldin, turning his bearded face Yellow Yakward once more.

"No," Hero denied him, "it can't."

"What?" Eldin was alarmed, then aggrieved. "But it could if you'd a lovely creature waiting in there for you, eh?"

"She's not waiting for you," said Hero. "She's serving her customers, feeding and watering them, and she'll be hard at it till the midnight hour. By which time we'll be high over Nir. Anyway, the last thing she needs right now is you!"

"She needed me this afternoon!"

"That's as may be, but now that you've laid ... *claim* to her, as it were, what's the hurry? She'll go off the boil, d'you think?"

"Unlikely!" Eldin preened.

"Then it's business before pleasure." Hero nodded, his mind made up.

As they headed for the harbor, Eldin continued to grumble. "I mean, what's in a night, eh?"

"Twelve hours," said Hero. "More, if you had your way!"

"No, no, lad," Eldin wheedled. "I'd be up bright and early, I promise; and we could skip just as sprightly for Nir in the morning."

"*I* could skip sprightly in the morning," said Hero. "You—you'd be knackered! Love-drugged and aching in every bone, and you know it. Right now we're sharp-eyed, clearheaded, hot on the trail. So let's not slack off. When the job's done, that's a different matter. Also, the wind's in our favor; we'll be in Nir even sooner than I thought. And anyway, I've got what's left of the money." Which was the best bit of his argument. For Eldin had his pride; he knew that if he entered the Yellow Yak without the price of a pint, then that Misha'd think he was only there for the booze!

Their sky-yacht *Quester* was tied up in the harbor. They boarded her, got the tiny flotation engine going, fed essence to the bags in the keel and up under the reinforced deck. *Quester* lifted off and Celephais sank below; the lights of hamlets along the coast began to come into view like far crowds of fireflies in the night; a warm, sweet wind off the sea filled out their sail and scudded them along with the clouds for Nir.

And cracking a bottle—just one, and middling stuff, for Hero's jaw was set—they toasted Naxas Niss' downfall, and laid their plans to that effect . . .

ON THE OUTSKIRTS OF NIR they set down in a farmyard, woke up the farmer who grumbled a lot and threatened to turn his bull on them, and placated him with tonds that got scarcer by the minute, or so it seemed. He helped them haul the wallowing *Quester* into a barn, where with engine stilled she slowly settled to a bed of straw. Then they inquired the way to the house of Mathur Imniss, and set off on foot into town.

Nir was a sleepy place even on big occasions. Tomorrow was one such: Fair Day! "Oh, joy!" (Eldin's sarcasm dripped like acid.) "There'll be rip-roaring cow-milking contests, slimy-pole climbing, roof-thatching orgies— the lot!" And there'd doubtless be Naxas Niss' tent, too, all yellow and tasseled and seeming perfectly innocuous, standing amidst the shies and sideshows on the village green.

Mathur Imniss was a retired quarrier, stonemason, and builder, and a faithful old friend of the questers. They found his house and got him and his good lady wife out of bed, slapped backs and kissed cheeks for a half hour. They took a bite to eat, then bedded down till morning. It was fortunate that Mathur's son, Gytherik the Gauntmaster, wasn't to house, else they'd have been up talking all night.

Early awake, the pair disguised themselves somewhat and sought out Tatter Nees, a troubadour of their acquaintance who lived in the town. Tatter knew everyone and everything; he called himself a wandering balladeer, but as Eldin was wont to have it, if he could sing better he wouldn't need to travel so much. However that might be, at least he was able to put them in the picture in re all manner of comings and goings. And indeed, yestereve, as dusk turned to dark, a caravan had come; aye, and this morning there was a stall in the market, where one Naxas Niss, a dealer in used clothes, was very cheaply selling off all manner of mannish finery. In their disguises (Eldin had grudgingly shaved off his beard, while Hero had applied one, and a foppish hat), they visited said stall.

Naxas Niss was busy as hell, selling clothes as quickly as he could hurl them out of his trunk, which he'd almost emptied by the time the questers arrived. Eldin's black leathers were still there, at least, tossed carelessly on Niss' folding table, but his shoes and coarse gray shirt had been sold.

"Now, he dies!" Eldin rumbled, forging forward toward the inner circle of bargain hunters. Hero dragged him back.

"No, he *doesn't!*" he hissed. "We're to bring him in, not do him in! You stay here—I'll get your gear." And he did, and paid three tonds for it, too. Niss, gathering up tonds like iron filings to a magnet, didn't notice him at all.

"God, we'll soon be broke!" Eldin moaned. "And I'm reduced to paying for my own stolen clothes!"

"No," said Hero, unrelentingly contradictory, "I am. But at least we now know what he does with them. Which makes it theft beyond a doubt. So now we've got him on all counts." He fished out Kuranes' letter from a pocket, read:

" 'Nakedness, imprudence bordering on madness, possible fraud and probable' (no, it's definite now) 'theft, and a lot of aimless running about.'

Niss is guilty of some and responsible for the rest. Add to that handling and disposal of stolen goods, and making fools of questers, and we can just about throw the book at him."

"I'd prefer to throw a fist at him!" growled Eldin; but Hero only smiled a wicked smile.

"No," said the younger quester, yet again. "Let's make the punishment fit the crime. And not just any crimes—or even all of them—but specifically his crimes against us."

And so they stood well back and watched Niss flog what was left of his rags, and pack up his trestle and hire a couple of lads to carry his stuff. And off he went chirpy as a cricket in the direction of the village green. Hero and Eldin followed him, stopping for a (quick) drink along the way, and when they got to the green, the yellow tent had already been erected and business was booming—or appeared to be.

"He's filling his damned trunk again!" Eldin spluttered, outraged.

"But not nearly so quickly," Hero pointed out. "Tonds are harder to come by here in cow country, old lad. See, he's pulling the crowd, all right, but your actual takers are few and far between."

As if to emphasize what he'd said: "What? A tond a tipple?" one onlooker cried. "Man, I only make ten in a week! Too rich for my blood, Naxas Niss, or whatever your name is." Others muttered low, shuffled their feet, began to drift away. Niss didn't fit here. Nir's fair had always been a fair fair, but Niss' prices seemed just the opposite. He might sell off his secondhand clothes cheaply, but his exotiques were something else. There were only a half dozen takers (one at a time, of course, of whom only four emerged from the rear, two running off like billy-o and two returning for a second pass; only *one* of whom exited, and then rushed off like billy-o) and then no more. Until Hero approached, wearing his silly hat and false beard. Eldin had meanwhile sneaked round the back.

"A tond a try?" said Hero, putting on a high-pitched voice and jingling coins in his pocket. "I think I can manage that."

Niss cocked his head on one side and looked at him curiously. His eyes narrowed a little—avariciously, Hero hoped, and not suspiciously. Finally the little man said: "But don't I know you from somewhere, sir?"

"Indeed," Hero squeaked at once, "for I purchased a good black suit from you just an hour ago. And a very good buy it was! So if these—er, exotiques?—these wines of yours are up to the standard of your hand-me-downs, why, there'll be no complaints here!"

Naxas Niss chewed his lip. So far he'd taken only eight tonds and three sets of togs. He'd do this latest lumphead, and maybe one more, and move on. Nir was a dump anyway; Ulthar should prove far more profitable; he'd get finished here, buy a yak and cart, and be on his way.

Still looking at Hero sideways and wondering where he'd seen him before, Niss ushered the quester inside and went straight into his spiel as before: "There's this ritual," the little man began to sing, doing his jig. "Now listen and you'll see—"

Eldin entered silently through the back flap and crept up behind him.

Hero said: "One wine sends me where I was before I was here—"

Naxas Niss said: *"Oops!"* He turned and made a leap for his table, fingers straining toward the bottle of black, and galloped straight into the arms of Eldin. Somehow, incredibly, Niss wriggled free, grabbed up his bottle of "medicine" and took a swig. This was more or less what the questers had expected him to try—something like it, anyway—and Hero was quick off the mark. He snatched the bottle from Niss and likewise glugged, then quickly passed it on to Eldin. For if this was Niss' bolt-hole, then by the many gods they'd surely bolt it for him!

Naxas Niss was already fading out, his tent, table, bottles, and trunk likewise, and Hero was wavering around the edges, when the Wanderer also tossed back a little black. And a moment later they were no longer in Nir, though as yet Hero didn't know it. The tent, unpegged, began to collapse around them as Niss, unfreezing, shot out through the front flap. But Hero was right behind him, leaving Eldin floundering in yellow silk. Outside the tent:

They were in a great cave of a dungeon, and along one wall stood a workbench supporting fifty or more bottles all of a different hue; and Naxas Niss shrieking and flying for the bottles as fast as his little feet could shift him. Alas for Niss, Hero was somewhat nimbler. The younger quester caught him by his red velvet collar, yanking and twisting at the same time. Niss went right on running, which made it look like he'd stepped on a banana skin; his feet shot up horizontal and his bubble-body spun facedown. And *thump* he came down on his belly, venting wind from both ends, while Hero jumped astride his fat back like leaping aboard some peculiar wobbly bronco.

Cursing loudly, Eldin ripped his way through the billowing wall of the tent, then stood stock-still and gawped all about; and in his bewilderment he almost took another pull at the black bottle. But:

"Don't!" Hero barked, from where he sat upon Naxas Niss' shuddering back. "Unless you're feeling especially adventurous, that is. Wasn't one nip enough?"

Eldin wasn't feeling especially adventurous; he crossed to the bench and put the black bottle down with all the others. And then, with Hero, he continued to gape all about.

The place they were in was literally a dungeon, and a strangely familiar one at that. It was lighted with green crystal glowstones which were imbedded in the ceiling, and with red ones piled in niches in the walls. They lent the place an infernal light. Stone steps cut from the virgin rock climbed one wall and through the ceiling; on the other side more steps descended; in the center of the floor, the raised rim of a dry well was loosely covered over with a heavy, rusty iron grid. And echoing up from below, indeed from that very well:

"Naxas Niss, is that you?" came a trembly old voice. And there was something familiar about that, too.

Eldin took a red crystal from its pile, crossed to the well, wrenched the iron grid aside and peered down into darkness. "Catch," he said, dropping the crystal. And down below, someone caught. The red glow in the well lit up a face wrinkled as a walnut, framed in shoulder-length white hair and a waist-long white beard, bearing a long white drooping mustache. Rheumy eyes peered, then widened in a glad, almost disbelieving smile of recognition.

"Eldin the Wanderer!" gasped the mage in the well.

"Nyrass of Theelys!" Eldin replied, nodding. "Reach up your arms."

Nyrass did as instructed, and Eldin clung to the wall's rim with one hand while dangling the other. And in a moment he'd hauled the ancient wizard to freedom. At which point Hero said: "All right, you two, let's have some help here. Bind this bugger's limbs, can't you, else I'll be sitting on him for the rest of my life!"

Nyrass found some rope and Eldin tied Niss hand and foot, then rolled him across the floor, propped him up in a seated position and roped him with his back to the wall of the old well. Silent now, the little crook tugged on his ropes awhile, then sat still and scowled at them all three while the ancient mage hugged Hero and Eldin each in turn. For the questers were his firm friends from a time when they'd helped him destroy Klarek-Yam, the mad First One who'd threatened to release Cthulhu and his kin into both dreamlands and waking world alike. He hugged them, and sobbed a little, too, explaining how he'd spent three months in the well, where Naxas Niss had kept him prisoned. As to how that had come about:

"My wizard ancestor, Soomus the Seventh of the Seventh, brewed many potent wines," Nyrass started to explain, nodding toward the variously colored bottles arrayed on the workbench. "Wines with a vast variety of properties, not all entirely harmless. Soomus also left a book, explaining their powers; but the book was encoded in Soomus' own runes, and I've never bothered much to decipher the thing. The wines I likewise left alone; left them down here, where they've been since those early days of dream, gathering dust and who knows what else to them. I thought from time to time I might destroy them, but even that could prove dangerous, and so I simply let them be.

"Well, one day there was a fair in Theelys, and that one"—he pointed a trembling hand at the trussed Naxas Niss—"had a stall there. There was a game he played with three brass cups and a glittering diamond as big as a robin's egg, which he called—"

"Find the gemstone?" said Hero, sighing deeply.

"Indeed!" cried Nyrass. "D'you know it?"

"Oh, we know it, all right," said Eldin. "But Nyrass, d'you mean to say you were taken in by that one? Why, it's sleight of hand—trickery—a game to filch farthings from the village idiots! And you a magician. Tsk, tsk!"

Nyrass bowed his head and eventually continued. "Well, Naxas also had a betting system called—"

"Double or nothing?" said Eldin. "Aye, an we know *that* one, too. And how many times did you double your bet, eh, trying to find the gemstone?"

Nyrass hung his head even lower. "A baker's dozen," he admitted. "Thirteen times, aye. Unlucky for some, thirteen, and especially me! But how could I lose every single time, eh? I'd seen the village children win, when they were gaming with Naxas Niss for sweetie-sucks and toffee-apples, so why couldn't I? Impossible that I should lose so often, and consecutively, but I did. Ah, but where the first bet cost me only a tond, the last one—"

"Cost four thousand and ninety-six of 'em!" said Hero, who was good at that sort of thing.

"Alas," said Nyrass, "I never was much of a mathematician."

"You're a daft old wizard!" said Eldin, but he put an arm round Nyrass' shoulders anyway. "What then?"

"I told him I probably had the money at home," said Nyrass. "He packed up his stall and came back with me. But when I looked I had only a few tonds, which he took, of course. But I did have goods. I offered him a cracked shewstone, not much good but better than nothing. And several books of outworn spells, and a pair of demagicked wands. None of which interested him. But then we came down here, and that was where I made my big mistake."

"You told him about Soomus' wines." Hero could see it all now. "And they *did* interest him."

Nyrass nodded. "Apparently he has a talent for translation. He snatched Soomus' book, tumbled me down the well—wandless and all, and no runebook in easy reach—and set about discovering what he could of the wines."

"But you're a wizard!" cried Eldin. "Couldn't you levitate out of there, or conjure assistance or something?"

"I'm a very *old* wizard," Nyrass corrected him, "and the older I get, the more I forget. In fact, I've just about forgotten everything! Anyway, as for the rest of it—"

"Let me tell it," now Niss himself spoke up, his voice sour as vinegar. "Else at this rate it'll take all day. Soomus' book started to disintegrate as soon as I opened it. I could only discover the secrets of three of his wines before the thing fell to dust. But I'd learned enough to make a start, at least. So . . . I took away with me the go-where-you-were, the be-where-you-most-desire-to-be, and the come-you-home—that's the black one, as you've discovered. Just those three, see, for I was cautious. I must walk before I tried running. I used the wines at various fairs and they worked for me like . . . like magic! But it wasn't all tonds and treacle, I can tell you. When threatened by the occasional punter who'd been where he desired but really shouldn't have been, I'd sip black and come back here in a flash, even as you've seen it happen. Each time I came back I'd feed the old fool, and attempt to decipher some of the labels on the rest of Soomus' bottles. Eventually I discovered the return-ye-here and the color-blinder; and with that last one, why, of course the rest were easy! But it was then I discovered how lucky I'd been. Dangerous? Those bottles are murder! The worst of 'em contained a liquid purple imp. Only try to sip from *that* one and he'd drag you in by your tongue, and you'd take his place! I weighted it and dropped it far out to sea, and then I reckoned I'd quit while I was ahead."

"Three months ago, all this?" said Hero.

"Forty-four fairs ago, aye," said Naxas Niss, more than a little surly now.

"And you didn't run out of red, gold, white, green, and black?"

"That's another of their properties," said Niss. "They replenish themselves."

"Bottomless bottles!" Eldin gawped. "Now, that's what I call magic!"

"But why hasn't anyone apprehended you before now?" Hero wanted to know.

"I've already told you," said Niss. "Whenever I smelled danger, I'd take a swig of black."

"But you'd think those you'd fooled would warn their friends, at least," said Eldin.

"Oh?" said Naxas Niss. "Really? And let on what clowns they'd been? Or how they'd gone through tens of tonds by coming back for one more sip of red? Or tell whose beds they'd found themselves in, naked as babes? And believe me, a forbidden bed isn't the worst place a man can most desire to be!"

Hero nodded. "And if someone with more guts than most came back to give you a thashing, then you'd simply sip black and slip back here—and your gear with you! Very clever."

"Too clever far," said Eldin. And to the magician: "Nyrass, I fancy you're getting too tottery to be left on your own. You could do with someone to look after you and your place both."

"A companion?" said Nyrass. "Maybe you're right."

Hero spoke up. "There's a homeless waif in Celephais called Kimp Lootis. He's a likable lad who lives by his wits, but given a home to call his own I reckon he'd be good as gold. What say we see what he thinks of the idea, eh?"

He ripped through the silk of Niss' tent to the table and its bottles, found and held up green. Then back to the workbench to retrieve the bottle of black. "Now you two hang on here," he told Eldin and Nyrass, pouring green into his palm and rubbing it into his jacket, pants, and boots. All done, he pocketed black, took a quick swig of green, and put the bottle down. "And keep your eyes on *that* one!" were his last words before he disappeared. Last to go was his finger, pointing at Naxas Niss. And . . . his clothes went with him!

Niss was furious. "He's not so daft, your spindly pal!" he snapped at Eldin. "Even I hadn't figured that out. Green affects only what it touches. Inside a man, it transports him where he most desires to be. Rubbed on his clothes, it transports them, too!"

Eldin beamed. "Right!" he said. "And right now he most desires to be wherever Kimp is. Not so daft, you say? Brilliant, says me!"

"What's he like, this Kimp?" Nyrass was uncertain.

"A good lad," said Eldin. "Needs a father, that's all."

"Well"—Nyrass shrugged—"it's true I've been feeling my years lately. They weigh on me like lead. And since I've no kin of my own—"

Hero materialized grin-first, likewise Kimp, still smacking his lips from the belt of black Hero'd given him.

Following which . . .

LEAVING NAXAS NISS BOUND (and double-bound) in the dungeon, the questers spent the rest of the day with Nyrass and Kimp. They wandered through the wizard's great castle and its gardens, tried fruits from a variety of trees; and all the while Nyrass performing small magics for the delight of the waif, and everyone feeling generally very light at heart. From a high turret as dusk began to settle, they watched the lamps flickering into life in Theelys, following which and as the stars also began to light, Eldin brewed tea and made them all a mighty plate of scrambled eggs on toast.

As for Kimp: he couldn't get over his amaze and delight that he now had a home and a father of his own; and Nyrass knew he'd never be lonely—or fall prey to the likes of Naxas Niss again—not with a lad sharp as Kimp around, he wouldn't.

Leaving the two to get better acquainted, Hero and Eldin went into town, came back an hour later towing a bunch of flotation bags purchased with the last of their tonds from a sky-ship's chandler. The bags were inflated, straining lustily inside a net but held down by massive lead weights in a huge wicker basket swaying at the ends of four ropes. And the questers hauled the weighted but weightless device behind them all the way to Nyrass' garden wall, where they fitted up Naxas Niss in a rope harness and forced a tot of white between his frothing, cursing jaws.

Off he went at once, heading full-tilt for Nir under a rising moon; and Hero and Eldin in the basket (along with Niss' trunk and Soomus' wines), having tossed out the great lead weights to make room, and vented a little essence to get the balance just right. Like a rickshaw-boy Niss ran, was Eldin's opinion—though he couldn't remember exactly what a rickshaw-boy was; something from the waking world, he supposed—going back where he'd last been, however far, his feet waggling for all they were worth but barely touching the ground because of the flotation bags he towed on high. The wind, at least, was in his favor.

And along the way, every now and then, Hero or Eldin would toss a bottle overboard, happy to hear it smashing as its exotique contents soaked the starlit path; and Niss groaning with each bottle smashed, knowing now he was done for and doomed to spend a spell (of the mundane sort, and if his legs held out that long) in Leewas Nith's Celephasian cells . . .

MIDMORNING SAW THEM BACK IN NIR, where finally Niss collapsed and fell into a sleep of total exhaustion. He was a lot thinner now, and his clogs worn through to his puffy, pulsating feet. They transferred him to *Quester* and sailed for Celephais, where in Leewas Nith's afternoon sessions he was found guilty and sent down for a twelve-month's rest.

Later, aloft aboard *Quester* (but tethered just twenty feet over the harbor, and safe from prying eyes), the king's agents found the false bottom in Niss' trunk and the little sacks of tonds he'd hoarded therein; which discovery was followed by a deal of hilarity, giggling, and thigh-slapping, as the questers counted their considerable profits and congratulated themselves that all had turned out so well.

But after a while Hero licked his lips and said: "D'you know, I'm dry? A splash of wine would go down well."

"Let's get ashore," said Eldin at once, "and find ourselves an eatery till the Yellow Yak's doors spring open!"

"No," said Hero, "I mean right now."

"What? Here, now, aboard *Quester*? But . . . there's not a drop aboard, lad, you know that!"

"I know you take me for a great fool!" cried Hero, reaching out and snatching the bottle of red from Eldin's huge jacket pocket. "As if you could resist saving just one of them—*you*, of all people!" He pulled the cork and took a massive swig, said: *"Ahhh!"* appreciatively and passed the bottle back.

"Actually," said Eldin, "I was going to tell you."

"Huh!" said Hero.

"No, seriously. See, it's no fun being color-blind on your own. But to tell the truth, you do look sort of cute in blue!"

"Cute?" said Hero. "Cute?" He chuckled and took back the never-empty bottle, tilting more of its contents into his throat. And smacking his lips as he once more passed the bottle, he said: "Well, that's more than I can say for you—*in puce!*"

"Puce!" The Wanderer almost choked on the biggest swig of all. "Puce!" he sputtered and coughed. "The *hell* with that!" And he hurled the bottle far out over the water.

For three days and nights the Southern Sea was green and gold and sky blue pink, and as for the fish which the fishermen brought in . . . why, rainbow trout had nothing on them at all!

THE STEALER OF DREAMS

Up there on the ocean-facing slope of Mount Aran, above the tree line but not yet into the snow (for the snowy peak of Aran had been forbidden to men immemorially, and especially to waking-worlders, and *more* especially to men such as Eldin the Wanderer and David Hero, called Hero of Dreams), up there, then, the atmosphere was thin but heady, the air cool and crisp, and the timelessness of Celephais amply apparent in the vista spread below: that same vista viewed by dreamers five hundred years ago, and one which others as yet unborn, or even undreamed, would view five hundred years hence.

Hero, on his own for once, or at least accompanied only by his hangover, which seemed to him far more noisy than any actual physical companion might ever be (with the single exception of Eldin, of course), appreciated the air of these higher regions and wished he could open doors in his ears, let the coolness waft through and blow out all the cobwebs, dead rats, indistinct memories and too-slowly evaporating muth fumes, and so leave an uncluttered brain to start functioning again as brains should, instead of stumbling blindly around in his skull and tripping itself up on all the junk in there.

Hero had a telescope with him, which he used periodically to enhance the gazing of his slightly bloodshot right eye down on Celephais. Each time he did so the pain was a little less penetrating than the last time—which told him that his head *was* clearing, however slowly—but still he couldn't look for more than a second or two, sufficient only for the glitter of a spire or minaret to stab through his pupil, or for bright flashes of

Naraxa water tumbling oceanward to set his senses spinning; and then, groaning, he'd turn his spyglass on the sea instead.

Now, normally that would be even worse, for the blue of the Southern Sea may fairly be described as a visual toothache; and Hero, who liked to do things with words (he wrote the occasional poem, and sometimes sang his own songs, too) had often wondered why no one had come up with a more descriptive color for it than simply blue. If a dark yellow stone could be described as ocher, then surely the Southern Sea's searing, indeed piercing color might better be titled acher? And by the same token shouldn't muth, so sweet on the tongue in the drinking, yet turning that same inoffensive organ to a vile, decomposing blanket during sleep, more rightly be called moth? For certainly he now felt that he had a mouthful of them!

As is seen, and for all the on-this-occasion-involuntary humor of his thinking, Hero was not in a good mood. But he was at least able to gaze down on the Southern Sea without doing his brain permanent damage, for last night's storm had left the ocean scored with ranks of marching waves, disrupting its "acher" to a bearable gray-green. And now we get to the other reason why Hero was here: for as well as the beneficial, purging effect of booze being burned out of his system by the climb, and the sweet, clear air of these heights to freshen his brain and lungs, there was also a nagging suspicion in the back of his mind that all was not well with the Wanderer.

Except to disguise this anxiety as Hero's "other reason" for being here is quite inaccurate; Eldin the Wanderer's welfare was indeed uppermost in Hero's mind, and all that nonsense about fresh air and beneficial climbing (?) quite spurious, or would be if he were willing to admit that he was ever at any time given to worrying about his fellow adventurer. They never did admit to such things, these two, and probably never would, but in fact they couldn't be closer or love each other more if they were twins. What's more, Hero half blamed himself for Eldin's absence on this occasion, and knew that he *would* blame himself forever if aught had gone seriously amiss.

But . . . last night there'd been drinking, and boasting, and wagering as well; as the muth had gone down faster, so the boasting and wagering had grown wilder; finally Eldin had declared that "alone, single-handed, on (his) own, without assistance and entirely unaided," (sic) he could sail their boat *Quester* to Serannian the sky-floating city, and there drink three bars dry; and when Hero had called his bluff, wagering his half of *Quester* that he couldn't, then the dippy old duffer had gone staggering off to do just that! Since when he hadn't been seen, and there'd been this sudden, vicious storm. So Hero's real reason for being here was that these heights were an ideal vantage point from which to scan the still-troubled waters beating on the strands for sign of Eldin's return. Except his return might well be in doubt. The trouble was this:

Without question Eldin could handle *Quester* on his own—when he was sober, and when the boat was in good repair. But a sail had needed mending, and a flotation bag had been lost in Baharna on Oriab at the end of a recent mission for King Kuranes, and a second bag had been losing essence for a long time now, so that the tiny engine had difficulty keeping it filled. And of course, worst of all, Eldin had been mindless on muth. Add to these objections the sudden storm . . . anything could have happened.

This morning Hero had come awake in their garret room to find his companion's bed empty; remembering the other's boast and his own wager, which had been nothing short of a dare, and rushing down to the wharf (or more properly staggering), he'd discovered *Quester* gone. Seeing the state of the sea, and already fearing the worst, he'd sought out Tatter Nees, a wandering balladeer from Nir who'd been their drinking companion last night. Tatter, none too steady on his own pins, had tottered off to make inquiry, and Hero had borrowed a spyglass and headed for Aran. And he'd counted a hundred and more boats coming and going this morning, some from the sky and some from the sea, but never a sign of *Quester.*

Which brings us to the present.

"Hero!" came a distant cry, echoing out of the trees and up the slope of scree and outcropped stone. Hero focused his glass, found Tatter down there in the ginkgos, hands cupped to his mouth, ready to fire another salvo.

Oh, God! thought Hero, knowing he'd have to respond. "What is it?" he finally bellowed—and immediately clapped both hands to his temples, fully believing that his head had cracked right down the middle.

"Two things," Tatter shouted back, staggering, repelled by his own voice like a cannon recoiling from a shot. And Hero could almost hear his low-muttered curses.

"Hold it, hold it." Hero waved a ceasefire. "I'll come down."

He stood up, slid on his heels through the scree, kept his balance remarkably well and used half-buried boulders to slow himself down when his plunging might get out of hand. And at last he was into the trees, and finally down to where the troubadour waited. Tatter, a long, thin specimen of Homo ephemerens, gloomed on Hero, saying: "Never again, never again," in time-honored fashion, without shaking his head.

"Likewise, I'm sure," Hero replied, remembering not to nod. And: "What's up?"

"First," said Tatter, "the king wants to see you." He half turned his face away, stared into the trees.

Hero could feel himself going white. "And second?" he said.

"Second . . . Hero, I—"

"Second?" Hero repeated.

Tatter took a deep breath, looked straight at him. "It's Ephar Phoog," he said. Phoog was an avaricious Celephasian auctioneer with the instincts of a ghoul. "He's dispatched a couple of his lads to Fang Rocks," Tatter continued. "There's a boat wrecked there, but not just any boat. There's a buzz in town that it's *Quester* . . ."

"And Eldin?" Hero's head was suddenly clear.

Tatter shrugged, bobbed about a bit, looked away again. "No sign of him. But that's not to say—"

"I know what it's not to say," Hero cut him short again. "Tatter, thanks. I know that wasn't easy."

"You'll go see the king?"

"Bugger the king!" said Hero, but softly. "I'll look for Eldin first." And he did. But when, in Ephar Phoog's auction house, they silently showed him a piece of shattered gunwale on which was painted *Ques*, the *ter* being lost; and when he recognized his own brush strokes . . .

SOME HOURS LATER Hero saw the king.

Kuranes was busy with the renovation of a wing of his Cornish manor house, and artisans were running about all over the place with buckets of paint and whitewash, platters of mortar and various mixes, while masons trundled wheelbarrows of carved stone blocks to and fro. Generally, all was in a turmoil. Hero scratched his head and wondered: *Is this how they achieve timelessness in Celephais? By refusing to let it fall into decay?* He was disappointed, for it would seem to take something of the magic out of things.

Hero was taken to the king in the great hall of the wing under repair, where Kuranes personally supervised the work; but when the king spied Hero he at once left off, took his arm, and guided him to private chambers. There he commiserated with the numb adventurer, and finished by completing Tatter Nees' previously unspoken:

"—But that's not to say that Eldin is, or has . . . come to harm."

Hero had bathed and smartened himself up a little. Not only for his audience with the king but also as a means of distancing himself from last night's idiocy, which had not only caused his current unease but might yet prove to have been entirely calamitous. For if Eldin were in fact dead and gone . . . then Hero knew he'd never drink muth again, nor carouse, nor do any of the myriad other things they'd so often done together. It would mean an end to all that, and to a great deal more. Possibly an end to Hero himself. But for now Kuranes had summoned him, and so he must do his best to pay attention.

Seated opposite the king, looking at him across his great desk through eyes grown a little less bloodshot in a face grown a lot more gaunt, what Hero saw was this:

Under a paint-splashed smock, the Lord of Ooth-Nargai and the Skies Around Serannian was slightly built but regally robed, gray-bearded but bright-eyed. The slant of his eyes and tilt of their brows might on occasion be thought sarcastic, even caustic, but the wisdom and compassion in the lines of his face, and the warmth and steadiness of his gaze, spoke of a love for and a loyalty to his fellow men—especially those domiciled in Earth's dreamlands—which was quite beyond mundane measure. And yet there was this *realness* about him which set him apart from Homo ephemerens; rightly so, for he too was once a waking-worlder, long departed from the conscious world to become a power and permanent resident now in the lands of Earth's dreams. But his origins were stamped on him like the face on a fresh-minted coin; nor were they absent from his voice, which contained in its accents thrilling, often tantalizing reminders of days long forgotten and lives spent in worlds *outside* or on a higher plane than the so-called subconscious.

Kuranes returned Hero's gaze, and what *he* saw was this:

Hero was tall and well muscled, yet lithe as a hound and agile as a Kledan monkey, and blond in the lands of dream as he'd been in the waking world. His eyes were of a light blue, but they could darken very quickly to steel, or turn a dangerous, glinty yellow in a tight spot. In fact he was usually easygoing, quick to grin, much given to jesting; but while he loved songs a fair bit and girls even more, still he was a wizard-master of fists, feet, knives, and any sword in a fight, of which there'd been no lack, as the crusty knobs of rock which he called knuckles avowed. A rough diamond, Hero, but one which nevertheless glinted exceeding bright.

Except now his shoulders were slumped and his face pale, where even the laughter lines seemed somehow faded. And Kuranes knew no less than Hero himself that if the Wanderer had indeed died last night, then that he'd lost the services of not only one good agent but probably both of them. And that was a loss he couldn't contemplate, for men such as these were hard to come by.

"Why did you send for me?" Hero eventually spoke up.

"Because I've a job for you," said the king, and he told him a little of what it was.

"Baharna, on the Isle of Oriab?" Hero's voice was dull. "But how can I leave Celephais now, not knowing? I couldn't." He shook his head.

"You can and must," Kuranes answered. "Indeed, it's the best thing in all the dreamlands that you *can* do! By the time you return we'll have found him. Or at least by then we'll know what's happened to him. It has to be better than moping around in Celephais, drinking every night and doubtless getting into trouble, and no earthly use to man or beast. You'll go and discover this monstrous Oriabian vampire and put him or it down—or I'll wash my hands of you."

This last was meant to shock Hero and stir him up, but it hardly touched him. Instead he merely looked at the king, and said: "We once sought out a vampire for you in Inquanok." And he shuddered. "On that occasion, without Eldin . . . I was a goner for sure."

"I know how you feel," said Kuranes.

"No, you don't."

"Very well, I don't. But listen: do this for me and strengthen our alliance with Oriab, and this is what I'll do for you. I'll have every boat in the harbor out searching for Eldin; I'll have men on every beach and cliff for twenty miles east and west of the city; each day you're away, I'll send you bulletins by carrier pigeon, so keeping you up to date. And when you return, I'll furnish you with a new sky-yacht to replace *Quester*. Who could say fairer than that? But you in your turn must promise to discover, or do your level best to discover, the terror stalking Oriab and eliminate it. And you set sail today, without delay, just as soon as we are finished."

"But as you've just as good as pointed out," said Hero without animation, "I've no boat."

"Chim Nedlar is the master of a sloop; he's waiting for you even now, tied up in the harbor but ready to sail as soon as you're aboard. Now, what's it to be?"

Hero stood up and headed for the door. He hadn't been dismissed but Kuranes said nothing. He merely waited, holding his breath. At the door Hero paused, looked back. "Oriab? Baharna? Me and Eldin, we've mutual interests there. We've had some good times there, too. And a few bad ones. There'll be a lot of memories sunk deep, just waiting to be disturbed so they can rise up again. My heart won't be in it."

"But your head will know it's for the best," Kuranes countered. "And stop talking as if he's dead! We don't know that, and only the future will tell."

Hero nodded, however slightly. "Baharna," he said again, but thoughtfully. And: "Only the future will tell . . ." He straightened up a little, and the king thought that perhaps some of the helplessness had gone out of him. "Very well," said Hero, going out and closing the door softly behind him . . .

———

HERO BOARDED the *Shark's Fin* an hour later. He chuckled inside a little (sadly, perhaps—or nostalgically, so soon?) thinking: *Now, what would Eldin make of this, I wonder?*

"What, the *Shark's Fin* sloop?" the absent quester would doubtless have commented. "A boat, you say? Sounds more like some weird Oriental delicacy to me!" And then both of them would have wondered what "Oriental" meant, for memories of the waking world came and went in exceedingly brief and usually inexplicable flashes. And now, as Chim Nedlar showed his passenger to his bunk, indeed Hero did wonder what "Oriental" meant. Which was strange because he'd known just a moment ago. But that was the way of it.

"Get some sleep," the sloop's master told him, "for you look all in." And then he went off about his business. A little later they set sail, and since the wind blew fair for Oriab they were soon airborne and out of the chop of waves which still hadn't settled from the storm. Then, far out over the Southern Sea—with the wind whistling in the rigging, and the flotation engines softly thumping like a pair of great hearts belowdecks somewhere amidships—Chim came down again and gave his cargo a shake.

Hero hadn't undressed, merely stretched himself out and fallen instantly asleep. Dressed in soft, russet brown leather, which was his usual garb, he wore a short jacket, snug-fitting trousers, and calf boots with his trousers tucked in to form piratical bells. His jacket sleeves were rolled up to show a tanned breadth of forearm, and a slightly curved sword of Kled hung from his belt on his right hip, loosely tethered to his leg above the knee. But asleep he tossed and turned, and mumbled to himself a bit, grimacing now and then and balling his fists.

For not only had he fallen asleep but straight into dreams within dreams: mental phantasms which, for all that they were only a repetition of what had gone—or what had probably gone—before, were exceedingly weird dreams indeed. His mind was exhausted, doubtless from worrying about the Wanderer, because of which it was perhaps only natural that his dreams should concern themselves with that selfsame worthy.

Eldin in trouble, aboard a storm-lashed Quester; *Eldin hurled overboard, tumbling down through leagues of sky to the heaving bosom of the Southern*

Sea; Eldin sinking through weedy deeps, ogled by fishes, finally feasted upon by crabs.

And Kuranes' voice sounding harsh in Hero's mind, saying very un-Kuranes-like things, such as:

"He's not dead, just resting his bones a bit. Now, leave him be, pull yourself together and be off to Baharna. You've a quest, remember? Seek out and slay me this vampire and I'll return Quester *to you—aye, and this dozy, drowned old duffer of a Wanderer, too!"*

"Watch who you're shouting at!" Hero mumblingly returned. "And especially what you're shouting at him!"

But casting about he discovered there was no king there at all—no ocean floor or recumbent, crab-nurturing Eldin—only a windswept, mountainous place where ghosts of vanished dreamers cried out to him for vengeance.

"Sucked dry!" they moaned. "Taken in our prime! With all substance drawn off, what are we now but fast-fading memories? Give us back our flesh, David Hero. Give us back to those who mourn us, and yet fear us for the voiceless wraiths we are become . . ."

Voiceless? They seemed to Hero to have voices enough! He might even have ventured to say so, but in another moment—

—He stood on the gently rolling deck of a ship. It was night now; ah, but he could tell by the feel of things that the night was unquiet! And sure enough, true to his instinct, a scarcely luminous ghost came striding toward him; burly and bearded it was, a sailor, by its rolling gait. And yet the stars shone through its insubstantial outline where it paused to peer at Hero, then put up a hand to its palid eyes to gaze far, far out to sea. Finally the ghost turned back to Hero and with a worried, puzzled expression, but quite conversationally, said: "The worst of it is, I can't seem to remember! My dreams have all been eaten up; and what's a dreamlander without his dreams, eh?"

"I—" Hero gaped, his eyes wide, astonished and not a little afraid of this conversation with a ghost. "I—"

"You?" the apparition frowned with faint-etched eyebrows. "Was it you took all I had been away from me?" Ghostly fingers—which yet felt real enough— reached to grasp Hero's shoulder and shake him. He gave a great start—

—Started awake!—sat up—saw Chim Nedlar there and gasped, remembered, then flopped down on his back again. But in a little while he once more sat up.

Chim Nedlar was a little overweight for a sailor, Hero thought, quickly recovering his wits. Somewhat puffy in the face and heavy in the frame, but jolly enough for all that. And there was that of the waking world about him, too, which seemed to add to his substance. He had loose lips, green eyes, dark hair parted in the middle and plaited down to his chubby shoulders, wore a shirt like a tent hanging loose to his shoes, which were wooden clogs with soles of rough hide to grip the decks. In height he came up to Hero's chin.

As Hero's heart quit hammering, so the other perched himself on the bunk opposite and said: "I could see you were nightmaring and so woke you up. Forgive me if I startled you."

"You did, and I do," said Hero. "Indeed, I thank you!"

Chim smiled, nodded. "So it's off to Oriab, eh? On king's business, too! I've heard of you, David Hero. Hero of Dreams, they call you, and you're a quester for Kuranes!"

Hero wasn't especially interested in conversation right now; though his dreams were fast receding, he still had his own private thoughts to think; but the vessel's captain was only being polite, and Hero could find no fault in that. "A small thing," he answered with a shrug. "We're the king's men, aye, me and ... and a friend of mine." He fell silent.

"Eldin, aye," the other answered gravely. "Eldin the Wanderer. Heard of him, too, and know that you're a pair of bold adventurers with many a tall tail to tell. And taller because they're all true! Me, I'm the wrong shape for derring-do, or maybe I'd have joined Serannian's sky-navy under Admiral Limnar Dass. But active service, me?" He jiggled his belly, gave a shrug. "Alas, no. So I sail the *Shark's Fin* here and there out of Baharna, finding what trade I can. I suppose we're a ferry, really. But I do get to meet some interesting folks, and I do like to listen to the tales they tell."

Hero yawned and at once apologized. "Knackered," he excused himself. "And I'm sorry, but I've no stories for you. Not now, anyway. Maybe we'll have a drink together sometime, and then we'll see." He carefully lay down again.

Chim Nedlar seemed a little disappointed. He sighed and said, "Ah, well—maybe I'll catch you in Baharna. Where do you pull your corks?"

Hero shrugged again, put his hands behind his head and suppressed another yawn. "The Quayside Quaress, usually," he finally answered. "Buxom Barba's place on the waterfront."

"Know it well." Chim chuckled. "A favorite haunt. Maybe I'll catch you there, then. The drinks are on me."

"Indeed?" Hero offered a weary wink. "Why, then you'll be welcome at my table any old time, Chim!" He closed his eyes, drawling: "Aye, and I daresay we'll meet there one night, in the old Quayside Quaress." And lulled by the vessel's gentle roll, he slowly drifted back into sleep. This time, however, there were no dreams within dreams...

IN BAHARNA, via a chandler's shop in the harbor, Hero made for Lippy Unth's place, the Leery Crab, standing squarish and squat as its namesake at the end of an ancient stone quay. Once upon a time the proprietor, Lipperod Unth, had owned another, similarly unsavory place, which as the direct result of a night's affray was wrecked and submerged in a scummy, disused part of the harbor. The Leery Crab, unlike its Craven Lobster cousin, was built of stone, not timber, and its door was guarded by Lippy's large son Gooba and an equally impressive friend. They stood one to each side of the entrance, young, olive-black Pargans, towering like gleaming, meaty monoliths in the dusk as Hero approached along the stone-flagged quay.

Recognizing him at once, Gooba stepped forward, grunting: "You're not welcome here, Hero." And he set himself squarely in the quester's way.

"Don't talk daft, lad," Hero growled. "Why, it was my money that built this place!"

"But my father preferred his *old* place," Gooba answered, showing his teeth in a snarl as he and his similarly mountainous friend fell into defensive crouches. "The one that you and Eldin the Wanderer sank!"

Hero paused only a few paces away. He carried a small sack which now he dipped into, coming out with a bomb as round and black as a cannonball, and a flint striker which he held up in plain view. He grinned humorlessly at their expressions, and low in his throat said, "Gooba, I still owe your old man a little something for feeding me to the scabfish. You

remember? And a crab's much the same as a lobster to me—crusty old
crustaceans both. Now, I'm not looking for trouble, but if you don't ease
up and let me pass I swear I'll light this fuse and lob all hell right in
through that door."

Gooba and friend blinked, looked at each other, seemed to shrink a
little. Creases showed in their black brows.

"I'll count to five," Hero pushed. "One . . ."

They stepped aside and he proceeded, or would have except now Lippy
himself stood in his way.

Lippy as a nickname didn't derive entirely from Lipperod, nor as one
might erroneously surmise from any great love of talking. On the contrary,
Lippy wasn't much for talking; he was far more a man of action. But
when he was annoyed, then he'd pout with his great black lips and thrust
them out ahead of him like a warning trumpet; and when Lippy Unth
looked like that . . . someone or ones was or were in big trouble! Hero had
witnessed Lippy's metamorphosis from bartender/owner to incredibly de-
structive device on more than one occasion; he had determined never to
see it again. Not if he could avoid it.

"No trouble, Lippy," he said now, studying the other's huge olive face
and brown, rolling eyes.

"Ah!" said Lippy. "No trouble, you say? But it seems to me I've heard
that before. And didn't I just now hear you threatening the Crab with
sudden and quite unwarranted annihilation?" His eyes settled on the bomb
in Hero's hand, mirroring it, which turned them to great black marbles
that stared accusingly out of his head. "Also," he continued, "you mentioned an unsettled score."

"Only to bolster my argument," said Hero. "In fact I consider all old
scores settled, and scars healed—or I will once this is over. Lippy, I'd no
more enter here than dive headfirst into the jaws of hell. But I'm looking
for Eldin and there might well be a certain customer of yours who can
tell me where he is."

Lippy let his eyes slowly wander beyond Hero, along the quay. "The
Wanderer's not with you?"

"See for yourself," said Hero.

Lippy's shoulders, which had been hunched up almost as high as his head under his stained, straining shirt, now relaxed a very little. He narrowed his eyes. "Very well, you can come in—but the bomb gets dumped in the harbor."

Hero shook his head. "Call it insurance," he said. "It not only gets me in but out again—unscathed! *Then* I'll toss it in the harbor."

"Hero—" Lippy rumbled warningly, his shoulders starting to hunch again. Worse, his great lips began to pout. Hero was aware of Gooba and chum straying fractionally closer on the flanks, knew it was time he restated the stakes.

"I'm short on time," he said, his voice very dangerous sounding. "So our little chat's over." He hefted the bomb, held his striker close to its fuse. "Now do I get in—or does everyone who's in get out?"

Lippy's lips retracted. "Who is it you're looking for?"

"The Seer with Invisible Eyes," said Hero.

"*Huh!*" said Lippy, at last standing aside. "Aye, he's here—damn his eyes!"

"They're already damned," said Hero, carefully stepping round the huge Pargan, through the door and into the Leery Crab's smoke-wreathed, muth-reeking gloom.

The Crab, like the ill-fated Lobster before it, was appointed in something less than opulence. The bar consisted of a stout, square wooden framework in the center of one huge room, from which Lippy, his wife, and massive son could take in the entire place at a glance. As for its clientele: They were hard men, loners, ex-pirates, sea captains from unknown parts on the lookout for a crewman to shanghai, seadogs and peglegs and others of a like ilk gathered to tell their tall tales, which got taller with every telling. But unsavory? It could be downright unhealthy!

But the place did have its good points. In high season, for instance, there would never be any overcrowding down here. There'd always be room to sit at a bench without tangling elbows; you'd rarely have to shout to make yourself heard; you wouldn't be bothered by ladies of the night. The *things* that used this place couldn't be called ladies of any description. And the proprietor, Lippy himself, demanded and maintained good order at all times. Or at least tried his best to do so. "Come and go in peace," was his motto, "or in pieces, as you choose."

Booze? It wasn't good but it wasn't the worst. Lippy's license was still intact, anyway. The muth-dew was watered (probably a good idea), the spirits tasted fishy, or at least of the salty element in which fishes swim, the ales had ailed somewhat and you could pickle eggs in the wine. But on the other hand it was very cheap, provided you had a cast-iron constitution. Most of Lippy's customers had, though for how much longer was anybody's guess.

In short, the Leery Crab wasn't the sort of place in which you'd expect to find one of Kuranes' most trusted foreign operatives, which was one of the two reasons why the Seer used it—the other being that he simply loved it! He was funny like that, the Seer with Invisible Eyes.

Funny in all sorts of ways, thought Hero, casting about in the glow of ceiling-suspended lanterns. But he very quickly found who (what?) he was looking for. The S.W.I.E. sat in one corner, with his back to the wall, hunched over a mug of muth. A good safe seat, Hero reckoned, sidling up and sliding onto the bottom-polished wooden bench behind its bolted-down table, ending up only a foot away from the silent Seer. He placed his bomb before him but kept the striker ready in his hand. Gooba came over, kept a respectful distance, inquired: "Are you drinking, Hero?"

"A small ale," Hero told him. "And if it tastes even slightly weird I'll be very annoyed. When I'm annoyed my thumbs twitch, see?" One of his thumbs twitched, anyway, and sparks flew from the striker—some of them passing dangerously close to the bomb's fuse. Gooba went off at a run to fetch Hero his ale, and several wise patrons seated nearby stood up, blinked or yawned in their fashion, then quickly put distance between and removed to more solitary areas of the great room.

Through all of this the S.W.I.E. had said nothing. Now Hero glanced at him out of the corner of his eye. As usual, the Seer was wrapped in a bundle of rags with the hood thrown up to make a shadowy blot of his face. All that was visible of the man within this cocoon of rough cloth was a pair of scrawny wrists and clawlike hands with long, sharp nails; these protruded from his tattered sleeves, trapping the mug of muth where it sat before him. He had seemed oblivious of Hero's approach, oblivious of all else, too; but Hero had noted that when he put his bomb on the table the Seer had visibly started. Now, however, he merely chuckled.

"A neat ploy, that," he commented without stirring, his voice like the scurry of mice in a bone-dry granary. "When is a bomb not a bomb? When David Hero is up to his—"

"—Neck in it, if you don't keep your voice down!" Hero hissed, out of the corner of his mouth. "What are you trying to do, get me crippled?"

The Seer shrugged. "No one can hear us." And then, straight to business: "What's on your mind?"

"Eldin the Wanderer. He's on my mind."

The Seer's head lifted a little and turned fractionally in Hero's direction. For a moment light fell on his face, which was gaunt, hollow cheeked, invisibly eyed. The sockets where those eyes should be contained an emptiness as deep as the spaces out beyond the stars, and certainly they looked just as cold, too. *Never give this one the old two-finger treatment*, Hero told himself, *or for sure you'll be left with a pair of crystallized stumps!*

The Seer winked, and for a moment one of the holes in his face vanished behind an eyelid. Then it was back again, deep and mysterious as ever. "Aye, aye!" said the Seer.

"Eldin," Hero repeated impatiently. "He's gone missing."

"And you want me to scry him out for you?"

Hero sighed. "Of course!"

"Better tell me about it, then. The dreamlands are vast and I'm not omniscient. Points of reference may help narrow it down a bit."

Gooba brought Hero's ale and retreated, and when he was back out of earshot Hero told the entire tale of Eldin's disappearance. When he was done the Seer grunted, *"Huh!* He deserves it—and so do you. What? You're like a pair of big kids, you two. Booze and birds, that's all you ever seem to think about!"

Astonished, Hero drew back a little. "Why, you callous old ... this is Eldin we're talking about! He and I, we're like one person. A team. A well-oiled machine!"

"Too well-oiled!" snapped the Seer. "And far too often. I really can't see what Kuranes sees in you. Not even with these invisible eyes of mine, I just can't see it."

Hero showed his teeth, puffed himself up—and deflated in a vast sigh. "Yes, you're right," he said. "All that you said and more—you're dead right. But even if we don't amount to much, still I'm only half as much without him. I'll be like a machine without an engine, doing nothing, going rusty. Also, I . . ." He fell silent.

"You love him?"

"Hell, no!" Hero was scornful, or tried to be. But he knew he couldn't deceive the S.W.I.E. "Of course I do," he finally admitted. And quickly added: "Er, in my way. The big . . . *heap!*"

"A heap," the Seer repeated, nodding. He cocked his head on one side a bit. "Yes, I can see that, now that you come to mention it. But we're wasting time. Now, listen: this right invisible eye of mine occasionally scans the recent past, and the left can sometimes scry on the immediate future. So since this is all very sinister, or at least fraught, that's how we'll go— sinistrally! Now tell me, what do you see in my left eye?" He closed the right emptiness and Hero gazed deep into the other. But there was nothing there, just a great yawning void that whirled and expanded until he felt he was being sucked into it. Suddenly dizzy, he looked away, shook his head to clear it of the rush and reel.

"Nothing," he said, after a moment. "Just a whirlpool of . . . nothing-ness!"

"Good!" said the Seer, with some satisfaction. "That's how it should be. Does you no good, knowing the future. I prefer to be kept guessing. Keeps me on my mettle. Now we'll try the right eye."

He opened the lowered lid, closed the other, and Hero looked again. At first there was nothing, but then—

—The Seer's invisible right eye began to fill in, tiny pieces of indeterminate action slotting into place like bits in a miniature jigsaw puzzle, gradually obscuring the absolute void which formed the board behind the picture. So fascinated was Hero by this process that he failed at first to take note of the emerging scene; but as it neared completion all leaped suddenly into perspective, so that now he gasped out loud and peered more closely yet.

It was Eldin and *Quester,* the one aboard the other, all tossed about in a storm that spun the little sky-yacht this way and that like a torn kite caught in high branches on a blustery spring morning. Eldin, fighting with the sails, trying desperately to cut them loose before they pulled the boat apart; and a boom swinging, striking him, hurling him against the side of the tiny cabin where his arm seemed awkwardly trapped.

Then the mast splitting and leaning over sideways to port, and the roof of the cabin wrenched loose and all the ship's gear sucked out into the maelstrom. And the Wanderer cradling his (broken?) left arm, lurching this way and that and looking all about in seeming desperation. *Quester* was breaking up around him; the mast, splintered at its base but not yet broken free, swung to and fro, clearing the decks and shattering the upper strakes. With each wild sweep Eldin must leap over the lunging mast or have his legs smashed. Then the mast swinging far out to starboard and jamming there, causing the aerial wreck to list at more than forty-five degrees in that direction.

And Eldin struggling with a hatch cover, slamming back the bolts until the door burst open with the pressure of the flotation bag contained beneath. The Wanderer's ploy was obvious; he took a knife and cut through one of the two guys holding the bag in place, so that it sprang out of its bay below the deck and strained like a balloon to be free. Then, tangling his arms and legs in the net which covered the bag, the Wanderer reached down and sliced through the second tether.

That did it; he was snatched aloft while *Quester* capsized and slid stern-first out of the sky, down toward the foaming Southern Sea far below.

The picture faded, broke up, vanished, and the Seer's right eye was once again invisible.

"He lives!" Hero breathed, mainly to himself. And to the S.W.I.E.: "I'll tell you what I saw—"

"Hold!" husked that worthy, with whispery breath. "What you saw from without I saw from within. Two-way, these windows of mine. What, d'you think I can't read these invisible eyes I've been gifted—or cursed—with? That would be like giving a crystal ball to a blind man! As for Eldin living, however"—he grew more whispery yet—"I'd not go daft on *that* theory, if I were you."

"Explain," said Hero.

"What you just saw was a day ago, during the storm. And it looked pretty perilous to me: floating off like that on a bag of mainly ethereal essence!"

Hero nodded. "Maybe, but we're old hands at ethereal-essence floating, Eldin and me. I say he lives! The question is . . . where?"

"You want to scry some more?"

"Can we?"

The Seer sighed. "It's a bit of an effort," he grumbled. "But now that I've picked up his trail . . . and anyway, what's a talent for if not to be exercised, eh? Very well, look again." And once more he shuttered his left eye while opening wide the bottomless pit which was his right. More than eager, Hero licked his lips, looked—

—And strained back from the Seer at what he saw, lurched to his feet with a cry of denial forming on his lips! Before he could utter it, the S.W.I.E. grabbed his wrist in an iron claw, dragged him down again. "It's a picture!" the Seer rasped. "Only a picture floating on the surface of my mind. Damn it, I'm not always right!"

"Liar!" Hero gasped. "It's real and you know it!" But nevertheless he looked again in the moment before the Seer blinked and erased the thing:

A backdrop of crags reaching to frowning mountains; great gray peaks rearing skyward; dark clouds scudding east on some secret, silent mission. And in the foreground: fangs of rock, scree slides, projecting outcrops like looming menhirs. Aye, menhirs, indeed! They set the mood for the rest of the scene. For caught fast halfway down a sheer-sided cliff, there was Quester's *deflated flotation bag; it clung crumpled to the fractured rock, the web of its rope net ripped—and empty!*

"Carried south, southeast by the storm," said Hero, his eyes halfglazed, "rushed along with the wind whistling in his rigging, Eldin eventually spied the Isle of Oriab. He deflated the bag a little, sank toward the island. But the wind was too strong or his judgment was off. He missed Baharna and flew on into the hinterland. Those peaks, the rocks, the mountain heights—those were the foothills of N'granek. I've seen it, been there, know the place. I *couldn't* be mistaken."

"But I *can* be!" the Seer insisted. "Did you *see* him crash into the cliff, rupture his bag and burst the net? Did you *see* him fall? No, you saw only—"

"—The *result* of that crash," Hero finished it for him. "I saw its result, and that's enough." His eyes had turned bleak, and yet moist, too. "Now I have to go and find his body, find Eldin, and deal with him before N'granek's gaunts find and deal with him. Or before he's found by other creatures of the night."

The Seer nodded, said: "*If* he's dead, and *if* you find him—what then?"

Hero frowned through his misery. It seemed an odd question. He shook his head. "I don't—"

"There are laws that govern the dead here in the dreamlands, Hero!" the Seer's voice was harsh. "Had you forgotten?"

Hero gasped as he saw the other's meaning. *If* Eldin was dead, then he'd died in an especially unpleasant manner. And those who died that way—in nightmarish fashion—all shared a common destiny: the Charnel Gardens of Zura!

"No," said Hero, shaking his head, "I'll not let that be! Zura shan't have him. Not the Queen of the Living Dead. I'll track him, find him, burn him before I'll let him go to her—and he'll thank me for it!"

He stood up again, and swayed a little from the sudden emptiness of his head, heart, limbs. "Now . . . now I have to look for him."

"Hero." The Seer again pulled him down, and was surprised that it took so little effort. "Aren't you forgetting something?"

"Eh?" Hero sat there cold and numb.

"Your quest?"

"What do you know of my quest?" His query was listless, automatic.

The Seer shrugged. "An hour ago, a carrier pigeon from Celephaïs found me as I was on my way here. From Kuranes. With a message. I was told you might seek me out, and the king asked me what I know of this Oriabian vampire. More than that, he also told me a couple of things. And it now appears your quest's more urgent than ever. I'm sorry, lad, but Eldin will have to wait."

Again Hero lurched to his feet. "Not for any king's quest!" he blurted.

This time the Seer made no attempt to seize him, but said: "Hero, do you trust me?"

Hero looked into his frozen, empty sockets, and said, "Yes—no—I don't know. How can I trust someone when I can't see what's in his eyes? Trust you about what?"

"About Eldin."

Hero's face was gaunt, tortured. "I have to find him."

"Sit down and listen to me."

Hero sat—but inside his pain and frustration were churning toward anger. "Hero," said the Seer, "there are many small lights in my mind. They glow there like fireflies in a dark lane, or stars mirrored in a still sea. They are people I've met, memories of which I've retained. I don't know these motes individually, can't tell which firefly is what man or woman. But I'm sure I'd know it if one of them were extinguished. None of them have been, not recently. A few have flickered now and then, but none of them have gone out."

"You're saying Eldin is still alive."

"I can't guarantee it, but I believe it. Now, do *you* believe me?"

"If I do, isn't that all the more reason why I must find him?"

"Hero," said the Seer. "This pain you feel, worrying about Eldin. Is it bad?"

Hero groaned. "He's more than a brother. I laugh with him . . ."

"How much worse is it, then, for those families and friends beloved of this vampire's victims? Now don't look away but answer me. Eldin is one man, and they are many. And again I say to you: I believe he lives."

"But a short time ago you told me not to rely too much on my theory of his being alive."

"Because if I'm wrong I don't want your hatred!"

They stared at each other for long moments. Finally Hero said, "Very well, but understand: If you are wrong, I *will* hate you. What must I do?"

"You go about your business for Kuranes," said the Seer, with an audible sigh, "and I'll look for Eldin. And who better for the job, eh? Me, with these invisible eyes of mine. But first, and quickly, let me tell you what the king told me, and also what I've learned for myself:

"Kuranes' message: The plague has spread to Celephais!"

"What?" Already the numbness was going out of Hero's brain; his mind was alert again, his grasp growing stronger. "The thing has taken a victim in Ooth-Nargai?"

"Victims!" the Seer corrected him. "Plural. Three of 'em."

"But how can that be?" Hero's brow showed creases.

The Seer shrugged. "More than one vampire, maybe? Or a creature who can fly in the night across the sea? I don't know how it can be."

Hero thought back on what Kuranes had told him:

Healthy men—hardy, adventurous types all, and usually in their prime—had been vanishing without trace in Baharna and its outskirts. They left neither hide nor hair, bits or bones behind but quite simply disappeared—almost. They *did* leave gradually dispersing wraiths—ghosts! But ghosts of peculiar habits. No rattling of chains or lopped-off head-carrying for these missing and presumably (what else?) dead persons; no, they were simply wraiths that haunted their old homes, their families, favorite places, and other "haunts" they'd known in more corporeal times.

Now, ghosts in the dreamlands were as rare as ghosts in the waking world. Oh, the dreamworld had its monsters and menaces, true enough, its regions of magick, mystery, and nightmare, but as for ghosts . . . Homo ephemerens (the people of dreams) didn't generally have much of true matter anyway. They *seemed* solid and real enough, as most dreams do, but there just wasn't enough of them to leave a great deal behind. Dreamland's legendary Enchanted Wood was rumored to be home for several departed spirits, but actual *sightings* of specters were generally few and far between. Or had used to be.

The trouble with the troubled spirits which the Oriabian (and now Celephasian, apparently) vampire left behind was this: that they were incredibly persistent in aspiring to ghosthood. Each and every victim had become a ghost, without a single exception. Also, instead of merely haunting, they went about like lost souls (which of course they were) in a sort of vacant, absentminded, and yes, totally *lost* condition. Not lost like virginity or lost in sin, but lost as in not knowing where they were. And perhaps more importantly, *not remembering who they had been*!

And having revisited that conversation with Kuranes, and now with something of animation, Hero said: "It suddenly strikes me that we can make a quick end of this thing!"

The Seer raised an expressive eyebrow over nothing whatsoever, and said: "How so?"

"Isn't it obvious? Use your right eye to scry the past, find the vampire in his/her/its vile pusuit—or better still red-handed at a victim's demise—and I'll take it from there."

"Oh?" said the Seer. "Obvious, is it? But if what you suggest were possible there'd be no more crime in all the dreamlands! Can't you see that?"

"Eh?"

The Seer sighed. "I can't scry on criminal activities—not consciously, anyway. My eyes for the most part are quite blind to all matters of larceny, thuggery, arson, etcetera. Crimes against persons or property are therefore outside my scope, especially in a supernatural context. On the other hand"—and he frowned, which, without eyes, was a sight to see—"in this case there does appear to be something of an ambiguity."

"Say on."

"Well, I've said I'm not much on scrying supernatural stuff—and that's a fact, even though the scrying itself is nothing short of supernatural! Ah, but I *can* see the ghosts of this vampire's victims!"

"Indeed? And can you show them to me?"

"Certainly! For I've made some preliminary investigations, and indeed I have the power to recall some of the scenes I've seen. Now look into my eyes again—both of them, this time—and I'll run a replay."

Hero looked as directed, and it was something like using the Viewmaster he'd owned as a child, except when he thought of it he couldn't remember his childhood and didn't know what a Viewmaster was. Just another brief flash of memory from the waking world.

The scene was Andahad, a small but opulent seaport on the far side of Oriab. Hero knew it well enough since he and Eldin's ladyloves Ula and Una Gidduf had lived there once upon a time with their well-to-do merchant father, Ham. As Hero watched, the picture in the Seer's eyes narrowed down to a house of some excellence standing on a hillside to the east of the town. Outside the house, relatives of the family, passersby, and curiosity seekers in general, stood about in a small crowd, some having visited or being about to visit and others simply waiting to see what they'd see. Hero scanned their faces and believed he saw one that he recognized; then the S.W.I.E.'s eyes took him through the main door and inside the privacy of the dwelling itself.

There, in the main room—the sitting room, with a wide window over-looking the ocean strand—the family of the missing-presumed-dead man sat around in great distress, wringing their hands and weeping, or else staring in astonishment at all that was left of the head of the family. His widow, the lady of the house herself, was quite distraught; wild-haired and -eyed, she all the time pleaded with the apparition, which stepped here and there about the room, peering this way and that, with an ex-pression of bewilderment—no, of utter mystification—written plain on its diaphanous transparency of a face.

Hero was fascinated. He watched the ghost in its perambulations, how it appeared to examine this or that object or item of furniture in the room, frowning as if desperately trying to recall something it should know. And a weird comparison struck Hero: that the specter's expression was not unlike Eldin's or even his own on those occasions when they would briefly recall some fragment from the waking world, only to lose it a moment later. Every so often, as it drifted about, the ectoplasmic revenant would deliberately move *around* a chair or table, as if subconsciously "remember-ing" that such items of furniture were there; but mainly it walked right through them, and occasionally people, too, even its own pleading, weep-ing, half-crazed widow.

Occasionally it would seem to recognize one or another of its children, stop and stare in its puzzled fashion, even begin to smile or cry; but then the three-quarters vacant, worried expression would return and off it would go again, fading and quickening in turn, insubstantial as moon-beams where it examined and reexamined the room. Eventually, not look-ing where it was going, it passed into a solid wall and disappeared.

"An explorer and adventurer," the Seer informed as his eyes went blank as space again. "He mapped half of Kled in his time, that one. A great lecturer on his travels and travails in far, foreign places. When you're too old for questing, Hero, maybe you should take a leaf from his book and become a lecturer. He didn't do too badly out of it."

"Oh?" The other frowned. "Well, possibly there's no connection be-tween who he was and what he's become, but in any case it doesn't seem to me that he's done too well! I mean, what is he now but a vacant vapor, eh?"

The Seer scratched his head through his cowl a moment, then offered: "Do you want to see more? I've looked into most of these cases as they've occurred. Since we're visiting in Andahad, as it were, you might also like to check out the shade of Shallis Tull."

"Shallis Tull?" Hero repeated the name. "Wasn't he big all those years ago in the antislave-trade lobby? Didn't he forge links with Parg, become the blood brother of Gunda-ra-Gunda, the Pargan king, and sabotage a Kledan slaver fleet?"

"The same." The S.W.I.E. nodded. "Hard as nails, Shallis Tull, but with a heart of gold. Alas, he too is now a ghost; he haunts the ship he once sailed against Kled!"

"He wasn't a family man?"

"No, not him. The sea was his mistress, and fair play for all men his goal. Care to visit?"

Hero nodded. "But make it brief; I fear for Eldin, and at this rate you'll never get after him."

Again the Seer's eyes clouded over . . .

So it went.

Through the Seer's invisible eyes Hero boarded Shallis Tull's sloop *The Silver Fish*, to witness that vessel's vampirized ex-captain vacantly exploring her length and breadth. There was something vaguely familiar about the ship's interior and belowdecks, but Hero was rather more interested in the ghost of Tull than the vessel it had chosen to haunt.

Finally he followed the blocky, bearded, bewildered, and disembodied apparition back up on deck, where in a little while it passed into the wheelhouse, through the wheel, and vanished into the woodwork.

Before the Seer's eyes could revert to their commonplace (?) vacuity, Hero gazed through them onto the wharfside, where as before a small crowd of curiosity-seekers had assembled, all of them staring in wide-eyed wonder at the ghost-boat. And again, among the milling faces of these perversely peering persons, Hero thought he saw one which he recognized. Indeed, the same one that he'd seen outside the house of the explorer-adventurer.

After that, in short order, the S.W.I.E. showed Hero the ghost of Eelor

Tush, a Baharnian vintner who'd journeyed to the edge of dream itself in the discovery of his rare wines; the spectral remains of Tark the Tall, mountaineer extraordinaire, whose recent expedition on the south face of Hatheg-Kla in the stony desert had been the talk of all the dreamlands (especially after his party, with the sole exception of Tark himself, had fallen to their deaths from the mountain's flank; indeed fallen *up* the mountain, for Hatheg-Kla is that sort of place); and finally the shade of Geerblas Ulm, fearless and fabled descender into holes, first man to ever clamber down a rope to the bone-strewn floor of the ill-regarded Pit of Puth. And always Hero was aware that the same figure and face were somewhere present in the vicinity, mingling with the mobs come to gawp at the ghosts of this string of unfortunate personalities.

And so fascinated and involved had Hero become with these ocular excursions that it took some little time for the fact to dawn that here he was back in the Leery Crab (from which he'd never in fact strayed), seated beside the Seer, who sipped at his muth as before. "Enough?" inquired that worthy, between sips.

"Quite enough." Hero nodded. "And I thank you for what you've shown me. What's more, I believe I'm onto something. Now make haste with that muth and get busy."

"Eh? Busy?"

"Searching for Eldin, of course, alive or dead. But alive, if you value my continued friendship."

The Seer drained his mug. "I shall proceed by yak to the western flank of N'granek, which I'll search most diligently," he promised.

"Good!" said Hero. "And when I've done with a spot of business—maybe even while I'm dealing with it—I'll make myself available for searching the eastern flank. Before we go our separate ways, however, perhaps you'll tell me: when exactly was Shallis Tull's demise?"

"Eh? Tull? He disappeared, oh, all of three or four months ago. One of the vampire's first victims, as it happens."

"And *The Silver Fish?* What became of her?"

"Sold in auction, the monies going to Tull's old shipmates."

Hero nodded and asked no more. They stood up and the Seer left a small (a very small) tip on the table, and in single file they took their leave of the place. Or would have, except that Lippy Unth was waiting just beyond the door.

"Hero," said the huge black man rumblingly. "I'll take that, if it's all the same to you." He glanced warily at the bomb in Hero's hand. Behind him stood Gooba and friend, along with a goodly number of scar-faced patrons.

Without pause Hero struck sparks and lit the fuse, which at once commenced sputtering and smoking and of course burning down. Everyone except Lippy, who seemed nailed to the quay's stone flags, burst into furious activity, diving this way and that like so many trapped rats, taking cover wherever such might be had. Some went so far as to dive headlong off the pier into the scabfish-ridden scum of the harbor. Lippy, as stated, merely teetered on his heels, his olive features somehow contriving to turn a dark gray.

"This?" said Hero, innocently, holding up the smoking bomb in plain view. "Take it, by all means!" And he tucked it into Lippy's wide trouser band under his bulging belly.

Finally Lippy unfroze, snatched the device from his trousers, lobbed it out across the greasy water. In doing so he noted how light it was; noted, too, that when it splashed down it didn't sink but bobbed—*exactly* like the green glass floats which the fishermen used to buoy their nets! What's more, there was a smudge of fresh black paint on Lippy's hurling hand . . .

"*Hero!*" he howled a moment later, when he'd had time to draw sufficient breath. But by then Hero and the S.W.I.E. both had quite vanished away.

HERO DECIDED HE'D CARRY OUT an aerial search for Eldin, and he knew exactly who he'd enlist to aid him in this venture: someone with a sky-ship, obviously. Night had settled and the Quayside Quaress was alive with music, lights and laughter as he hurried along the dockside. At the door he bumped into the very man he sought, Chim Nedlar himself, master of the *Shark's Fin* sloop.

"Ahoy there, Cap'n!" Hero called out in a voice darkly jovial.

The other peered at him a moment in the gloom, then chuckled. "Ahoy, Hero! So we get to have a drink together after all!"

"Later, maybe," said Hero. "But right now I've need of your boat."

"Eh?" Nedlar seemed uncertain. "But I've given my lads shore leave for the night. Whatever it is, I'm sure it can wait till morning."

"No." Hero shook his head. "It can't. My friend and fellow quester Eldin the Wanderer is wrecked somewhere on N'granek, where the foot-hills meet the mountain. I've come here, to the Quaress, to borrow a bit of gear, and then I was on my way to find you. By being here you've saved me the trouble. Don't worry, I'll pay you well for your time and the hire of your sloop. As for being shorthanded: how many crew do you carry?"

"Myself and two—when they're here," said the captain. "She's easy in the handling, the old *Shark's Fin.*"

"But built for speed!" said Hero. "Which is what's required. And the wind's dropped, and we're both of us sailors. Man, I reckon we can handle her well enough on our own. Now, look, while I get me an aiming-lamp, maybe you'd like to pick up a bottle or two? Then while we search we can pull their corks, eh?"

Chim Nedlar brightened a little. "And perhaps you'll tell me a handful of your tall tales?—er, while we search, I mean?"

"A deal's a deal." Hero nodded.

As Chim made his way to the bar to buy booze, Hero's eyes narrowed a little. He watched the other's broad back disappear into the crowd . . .

Then someone tugged at his elbow and a foul, familiar female voice blasted in his ear: "Hero, by all that's unspeakably clean and healthy!"

"Buxom Barba!" he returned, recoiling from her breath.

Gigantically bosomed, gap-toothed from many a fistfight, and beaming very unbeautifully, Barba grabbed and hugged him. He felt his ribs give a little and fought free. "And Eldin?" she said, punching Hero mightily in the shoulder as she glanced this way and that. "Now, where's my fa-vorite boy?"

"Lost," said Hero, and he explained the other's possible plight. "That's why I'm here, to borrow one of your stage-lighting devices."

She went and brought one for him: a lantern with a curved lens, to throw the light in a beam. Onstage, the amazon Zuli Bazooli's dance was made that much more sensuous where now only five lights played upon her gleaming body instead of the customary six. "My thanks, Barba," said Hero. "I'll not forget you."

"When you find him drag him back here for a drink!" she shouted, as he hurried toward Chim Nedlar waiting at the door . . .

AFTER THAT IT TOOK TEN MINUTES to get aboard the *Shark's Fin*, cast off, and climb up into the night sky, and in a little while the gentle breeze off the sea was hushing them inland toward N'granek. Hero fixed up his searchlight in the prow, and Chim let his vessel drift along silently under half sail, crossing Baharna's hinterland plateau toward the central peaks. Then the captain joined Hero as he scanned the way ahead, and each pulling a cork they drank a little wine. The stuff went straight to Hero's head, which in the circumstances was perhaps to be expected.

"The engines are off, bags three-quarters full, altitude steady," said Chim. "Twenty minutes or thereabouts and we'll be over the foothills. Then we can start hallooing and hope your friend hears us, and your searchlight can double as a depth gauge. There are fangs aplenty I wouldn't care to bang into. Closer to N'granek I'll start up the engines, gain a little altitude, head for the eastern flank. If Eldin the Wanderer's there he should see or hear us. I still think it would have been better by daylight, but—"

"But he's lived through one night out there already," said Hero. "*If* he's still alive. So by now he'll be a bit desperate—especially if he's hurt. That's why it couldn't wait till daybreak."

"Of course, of course," said Chim, falling silent and thoughtful.

"Oh?" said Hero in a little while. "Is there something? Did I perhaps snap at you just then?"

Chim shrugged. "Only because you're under stress," he said. "But I suppose in the circumstances you'll not be much for recounting your adventures. A shame. For it's my hobby, you know: listening to swashbuckling yarns. And with such as you aboard . . . why, to hear firsthand accounts of *your* adventures would be . . . but probably not at a time like this, eh?"

Hero looked at him sideways. "I've nothing against it," he said. "Indeed, it might help pass the time." At which . . . it was as if a chill breeze blew on the back of Hero's neck, so that the short hairs stiffened there and made him shiver. He looked to see what had caused this sudden, icy gust, and there—

—Not three paces away, there stood a burly, bearded figure, peering in a puzzled fashion across the gunwale and out into the night! At first Hero almost cried out, for he thought that it was Eldin. But then he saw that for all its burliness the figure was ephemeral as fluff, less than a shimmer on a hot day. Rightly so, for it was the not entirely unfamiliar ghost of Shallis Tull! Its familiarity had two sources. One: this was one of the apparitions that the S.W.I.E. had shown to him; and two: it was the ghost he'd seen in his dreams during the crossing from Celephais to Oriab. What's more, it seemed to Hero that the specter was a warning . . .

"Ah!" said Chim Nedlar, "You see him, do you? From where I'm standing he's the merest outline. You see, it's all in the angle. Well, nothing to be afraid of. He's perfectly harmless. Give you a start, did he?"

The ghost quit its peering, wandered off along the deck and into the wheelhouse. Its face looked out for a moment through a window, and then gradually faded away . . .

"Eh?" said Hero, shaking himself. "A start? Aye, a bit of a one." He looked hard at Chim and his eyes had gone a fraction glinty. "Though why that should be I can't really say—since this was once his ship! P'raps I should have expected him."

Chim nodded. "Oh? And you know all about him, eh? Aye, the old *Shark's Fin* was once *The Silver Fish*; I thought it wiser to name her anew. I mean, it's one thing to be haunted but quite another to advertise the fact! How much trade d'you think I'd do if my customers knew this was Tull's old vessel?"

"Not much, I suppose," said Hero. "But doesn't it—he—bother you? Aren't you a bit chary of him?"

"He's a ghost." Chim shrugged. "And gradually fading as all ghosts do. I see less and less of him. Another week or two and there'll be nothing left of him at all!"

"But he's the victim of a vampire." Hero was coldly logical. "I mean, what of the legends? What if he should come back in vampire guise and vampirize you?"

"*Hah!* Twaddle! Stuff and nonsense!" Chim snorted. "Superstitious claptrap!"

"Oh?" Hero feigned a look of surprise. "You're not a superstitious man, then?"

"Me? No, of course not."

"And yet you admit that your boat's haunted . . ."

Chim narrowed his eyes. "I—"

"Indeed, it *is* haunted, for just a moment ago we both saw the ghost."

Chim sputtered. "A common or garden ghost is one thing," he declared, "and a vampire quite another. The first I believe in, not least because I've seen it, but the other—"

At which point the *Shark's Fin* bumped shudderingly into something, and from down below there came the rumbling echo of falling boulders. "Crags!" Hero cried, aiming his searchlight down into darkness.

"Fangs!" Chim leaped to the wheelhouse, got the flotation engines going.

They'd been lucky, merely brushed a pinnacle and blunted its stony tip. But sure enough they'd drifted well into the foothills, and southward rose the central peaks, where N'granek was lord and master. Gaining altitude, the ship bore them up above the danger zone.

"East," said Hero a little breathlessly. "Tack east now, while I sweep with my beam and we will both call out as we go. If Eldin's somewhere down there he'll see and/or hear us."

East it was, searchlight flashing, voices calling, and down below a thin mist crawling on the crags and in the hollows. But never the sight or sound of Eldin the Wanderer. And after a while: "Let down your anchor," said Hero gruffly. "It's dawned on me that if he's hurt, he may well be gathering his strength to make reply. I'd hate to overshoot him and leave him cold and broken in the mist."

Chim Nedlar did as instructed; the *Shark's Fin* swung gently at anchor some thirty-five feet over the crags, with frowning N'granek as backdrop, shrouded in a mist made yellow by the rising moon. And for an hour Hero aimed his lamp this way and that, until its oil was all used up; and all the while the two men bellowing their lungs out—to no apparent avail. "I'm hoarse," Hero finally admitted.

"Me too," replied the other.

They drank wine, Hero perhaps a little too much.

Then the *Shark's Fin*'s master spotted a tear in the inside corner of the quester's right eye, and another forming in the left. He nodded his understanding, said solemnly: "You think he's a goner, right?"

Hero looked away.

"You've adventured a lot together, you two," Chim prompted.

"Aye." Hero's voice came gruff from where he averted his face. Then, with more animation: "Adventured? *Hah!* That's not the half of it! How many men have been to the moon, Chim? We went there, got turned to moon rock—almost, and returned to tell of it. What do you know of Lathi and Zura? They've been enemies and allies both—until now I don't quite know what they are! We've chased horned-one pirates aboard Admiral Dass' flagship, burned old Thalarion to the ground, sailed dreamland's skies on the life-leaf of a Great Tree. Adventure?"

"Go on," Chim Nedlar urged. "Tell me more. Only paint a fuller picture, Hero. These are mere scraps you're tossing me."

And so Hero began to talk.

It was the wine, his grief, the misty night. It was his loneliness. And of course it was Chim's urging. The man was a good listener: he was like a sponge, soaking up all that Hero told him. But he was much more than a mere sponge.

Hero told of his part in the destruction of Yibb-Tstll's avatar idol in the Great Bleak Mountains; and of how he'd lulled the eidolon Lathi with a lullaby, thus enabling her hive city to be razed to the ground. He talked of the aerial plank-walk he'd taken, with Zura's zombie-pirates' swords at his back, and of his rescue from that miles-high tumble by Gytherik Imniss' night gaunts; and he told of the time he'd been vented from the bowels of Serannian in a great gust of scented flotation essence, when again Gytherik's grim of gaunts had plucked him from gravity's "fell" clutches.

And as time passed and his tales grew more detailed, so their telling became an almost automatic process; it was like siphoning water: one suck to get the thing going, and that's your lot till the lake's dry. Tonelessly, with neither affection nor detestation, he told of trials both titillating and terrifying; and all the while it seemed that he unburdened himself, that a great weight was lifted from him *as* each tale was told. And strangely, *as* each tale was told, so he forgot it—utterly, so that it didn't even cross his mind to wonder why—as he went on to the next story.

Worse far, however, than the mental depletion taking place in Hero, was the physical one. He was growing . . . flimsy! The more he divulged of his life and loves, his adventures and misadventures, his windfalls, pitfalls and pratfalls, his lucky and losing breaks, the less of *him* there seemed to be. It was as if Chim Nedlar were absorbing his *substance* as well as his words. And yet, once started, there was no stopping. His life came out in an endless stream, like a vein slashed through. And the water of a tepid tub turning pink, then red, as the poor doomed soul lies back and oh so gently expires. But there was no blood, no pain, and very little of conscious awareness of the murder taking place. Of Chim Nedlar's murder of David Hero, Hero of Dreams.

No blood, no—for Chim was not that sort of vampire.

But a vampire he was, to be sure.

"More! More!" he gloated—and bloated as he fed on Hero's heroics. "Except . . . tell me more about Eldin, too, and Limnar Dass, Gytherik, Kuranes, oh, and all the others you've known. I want to know all of their adventures, too!"

Hero looked at the other through eyes that swam like small fishes in a bland bowl ocean. Chim Nedlar, grinning, drooling, his fat face full of spittly teeth, his eyes pinpricks of passion in a puffy mass of dough. Chim, all swollen with Hero's stories. No—with Hero's life!

And now Hero knew (however dimly) what he'd more than half suspected anyway. Except it was too late to do anything about it. And anyway, did he *want* to do anything about it? This way there'd be nothing of him left at all for Zura. And certainly it was painless enough. But what would the worlds of dream have been like without Eldin? It was something he hadn't intended to discover.

Maybe there were dreamlands ulterior to this one, and maybe he'd meet up with Eldin again in one of them. Why not? They'd named the old lad Wanderer, hadn't they? A ways to wander yet, perhaps. Now, *there* was a thought!

"More! *More!*" Chim demanded, his voice a gurgle.

"One last tale," Hero whispered, the merest shadow of a man where he sat with his pale head lolling on the gunwale, his barely opaque hand listless where it tried to grasp and lift his bottle, but wasn't quite solid or strong enough to manage it. "The last one, Chim—for it's *this* one!"

"This one?"

"Aye." Hero nodded. "The story of how I came to Oriab in search of a monster—and found him!"

"Ah!" said Chim. "Ah! But discovered him too late!"

"I've known for some time." Hero sighed, his dying searchlight's beam beginning to show through his flesh. "Not the how of it, until now, but certainly I suspected the who."

Chim nodded. "That's as it may be; it detracts not at all from my enjoyment. Out with it, then, this last tale. Tell it all—and then you're done. And me? Glutted, I'll first sleep it off, then live on your fat dreams for quite some little time before I'm hungry again."

And Hero, unable to resist, began to comply:

"It started with drinking," he said, his voice very ephemeral now, "and with boasting, and of course wagering as well. As the muth went down faster, so the boasting and wagering grew wilder. Mine and Eldin's, of course. Finally the great buffoon declared that 'alone, single-handed, on (his) own, without assistance and—' "

The anchor chain rattled and Chim gave a start. Beneath his ballooning shirt the great mass of him quivered. His piggy eyes left Hero's fading face to scan the dark deck. There was a streamer of creeping mist; there were shadows, splashes of yellow moonlight. Nothing else.

Chim faced Hero again. "Go on," he said.

"No!" came a gruff, grim, croaking voice from the darkness of the wheelhouse. "No, lad, say no more. For it strikes me you've damn near talked yourself to death already!"

Shallis Tull's ghost came lumbering, bearded, and burly. Except it wasn't Tull but Eldin!

"Gah!" said Chim Nedlar, who knew the game was up. *"Gah!"* He drew a long thin knife from its sheath sewn into his shirt. Eldin disarmed him with a lunge and a twirl of his great straight sword. And, "Gah!" the soul-stealer said again, shrinking against the strakes.

"Eldin!" whispered Hero, unable to rise. "Eldin!"

"The same," said the Wanderer, his own voice scratchy as sandpaper. He reached down, took up Hero's bottle, drained it in one massive gulp.

"Did you hear?" Hero was thin as water, blurred at the edges, gradually going gaseous.

"Enough." Eldin nodded. "I've been clinging to the anchor chain for some little time, waiting to be sure I knew what it was all about. Now I know." He placed the point of his sword on a spot a little below Nedlar's fat, bobbing Adam's apple. "Now tell it back," he ordered. "All of it, exactly as you heard it."

"He told the stories of his own free will!" Chim Nedlar babbled.

"And so will you," said Eldin grimly.

"What? At swordpoint?"

"You have a choice: untell the things, and unspell Hero—let out those tales of his which you've somehow trapped—or I'll let *you* out all over the deck here!" He pressed harder with his sword and the other's throat was indented, where the tiniest prick of red showed.

"I'll do it," the vampire gulped.

He retold Hero's stories. In the telling, his bulging shirt subsided a little and some of the puffiness went out of him; Hero put on flesh, or rather his outline began to fill out and look less like that of a jellyfish in the sunlight. Soon he was able to stand up. He looked more his old self, and yet still a little vague.

Chim Nedlar had come gaspingly to a halt.

"Did he retell all?" Eldin was suspicious.

Hero scratched his head. "How'm I supposed to know? I re-remembered everything he said, but how can I say he said everything?"

"Lathi?" said Eldin, and Hero nodded.

"Zura? Kuranes? Gytherik? Serannian?" Nods to all.

"The Mad Moon? Yibb-Tstll—"

"Eh?" said Hero. "Yibb-who?"

"*Hah!*" Eldin prodded again.

Chim Nedlar, looking very pale, gave a little shriek and quickly spilled the rest of the beans—spilled the rest of Hero's memory and being back into him. And: "That's it, that's all, I swear it!" he finally cried.

"Not by a long shot," said Hero darkly, entirely entire again.

Eldin didn't understand.

But Chim Nedlar did. "You're out to destroy me," he whispered, his lips aquiver.

"Too true," Hero agreed, "one way or the other. My turn, Eldin." He unsheathed his slender, curved Kledan sword with a steely whisper, held its keen edge to Nedlar's windpipe. "Let's start with Shallis Tull," he said.

Weeping and babbling, and cursing a lot between stories, the vampire retold Tull's tales, and so revitalized the man. In a little while something more than a ghost came bowling up from belowdecks, beard bristling and eyes ablaze—with astonishment, with joy! "It's coming back!" Cap'n Tull cried. "*I'm* coming back!"

And as he in turn filled out, so Chim Nedlar continued to diminish.

After Tull, in short order, it was the turn of Eelor Tush, vintner extraordinaire; but he did not materialize here but in Baharna, no doubt. Then Tark the Tall, mountain man, who probably came back clinging to some pinnacle somewhere. And Geerblas Ulm, doubtless fattening out in one of his favorite underworlds; and so on, and so on . . .

Finally Chim Nedlar was a wisp. Toward the end he'd been unstoppable (the siphon principle again) and simply spilled all the life he'd taken in back out into dreamland's aether, through which it sped back to its rightful dreamers. They knew when he'd told all, for his eyes—about as invisible now as the S.W.I.E.'s—suddenly went extremely vacant.

He floated to his feet, leaving his voluminous shirt and empty clogs behind, and looked this way and that without recognizing anyone or anything. Then, seeing Hero, Eldin, Shallis Tull, perhaps he did remember something. He backed off from them, passed through the ship's strakes and stood for a moment on thin air over misted, unknown chasms of night. Then he began to fall, and falling dispersed entirely.

A thin, thin cry of empty frustration and lost longing drifted back to them. Or maybe it was only the wind rising in the crags, blowing the mist away in tatters which vanished almost as quickly as Chim Nedlar . . .

SITTING IN SUNLIGHT upon a pile of nets where they dried on the wharf side, Hero and Eldin watched Shallis Tull painting out *Shark's Fin* on the upper outside port strakes of *The Silver Fish*. He'd promised to sail them back to Celephais, but not until his vessel bore her rightful name once more.

Meanwhile, Eldin had told his own tale, which Hero didn't steal but merely listened to: told how he'd crashed among the crags and his flotation bag was bust; how he'd clung to a ledge while his numbed arm regained its strength and feeling; how then he'd yelled himself hoarse, yelled till he had no voice left to yell with, for the better part of a day and night. But when the mist had thinned a little he'd seen his way clear to climb up from the chasm, to where the S.W.I.E. had found him hungry, thirsty, and a bit banged-about, but otherwise well, and helped him up on to the back of his yak.

Then, on their way down to Baharna, they'd spied the *Shark's Fin* and heard Hero's and Chim Nedlar's shouting. Following voices and fading searchlight beam both, soon they'd come to the place where the sky-ship was anchored. By then all was silent.

Eldin would have called to those aboard but couldn't: he had no voice.

And anyway, the S.W.I.E. had cautioned him: "Something's wrong here! I can smell it!"

Following which Eldin had shinned soundlessly up the anchor chain . . . and the rest is known.

"Who was he, d'you suppose?" Now the Wanderer wanted to know.

Hero shrugged. "Someone from the waking world, I should think. Somehow, when his time was up, he found his way here. Maybe he was the kind who lives on the glories of others. You can find his like in any bar you choose: poor souls whose own lives are so drab they may only color them with the lives of others—whose nature it is to bask in the glow of adventures they've never experienced for themselves, except as recounted by their heroes. And in his transition from waking- to dreamworlds, his dependency grew strong while his will weakened. Until he emerged here as a weird sort of vampire, as—"

"A stealer of dreams?"

"That's my guess, anyway." Hero nodded.

Eldin said: "Hmmm!" and changed the subject. "Well, lad, it strikes me I've saved your life—again."

Hero snorted. "It was you put it at risk in the first place!" he accused. "You drunken old—"

"Not so much of the 'old,' if you please!" Eldin cut him short.

"And that's the end of *that,* too!" said Hero, threateningly.

"Eh? End of what?"

"Boozing! We've done much too much of it. It's what started all of this in the first place."

"What!" Eldin was aghast.

"No more muth," Hero declared.

"You're joking! What about wine?"

"No," Hero pursed his lips, shook his head. *"All* booze is out—as of now."

"Immediately?" There was a frog in Eldin's throat.

(A moment's silence.) "Tomorrow."

"Good!" The older quester's grin split his face. " 'Cos right now I've a hell of a thirst on. How about a pint?"

"I could murder one." Hero sighed . . .

HARRY KEOGH:
NECROSCOPE

DEAD EDDY

Sometimes Harry felt that he'd lost a lot of time, years even. He wasn't able to say how or where all that time had gone, but every now and then he'd get this paranoid feeling—a sort of nervous anxiety—that he should try to catch up, grab a hold of the minutes, hours, days before they passed him by entirely. On the other hand, at other times and far more rationally despite the peculiar circumstances of his life (or perhaps because of them), he would simply put it down to the fact that his was a young mind inhabiting a somewhat older body. Which meant, of course, that he really *had* lost a great deal of time, and that he'd been shortchanged on several years that his *current body* had enjoyed without him . . . but that's another story.

And sometimes when that weird paranoia was on him—that niggling notion that he was missing something, that things had sneaked by him unnoticed—then he'd stir himself up and go to work on something, on anything, in a burst of frantic activity, aglow with frenzied energy, in a vain attempt at catching up.

Harry's old house by the river was to have been the latest beneficiary of one of these rages. He'd determined to clear out the attic, then to reduce all of the wormy old sticks of broken furniture that he knew were hiding up there to so much ash on a bonfire in his garden. Except that wasn't how things would work out. For up there under the rafters, under the dusty, cobwebbed eaves, that was where he'd found the money.

But there's money and there's MONEY! And this was money of the latter variety. It was a hoard: quite literally "a treasure trove, deposited in secret." It could only be, for despite that it was in *his* attic, Harry knew that *he* hadn't put it there . . . had he?

And yet, seeming to fit in with some half-formed theory of time lost and events forgotten—or perhaps erased?—his discovery did ring a bell . . . albeit one whose tolling was quickly smothered, drowned out by his astonishment at the sheer size of his find, the as-yet uncalculated value of all this "loot." For surely a hoard such as this must be someone's ill-gotten gains, else why hide it? (And then again, why in Harry's attic?)

Great wads of pounds, dollars, and deutsche marks, all in high denominations, stuffed carelessly, haphazardly into two motheaten pillowcases like so much old packing paper—and that was *only* the paper!

But in that same dark space under the eaves, in a matching pair of heavy, triple-stitched burlap bags . . . what in the name of . . . ? Pieces of eight?

No, no pirate's hoard this—no Spanish gold here, not in the Necroscope's attic—but gold nevertheless. And every coin a troy ounce! South African gold: Krugerrands! And morning sunlight coming through the gap where a tile had slipped, striking glorious fire from twin clunking, chunky piles, as Harry tipped out the contents of the burlap bags onto the attic's warped old floorboards.

For a split second, in the blink of an eye, a scene formed on the screen of his oddly reluctant memory:

He pictured a hugely sprawling house or fortress, a walled villa or manse on the rim of a gorge. But a manse? Hardly that! How could he have thought to designate a name like that to such a doom-fraught old place? What, that awesome pile—that aerie, glooming with seemingly sinister intent upon some foreign land, and from there leering out across the very world—that place, the home of ecclesiastics?

And that was it, that was all. In the next blink of an eye it was over; the picture had dissolved, melted away—likewise the thoughts it had conjured—like a name on the tip of one's tongue that recedes deeper into limbo the more one tries to remember it. And Harry was alone with his "loot," the crisp paper and glowing coins . . . *and* with his bottom jaw hanging open.

Those coins: why, there had to be five hundred of them! And despite all of the wonders and horrors of Harry's life, and the fact that there was very little in the whole world which could actually shock him, still he felt stunned—actually considered the notion that he might be dreaming—as he meshed his fingers through one of the piles, gradually eased them apart again, and let all of that gold settle into a single, solid-seeming nugget that burned yellow as coals in a hearth fire . . .

MAN AND BOY THE NECROSCOPE had never been wealthy. He'd made a little money from what he now thought of as his "ghostwriting" period, but that was all. Yet now, making a few quick calculations, suddenly he was rich, almost 2 million pounds sterling rich! As for what he'd do with the money: no problem. It would fund his continuing search, paying the wages of all the people he'd engaged to look for his wife and child around the world.

But that, too, is another story . . .

A LITTLE WAY DOWNRIVER FROM THE HOUSE, in a grassy bight where the water stood deep and mainly static, with only the occasional surface swirl to indicate influxes from the central current, Harry sat with his feet dangling over the rim and talked to his Ma. She was down there somewhere, or what was left of her after all this time.

That last wasn't a thought that bothered the Necroscope too much; he remembered her as she'd been—through the eyes of the infant *he* had been—and that's how she would remain. It's how most mothers remain after they've gone.

But in any case they conversed, and of course he mentioned the money.

Money? she repeated. *Under the eaves?* (And Harry could almost see her raised eyebrow.) *I know nothing about that, son.*

"Actually," he told her, "I didn't expect you to know anything about it. The notes are crisp, new, recent. And the coins were minted only ten years ago—er, since your time, that is. No, the reason I mentioned it is because I thought you might be able to ask about it among the Great Majority, see if they have any ideas about it."

The only one I can think of who might know . . . She began to answer, then paused before continuing: *but he doesn't have very much to say anymore.*

In fact I haven't sensed his presence for quite a long time, and I think it's entirely possible he's gone now, "moved on," as it were. Viktor had no friends here, and he definitely didn't like being this close to me!

Harry knew who she meant: his stepfather, Viktor Shukshin, the man who had murdered her, pushed her under the ice when the river was frozen over and the Necroscope was just a child. That was a crime that the Russian spy had paid for some years ago—paid for in spades when he'd died a death as weird and gruesome as any that might be imagined—yet the Necroscope still hated the very thought of him. And:

"No," he answered, trying not to growl, "I don't think it was his money. The time frame is right, but the last time I saw Shukshin—on the night he tried to kill me, when you, er, intervened?—he looked pretty much down at heel to me. The money *could* have been up there in the attic, I suppose, but if Shukshin had known about it I'm sure he would have been using it."

Now, Harry's Ma sensed the nervous anxiety in him, and knew its source: He was still trying to figure out where all of the time had gone. And assuming that the money in his attic had found its way there during those lost years—that it had been put there by Harry himself—she also knew that it was time to change the subject. There were things Harry would never be able to remember however hard he tried, and it would suit her better if he didn't try at all.

And so, with an ostensibly innocent incorporeal shrug, she said, *Anyway, why do you concern yourself so? I mean, if you're suddenly well off, won't that make life a lot easier for you?*

"Eh?" said Harry, who had fallen into a kind of reverie or more properly a mood of dark, thoughtful introspection, as he'd remembered the events of that fateful night when his stepfather had gone down in mud and weed and bones—the bones of his dear Ma—down to the riverbed, never to come up again. But now her query lifted him out of it, brought him back to the present.

What was that she was saying? he wondered as he resurfaced from the darkness of those memories. Something about life being easier?

It's time you had some fun, *Harry!* she said. *It's time you let go of the past and started to think about the future. Those of us who don't* have *any futures—*

the teeming dead—we can't help but think you're wasting your time. I mean, life's not for being morbid, son. There's time enough for that, er . . .

"Later?"

Yes, later, his Ma answered with a sigh. *For we all end up here sooner or later. And right now's your time to live.*

Which was when he decided to forget what was past or lost, forget what couldn't be recalled, and start to live again. That is, if his search would let him . . .

LATER, downstairs in his living room, scarcely conscious of the travel show on the TV and occasionally pausing to blink wonderingly at a short stack of gleaming gold on a coffee table close to hand, the Necroscope riffled absentmindedly through a wad of fifty-pound notes. The reality of his find—the opportunities it had opened up—was starting to get through to him now. And as for his original plan: to use this money to fund his search, paying the wages of a great many private detectives worldwide: oh, it would do that all right, *and* a whole lot more.

In fact his Ma was absolutely right: from now on, certainly as far as money was concerned, Harry could do whatever he fancied. Of course there hadn't been a hell of a lot that Harry couldn't do *before* this windfall, but being the soul of honesty and unwilling to use his metaphysical talents outside the law—or outside what he himself considered ethical use—he'd had to suffer the same restrictions as any other moral person.

For instance: he could easily rob a bank—Fort Knox if he so desired—but wouldn't because he wasn't a thief. Similarly, despite that Harry had put many men and monsters to death, he'd never considered himself a murderer. And for all that he talked to dead people, the Great Majority, he most definitely wasn't a necromancer!

By his reckoning, the difference lay in one's approach; it was the way one saw and did things, a matter of one's humility, decency, and ethics.

This newfound wealth: it was tainted, he felt sure of it, knew it without knowing how. But now, by some mechanism unknown to him, it had ended up in his hands. Stolen it most surely had been, but by whom and for what reason, there was no way of knowing. He only knew he could make use of it, and if he made *good* use of it . . . then that was all to the good! It was only right and proper, after all—

—*But* at the same time he knew his Ma was right, too. If he were to use just a little of the money for his own personal pleasure, well, what harm in that? None at all that Harry could see. Because for a fact there hadn't been too much "fun" in his life so far . . .

BRIGHT LIGHTS ATTRACTED Harry's notice.

Outside, beyond glazed patio doors, the day was suddenly overcast by unseasonal clouds that painted the mainly untended garden a sickly gray-green. Distant lightning silhouetted hazy Scottish hills, and in a little while there sounded a far-away rumble of thunder.

The sudden gloom made the moving pictures on the TV screen that much more stark, glaring. For it wasn't the lightning that had caught Harry's eye but the flickering colors of a million lightbulbs and neons that formed moving pictures, legends, and electrical life in the corner of the room.

"The Flamingo Hilton," said one such legend, in a blaze of pink neons atop a huge illuminated hotel. Then the camera angle swooped down to the entrance, revealing the same legend over an amazing facade shaped like an exotic globular fruit, or flower, or flame, all etched in pink, gold, and orange light.

Harry's eyes were now glued to the screen as he groped for the remote, adjusted the subdued sound until it became audible, and picked up on the last few phrases of the commentary:

". . . And that's it, folks, that's Las Vegas—called variously the Land of Illusion or Sin City—ultimately a gambler's paradise and oasis in the Nevada desert. But before we go let's take a last look at the Strip at night. And here's a parting thought for you as we say a fond farewell to all the bright lights, the loose slots, and those beautiful leggy showgirls—

"—Wouldn't you just love to have the lightbulb concession in fabulous Las Vegas?

"So there you go. It's been great to have you. This is Joe Frazell, signing off on this week's *Travel Extravaganza* . . ."

The camera panned across an ocean of colored lights, came to rest on

Frazell in an Elvis Presley outfit, standing central in a long straight road—the famous Vegas Strip itself—with his outspread arms and legs forming a stylized Elvis X in the midst of a vast panoply of neon dazzle. For a moment the show's host held the pose, then lowered his arms to his sides, lowered his head to his chest, turned and exited stage left in dejected mode. The camera (mounted on a vehicle, no doubt) began to move forward, panning left and right as the casinos lining the Strip commenced flowing by in a luminescent stream, each bent on outdoing the next in garish splendor.

From the Flamingo Hilton to the Imperial Palace—accelerating toward Nob Hill, Castaways, the Holiday Casino, and the Sands—and more yet toward the Desert Inn, the Frontier, the Stardust, and Westward Ho—then blazing on past Circus Circus and the Riviera, toward El Rancho and the Sahara. A stream of lights, neons and brilliant facades, all fusing together, blurring into a tube of radiance that was so reminiscent of a trip through Möbius time that Harry ... that he held his breath!

—Only to slowly expel it as the TV screen faded to black, and the end credits commenced rolling in a comparatively somber white, and finally the channel's insignia took center screen.

The End ...

But only the beginning for a thought that was now blossoming in the Necroscope's mind. Fun? Now, *that* would be fun! Moreover, Las Vegas was a place where he'd never thought to search, where he hadn't ever imagined Brenda might go. Now, however ... well, why not?

Hadn't she always loved fairgrounds? And wasn't Las Vegas the biggest, most magical fairground in the world? Harry didn't know too much about it—he'd never been to America, let alone Las Vegas—but he knew this much at least: that Vegas was the place to go if you loved fantasy, razzle-dazzle, and the bright-eyed excitement of thousands of thrill-seekers, radiating from them like so much glitter dust, so much magical aether into the Nevada desert nights.

Such a potent magic, and so very tangible, that Harry had felt it himself—even though it had only come to him via a TV screen!

But Brenda? Brenda and her infant son, Harry Jr., not five years old as yet, in Vegas? Or were they just an excuse because he would like to go there himself and have some "fun"? If so, he knew how to reinforce that excuse. When they were kids in their middle teens, sweethearts and even lovers way back then, wasn't Brenda the one who couldn't wait for the summer to come around, so that she could drag him down to the Seaton Carew resort with its seafront slot arcades, fish-n'-chip shops, dodge 'em cars, and wide white-sand beach? Wasn't she the one who would (if he had let her) roll their last few copper coins down those swiveling chutes onto traveling "win" lines which were almost impossible to hit? She'd actually done that once—used the last of their money—so that if he hadn't bought return tickets they'd have had to walk home. Harry remembered how he'd tormented her, kidding her along that in fact they only had single tickets, until it was time to catch the bus. She'd paid him back by turning up half an hour late on their next date.

There had been some good times, would have been a lot more if Harry hadn't been Harry. If he hadn't been called upon to do the things that he'd done. But he was what he was—the Necroscope—and he had been called . . .

Brenda, in Vegas. Was it possible? Surely not—how would she have supported herself? With her hairdressing? She had been very good at it, first class, and you could pretty much guarantee there'd be plenty of demand for good hairdressers in Vegas. And as for a place to lose oneself: what, among all those year-round crowds? Why, Las Vegas would make the ideal hideaway. And you could forget that old saw about a needle in a haystack, for this would be more like looking for a jackpot in a slot-machine arcade.

In a certain way, that last thought would prove prophetic. But paradoxically, the task it had set wouldn't prove nearly so problematic . . .

HARRY WENT TO LAS VEGAS—he simply "went there," in his usual, unusual way. He had no coordinates to begin with, but the dead of the Charleston Heights Cemetery were eager to oblige. It was more than worth it to them: the opportunity to have a few words with the Necroscope, the one man among all the living who could actually speak to the dead.

And so he homed in on them and talked for a while, because he believed that one good turn deserves another. (And of course at the other end of the scale he also believed in an eye for an eye, that evil deeds should be repaid in kind.) But in a little while it was time to move on.

"Where exactly am I?" he asked an old silver miner who had been down in the ground here for almost one and a quarter centuries—deep down *below* the modern cemetery—since a time when this land was farmed by a party of Mormon settlers sent here by Brigham Young. The Mormons had given Jack Black (as the old boy was called) permission to dig for precious silver metal here in what was once the corner of a stony field. And here he remained to this very day.

Eh? said Jack. *You don't know where you are?*

"I mean," Harry patiently explained, "I need directions to the Strip, the bright lights, the casinos."

Heh-heh! came the answer. *Well, Harry, 'scuse me laughin', but it seems to me you just might be askin' the wrong one. The name's Jack Black, not blackjack! And I been down here so long, why, there* weren't *no Las Vegas the night it rained and my diggings done caved in on me! But hey, I knows exactly where 'tis anyways, this bright-lights Las Vegas that you're lookin' for. 'Cos old Jack Black and silver, we always did have this—how-do-you-call-it?—this here affinity. I mean, it* draws *me, you know? Even now, after all these years, still it draws me.*

Speaking like this to the dead—using this weird, metaphysical telepathy—often conveyed more than was actually said, and Harry Keogh was its lone exponent. He knew immediately what the old-timer meant: that lying down there in the cold earth he had actually *felt* the ebb and flow of money, of silver dollars, into (and occasionally out of) Las Vegas as it grew up into the greatest massed gambling concern the world had ever seen, which was mainly responsible for earning it its name, Sin City.

A sin? said Jack. *Damn right! To think I burned myself out—then buried myself alive—in my search for silver, and all they does with it these days is stick it in machines with spinnin' reels. But lyin' here I feel it all, every dollar in every slot, and my bones still ache with the longin' for it. And naturally I knows the whereabouts o' the ache, where it's a-comin' from.*

And then, after pausing to point the way: *It's maybe three or four miles,* said old Jack. *But no more'n that. And if you're here to gamble, well, I surely wish you luck, Necryscope. But if you was to win . . .*

"Yes?" said Harry.

...Then you might just think to come back here and stick a silver dollar piece deep down in the soil with the heel of your boot. Sumthin' for me to feel real close to—to ease the aches in these old bones.

"It's a deal," said Harry. And on afterthought: "Actually, it makes a change to meet someone who's *drawn* to silver as opposed to fearing it."

And Jack Black answered, *Oh, we knows all 'bout that, Necryscope: you and vampires and what-all. So maybe you've come to the right place after all.*

At which Harry felt the hairs stiffening at the nape of his neck. And: "What's that about vampires?" he growled, his eyes narrowing.

Calm down, Harry! the old-timer was quick to reassure him. *It's a joke, that's all.*

"A joke?"

Sure. About Las Vegas—how there's more damn bloodsuckers in Vegas than anywhere else in the whole damn world!

And as Harry took a deep breath and relaxed again, the old man—the dead man, who would never get any older—chuckled in his fashion and then fell silent.

With which Harry offered his thanks and a silent farewell to the other members of the Great Majority who were buried here (silent because a young woman had come into the cemetery, where she now arranged a wreath on a nearby plot), walked quietly out of the place, and strode off along the road in the direction of downtown Las Vegas ...

IT WAS TEN AFTER EIGHT IN THE MORNING; since Harry had departed Bonnyrig at four in the afternoon of the same day, he might now be thought of as being ahead of himself. And the frivolous idea occurred: crossing the time zones instantaneously was a different kind of time travel! As for jet lag: that wouldn't pose any great problem for the Necroscope, whose trip home could be accomplished as quickly as his trip out.

He was reminded of a clever old limerick:

> There was a young fellow called Bright,
> Who traveled much faster than light,

He set off one day in the usual way,
And returned on the previous night.

And Harry wondered—was that the secret of time travel in the Möbius Continuum? For obviously "instantaneously"—the way *he* traveled—must be faster than light. Was that perhaps the key to an understanding of Möbius metaphysics, the existence of those enigmatic past and future time-doors on the Möbius strip?

The thought passed as quickly as it had come; right now he was heading for an entirely different kind of strip, and he was supposed to be having fun . . .

BEHIND GREEN LAWNS LEFT AND RIGHT, modest plaster-walled, wood-floored houses stood row upon row, showing no evidence of their proximity to Sin City. This could be any '50s development almost anywhere in North America: simply a neighborhood where "ordinary" people lived, the working people and the retired.

But as Harry reached a crossroads he spied in the distance a skyline of glittering, much taller buildings. And always seeking cover, making sure that he wasn't observed, he commenced a series of rapid-fire Möbius jumps toward that district. So that in no time at all (quite literally) he was standing in Fremont Street, central to the downtown casino area.

Then, despite that he had eaten that morning, he couldn't resist break-fasting again on steak and eggs, so-called silver-dollar pancakes and syrup (all on the same plate), and a huge pot of coffee to wash it down—all of which cost just ninety-nine cents! Harry could scarcely believe how cheap things were. But at the same time it just might have been a problem, for as yet he didn't have any American money. All of those dollars at his place in Scotland, and he'd been so eager to get here that he hadn't brought a one with him, only English paper money and a dozen or so Krugerrands from the hoard in his attic.

He was in a coffee shop just off Fremont. It was a little after nine and the place was half-empty. While it appeared that most of the customers were still waking up, there were some who looked like they hadn't yet been to bed! Harry suspected they'd be all-night gamblers who had managed to save the last of their dollars for breakfast—with which he felt a sudden stab of anxiety. And groping in his pocket, his face fell as finally he realized his gaffe.

At the same time his huge, white-aproned server approached and cocked his bald head on one side. Having noted Harry's consternation, the man growled, "Is dere perhaps a problem?"

"Er, no," Harry answered, handing him a heavy coin. "It's just that I've no change, that's all."

"Oh yeah? So what's dis?" The other's brows came together, trapping the bridge of a bulbous nose. "Some kinda foreign coin—and a copper one at dat?"

"Er, not copper," said Harry, aware of the server's shadow looming over him. "That's gold. It's a Krugerrand. It's good as money anywhere, and worth an awful lot of your silver dollars."

The other's jaw dropped. "It looks real, and it sure feels real," he said. "But if it *ain't* real..."

The Necroscope could only offer a helpless shrug. "I don't know how I can prove it," he said.

"Is dat so?" The server squinted out of the window, across the narrow street. "But I do. Gimme ya shoes."

"My shoes?" Just for a moment Harry was mystified. Then he followed the server's gaze and made the connection: there was a hock shop and currency exchange almost directly opposite on the other side of the street. And while this big fellow checked out the coin's value—or its lack—Harry wouldn't be going anywhere without his good shoes! Of course, he *could* go somewhere, just about anywhere; but the big man didn't know that, and anyway Harry didn't intend to run out on him.

Pouring himself a last cup of coffee, he watched the other dodging the morning traffic and entering the hock shop. Perhaps two and a half minutes later, no more than that, the man reappeared and came running back across the road with Harry's shoes in one hand and money in the other.

"Pal, I got ya a wad," he said breathlessly, as he handed over a thick bunch of five-dollar bills. "I mighta been ripped off, but hey, I only woik here!"

"I'm most grateful," Harry replied, giving him back eight bills. "And if I might ask your help in hailing a taxi?"

"A cab? Sure." The server gaped at his thirty-nine dollar and one cent tip. "But . . . dis is way too much!"

"Not at all." The Necroscope waved aside his protests. "I . . . well, it's like I've had a lucky break, you know?"

"Jeez!" said the other. "A lucky break? It seems ta me ya musta broke da bank! Tanks a million! And, er—sorry about da shoes."

Harry slipped his feet into his shoes and followed the big man out onto the street. There he shook the other's hand, and a moment or two later seated himself in the back of a taxi headed south for the Las Vegas Strip. The server stood at the curbside scratching his shiny head, and watched him go . . .

HARRY DIDN'T EVEN THINK about checking into a hotel. Why should he when he'd be sleeping at home tonight? (At about 5:00 or 6:00 in the evening in fact, Las Vegas time of course.) But that was only if by then the adrenalin had stopped flowing, which at the moment didn't seem at all likely. It was the place; it had this frenzied life of its own, this energy, this enormous electrical heartbeat. And his heart was beating to match it.

"Fun?" Well, so far so good. Now he could try out his luck. Except this time he wouldn't have to worry about losing all of his money and having to walk home. Heck, he could lose as much or as little as he wanted and it still wouldn't matter a damn! And as for walking home—not anymore he wouldn't!

But the sun was very hot on his back now, and the casinos looked so very cool and inviting.

IT WASN'T MUCH FUN. Harry discovered that he might easily lose himself in the acreage of slot-machine mazes; he saw his money disappearing into the slots as fast as he could feed them. Now and then lights would start flashing from this or that machine on the other side of the floor, where someone—some "winner," Harry supposed—would start dancing and shouting. But no such luck where he was concerned.

Attracted by one such clamor nearby, he joined the small crowd who went to ooh and aah at the jubilant punter's lucky strike. Five hundred dollars for a line of fives? It didn't seem so very much to Harry, and this a dollar machine at that. It certainly wasn't this particular slot's top jackpot of five thousand. And already Harry's American money was gone, so that if he wanted to carry on he would have to exchange some sterling . . . or Krugerrands. But he'd try to avoid that last if he could. It could only bring him under unwanted scrutiny.

But as Harry thought these thoughts, someone else thought this one:

The loosest slots are downtown, Necroscope. I can perhaps teach you how to win some jackpots—small ones, maybe—but this place is too classy and the machines are too new. Looking at them through your eyes—seeing and feeling them as you see and feel them—I mean, I don't even recognize a lot of them! The simplest slots are the best. They're the ones I understand best, and brother do I understand them!

"You have me at a disadvantage," Harry mumbled (apparently to himself) as he peeled English fifty-pound notes from his wad and approached the window of a cash exchange booth. He could as easily have thought his answer at this unknown newcomer, but he preferred to speak it . . . it felt more natural that way.

Eddy, said the other. *Once "Slots" Eddy, the sharpest mechanic in town. But now I'm just Eddy, or Dead Eddy, as they call me around here.* Huh! *"Dead Eddy"—they say it has a nice ring to it.*

"Mechanic?" Harry raised an eyebrow. One of his newfound friends in the Charleston Heights Cemetery had warned him about mechanics (also known as card sharps) dealing card games in the casinos. *Avoid the blackjack tables, Necroscope,* he'd been told. *Some of those mechanics can deal you ten face cards in a row!*

But now: *No, I'm not that kind of mechanic!* Dead Eddy protested. *And I wasn't a car mechanic either. We're talking slots here. I was a guy who fixed the slots when they broke down! But I mean, I wasn't just any guy—I was* the *guy!*

"Ah!" said Harry, whose mind was more in tune now. "I know what you mean...I've seen such people working in the pleasure arcades in England. Fixing the slot machines, yes."

Pleasure arcades? said Dead Eddy. *You mean those one-armed bandits like at the seaside? Next to the fortune-telling puppet Gypsy and the roll-a-penny stalls? Well, let me tell you, Necroscope, the principle's the same—to empty your pockets—but here in Sin City it's an entirely different ball game. Which is to say, they're trying a whole lot harder!*

"That's a fact," Harry muttered, slapping two fifty-pounds notes on the counter of a teller's window. "Trying harder—and doing it a whole lot faster!"

"How's that?" A tiny, bright-eyed, middle-aged lady behind the counter stared hard at him. "Did you say something?"

"Er, dollars please," said Harry. "For the slots."

"Sure, we can do that," she said, eyeing him appraisingly as she held one of the fifties up to the light. "What else?"

"Er, nothing else," Harry answered.

Amused, the teller shook her head. "No. I didn't mean what else do you want. I meant, why else would you want dollars? But at the same time it wasn't a question. It's an American thing."

Harry blushed, and said, "You'll have to excuse me. I mean, I'm not an American."

"Oh, really?" Grinning wickedly, and just a little sarcastically, she tipped a bag of heavy metal tokens into a plastic bucket. "I'd never have guessed."

Feeling yet more stupid, Harry nodded. "My accent, right?"

"That and these big English fifties," she told him. "Fives we see often enough, but not too many of these."

And as Harry moved away from the booth: *You're trying real hard to get yourself noticed, right?* said Dead Eddy. And before Harry could answer: *I mean, you're not quite what I expected. I heard you were a tough guy, but from what I'm hearing and feeling it's more like you're sort of...what, in-nocent?*

"Me, innocent?" said Harry, thinking back in brief flashes to some of the things he had seen and done—telepathic scenes, from which Dead Eddy immediately, abruptly recoiled. And:

Whoa! Scratch innocent! said the dead man. And then, in a little while and far more thoughtfully: *So, if you're not exactly innocent, could it be you're sort of naive, maybe? How about naive in its most basic form? Are you amoral, Harry?*

"I have my own ethics," said Harry, beginning to feel just a little annoyed. "My own morality. Anyway, what's that to you? Do you always ask so many questions of strangers?"

Hey, no offense! said Dead Eddy hurriedly. *Like I said, I'm here to help you out, Necroscope. I didn't mean to break your balls! Can we start over? As for being strangers: from what I've heard of you, you don't admit to strangers among the Great Majority—just friends.*

"I'm friends with those who are friendly," Harry answered. "People who don't try to pigeonhole me but simply accept me for what I am."

Well, that's me! said the other. *I accept you for what you are. And if you'll accept me the same way—for being the best of the best when it comes to knowing slots—then you and I can do each other some big favors.*

"Favors?" said Harry, cautiously.

You want to have fun . . . you want to win, don't you?

The Necroscope nodded. "That would be nice, yes. But what is it that *you* want?"

I only want to play, said Dead Eddy, perhaps guardedly. *I only want to do what I've missed doing these three years. See, I didn't simply fix the slots but I loved them, too—I loved studying them, playing them—and that's how I became the best damn slot-machine player in all Las Vegas! So if we could play together, well, I'd get what I want—the fun of it, the excitement—and you'd get what you want, whatever that is.*

"The same thing," said Harry. "That's why I'm here: to try and have some fun, a little excitement."

So, what do you say? said Dead Eddy.

And Harry shrugged. "Where do we start?"

Attaboy! The other chuckled. *Okay, first we find a machine I understand, one I can work with. Then we'll start small, give me a chance to get my hand in . . . like, I can use the practice, you know? Then, if things haven't changed too much around here, pretty soon you'll see me prove myself.*

"If things haven't changed?"

The machines, Harry. The slots. All the time they make new slots: new designs, new gimmicks. In Vegas almost everything is subject to change. Casinos go up, others come down; their names change. The Strip gets longer and longer. Owners go broke; they get bought out, and Vegas moves on. Likewise the slots, they're always changing. But like I said already, the simple slots were always the best, and I'm betting they still are.

"Yes, and betting with my money," said Harry.

Dead Eddy offered an incorporeal nod. *Right. But also with your good right arm, your sharp eyes, and especially your thing with numbers.*

"My thing with numbers?"

Which should help you to get ahead of the game—but literally. It's all math, Harry: being able to recognize certain patterns, and knowing what's coming next.

While talking, Harry had allowed himself to wander to the central area of the casino's vast gambling hall, a region where the massed ranks of slot machines stopped short and gave way to green baize tables. At one of the tables, four or five gamblers stood round a roulette wheel where the ball was even now clicking and jumping at the end of its dizzy chase. Coming to a halt on the double zero, it caused the people at the table to groan as one man. And as Harry stepped forward for a better look:

Don't even think about it! said Dead Eddy. *Roulette? It's the Devil's game.*

"Careful how you use that word," said Harry. "There really are devils, Eddy—well, devils of a sort—and you don't want to go invoking something you can't put down."

Sure, there are devils, the dead man agreed. *Didn't I have one of my own? And don't I still? Doesn't every addict? Anyway, I know what you mean, Necroscope, and yes: I was talking about Old Nick, but not the real Devil. Just this peculiar superstition, is all. One that goes with the roulette wheel. Any one of these croupiers—these dealers—could tell you about that. But who needs them when you've got me?*

Harry was interested. "So tell me about it," he said.

Well, said Dead Eddy, *to start with we have these numbers from one to thirty-six. Do you know what they add up to?*

Harry did a rapid mental calculation, a matter of just a few seconds, and said, "Six hundred and sixty-six." And then, after a brief pause to think about it: "Oh! I see what you're getting at. 666: the number of the Beast in Revelations."

The very Beast, yes, said Dead Eddy. *And then there's the colors. Red for blood and black for darkness. And if you care to follow the flow of the red numbers from one through thirty-four, you'll see they make the snake in the Garden of Eden.*

"But all superstitious nonsense, of course," said Harry.

Dead Eddy shrugged. *Sure. Utter nonsense. And here's you talking to a dead man, right?*

Harry didn't pursue it but headed out of the central area and back toward the marching rows of slots.

Sitting at one such row, a long line of little old ladies yanked on the metal arms, watched the reels, fed the slots and yanked again. They all had plastic buckets, some near full but most near empty. Occasionally a little old man would put in an appearance, checking on how his particular little old lady was doing.

See those faces? said Dead Eddy. *Come back tonight, maybe even tomorrow, you'll see most of 'em again. This is what they do. It's all they do.*

"Addicts," said Harry.

Sure, Dead Eddy agreed. *But they don't know it until they can't afford it anymore. That's when it starts to hurt. And I should know, 'cos me—I was an addict's addict!*

Harry was passing an area where three or four slots in a row stood unoccupied. And:

Whoa! said Dead Eddy. *Now, there's a machine I recognize.*

The Necroscope knew which one Eddy meant: the one that he was looking at, obviously—the one Eddy was seeing through his eyes. "But that's a twenty-five-cent machine," he said. "I only have dollars."

So go to the cashier, Eddy told him. *Change twenty-five of those tokens for quarters. And Harry, we don't call 'em twenty-five-cent pieces. We call 'em quarters. Quarter dollars, right?*

"Right," said Harry, feeling stupid again, and more than a little frustrated.

And having followed his dead friend's instructions, on his return to this worn, weary-looking machine, and as he slipped a quarter into the slot and reached for the handle—

—*Three,* said Dead Eddy.

"Eh?"

Three quarters. What are you, cheap? Play three *coins, Necroscope. That way if you win it's three times the payout.*

"Are you sure you know what you're doing?" Harry frowned, discovering that he really didn't much like being ordered about like this. Also, there was this overanxiousness—this hard-to-define eagerness—about Dead Eddy. "I mean, it's not just the money, but—"

I do know what I'm doing, yes, Dead Eddy snapped—and at once apologized. *I'm sorry, Harry, but my nerves are jumping. I feel like a guy who's hooked on cigarettes: it's a new day, and I really need that first drag. I mean, it's such a . . . oh, hell, such a long,* long *time since I was this close to a slot! And do you know how bad I'd feel—or how much worse* you *would feel—if you should hit a jackpot with only one miserable coin in the slot? That's what makes it all worthwhile: hitting the big ones. It's the difference between six hundred coins and two thousand! It's what keeps the old ladies sitting there like they were hypnotized, with their watery old eyes hanging out. Because you can bet your life that every single one of those grannies has had a jackpot or two in her time.*

"Addicts." Harry nodded. "And now they're back for more."

Absolutely, said Dead Eddy.

"Just like you, through me," said Harry.

But it's not hurting me like alcohol, cigarettes, or dope, the other answered desperately. *Nothing is hurting me anymore, not where I am. This is . . . it's just for the memory, just for fun. So do me—us—a favor and play three coins, will you?*

So Harry did as he was told. Spent three coins. Again, and again, and again. And on the fifth spin—the fifteenth coin—he was rewarded with a bunch of cherries on the first reel, for which he got back just five of his fifteen quarters!

"This isn't my lucky day," he said then. "Frankly, I can't see the point of this." But:

Keep playing, said Dead Eddy. *We only just got started and already the patterns are forming. Can't you see them? Hell, you* can't *stop now—not when I'm excited as all get out!*

"Patterns?" Harry fed the machine yet again, albeit reluctantly.

Okay, said Dead Eddy patiently. *I'll play with your eyes, your arm, and you'll play with my mind. That way you'll see the patterns. I mean, like use your numbers thing, Necroscope!*

Harry let go of physical things, concentrated on the metaphysical, and yanked on the handle. And now Dead Eddy was more surely in control. Now, too the Necroscope felt the thrill that the dead man was feeling—and also something of Eddy's talent. For sure enough he did have a very real talent.

And certainly there were patterns. They were in the reels, the combinations; in the whirling, drifting, strobing effect of the bells, bars, and cherry symbols, all sliding down the machine's bottomless triple chutes.

And indeed the patterns rang a bell. For in their way they were akin to Möbius equations, those constantly mutating mathematical formulae with which Harry conjured the Möbius Continuum. The main difference being that he couldn't stop them, couldn't bring them to a halt. Only the machine itself could do that—couldn't it?

But you can *read 'em,* Dead Eddy told him. *You can line 'em up—fix 'em in your head—make 'em* appear *to stop spinning! Do you know what I'm saying? Like the spokes in the wheels of a speeding auto, when they seem to stand still or turn backward?*

Yes, of course Harry knew what he meant. But not this time. Already the reels had snapped into immobility, one, two, three: another losing line. And:

Again! said Dead Eddy. *Again, Necroscope—again!*

And again and again. By which time Eddy had got his thing working, and Harry's was working in tandem. If he concentrated hard enough he could "fix" the symbols on the central, winning line, and read them almost as well as if they were stationary.

"But what's the good of that?" he wanted to know. "I mean, it still doesn't determine the end result."

But it does give you a forecast of what's coming. See, the way I play, I can tell by the spinning symbols—the ones that I "fix" on the win line—what's

coming up in the next dozen or so spins. It's practice, that's all. And brother,
I've had more practice than anyone else in the world!

"You mean like this," said Harry, as he focused his eyes, staring hard, intently at the win line.

I mean exactly like that! Dead Eddy gave a whoop, as three "wild" jackpot symbols, all blurred and wavering, tried hard to firm up behind the slot's glass window. And: *You know what that means, Harry?* he said. *That means that in the next dozen, maybe two dozen spins, we're in line for a jackpot!*

"You're sure? But I still don't see how it works."

Well, me neither, said Dead Eddy. *But who cares, as long as it does work. Trust me, Necroscope.*

Harry did trust him—for now, anyway—and kept on playing. And with every spin the winning symbols in the window lost more and more of their blurriness, until Harry, too, could feel the jackpot just around the corner.

But it didn't take two dozen spins or even one dozen. Just ten. And in the few brief seconds of that tenth spin—even as the reels whirled in their dizzy round—somehow the Necroscope knew that this time was *the* time. The "wild" symbols were holding firm on the win line; so firm that as the slot clunked one, two, three times, Harry could scarcely accept the fact that the reels had stopped spinning and the game was over.

Oh, they've stopped, all right! said the dead man, triumphantly. *And yes, it's over—and we just hit a jackpot! Now you have to face the music.*

"Music?" said Harry, slightly alarmed.

With which a light started flashing on top of the machine, and coming loud from somewhere inside the thing there commenced what sounded like a jaunty, organ-grinder's version of "We're in the Money."

Music, said Dead Eddy. *Sweet music!*

"So that's where it's coming from," said Harry. "Every now and then, a burst of 'We're in the Money,' or maybe that marching number I keep hearing."

That's right. (Eddy's incorporeal nod.) *Happens every time a slot hits, which lets all the other punters know that another jackpot's gone down. It's great advertising for the casino, and it keeps the flagging gamblers going—gives even the shy guys an incentive to try their luck. Let's face it, Harry, if no one ever won nobody would want to play.*

Harry glanced at the machine's tally board, and the legend said that three "wild" symbols were worth two thousand coins.

Five hundred dollars, yeah. But Dead Eddy didn't seem too impressed. *Nothing to write home about, but it's a good omen.*

Was that all? Harry thought, while keeping the thought to himself. Just a good omen? Well, maybe, but the fact of it was that he was excited as . . . "as all get out," as Dead Eddy himself would have it.

"And we can do it again, right?" said Harry, looking left, right, and all around, trying to catch the eye of an attendant. That shouldn't be a problem, for already a small crowd of oohers and aahers was gathering.

Oh, we're going to do it again, said the dead man. *But not here.*

"Not here? But why not?" said Harry. "I mean, just looking around I can see plenty of models of this selfsame machine. The same name, make, everything. So why not here?"

Because, er . . . because this is a high-class joint, and we can't be too conspicuous, the other replied, albeit vaguely and unconvincingly.

The Necroscope might have said as much—might have asked if there was something Dead Eddy wasn't telling him—but just then he saw a uniformed slot attendant wheeling a narrow, boxed-in trolley in his direction. And:

Quiet now, said Dead Eddy (relievedly, Harry thought). *You don't want to be seen talking to yourself, do you?*

The attendant, a small, pockmarked man glanced at the Necroscope, then at the machine, and nodded. "Nice!" he said. And: "Are you staying here, sir?"

"Er, no," said Harry. "Is that a requirement?"

"No, sir, not at all," said the other. "It's a house rule, is all. We like to keep a check on the winners. Helps sort out the comps at the end of their stay, you know? That's if they're staying here, of course."

"Er, of course," said Harry, who hadn't understood a thing he'd heard.

Comps? he thought at Dead Eddy, while the attendant opened up the front of the machine and did things to its innards.

Complimentary cash-back, free meals, nights on the house, the dead man explained. *The more you play, the better they take care of you. Especially if you're a high-roller.*

Harry understood high-roller. But: *Even when you win their money?*

Sure, said Dead Eddy. And then, less definitely, *Er, most of 'em, anyway. It's like I said: very good advertising for the casino.*

The attendant was locking the machine again, so Harry told him, "Er, she hasn't paid out yet."

"She doesn't, not on jackpots," said the other. "That's my job. The slots only pay on the smaller stuff." And then, glancing again at Harry, curiously this time: "You're kind of new to this, right? Are you English?"

"Er, yes," said Harry. "To both questions."

The other nodded his understanding. "Beginner's luck." And with that he counted out five one-hundred dollar bills into the Necroscope's hand, then got him to sign for the money.

"Thank you," said Harry.

"Not at all. Don't mention it. And now maybe you'd do something for me? Put a coin in and pull the handle. Let's bury the jackpot or no one else will want to play this machine."

Harry obliged and the attendant went off with his trolley.

Watching him go, Harry asked, "So what now?"

Now we go upmarket, said Dead Eddy.

"To the dollar slots?"

And then to the five-dollar slots, yeah!

"But not here?"

I said upmarket, said Eddy. *And up is down—downtown, to you.*

"But downtown is where I came from," Harry answered, as he headed for the rest rooms. "And not too long ago at that."

Good. So you know the way, said Dead Eddy logically.

"I know some coordinates, yes," Harry nodded, (apparently to himself) as he conjured Möbius equations. "Do you think you can stay with me?"

Well, if not I can catch up with you there, said Dead Eddy. *I'll find you easily enough, Necroscope.* Huh! *Like the proverbial moth to a candle's flame. Hell, you're the only warm thing around here!*

Following which Harry walked into the men's rest room and passed through two doors simultaneously. One of them—a solid door—accessed a toilet cubicle; the other, totally invisible to anyone other than the Necroscope, opened into the metaphysical Möbius Continuum . . .

AT 11:10 LOCAL, the Necroscope stepped from the Continuum onto the corner of First and Fremont. Normally he would have been more discreet—he'd have chosen a more suitable coordinate, a less populous exit point—but excitement had made him careless. Not the cold, morbid excitement which had been such a regular feature of his previous existence but the excitement of Las Vegas: a lust for life as opposed to a battle with undeath.

This time he was fortunate: no one noticed his abrupt appearance on the now busy corner; no one collided with him or had to sidestep.

He felt Dead Eddy's presence, and asked, "Do you recognize the place?"

Yeah, said the other. *Couldn't possibly forget it. Nothing has changed too much around here. But we're at the wrong end of Fremont.*

Now the Necroscope detected a definite edge to Eddy's dead voice, more than a tinge of tension—or perhaps apprehension? And so, as he moved in the direction indicated, he said, "Maybe we should talk as we go. I mean, considering we've become partners—well, of a sort—I still don't know too much about you. In fact, you know far more about me."

Is that surprising? said the other. *Heck, everyone down here knows about you! But me . . . ? You'd like to hear my story . . . ?*

"Why not?" said Harry. "A friend of mine has a coffee shop just along here. You like coffee, don't you? You can talk while I drink, and maybe you'll get something of a taste."

Then . . . he could almost hear Dead Eddy smacking his lips. And: *Now, that is an offer I can't refuse!* said the dead man . . .

"HEY!" said the massive, bald-headed server, grinning a welcome as he wiped his brutal hands on his apron. "Back so soon? Well, I knew da food in dis joint was good, but—"

"Just for coffee," Harry told him, and silently added, *for two.*

"Coming right up," said the other. "On da house."

I'm impressed, said Dead Eddy. *Do you always make friends this easily?*

But then, remembering certain scenes he'd glimpsed in the Necroscope's mind earlier: *Er, not always, right?*

"Not always," Harry agreed. "But it's usually fairly easy to get folks to talk about themselves—er, *usually.*" He put a lot of emphasis on the last word.

Okay, you win, said Dead Eddy. *But where do I start?*

"How about at the beginning?" said Harry. "Like, when you first came to Las Vegas?"

Sure, said the dead man, *why not?*

And this is the story he told . . .

I CAME HERE in the early '60s. Before Vegas I was a wanderer and a gambler, yes, and some would say a welcher, too. It wasn't an easy life I'd chosen. But honestly, in a way I was innocent—I was more ripped-off than a ripper. I played some bad hands with some awfully bad people— people who'd take your teeth if there was gold in 'em—and on those several occasions when I made a run for it, it was usually to save my skin. When debt loads got too heavy, I would move on out from under them.

But you have to understand, this was all cards. Those days I played cards, and did it well. If the deck was clean I'd win, but as often as not it was dirty. I would lose, heavily, and it would be time to move on. And horses? . . . well, yeah, it's true, sometimes I played the gee-gees, too. But as for slots—

Slots didn't enter into my life till I came to Las Vegas, and even then not immediately. I had somehow managed to get my self married to Mary-Jane; I didn't want to put her through the hell of up-and-running when-ever I hit a losing streak; I had to get a job and settle down.

Now, I'd always had this thing with machines . . . not just slots but any machines. Even when I was a kid I could take a watch to bits and put it together again, and if it wasn't working when I started it would be when I finished. Sewing machines, typewriters, Hoovers, locks and clocks—if they had cogwheels, batteries, springs, and/or levers in any combination I could fix 'em.

One night I was in the Sands—the casino, that is—and I was down. I'd been working, doing a little rewiring on a set at Circus-Circus, but that was finished now and I didn't have a job; didn't know how I was going to tell Mary-Jane, either. She was doing this and that, some typing, a little desk work for an auto-rental outfit: nothing that was going to buy us too much.

Anyway, maybe I'd dropped in to get a drink under my belt, I can't remember. Or it could be I was looking for a program, a souvenir from the Copa Room. Hey, *now* I remember! It was the fall of '63 and Frank Sinatra, Dean Martin, and Sammy Davis Jr. were headlining right there at the Sands. When those guys were in town it was like all Hollywood was here! You never knew who you'd bump into.

Me, I bumped into a guy with his head in a machine and all I could hear was his cursing. He was fixing the slot—supposed to be, anyway— but it had him beat. When he came up for air I said he should let me try. He might have argued but right about then Jack Entratter (he was one of the Sands' big bosses at the time, probably the biggest) was passing by. And he told me, "Go ahead and try."

Two minutes and the slot was working perfectly. So I had a little oil and grime on me—so what? I had a job! And Entratter was so pleased he paid to have my clothes cleaned and gave me a bunch of free passes to the show. Me and Mary-Jane, we actually got to see the Rat Pack in action three nights in a row!

And that was the start of it. I became a slot mechanic, or *the* slot mechanic, at the Sands Hotel and Casino. I didn't know it then but as I was getting under the skin of the slots (well, so to speak) so they were getting under mine, but a lot deeper. And, to cut a long story short, it wasn't too long before I was giving half my wages back to the house— then three-quarters—then . . .

But need I go on?

And dammit, I'd *never* been hooked on slots! Cards? I admit to my failings, yes, at least where card schools were concerned. But slots or the casino tables? Not me! It was—I mean it *had* to be—the proximity, Necroscope! I was just too close to those one-armed thieves. Hell, they were my job! There was just no escaping them. In Vegas they're everywhere.

You'd think I would know better, eh? Me working in a joint like that, knowing the score, the odds, and still drawn to play those bandits like some kid in short pants in a penny arcade? I was a clown, right? But there were bigger clowns than me. A lot bigger. Did you know that Frank Sinatra and his pals were doing the same dumb thing? Do you think Dean Martin—or Dag, as Sinatra called him—was just kidding around when he cracked jokes onstage about losing his salary on the tables? Yeah, and Sinatra, too, for that matter; and would you believe it, Frank actually *owned* a piece of the Sands!

"Everyone's a winner in Vegas," is what they say, Harry—but as a certain song disagrees, it ain't necessarily so . . .

I STARTED TO STEAL. Not much at first, enough to balance things out, is all. Mind, I didn't think of it as stealing; hell no, I was just getting back what the slots were taking off me. I'd do my thieving at the Sands: a dip into this or that machine while I was fixing it (when often as not I'd be fixing it to go wrong again), and the occasional, er, sleight of hand if I had to top up an empty slot with coin. But of course by then I was part of the furniture and nobody was watching me too closely. At least, I didn't think they were.

After a while, though, someone must have noticed, got suspicious or something, because whenever I had to do work on a machine there always seemed to be one of the pit bosses around. Pit boss? That's a guy—usually a *big* guy—who watches other guys watching the dealers at the tables. And believe me, Harry they don't miss too much.

I had been at the Sands quite some time by then, and obviously I had to stop playing the slots there. I mean, that would have been really stupid; it would have given the game away, you know? What, a guy who fixes slots who also spends all his spare time playing them? On *his* wages? Not likely . . . or *very* likely if he's also ripping them off.

No, I'd do my, er, "gambling" downtown. The slots seemed a lot looser there, and anyway by then I had this thing going for me. That's why I emphasized gambling, because really I was just milking the slots. And I remember how it got started, so let me go back a ways. And excuse me for jerking you around like this, okay?

I was still working at the Sands—or you might say I was simply *working* the Sands—when it started to happen. As I was fixing the slots I'd have occasion to play 'em just to try them out, the way you'd switch on a flashlight after fitting it with a new battery: a trial run, so to speak. And finally, after all the time I'd spent working with those machines, I suddenly discovered this knack of mine, found that I could forecast the big jackpots by concentrating on the spinning reels. By doing that, I could see what was coming, just as you saw back there on the Strip.

But by then too it was fairly common knowledge that I was, er, taking liberties with house profits. Not big stuff, no, but definitely against the rules. It was early September 1967 and I was getting the push, being told not so gently that it was time I left...and would I please empty my pockets first?

It might have been bad for me but just then Jack Entratter was in a very good mood. I guess he'd made a pile of money when he and the other owners sold the Sands to Howard Hughes, who was buying up most of Vegas right then. So I got off real light and along with a "fatherly" talk Entratter actually gave me a great reference. Could be that now he was out of the casino business he figured fuck 'em—or maybe he just liked me? I really don't know.

Anyway, I didn't get another job immediately but honed my talents in off-the-Strip back-street joints where my face wasn't too familiar. And to make sure it didn't become too familiar, I took to wearing various disguises.

Years went by (I mean literally), and I somehow managed to stay ahead, but only just. Oh, I'd cracked the machine thing—cracked it wide open, the way you've seen—but I was also back to playing cards, playing the horses, playing the fool. In fact what I was winning on the slots I was losing on the other shit. I was gambling again, but big-time.

Well, Mary-Jane knew about it and threatened to leave me. I wasn't so far gone that I was about to let that happen, so it was time to rein back, stop gambling—as opposed to the other thing I did—and get a job again. Which I did, downtown.

After that...there's not much to tell. My skill with the slots was fully developed; I stockpiled a little money in Mary-Jane's name—not a lot but she wouldn't go hungry if anything happened to me, which as it happens it did—and from then till the end I was a mechanic again...

WHEN IT SEEMED Dead Eddy was finished Harry said, "The end? The very end? That sounds sort of ominous."

An accident. The other offered an incorporeal shrug. *Hey, accidents happen, Necroscope. We've all got to die sometime. My only regret: I should have left the horses and the cards alone; should have concentrated on my slots thing. Like, maybe I could have spread it around. Atlantic City, Reno, anywhere where they have high-roller slots. See, in those days, I mean when I first started out, a man had to be very careful. The Mob ran Vegas in those days, in the '60s and early '70s before the joint went legitimate, and the fact is there are still a few wiseguys around. And no one steals from the Mob—not even when it isn't stealing! A guy who knew the machines and hit too many jackpots—hell, it wasn't at all unlikely he'd get hit himself . . . !* And then, hurriedly, as if the conversation had suddenly become too morbid for him:

Anyway, that's it. You wanted to know about me, so now you know. Dead Eddy in a nutshell. Once king of the slots—tarrah! But alas, the king is dead. Long live the king. Huh!

"You had an accident," Harry mused almost to himself while letting Dead Eddy guide him into a shaded side street. "Can you talk about it? What happened, Eddy? Did you get hit by a car or something?"

Or something, said the other. *Hey, do you mind if we don't go into the details? I mean, dead is dead, right? And for three years since 1980 I've been dead. You wouldn't want me to relive it—or re-die it—would you? Anyway, we're there.*

The dead man had steered Harry in through the smoked-glass doors of a casino before he'd even had time to read the name on its electronic facade, but he saw at once that the place was by no means typical of its Strip counterparts. And while Dead Eddy had asserted that they were going "upmarket," it was obvious to the Necroscope that this was a reference to Eddy's own state of mind, relating only to the way he viewed his ability to control the slot machines.

And his formless companion agreed. *You can say that again, Harry. Unless there've been some big changes around here in the last three years, this joint has some of Vegas's loosest slots. That is, er, if you know how to play 'em.*

Looking the place over, Harry observed that: "It also has some pretty poor decor, badly stained, cigarette-burned tables, worn carpets, and a generally sleazy atmosphere."

Yeah, you got it in one, Dead Eddy agreed. *But at the same time it covers both ends of the spectrum. It's cheap and cheerful, sure, but while you're looking at those beat-up nickel-and-dime slots in the corner there, you might also like to consider the five-dollar babies up those steps in that roped-off area on the central dais. Likewise the table games: this joint has minimum bets that range from quarters on one table to ten bucks on the game next door. No fiscal discrimination here, Harry. Money—be it in large bills or small coins—is all that counts in this joint!*

"I don't see too many people in here," said the Necroscope. "And those I do see look a good deal different to the people on the Strip."

Right, the dead man agreed. *That's the difference between tourists and locals, wannabees and has-beens, amateurs and pros. Up on the Strip everything's glitz, it's all for show. But down here—and more especially in a joint like this—it's the real thing. It's all about money, gambling. Oh, sure, they'll relieve you of your loot at both ends of town, but on the Strip they'll at least smile while they're doing it. Here . . . well, they don't so much pretend it's for laughs. The "complimentary" drinks are watered, the machines are fixed, and the guys dealing cards are . . . a whole lot cleverer than I ever was!*

And sensing the bitterness in Eddy's voice, the Necroscope inquired, "Why do I get the feeling you're not *just* having fun, Eddy? What is it makes me think you're out for revenge?"

For a moment there was no answer, but then Dead Eddy said, *Let's put it this way, Harry: in this case fun and revenge are two sides of the same coin. Fun for you and—if you insist—revenge for me. It's payback time, is all. And anyway, I don't want to be the one who breaks the golden rule.*

"The golden rule?"

The one which you discovered for yourself, said Dead Eddy. *That in death the Great Majority will continue to do what they did in life. I was always trying to take money off these slots and the rich, frequently crooked bastards who owned them. Well, I still want to. So come on, why don't you admit it, Harry? So do you.*

"And that's it?" Harry answered, admitting nothing of the sort. "There's nothing else to it? No ulterior motive?"

Again a moment's silence from the dead man. And then: *You and I, we believe in much the same things,* said Dead Eddy. *You like to feel you're on the side of right, right? Well, believe me, Necroscope, if you and I cleaned this joint out—which we can't, because even the two of us together don't have the luck of that guy who broke the bank at Monte Carlo—but if we did somehow manage to strip this place to the bones, that would be honest-to-God justice. It would be just, and it would be very,* very *right!*

Harry saw that he wasn't going to get to the root of this, and so: "Okay, since we're here I'll do this for you," he said. "But you're wrong about one thing, Eddy: I'm not interested in the money. So I'll be doing it for . . . well, for fun, yes. And then I'll think about what to do with our winnings."

Let me make a suggestion, said Dead Eddy. *Give it to Mary-Jane. Let's face it, you don't need it and I can't use it. But whatever she's doing now, she'll probably find it very useful.*

Harry nodded. "It's a deal. So then, where do we start?"

We start with the quarter slots, said the other. And if he had been a live man, then Harry might have thought he heard him sigh. *Those ones over there in the central floor area.*

Harry made his way to the cashier's window and changed one hundred dollars into quarters, then proceeded to the slots that Dead Eddy had indicated. And en route he gave the casino a somewhat closer inspection.

The place wasn't nearly as big as the massive complexes on Vegas' famous Strip, but then again it wasn't a hotel. It was just a casino. And since there were no guests there was no need for a restaurant. It had bars, certainly—three that the Necroscope could see—and snack bars with a limited amount of seating at both ends of the long main gambling hall. But there were no show bars tucked away in the corners here; there was no gift shop or ornate theater foyer; and there was definitely no night-club or carnival atmosphere, not in a place where even the cocktail waitresses were dowdy and, to be a little cruel but truthful, much too long in the tooth.

Cheap and cheerful, sure, said Dead Eddy. *But didn't I say so already? However, I'm sure you'll note the one thing it does have in fair measure.*

"Floorwalkers," said Harry, with a curt nod. "Big fellows, all of them."

Yeah, and nearly twice as many as in most downtown joints, Dead Eddy concurred. *To keep an eye on the, er, clientele. See, most of the punters in here are down-at-heel addicts, slots and blackjack junkies, no-hopers, Necroscope. They're losers—but losers on their last legs can sometimes get a little, er, shall we say restless?*

"They can cause trouble?"

Sure. You'd be surprised how many of these slots—expensive items, Harry— get thrown down on the floor and jumped on. Or you'll get the drunk who insists on betting his Rolex on one spin of the wheel, then says he was robbed when he loses. Well, the chances are he was *robbed, but in a joint like this—*

"—Who's keeping score?"

Exactly. And if these people can't take your money one way . . . well, there's always the other way, right? And if you should even think *of fighting back . . .* (But there the dead man came to an abrupt halt, just a little too late to conceal the unmistakable venom in his voice.)

"I think I may be starting to understand your anger," said Harry, whose mind had now definitely accepted a revenge motive. For Dead Eddy must have wasted a good many years of his life in "joints" like this. And the Necroscope wondered—how often had Eddy considered that he *himself* was being robbed? And hadn't he admitted it was payback time? But . . . was that all there was to this thing? A niggling doubt persisted in Harry's mind.

You believe you understand my anger? Good, said Dead Eddy. *So should we start by taking some of it out on these here machines?*

And with that Harry—but in fact both of them—began to play . . .

FIFTEEN MINUTES LATER:

Sy McMahn, a squat, cauliflower-eared torpedo of an Irishman, got his boss, Joey Randazzo, on his belt walkie-talkie. Sy was at one end of the floor-between-floors—which is to say in the workspace over the main gambling hall—and Joey was in his office at the other end.

"Yeah, what now?" Randazzo growled, annoyed at being disturbed, just as he and his accountant were managing to "balance" the casino's books for the last quarter. "Here's me in the middle of delicate financial adjustments, and people keep calling me with this or that dumb question or problem. Who the fuck is this anyway? Is that you, Sy?"

"It's me, yeah," McMahn replied. "What, are you working on the books or something? Well, I'm involved with a little financial shit of my own. Believe me, Joey, the books'll look a hell of a lot worse if we get too many guys like this one."

"Eh?" Randazzo grunted. "Eh? What guy? Are you scoping on somebody?"

"Guy on the slots," McMahn answered. "I'm almost directly on top of him. He's bagged two jackpots in ten minutes."

"What?!" Randazzo snapped at his walkie-talkie. "Have you fucking lost it that you should call me about this? So there's some lucky fuck down there, so what?"

"I'll tell you so what," said the other. "Those books that you're balancing, they ain't nearly as balanced as these slots. Joey, this guy is doing the impossible, winning jackpots out of machines that can't pay jackpots!"

"He's doing what?"

"He's hitting on slots we had fixed. Two spayed slots down there, and the bitches just gave birth! The occasional winning line—a couple hundred dollars now and then—we accept that, it's like peanuts. But nobody takes jackpots out of *these* machines. They're fixed, weighted. Yet this guy's winning jackpots! Only the smaller ones, sure, but they're still jackpots. What's more, he's just changed his quarters into dollars, so it appears he's looking to up the ante."

"He won on the weighted machines?" said Randazzo, scowling at his handset. "So . . . maybe a weight came loose. That's happened before, right? Sometimes a weight shakes itself loose?"

"What, on both machines at the same time?" If nothing else McMahn was logical. "I mean, those are *very* long odds, Joey!"

Slamming his ledger shut, Randazzo almost shouted into his handset, "So who is this guy? We seen him before? Is he tooled up or what? How's he fucking doing it?"

"Never seen him before in my life," McMahn answered. "But if this is breaking and entering, then he's got to be some kind of Houdini. You're asking how does he do it? He puts his money in, yanks on the fucking arm! No magnets, jimmys, or mechanical aids of any kind. Not that I ever heard of, anyway."

Puffed up almost beyond endurance, with rage and frustration both, Randazzo snarled, "Okay,"—and to himself, *You dumb fuck Mick!*—"I'm on my fucking way." Then, slamming the walkie-talkie down on the desk he jerked to his feet, kicked his chair away, and headed for the door.

His accountant, Arnie Goldstein, a round-faced bulge of a man with several quivering chins, asked, "Trouble?"

"What?" Randazzo grunted, glancing back at him from little piggy eyes. "Trouble? Shit, no—I'm always this fucking color! Just fix the books, will you?"

Then he was through the door, slamming it behind him . . .

HARRY (AND DEAD EDDY) had moved just a short distance, to a row of dollar slot machines. There were one or two other players in that area but there was very little noise—a distinct lack of coin clatter—from the machines.

Just one look at their faces, said Dead Eddy, *and you know there's been no action worth mentioning around here in a while. Yeah, but now that we're here all that's about to change.*

Harry seated himself at a slot clear of the other players, and commented, "This is the same make of machine that we played on the Strip, right?"

Right, said the other, *but not quite the same. I mean, you can actually win on those slots in the big Strip casinos.*

Harry almost stood up again. "What are you saying? That we can't win on this one?"

Oh, we can *win,* Dead Eddy answered. *Of all people, you and I can very definitely win. Absolutely! It's just that we're not supposed to, is all.* His words conveyed more than he'd actually said.

"The machine is fixed?"

In this place it's fifty-fifty, said Dead Eddy. *About half of these machines are fixed, or at least they used to be. We're about to find out if this joint is under the same management as when I was last here.*

But once again something in Dead Eddy's voice, incorporeal though it was, had given the Necroscope cause for concern. "The management? What have they got to do with us?"

I mean, er, if *these slots are fixed,* said the dead man, hurriedly, *then we'll know that the selfsame people are running the show. But don't get me wrong, Harry: they're not all crooks in downtown Vegas. On the contrary, there are very few wiseguys left here. It's just that in this joint, er, there used to be.*

Harry had started to play at three dollars a shot. "You're saying the Mob owned this joint—er, this place?"

They owned most of the casinos, once upon a time, the dead man answered. *But legitimate concerns gradually bought or drove them out, like when Howard Hughes was buying up the place. That was something, eh? A guy so rich he could make the mafia offers that even they couldn't refuse!*

"But they owned *this* place?" The Necroscope was insistent. "Just a few years ago, in your time?"

Yeah, they did! Dead Eddy almost spat the words out, would have if he'd been flesh and blood. *A guy called Randazzo—Joey Randazzo—ran the joint. He probably still does. But so what?* Then, as if realizing he had been snarling, and abruptly changing the subject: *Hey, how about giving me a hand concentrating on these reels, Harry? Shit, will you look at these "wild" symbols slipping all out of sync! That's because* you *are slipping, Necroscope! I mean, it's like I could use some assistance here, partner!*

"Dead Eddy," said Harry grimly, "as soon as we're through playing here there's something you're going to tell me. In fact you can start right now— by explaining why I keep feeling the urge to look all about me. It's got to be you doing it, because *I* am not normally this nervous. What are you looking for, Eddy? What are you expecting? And why is it I feel that I, or we, are under close scrutiny?" But:

Look! the dead man shouted. *They've lined up! Harry, she's going to hit any time now! So do me a favor, will you? For the next two or three spins stop breaking my balls and* concentrate, *okay!?*

Harry tried to look deeper into the other's mind . . . would have tried even harder if his eyes hadn't been attracted to the reels—where sure enough the blurred "wild" symbols on the win line were rapidly firming into stroboscopic solidity.

And a moment later:

Click! Click! Click! Followed by Dead Eddy's cry of, *Jackpot! A fifteen-hundred dollar jackpot this time, Necroscope!*

To corroborate that fact the slot's light started flashing, while a raucous if tinny rendition of "We're in the Money" commenced playing from within its mechanical heart.

But did you notice that third reel, Harry? Dead Eddy inquired. *How the last "wild" symbol really fought against dropping in? That's because the reel's been weighted and the slot fixed. Oh, yeah. But we've unfixed her! And now the man's on his way.*

"The man?" Harry repeated him, sharply.

The guy with the money, said the dead man. *He'll be arriving any time now. The quarter slots were able to pay out all by themselves on smaller jackpots, but when these big ones go down the machines stop dead and it's people who come running.*

Harry glanced through the milling forms of a half dozen or so oohers and aahers (but harder, more cynical, less obligingly "agreeable" types than the gamblers he'd seen on the Strip) to where a casino employee came trundling his wheelie cash trolley in Harry's direction.

And: *Fifteen hundred dollars,* Dead Eddy chortled. *You know what that means, Harry? At fifteen dollars a throw, one hundred spins of the reels! Not that we're going to need that many.*

"What's that?" The Necroscope's eyebrows shot up. "Fifteen dollars a throw? What on earth do you mean? Have you gone crazy or something?"

Crazy, me? Hell, no, said the dead man. *You see those five-dollar slots up there on the high-roller dais? It's three five-dollar tokens for each yank on the handle if you intend playing hardball with those babies! Which I reckon is only fair considering that the big jackpots on those machines are worth thirty-five thousand dollars!*

"And of course we do intend to play," said the Necroscope, just knowing it was so and wondering where all this was leading him.

For thirty-five thousand dollars? You'd better believe we intend to play! said Dead Eddy. *So go ahead and tell me, Harry: is this "fun" or is this fun?*

Harry didn't answer him. The payout person was almost upon him; the small crowd of onlookers had dispersed; several large, unlovely, shirtsleeved floorwalkers had gathered seemingly out of nowhere. For the moment these dealers and pit bosses, casino employees in general, just lounged there, keeping their distance and hardly seeming to notice Harry at all. But he thought differently. It would be completely impossible to remain inconspicuous, unnoticed, beside a slot that was flashing its light and singing its head off!

The man with the cash trolley had come to a halt in order to answer his walkie-talkie. He was only a few paces away when he began speaking into his handset, and Harry thought he heard him say something about ID. Just a moment or so later, however, the man had turned his face away and was now mumbling into the handset in lowered tones. Occasionally, while he continued his furtive conversation, he would cast curious glances in Harry's direction.

What's going on, Eddy? (Harry spoke now in the dead man's own medium.) *It seems to me that something's wrong here.* And:

Necroscope, tell me something, Dead Eddy came back. *Is it really true what they say about you? Like, you can handle yourself in just about any situation?*

Now Harry was genuinely alarmed. *Eddy, I think maybe you'd better tell me now. Am I in some kind of trouble? Have I made a mistake, done something wrong here? What's going on?*

Stay cool, Necroscope, the dead man answered. *What are you worrying about? The guy's checking if it's okay to pay you out, is all.*

Why wouldn't it be okay to pay me? I won—er, didn't we?

But the payout person—a tall, thin man with slicked-back hair, bushy eyebrows, and a hawk nose—had taken two more paces forward and was now speaking directly to Harry:

"Your lucky day, sir! Three jackpots in a row. I don't see that too often."

"Likewise," said Harry uncomfortably. "It seems I've been, er, extremely fortunate."

"You can say that again." The other smiled a tight smile.

Hey, Necroscope! What's with all this polite conversation? Harry's dead companion seemed eager to get on with things. *Tell this guy you want payment in five-dollar tokens. And don't worry about all the goons—I mean the muscle, the pit bosses—among these onlookers . . . they're just curious, is all. Most of these people won't even know these slots are fixed. And the fewer who do know the better . . . from Joey Randazzo's point of view, that is. See, Las Vegas has laws against this kind of shit.*

In for a penny, in for a pound . . . or thirty-five thousand dollars. And Harry did as Eddy had asked and said to the payout man, who was opening the front of the slot to reset it and turn off the music, "Er, could you possibly pay me in tokens? Maybe five-dollar tokens, for the slots on the dais back there?"

The man had finished resetting the machine. Locking it, he looked at Harry, and said, "Give me a moment and I'll check that out for you, okay?" And stepping aside a few paces, he used his walkie-talkie again.

Harry waited, and so did Dead Eddy, who for once had nothing to say. Then:

"Sure," said the payout man, "that's okay. But let's first get rid of this jackpot, then we'll go get your tokens from the cashier."

Harry put a single coin in the slot and obliged by pulling on the handle. But this time he averted his own—and therefore Dead Eddy's—gaze and concentration from the win line.

Then, as Harry and the payout man headed for the cashier's booth: *See,* said Dead Eddy, *Nothing to it, Necroscope.*

Well, maybe so—but Harry could have sworn he'd heard the dead man sighing his relief into the metaphysical aether . . .

WHILE UP ABOVE, on what was euphemistically called the observation deck:

"What's up, Joey?" Sy McMahn was fascinated by the change that had come over his boss, the ex-wiseguy thug called Randazzo, while the latter had watched Harry Keogh playing the dollar slot in the gambling hall below. Even now Randazzo's eyes were rapt upon that unknown figure on the CCTV screen, as the Necroscope, in the company of the payout man, went to the cashier's booth and collected his winnings. "I mean, aren't you going to check this guy's ID? He just won big, and that's taxable money he's taken off us. Also, that's *three* no-win slots he's busted jackpots out of. Shit, we really need to know a lot more about this guy, Joey!"

Randazzo frowned, squinted his piggy eyes at the screen, half shook his head in a puzzled fashion. "There's . . . there's something about him," he finally muttered, his normally gravelly voice so faint it seemed he was speaking to himself. "Something . . . something *about* him, yeah. And maybe I'm crazy but I think . . . I think it's something I may have seen before."

"You know the guy?" McMahn leaned forward and touched his boss on the shoulder where he sat hunched before the black-and-white screen, causing him to start. But instead of snarling at this intrusion—a reaction which the big Irish bouncer might well have expected from a man like Randazzo—the other merely hissed his irritability and shrugged him off.

And presently: "No," Randazzo answered, with a slow shake of his head of greasy, jet black hair. And in that totally uncharacteristic near-whisper, "No, I don't know him. But I once knew someone with—I don't know—similar mannerisms? Someone just as nervous and shifty-eyed, always looking around like he was up to something. Yeah, and I sure as hell knew someone who played the slots like him and won on machines where you're not supposed to win."

"Yeah?"

"Yeah," Randazzo breathed his confirmation. "It was maybe three, four years ago—before your time here, right? Or maybe not. Do you by any chance remember Eddy Croker?"

"Eddy Croker?" As McMahn searched his memory, so his scarred brow wrinkled up and his eyebrows came together in a frown. Then: "Yeah, I remember Eddy," he said. "But only just. I never got to know him too well. You took me on maybe two, three weeks before he moved out. He was here . . . and then he wasn't. He was a mechanic; he fixed quirky slots, right? Yeah, sure I remember him—'Slots Eddy.' But we was like, you know, ships that pass in the night."

"Yeah," the other whispered. And under his breath, but not quite inaudibly, even derisively: "Shits that pass in the night, right."

If McMahn had heard he would have preferred not to. And so he ignored Randazzo's comment, and said, "So what's this guy got to do with Eddy Croker?"

Randazzo's customary growl was back in his voice as he sat up straighter, glared contemptuously at McMahn, and said, "Don't you ever fucking listen to anything, Sy? Haven't I already told you the guy reminds me of somebody else? Well, that somebody is Eddy Croker. Eddy who fixed the slots, yeah—fixed them so he could win!"

"Really? He did that?" McMahn's eyes opened wide. "Is that why you got rid of him? I don't remember you being mad or nothing."

"Oh, I was mad all right." Randazzo nodded, his piggy eyes returning to the CCTV screen, while his stubby but expert fingers controlled the ceiling camera whose lens tracked his quarry, keeping the Necroscope on-screen where the latter was now carrying a bucket of heavy five-dollar tokens toward the dais with the high-roller slots. "I was mad as could be, as mad as hell."

There could be no mistaking the menace in his voice, which caused the Irishman's jaw to drop at about the same time as the penny. "So that's why he...why he wasn't here no more. That's why...why he went away!"

"Right," Randazzo grunted. "That's why he went away." Then, feeling the big bouncer draw back from him:

"What's wrong, Sy? Squeamish, are you? Listen, Eddy Croker was a lousy cheating thieving degenerate gambling rat-fuck! The guy got caught with his nose in the trough when he shoulda been fixing the slots. And like I said, he *was* fixing the slots—but only so he could beat the fucking things! I mean, he knew stuff about certain slots that nobody else knew. But *I* wanted to know and gave him plenty of opportunity to tell me, a whole world of opportunity. *Huh!* Well, at least he deserves some credit in that respect: whatever his secret was, Slots Eddy took it with him."

McMahn had now accepted the fact of Eddy's fate. "The fink didn't cough, right?"

"Oh, he coughed some," Randazzo answered. "Coughed, cried, gasped, choked, threw up, and bled. But if you're asking did he talk—no, he didn't talk except to lie. Lied his fucking head off. Said he was the only one who could do what he could do, as if it was magic or something."

"But of course, you didn't believe him."

"Didn't I tell you he was a lousy liar?" Randazzo snarled. "No, I didn't believe him. And whatever it was that Eddy knew—even if I *had* believed him, that he had this special talent—I couldn't take the chance that he wouldn't pass it on to someone else, now could I? Hey, am I a responsible

Las Vegas citizen or what? I mean, think about it: what something like that could do to a town like Vegas."

"I'm thinking," said the other.

"Right," said Randazzo. "Apart from which—my civic duty and all, and the fact that when I had him checked out I learned he'd been scamming every casino up and down the Strip for years—well, apart from *that,* I was more than somewhat pissed off at the thought that this stupid little shit had the balls *to steal from me!*"

"I can see how that would annoy you," said McMahn, his eyes drawn to the screen, where Harry Keogh had just now sat down in a swivel chair in front of a five-dollar slot. "And now there's this guy."

"Yeah," Joey Randazzo muttered. "Now there's this guy. And while he isn't Eddy Croker—while he couldn't possibly be Eddy because there *is* no Slots Eddy—still there's something about him, something weird that reminds me of my ex-pal. So maybe the cheating bastard had an apprentice after all. But you know, Sy, there are only so many casinos in the world and eventually this new guy, whoever he is, was bound to turn up here."

"And where there's one," (McMahn was beginning to catch on now) "there could be more, right? Is that what's bothering you, Joey?"

"Right," Randazzo growled. " 'Cos like I said, I get pissed off at the thought of bums stealing from me. So you and me, Sy, we're gonna watch this one. Like cats on a nest of mice, we are gonna watch him. And then— if he really is what I'm beginning to think he is—well, you know what happens to the little mice when the big cats move in, don't you, Sy?"

In answer to which the big bouncer said nothing at all but simply backed off another pace . . .

WHEN THE BIG ONE HIT the Necroscope didn't leap to his feet but simply sat there watching the jackpot prize—a massive thirty-five thousand dollars—flashing on and off on the slot's front panel. The illuminated legend, the signal light, the music: all the razzmatazz of the Big Win, the high-roller hit, washed over him without really meaning anything. Because he knew that he—Harry Keogh, Necroscope—hadn't had anything to do with it.

Oh, he was responsible for bringing Dead Eddy in here, but in fact this was Eddy's show. Eddy was the one with the talent, even though he'd only been able to use it through Harry. And it wasn't that he could see or control the future, not at all. But it *was* that he could control the reels. Eddy wasn't a precog or a seer—no way, because the future will be as it will be, immutable as the past, which nothing and no one can ever change—but he *was* telekinetic.

Harry knew that now for a certainty, because this time the Necroscope had deliberately abstained from exerting any kind of influence over the slot machine—yet still the winning symbols had fallen neatly into place! So that once again the golden rule was holding true: that whatever a person did in life—be it a habit, hobby, vocation or avocation—then frequently he or she will continue to pursue it in death, and that over time it will be perfected. Alas, that all the knowledge that's in the ground or gone up in smoke can't ever be realized; that there's no way the Great Majority may ever reveal their secrets to the living. Or rather, that there was no way before the Necroscope.

The dead man had "heard" Harry's thoughts, and said, *What's that? It's all me? Is that what you're saying—or thinking?*

"It's all you, Eddy," Harry answered, out loud, because as yet he was still alone on the dais. "In London there are people who harness talents like yours. That's a fact. I know because I worked with them . . . for a while, anyway."

So, you're saying I didn't need you?

"Only in order to bring you here. And now that you've done what you wanted to do, why don't you tell me the whole story? I know you haven't told me everything, Eddy."

"What's that?" said the payout man, who had come upon the Necroscope unnoticed, causing him to start. "Did you say something?"

"Er, I was talking to myself," Harry lied (but not really, for of course there was no one else there).

"Well, you've really hit it big this time," said the other, and he whistled his appreciation. "You're going to be something of a celebrity when they get finished with you upstairs."

"Upstairs?" Harry stood up and looked questioningly at the payout man.

"Yep," said a third voice, that of a heavily built, flustered-looking man in a dark suit, the uniform of a pit boss, who had just now climbed up onto the high-roller dais. And with his hamlike hand on Harry's shoulder, in a vaguely Irish accent, Sy McMahn continued, "We'll be paying you by check, sir, and naturally we'll be wanting your photograph for our, ahem, 'rogue's gallery'—ha, ha! Just for promotion purposes, you understand. It's casino policy, is all, so we can place a framed picture of you on the wall with our other big winners. Real good for business, you know? Also, you get to meet the boss—er, the owner, that is."

The Necroscope found himself being led away, and no reason whatso-ever why he shouldn't go. As for the money: he would have the check made out to Mary-Jane Croker, per his arrangement with Dead Eddy.

Hearing his thoughts, the dead man said, *Thanks, Harry . . . but first we'll have to collect the check.* His voice came over so bleak—like a cold draft in an empty old room—that Harry might well have queried his meaning. But by then they were into the elevator, and Sy McMahn had turned a special key in a metal panel to bring the cage to a halt on the floor between floors.

After that it all seemed to happen very quickly.

When the elevator jerked to a halt and the doors slid open, Harry found himself whisked through the low-ceilinged but otherwise spacious obser-vation level from which Joey Randazzo's team of watchers kept electronic surveillance on the gamblers in the casino below. Noting the many CCTV screens in the various rooms and partitioned areas, through which Mc-Mahn hurried him toward his boss's office, Harry couldn't help but wonder if his image, too, had appeared on-screen during his and Dead Eddy's assault on the machines downstairs. But even if that were so, so what? For while Harry himself would have been visible on the screens, Eddy Croker certainly wouldn't. At which thought:

Harry, said the dead man, his mental voice nervous, hushed, and hur-ried, *ask the big guy where he's taking you. And ask him who you're going to see.*

The Necroscope took Eddy's advice and spoke to McMahn. "Er, you say I'm to have my photograph taken up here? Well, fine, but just exactly who will I be speaking to? Who runs the place, and what do I call him? And for that matter, what do I call you?"

"I'm Sy," the big bouncer told him. "And the owner of this place—the guy you're gonna see—is called Joey. Yeah, Joey Randazzo."

Harry, said Dead Eddy at once, *it seems nothing's changed around here. That's the Randazzo I told you about. But I didn't tell you* all *about him, or about anything else; but hey, you've already worked that out for yourself. So now I've really got to ask you: Are you* all *they say you are? I mean, if I didn't know better I'd simply describe you as a young guy who talks to dead people. Maybe a little bit cold deep inside but, well, a humble guy, really. I haven't sensed any kind of tough guy in there at all! So what I'm asking you is this: can you really,* truly *look after yourself?*

That's the second time you've asked me that, said the Necroscope, feeling his skin prickling. *But why? What is it you're worrying about, Eddy? Is it this Randazzo fellow?*

Yeah, said the other, his dead voice pitching close to hysterical now. *Yeah, it's this Randazzo fellow. 'Cos just in case I forgot to mention it—and if you're* not much *good at taking care of yourself—then you really don't want to be meeting up with Joey Randazzo!*

Now, listen, Eddy, said Harry . . . a single moment before Sy McMahn twisted his arm up behind his back, put a forearm across his throat, and almost lifted him in through the door of Randazzo's office.

But the dead man had already cut him short with: *No, Harry, that's not just any Eddy you're talking to, it's Dead Eddy. And I'm really sorry, Necroscope—but now you know why!*

Almost as a reflex action Harry's mind had already reached out—to the coordinates of an old friend in a cemetery in England six thousand miles away. And without pause, *ex*-ex-army PTI Graham "Sergeant" Lane answered his call:

No problem, Harry. I'm right on it! Just let me handle it my own way.

Harry relaxed his body to let Sergeant in heart and soul, but mainly soul. And under Sergeant's control Harry's head and right elbow slammed back in unison with pile-driver force, the first striking McMahn's nose and mouth, and the second sinking nine inches into his gut, driving all the air out of his body. And using his hip as a pivot and McMahn's arm and wrist as the lever, Harry (or Sergeant) threw the bouncer like a huge, powerless rag doll against the makeshift wall, caving it in.

Behind his desk Joey Randazzo sat up straight at the sight of this modestly built young man throwing Sy McMahn around like a sack of straw, his bottom jaw falling open and his eyes standing out like marbles—but standing out in rage, not fear. And now those eyes glanced off to one side as Randazzo gave the nod to someone who stood out of sight, behind the door.

Naturally, because Sergeant "saw" through the Necroscope's eyes, he could only see what the Necroscope had seen; fortunate for the ex-PTI that he couldn't feel what Harry felt: the vicious *smack!* of a lead-weighted cosh that brought the whole world crashing down on Harry, simultaneous with an implosion of darkness that hurled Sergeant out of Harry's mind, back to the even greater darkness of his grave.

And for a little while Harry was out of things, too . . .

WHEN THE NECROSCOPE CAME to he found himself tied to a chair in the same office; that was made plain by the sight of the caved-in partition wall, plus the figure of a bruised and bloodied Sy McMahn slumped in another chair in one corner of the room.

Harry's regaining consciousness hadn't been a natural awakening; the sharp, choking sting of smelling salts was almost as painful as the lump now rising on the back of his head. And the warm trickle in that same region told of his scalp having split where he'd been coshed. As for his being trussed: when movement and the pain in his head allowed—which is to say a second or so after opening his eyes—Harry discovered that in fact movement wasn't allowed, or only a bare minimum. Whoever had roped him to the chair was an expert.

And as his eyes focused more yet, again he saw Joey Randazzo, now chewing on a slender cigar, blowing smoke rings where he sat behind his desk. And from close behind Harry, the shadow of a third person fell upon him where he sat. This would be the one who had administered the sap and then the smelling salts.

With his head quickly clearing of all but the pain of his injury, the Necroscope tested his bonds again, only to discover that his best efforts were worse than useless . . . far worse, in that they'd attracted Randazzo's attention.

"So, our boy's awake," the thug said, rising from his chair and coming round the desk to stand in front of Harry. "Mr. Magic is awake and hurting, and is going to hurt a hell of a lot more if we can't come to some kind of agreement." Grinning a shark's grin, he blew cigar smoke in Harry's face.

Harry's mouth was dry as tinder, but somehow he managed to mumble, "A . . . an agreement?"

"Yeah." Joey Randazzo nodded and offered an expansive wave of his cigar. "You agree to tell me how you do it and where you learned it—the trick of it, so to speak—and I agree not to kill you but merely break a few bones as a reminder to you that you're never gonna do it again, especially not to me!"

"How I do what?" Harry asked, knowing full well what Randazzo meant, but trying to give himself enough time to think his way out of his predicament. And think he did, as quickly as the hurt in his head would allow.

Dead Eddy was no longer with him; like Sergeant, he'd gone back where he belonged, to a local graveyard . . . at least, that was Harry's assumption. Reasonable advice he might—but probably wouldn't—have got from Eddy; in any case he didn't need any kind of confusion right now. For it was obvious to him that the reason he now found himself trussed up had a lot to do with Eddy and his telekinesis. Randazzo's comment (the fact that the wiseguy boss of the casino *knew* that Harry had a system to beat or cheat doctored slots, if not what that system was) more than hinted of a previous meeting between himself and good old Slots Eddy. And anyway Eddy had admitted as much himself. It was only a pity that he'd left it so late.

At which point Harry stopped thinking, or at least stopped trying to straighten out his thoughts, because a scowling Randazzo had bent over him and yanked on his bloodied hair until he looked up directly into the hoodlum's threatening piggy eyes.

"Hey, guy!" said Randazzo. "What are you, trying to test my patience or something? Well, let me tell you something about my patience—I don't have any! So don't you go asking me what I'm talking about. Don't you play innocent with me—asking how you do what. You fucking know how you do it 'cos I was *watching* you do it!" He let go of Harry's hair, dragged heavily on his cigar until the tip glowed red, shook warm white ash into Harry's lap, and continued.

"Okay, last chance. Only now I'll try to be more specific. How come you fucked with my slots? Maybe you learned a trick or two from Eddy Croker, right? He had a way with him, Slots Eddy, which got him in trouble. The fact is you seem to have the same knack. A coincidence? Well, see, I don't believe in that kind of coincidence. So talk." Looking beyond Harry, he jerked his head to indicate that someone should come forward. "Slim?"

The tough behind Harry's chair stepped into view. He was a spindly, chalk white man with sloping shoulders and pockmarked, hollow cheeks. And slapping his cosh into the palm of his hand, he said, "You got no paperwork, no driver's license, no IDs, no nothing but these." He put the cosh away, dug in his pocket, and held out a slender hand full of heavy Kruggerrands. "You're English, which is as much as we know about you. But no one saw you come in here and no one needs to see you go out. So whoever you are, we really do think you should talk."

Meanwhile, Harry had considered his options. He couldn't rock the chair enough to topple himself through a Möbius door. He *could* perhaps create a door directly beneath him, but if he did that the chair would go with him into the Möbius Continuum. Still unable to free himself—and uncertain as to whether he could control his movements or direction through the Continuum while fastened to a chair—it wasn't a pleasant thought that he might find himself tumbling end over end, endlessly through Möbius space-time! So that was out.

Or he could talk. In which case he'd have to lie, because the truth just wasn't believable.

"Nothing," Randazzo growled. "I'm not hearing anything at all. Well, you know something, guy? Even a yelp would be better than nothing at all." And leaning closer: "Is that a dimple in your chin? Well, shit, I think a dimple would really suit you."

He reached toward the Necroscope's shining face with his cigar, and as

Harry instinctively inched his head back, the thin thug grabbed his ears to hold him still. And snarling his sadistic pleasure, Randazzo pushed his cigar into the cleft in Harry's chin until the hot tip was forced back into the wad of tightly coiled tobacco leaves.

There was a barely audible crackle of burning stubble, and its thin but acrid stink, before the Necroscope yelped his pain and outrage. And as Randazzo withdrew his instrument of torture Harry talked, or rather babbled:

"I'd gladly tell you how I did it," the words tumbled from his dry lips, "except it wasn't me but Dead Eddy. Eddy used me, but he's the one who did it!"

A bad choice of words. An error. But would a lie have been any better? And it wasn't as if he was ratting on Eddy, because Eddy had paid his dues and was beyond all that. Beside which he had dropped Harry right in it.

Randazzo's jaw had fallen open again. "Eddy Croker did it? Slots Eddy? But Eddy Croker's *croaked!* Except...did I hear you say 'Dead' Eddy? How come you'd know about that? I mean, *nobody* knows about that!" And pushing his face close to Harry's again, so close that the Necroscope shrank from his tobacco, beer, and bad-lobster breath, he whispered, "Who the fuck are you, guy?"

Harry began to struggle, fighting like crazy against ropes that hadn't an inch of give in them, until Randazzo's hand shot out and grabbed his throat. By now the flesh of the thug's face was so screwed up, so twisted into a livid mask of hatred, that his eyes showed only as evil, blackly shining slits.

"Fuck you!" Randazzo spat the curse into Harry's face. "It really doesn't matter who you are, because you know too fucking much! Slim." And once again he gave the nod to the man with the cosh.

Even knowing what was coming, Harry hadn't enough time to squeeze his eyes shut before the world caved in on him a second time. But it made no difference, for in just another moment his eyes were only too pleased to close all by themselves...

———

HARRY, WAKE UP! Dead Eddy was going frantic in the Necroscope's mind. *For God's sake—and mine, and yours—wake the fuck up, while you still can!*

"What—*ulp?*" Harry tried to mumble, finding it hard to do because of all the dry soil that was trying to push itself into his mouth and the weight of the stuff on top of him. Dirt below him and his jacket above, and maybe an inch or so of air squeezed in between. But that was all, because each time he breathed the lining of his jacket got sucked into his mouth. And the air was stale because he'd already breathed it more than once.

Are you awake? Dead Eddy sounded louder, closer than ever before. So close that his shouts were actually hurting. Or maybe it was everything else that was hurting, Harry's whole body. And then there was the darkness, the dirt, the weight pressing down on him, the fact that no matter how hard he sucked . . . he couldn't . . . any longer . . . breathe!

He was lying facedown, flat out—flattened out!—with his jacket riding up over his head. But still he should be able to breathe. Why couldn't he breathe?

For the same reason I couldn't breathe when they did it to me, Dead Eddy was screaming at him. *It's because you're* buried, *Necroscope! It's because they've fucking buried you!*

It was the only explanation, and it hit Harry like a trip-hammer, harder than any cosh.

His head cleared of all but its aching; his thoughts gathered and ran true; he tried to breathe again, got a mouthful of dirt and jacket lining, and knew it was the last breath he'd be taking in this place—but not his last breath.

With no time to spare, Harry used a familiar metaphysical formula to conjure Möbius equations. Then, as mutating mathematical symbols coalesced into a door that opened inches beneath him, he let gravity do the rest. Along with a ton and a half of sand, soil, and pebbles, he fell into the Möbius Continuum—and almost at once fell out again at well-known coordinates, in the gloom of late evening, on the grassy bank of a Scottish river.

Nevada desert, dry dirt, and dust rained down on Harry, at least until he'd drawn breath, coughed his lungs out, and blown plugs of soil and snot from his nostrils. Finally he thought to collapse the door, then simply lay there panting, feeling sore, sucking on the sweet night air—

—And getting angry—

—Very angry . . .

DEAD EDDY CROKER was sobbing—*still* sobbing—all of twenty-four hours later. That was because the teeming dead hadn't let him in on the fact that Harry was alive; their way of teaching him a lesson. For when Harry had exited his shallow Nevada desert grave through the Möbius Continuum, all Eddy had sensed was his absence, the unbearable but inescapable fact that the small warm flame of Harry's being had been extinguished. He couldn't know that it hadn't gone out but simply moved away, beyond his sphere of reception.

So that when Harry returned—

Eh? Who? Whazzat? said Dead Eddy, abrupt, startled questions that hovered in the psychic aether as his sobbing gradually subsided. *I mean, is someone . . . someone there?*

"Yes," Harry answered, gruff but not entirely unforgiving. "Yes, I'm here, Eddy. I'm here because the Great Majority can't take anymore, because we could hear your sobbing from halfway round the world! Well, that's one reason I'm here, anyway."

Harry? said Dead Eddy, his astonishment—and sheer burgeoning joy—sounding loud and clear. *Necroscope? Is it really you? But how can it be? I thought . . . I thought that you . . .*

"I know what you thought, Eddy," Harry told him. "You were very nearly right, too. If you hadn't managed to get through to me when you did . . . well, I might still be down there with you, or if not *with* you, right alongside you. So it seems I'm in your debt. Mind you, I don't feel I owe you anything; it's more like you owe me—an apology. So that's the second reason I'm here."

Just a moment ago Harry had arrived back in Nevada via the Möbius Continuum. It was midafternoon and the sun was high and hot. Harry stood in a shallow declivity, the bed of an ancient, long-since dried-out river, an arroyo. In the distance, a range of mountains was silhouetted purple against an aching blue sky; while in the opposite direction, along the length of the arroyo . . . was that distant silvery glint a reflection from the gleaming metal spire of some tall building, perhaps a casino? Or was it the high window of an airport's control tower? Probably the latter, because high overhead a passenger-carrying airplane was creating a vapor trail as it descended in that same direction.

An apology? Dead Eddy was beside himself with relief, with joy, with emotions he hadn't known since he was alive, and then only rarely. *I should say I'm sorry for what I did to you—for what I* didn't *tell you? You mean you don't already know exactly how sorry I am, why I feel like I've been breaking my heart for days now, ever since the moment I thought that you . . . that you were dead? Well, then, I'm sorry, Harry. I'm really, truly sorry. But you know—*

"No 'buts,' Eddy," Harry cautioned him, looking around and examining the area more closely, noticing tire tracks and footprints in the dry soil.

No, you're right. No buts. Of course not. Only remember: I did try to check it out. I really did *try to make sure that you were the toughest of tough guys, and that you were up to it.*

"No, that's not good enough," said the Necroscope, shaking his head. "You conned me, Eddy. You tried to avenge yourself by using me. But I'm flesh and blood. They could have poisoned me, shot me, knifed me. Any one of those methods and a hundred more would have worked. They could have broken my bones, or—"

—They actually did *break my bones!* Dead Eddy interrupted. *They broke my good right slots-playing arm—broke it in three places, to remind me not to use it like that again. It was Randazzo. He didn't need to cause me that kind of extra pain, 'cos he'd already decided to kill me. But, well . . . that's how it is with Joey Randazzo.*

For a second or two Harry said nothing, simply stood there letting Dead Eddy's words sink in; their mindless brutality, and the brutality of the man whose actions had prompted them. Until finally he asked:

"How was it for you, Eddy? Was it really as . . . as—"

—As bad as all that? Dead Eddy's voice was painfully cold now, as cold as his memories of the day he'd died. *Yeah, it was as bad as all that. Dying*

is never easy; who'd know that better than you, Harry? But I think I could have done without the, er, additional complications.

"Complications?"

The beating. Dead Eddy shrugged. *The broken arm, and probably half a dozen ribs—done with a hammer. The getting kicked in the face when I was trying to crawl out of my shallow grave. The lying there only half-conscious, listening to Joey Randazzo laughing as his boys heaped dirt on me. The noise their shovels made slicing soil, until my ears got blocked so I couldn't hear it anymore. The trying to breathe dirt—if only to get enough air to belt out one last scream.* Eddy shrugged again. *The complications, you know?*

Harry stood there with his bloody chin, where the big burn blister had burst; his sticking-plastered head, with its twelve stitches in the back of his scalp; his headache, which a doctor had said was due to concussion, and that he should take it easy for a day or two. He stood there and nodded, and said, "Well, I know about some of that. Especially that last bit. So I suppose we'll accept your apology and let it go at that."

We?

"Me and the Great Majority. But really, it would have been better if you'd just been straight with me."

I realize that now, said Dead Eddy. *But since I was—you know—like a sneaky bastard in life, how could I expect to be any different in death? I was hardly the salt of the earth, now, was I?—even if I am now! No, I was just following the rules, Necroscope. And if I had been straight with you, would you have done anything about it?*

"That's academic," said Harry, "because the Great Majority have now seen fit to vote on it, and I'm with them all the way. You see, while we mightn't much care for your methods, Eddy, we like Joey Randazzo's even less."

Which is what I wanted all along, said Dead Eddy, *except I went about it the wrong way. But you should know, Necroscope, I can tell from the way you said it—your tone of voice—that your last "we" should have been an "I." It's you who wants revenge on Randazzo now, right?*

"Can you blame me?" said Harry. "But where I was your tool before, now you'll be mine. That way we'll both get some satisfaction."

Eh? Me, a heap of bones down here in the ground? Dead Eddy was mystified. *What can I do for you from down here, Harry?*

"From down there, not much." Harry had to agree. "Which is why I brought this along." And he tossed down a brand-new spade onto the dirt and pebbles. "But on second thought . . . well, who knows? We may not need it."

Dead Eddy saw what was in Harry's mind without him having to spell it out, and said, *You really think I can do that?*

Harry nodded. "Sure. What you did with those slots doesn't even come close to your full potential. It's telekinesis, Eddy. You can move things with your mind. And as we saw in Randazzo's casino, you do it better now than when you were alive."

But still I'll need your say-so.

"You've got it," said Harry. "I give it gladly. I call you up, out of the earth."

As easy as that? But I've always believed no pain, no gain.

"Oh, it will probably cost you," Harry told him. "Getting mobile again is no easy thing, or so they tell me. But for you, with that talent of yours . . . maybe it won't be so hard. It all depends how badly you want it."

How badly I want it? You're kidding! When do I start?

"Any time you like," said Harry, and he looked down at the earth under his feet. Nearby, he saw a rough hole in the ground six feet long by three wide by three deep. This would have been his grave. The dirt that had once filled it was now lying where it had fallen from the Möbius Continuum, on the bank of a Scottish river. While directly underfoot—Eddy's grave was barely perceptible, an oblong depression where the earth had settled a very little. He and the Necroscope had lain only fifteen inches apart. Small wonder Eddy's "shouting" had been so loud!

Here goes, said Eddy, as Harry stepped aside.

A layer of dust blew away from the surface of Eddy's grave and settled elsewhere. It was followed by a fistful of pebbles, rising up and moving aside, then plopping down onto the earth.

Then, a moment's pause before Eddy said, *This isn't easy.*

"I didn't say it would be," said Harry. "Moving is likely to be harder still—but there's a long way to go before that. Try again with the dirt."

Two fist-sized rocks wobbled into the air and tossed themselves aside. And:

Phew! said Dead Eddy.

"You want some help?"

Nope, said the other determinedly. *I got myself down here and I'll get myself out.*

"Okay, but that's going to take you some time. So I'll go away now and leave you to it. I'll take my doctor's advice and rest up awhile. But tell me, when is Joey Randazzo's place at its quietest?"

Two in the morning, said Dead Eddy. *It's, er, pretty dead around then.*

"Then that's when I'll be back," said Harry. "But are you sure you don't want any help? Maybe you'd like to quit now and lie still? Maybe it isn't worth it. Do you want to quit, Eddy?"

Over my dead body! said Eddy, as the shovel picked itself up and made a tentative stab at the earth.

The Necroscope smiled, and nodded. "Well, I have to admit you've got guts," he said, admiringly.

Once upon a time, for sure, said the other. And amazingly he chuckled, however grimly . . .

A FEW MINUTES BEFORE 2:00 A.M. Las Vegas time, it was just as Dead Eddy had said it would be: only a handful of die-hards propping up the gaming tables or playing the slot machines in Randazzo's downtown casino. All of the out-of-towners—the tourists, the people with the money—were in the flashier places on Fremont Street; the places with mobile, illuminated facades and smiling late-shift dealers, and long-legged cocktail waitresses serving free (slightly watered-down) booze to thirsty punters. And this was also the hour when Joey Randazzo called it a night and made for home, or a piece of ass, or a joint with straight tables to do a little gambling of his own, depending on the receipts.

But not tonight.

Tonight there was something in the air—a feeling of apprehension: some tension left over from the unsettling events of yesterday, perhaps?—a certain expectancy like the calm before a storm. Randazzo's nose for trouble, which had saved his gangster's hide on several previous occasions, had him sniffing the air, wondering if he should put the bent slots in for "repairs" and change the rigged roulette wheels before investigators from the gaming commission dropped in on him—that kind of feeling. Randazzo had been *expecting* something to happen, but never in a million years could he have foreseen what was coming.

Finally, as he gave a wry snort and tried to shrug off the feeling of impending...well, impending *something*—as he prepared to vacate the premises, leaving the night shift to his pit bosses and Sy McMahn—that was when it happened.

Pausing in the doorway of the main CCTV room, where McMahn was at his post with his eyes rapt on the viewscreens, Randazzo saw from the hunched condition of the Irishman's shoulders, his frozen attitude, that something wasn't right. And McMahn's battered, recently patched-up face—his gaping mouth and bulging eyes as he sensed Randazzo's presence and spun his swivel chair toward the door—confirmed that fact.

"What?" Entering the room, Randazzo spat the word out like a bullet. "You dumb fuck Mick! Stop gawking, will you, and tell—me—*what?!*"

But McMahn could only point a stubby finger at the central screen and say, "That—*that's* what, Joey! So tell me I'm nuts, but don't I recognize that guy?"

Randazzo's florid face turned white in the several seconds it took to skid to a standstill and glance at the screen. Then:

"Holy fuck!" His jaw fell open to match McMahn's.

"Me and Slim," McMahn's voice was a hoarse whisper, "last night we spent two, three hours digging this hole for that guy. Then we tossed him in, and let the truck's tailgate down—just like you told us to—and used it like a blade to sweep the shit back in on top of him. Slim knew what he was doing...Hey, this wasn't the first time for Slim! So, Joey, this guy—"

"Holy fuck!" Randazzo breathed the blasphemy again, as if it were indeed holy; and he ignored the Irish bouncer as if he wasn't even there.

"—This guy playing the slots down there," McMahn continued, "it isn't, it *can't* be him! It has to be his twin!"

At which point Harry hit the jackpot and looked up at the CCTV camera angled down on him. And now Joey Randazzo—and Sy McMahn, too—saw that it was indeed "him," the selfsame man. They couldn't mistake that ugly, weeping burn on his chin where a Band-Aid had come loose, or the wad of sticking-plaster like a small white skullcap at the back of his head.

And calm and almost expressionless (but oh so cold-eyed), Harry Keogh, Necroscope, stared back at them—not seeing them but guessing they were there—while he waited for the payout man who was already approaching, trundling his trolley as fast as he could go.

"W-what?" The payout man's eyes stood out like organ stops. "Y-you again? A-another jackpot? J-J-Jesus, I didn't expect I'd be seeing *you* again!" No, of course he hadn't—because he must have suspected at least something of what was waiting for Harry upstairs last night, especially after the big bouncer Sy McMahn showed up. Also, he'd been in receipt of instructions from Joey Randazzo, who he'd spoken to on his walkie-talkie.

"Oh, I'll *bet* you weren't expecting to see me," the Necroscope answered, snatching the man's walkie-talkie from his belt and hitting him with it. (Except it was Graham "Sergeant" Lane, not Harry, who did the actual damage.)

And as the man went down, clutching a bloodied ear: "Good grief, Sergeant!" said the Necroscope. "I hope you haven't damaged this thing." Harry needn't have worried; the walkie-talkie was a heavy-duty model; now he examined the buttons on its call pad, and saw that one of them was marked "Sy." Pressing it, he held the receiver to his ear.

In the CCTV room overhead, McMahn and Randazzo saw what he was doing, heard the *bleep* from McMahn's walkie-talkie where it lay on a console. Randazzo snatched it up, and said "Yeah? What can I do for you this time, creep?" And to one side, behind his hand as he listened to Harry, he whispered, "Sy, get Slim while I keep this bastard busy. You know what to do."

"What you can do for me?" Harry repeated him. And thinking back on yesterday: "Nothing much. Actually, it's what I'm doing for you—and for this entire stinking fleapit. You see that?" He pointed to a brown paper parcel—a six-inch cube—wedged between two slot machines. "That's a bomb, Joey. Enough plastic to reduce this place to rubble. And this"—now he reached into his pocket and produced a TV remote, but Randazzo didn't know that, just like he didn't know the bomb wasn't a bomb—"is the trigger I'll press as soon as I've walked out the door. That is, unless we can come to an agreement."

"Agreement? What fucking agreement?" Randazzo was sweating now.

"Something better than the one you offered me," said Harry. "I want your apology, Joey." (He wanted no such thing.) "I also want the Krugerrands you stole from me, and thirty-five grand's worth of winnings. I'll wait right here for all three, but only for three minutes."

Where are my fucking pit bosses!? Randazzo wondered—just a moment before Harry said:

"Oh, and if you're wondering where are all your heavies"—he put the remote away and cupped a hand to his ear. And coming faintly over the walkie-talkie Randazzo heard glass shattering, followed at once by the howl of fire alarms—"a mutual friend of ours has just taken care of them. One: they didn't much like the look of him, and two: it's in the SOPs— standard operating procedures, Joey. Everybody has to vacate the place— except you, me, and the bomb. Oh, and by the way, they all know about the bomb, too, because of the note I left at the cashier's booth."

"Fuck!" Randazzo snarled. And then, but grovelingly: "Now listen, wait. I'll need more than just three minutes. The money and those gold coins— I'll have to go down to the vaults, the counting room."

"So maybe I'll give you four minutes," said the Necroscope reasonably. "But that's all." And smiling a cold smile into the CCTV camera, he drew back his arm and smashed the walkie-talkie down on the floor, then stamped on it until it flew into little bits and pieces . . .

FUCK THE MONEY AND THE KRUGERRANDS! (Descending in the elevator, Randazzo slapped a full clip into his piece.) *This English fuck won't be pressing any buttons with a bullet in his head, and he won't be digging himself out of his grave a second time, that's for sure!* For by now Sy McMahn and Slim would be on their way—*They'd better be—and fuck the SOP's, too!*

But the big bouncer and Randazzo's hit man were not on the way, because they'd now seen who—or what—the pit bosses and a good many others in the casino had seen: Harry and Randazzo's "mutual friend." Combined with which the threat of a bomb blast and a fire had provided all the incentive they'd needed to make a run for the safety of the streets. It seemed kind of obvious, especially to McMahn and Slim, that this time Joey Randazzo had made himself one enemy—or maybe two—too many.

Meanwhile:

Harry had positioned himself where he could remain out of sight yet still see Randazzo coming. And from the same location he'd been able to keep an eye on a door marked PRIVATE that led to the vault. Just a moment ago, the last of the casino employees, three men in rolled-up shirtsleeves, had made a confused, bumbling exit through that door, locking it behind them. Good!

As for the vault itself: the Necroscope had memorized its coordinates direct from Dead Eddy's mind; and now, as the elevator doors hissed open and Joey Randazzo hurtled into view, he conjured a Möbius door and used the Continuum to go there. For Randazzo was no longer Harry's problem—

—But he remained someone else's . . .

FOUR OR FIVE PACES OUTSIDE THE ELEVATOR, Randazzo skidded to a halt. *Now what the . . . ?*

There was no sign of Sy McMahn or the sadistic thug known only as Slim, and at the far end of the long gambling hall the last handful of patrons was fleeing the blaring alarms, vacating the casino. A minute more and the place would be empty.

But if the place was empty—and from what Randazzo could see, it was or soon would be—then who was playing the slots? Who was playing a hell of a *lot* of slots, and more of them moment by moment? What crazy shit was going down here?

Fumbling his automatic from its underarm holster, Randazzo started forward again, very slowly at first, his pace gradually gathering speed as he drew near the first triple-ranked bank of slots on the perimeter of the central area's gaming tables. And there, once again, he skidded to a halt.

There was no one at the machines, but they were playing—playing themselves! Their metal arms yanking, their reels spinning, small winnings tinkling into their trays, and all accompanied by the hypnotic, idiot burbling of their machine noises!

Randazzo's bottom jaw fell open and his piggy eyes opened as wide and wider than ever before. He gurgled obscenities that went unheard, as suddenly—slot after slot, and row after row, in a dominolike procession—all of the machines began hitting jackpots, and the multiplied, amplified fairground cacophony of out-of-sync versions of "We're in the Money" set the casino's cheap chandeliers dancing on their flexes.

"What the . . . ?" Randazzo started forward again, his weapon held out before him, aiming it here, there, and everywhere without finding a target. And the sound of the music, and of dozens of lesser jackpots emptying their guts into metal trays, became deafening as finally he reached the spot which Harry had occupied on the CCTV screen.

But it wasn't the Necroscope who was waiting for him.

Randazzo saw the *thing* standing there—this rotted thing of white bone and flaps of brown leather, this entirely impossible dead thing with crusts of earth plopping from its skeletal frame—and knew without being told, without guessing, and without the slightest shadow of a doubt, exactly what it was.

Not an "it" but a "who," for there was no mistaking Eddy's right arm— broken in three places and fallen from his mouldering shoulder—*whose bones came creeping over the polished floor in Randazzo's direction!*

Everything that had happened in the last day and a half—all of the anomalies, suspicions and forebodings, and not least this evening's weird atmosphere—it had all been a prelude to this: Eddy Croker's revenge!

Randazzo's dizzily whirling thoughts righted themselves as best they could and fled back to yesterday's meeting with Harry Keogh. What was it that the British fuck—that guy who should be dead now but wasn't— had tried to tell him? That it wasn't him but Eddy, "Dead" Eddy, who'd done it to the slots? Well, so it had been . . . *because he was still doing it!*

"Shit!" said Randazzo, finally finding the strength to aim his weapon and squeeze the trigger.

Chips of white bone flew, but in the next moment something else was flying. Silver coins were flying, out of the slot machine trays! Dimes and quarters and dollar tokens—all gathering together and whirling in the air in a mad spiral of silver like a glittering dust devil. More than one hundred thousand dollars worth of minted metal disks—each and every one of them balanced against gravity by Dead Eddy's telekinesis.

And just a moment later, all of them *directed* by that same vengeful force . . .

HARRY READ ABOUT IT IN A LOCAL NEWSPAPER the next day: how when the bomb squad had finally entered the casino they'd found Joey Randazzo dead and buried in a heap of coins that had apparently suffocated or squeezed the life out of him. But the police were still looking into one other as-yet unexplained feature of Randazzo's death.

Harry also read how Francis "Slim" Avigliano and Sylvester McMahn, "former associates and employees of Mob-connected Randazzo," were under arrest and being questioned about the affair. This last hardly surprised the Necroscope: his anonymous letter to the law had supplied them with a detailed description of the location in the desert where they would find evidence of recent exhumations . . . which would further explain—or at least *help* to explain—how come they had found a human skeleton close to Randazzo's corpse. (For of course the Necroscope had known that when the sinister arroyo was investigated the police would discover the same footprints and tire tracks which he had seen on "visiting" with Eddy.)

SINCE THEN, having done all that he could, Harry had let things work themselves out; which they had, most satisfactorily. And a fortnight later he contacted Eddy again, tracing his new coordinates to the Charleston Heights Cemetery where Harry's adventures in Nevada had begun and where Eddy Croker's mortal remains had at last been laid to decent rest.

But before talking to Eddy he went to see Jack Black, that oldster who had once mined silver here, however unsuccessfully. And: "Jack," he said, "I've come to say I'm sorry."

Eh? (Half-deaf in life, Jack Black's hearing showed little improvement in death.) *Is it you, Necryscope? What in hell have you got to be sorry about?*

"Nothing in hell," said Harry. "Just a promise I made you: that I'd come back here with a silver dollar, and shove it down in the earth where you could feel it."

Oh, well. The old boy sighed. *I suppose it fits the story. I never did find too much of that good stuff in life.*

"But I'll tell you what I do have," said Harry. "That's if you think it will serve instead. I have a gold piece, Jack—if that will do?"

Did you say a gold piece? In Harry's metaphysical mind the old man's amazement, his childlike joy, was like the sun emerging from behind a cloud. *And did you ask if it would serve? You* bet *it would, Harry! Why, I was never so rich in my whole life!*

"Then it's all yours," said the Necroscope. And he drove a stick into the earth to make a hole, dropped one of his rescued Krugerrands in, and scuffed everything over with loose soil.

And finally he walked over to Eddy's grave...where oddly enough there were fresh flowers! But not really surprising, not after Harry had thought things through. That was something else that had appeared in the local papers: Eddy's identity, checked against dental records—which was why Mary-Jane Croker had had him buried here.

Necroscope, said the dead man when he sensed Harry's presence, *you can't know how pleased I am that you've remembered to come back and visit. And I can't wait to hear how it all worked out on your side of the divide.*

"Much as planned," Harry told him. "Your killers have been charged with Randazzo's and your murder, though the police are still working on that; I got all my Krugerrands back; your wife found a sack of paper money on her doorstep—a hundred thousand dollars, as I reckoned it— and it looks like, er, 'someone local' has seen fit to look after your grave. Might I hazard a guess that it was Mary-Jane?"

Dead Eddy offered an incorporeal sigh, and said: *Oh, I knew it was her right away. She felt almost as warm as you, Harry.*

"So all's well that ends well," said Harry. "She found you again, even if I didn't find the ones I was looking for."

Oh? said Dead Eddy. *You didn't say anything about that.*

"Well, it's sort of personal," said Harry. "Let's just say that everything *else* has worked out well."

Except for Sy and Slim, said Dead Eddy. *Oh, and Joey Randazzo, of course.*

Harry frowned. "Yes, Randazzo. That was a very—what?—novel sort of way to kill him?" He was thinking about that last "unexplained feature" of the gangster's death, which the police were still working on.

Eddy shrugged. *That crazy man. He tried to fill me full of lead!* Hah! *Me, a heap of bones! And so I—*

"—You filled him with silver," Harry finished it for him. "His intestines, guts, lungs, and windpipe—every cavity in his body—crammed with silver from the slots." And thinking about it the Necroscope (even Harry Keogh) felt an involuntary shudder drilling through his body. "But what prompted you, Eddy?"

I dunno, the other mused. *Maybe it was the music.*

"The music?"

Yeah, all that music from all those slots, said Dead Eddy. *"We're in the Money," Joey Randazzo's favorite tune . . . except this time the money was in him!*

In answer to which, the Necroscope said nothing at all . . .

DINOSAUR DREAMS

I

Finally, after finding a small, glistening fossil—a slightly chipped belemnite or "elf-bolt," looking for all the world like a leaden, elongated stone bullet—among the washed pebbles at the ocean's rim, Harry had come to recognize that elusive sound for what it really was. Not a "sound" at all but an oh-so-faint tingling sensation in every fiber of his extraordinary being—an *awareness* in his weird mind—which only a Necroscope, only *the* Necroscope, could ever experience. It was the residual aura of dead things, the remote resonance or sympathetic vibrations of long extinct, even prehistoric things.

Paleontologists thump the ground, and the echoes bouncing back to them indicate the size, shape, and substance of things buried in the earth. They hammer with machines and explosives, and their receivers are seismometers more sensitive than sonar, linked to computer monitor screens with pictures as detailed as X-ray photographs. Thus they look into and investigate Earth's innards. And like Harry on this warm summer day on this lonely Yorkshire beach, they look for fossils. Unlike the paleontologists, however, Harry Keogh didn't need to thump the earth; he simply (or not so simply) "listened" or experienced.

For Harry was sui generis, and unless we accept that odd but apt word of his own coinage, *Necroscope,* there isn't one for what he was, what he did, or the sixth sense with which he had been . . . what, endowed? For *psychic,* or even *spiritualistic medium* simply doesn't describe or do it justice . . .

Four or maybe five summers ago (the last few years seemed all unreal and shadowy, blurred and confused in Harry's memory, as if they hadn't really happened at all, or as if in the main they'd been erased), he'd searched for his wife and infant son among the towns along this eastern shore, searched here, there . . . just about everywhere. Until more recently—believing his family irretrievably lost, and those fruitless years of searching with them—he'd given up. For love dies after a time, and more quickly where there's blame.

His wife, Brenda—or more probably his son, for certainly the infant had possessed the skill; she or he, then—had taken the pair out of harm's way, beyond any means of discovery currently available to Harry, beyond the stranger he had become and far beyond the danger, the threat posed by simply knowing him. Which had left the Necroscope bitter and alone. But the bitterness had faded with the years—those strangely obscure, oh-so-dimly remembered lost years—until Harry was more his old self again, and as much his "own" self as he ever could be.

Back then, however, while still he had searched—

Harry had rested up in Bridlington, Yorkshire, awhile, and this tiny bay and stony beach, which was only accessible at low tide (except to Harry, of course, who had his own unique way of getting into and out of places), had been an excellent place to be alone, where he could bathe in the surf or drowse in the sun undisturbed. Sometimes he'd lie on his towel and think; others, he'd just lie there; now and then he would sleep and dream.

That was when he had first heard the sound—as he'd woken up when the sun slipped behind a cloud and a breeze off the sea blew sand in his face—and from then until now he had wondered what it was. The sound that wasn't a sound, like and yet unlike holding a conch to your ear and listening to some distant ocean in its sounding coils. Except he had no conch, and it certainly wasn't the sound of waves on some imagined shore.

What, then?

An echo of very real waves, geological echoes, coming back to him through the sand and the pebbles under his towel? Hardly that; the sea had been flat as a millpond, with barely a ripple stirred up by the summer breeze. So maybe it was his own breathing, the blood singing in his ears, or that more-imagined-than-real sizzling of the sun on the sea on especially hot days. All well and good, except the day hadn't been all that hot.

But it *had* been a very drowsy day, and laying his head back down Harry had quickly fallen asleep again. Which was when he'd dreamed an odd and peculiarly vivid dream; vivid in its colors and textures, and odd in that it had seemed so far removed from what he would normally expect of his dreams . . . but far removed in time rather than space, and on this occasion the Necroscope had been merely an observer, a witness.

An ugly, leathery, bat-bird Thing *ran or flopped, while a grotesque, massive, hungry* Something Else *thundered in hot pursuit. The runner (the prey) was winged, furred rather than feathered, and fragile rather than ferocious, at least by the standards of its era. It tried again and again to get airborne, making frantic hopping leaps on short, clawed hind legs, only to fall back in tangles of membrane—tangled because one of the creature's wings had been ripped through its sheath from elbow to trailing edge by three nine-inch claws. And this keening, crippled flyer skittering and tumbling on the stony ground like a crashed kite when the string breaks, only just managed to keep two or three spastic lurches ahead of the hunter.*

As for the latter: he looked a little like a T-Rex but far smaller, with a tall blue head crest, far-reaching taloned forelegs, massive hind legs, a lashing tail, and jaws that were . . . simply unbelievable. And despite his earthshaking, jarring gait through thorny fernlike foliage, the big lizard's scarlet eyes never once blinked but held fast to the tortured, flopping rag-thing whose pinion he had torn in a surprise attack.

The scene was prehistoric, of course. That much Harry knew and no more. He wasn't any kind of paleontologist and his knowledge of prehistory was scant to say the least. As a youth he'd read Sir Arthur Conan Doyle's The Lost World; *he'd seen an old monochrome print of the original, superior* King Kong, *and maybe a handful of less worthy monster films, and he'd gone the usual route of building a plastic model dinosaur or two . . . which was about as far as it went. So he was hardly qualified to know the actual names of such creatures, other than that they* were *dinosaurs, one of which was some kind of pterodactyl.*

As for the earthbound predator: not a snowball's chance in hell that Harry would know that one's name! But he did know for sure that it was no herbivore. Things weren't put together like that, with teeth and claws like that, in order to eat grass and leaves.

The terrain was sloping, a rugged decline along a fault in the earth: on the one hand the boulder-strewn ground, gradually falling away, and on the other the base of sheer, rugged cliffs that soared a hundred feet or more. Under normal conditions the pterosaur would consider the slope along the base of the cliffs an ideal launch site. And now—too terrified to appreciate its incapacity, traumatized beyond thinking of anything but flight, escape—it kept right on trying to do just that. To no avail.

Now, too, the predator was once again within striking distance. And where before he had tried to grasp a wing and only succeeded in tearing it, now he stamped on the back end of the flyer's body, drawing forth a shrill shriek of agony that very nearly drowned out the snapping of lightweight bones. And that should have been the end of it—was the end of it, almost—but not as the predator intended.

The cliffs at this point formed an overhang, a chimney of crumbling shale like a column of gigantic, badly stacked dominoes. In stamping on his prey's rear end—a clumsy and unintentional act that might *have worked out fortuitous, at least for the predator—the greater monster had thrown himself off balance and crashed his bulk into the base of the fault. Shale shards flew and the chimney shuddered, bulged outward from the cliff, flew apart under its own suddenly disturbed weight. And whole sections of the cliff went with it, thundering down from the heights like the undercut front of an iceberg at the sea's rim.*

The entire subsidence, lasting some twenty to twenty-five seconds, was like a chain reaction of fractured slate slabs, a deluge of riven rock. No living thing could have withstood the battering of so many crushing tons, and when the hurled debris settled the flyer was completely buried and only the bent back of the hunter stood up from the sliding slate and scree jumble. That armored back shuddered for a moment or two, and a muffled roar, more a suffocated snort, found its way out of the pile—which only served to initiate a second, smaller avalanche that broke the predator's back and completed his interment.

And that was that. No more movement other than a few rills of dust from on high, no sound other than the spattering of the last few handfuls of falling pebbles, and no further indication of life from that brand-new smoking scree skirt at the foot of the cliffs.

THE DREAM HAD STAYED with Harry a little while—stayed in his mind through that period between sleep and waking—until like most dreams it slipped away as he came fully awake. So that all he had remembered at the time was that he'd witnessed something out of earth's prime.

All of which had occurred some two or three years ago, and at that time he had yet to find the belemnite...

NOW, HOWEVER, HE WAS BACK. And it was mainly the sound, or what he continued to think of as a sound, that had brought him back. That and the fossils exhibited in the natural history museum in Sunderland, County Durham, a town on England's northeast coast only a few miles from where Harry had grown up.

He'd gone there to test a theory, pass a little time, and maybe to recall something of his boyhood. Saturdays when he was nine or ten, he and Jimmy Collins would take a bus into Sunderland and spend an hour or so at the public swimming pool. Then, on the way back to the bus terminal, they would sometimes visit the museum. Jimmy, ever the athletic, open-air type, had never been enthusiastic about these visits. ("What? You don't want to go to that dusty, airless old place again, surely?")

But for Harry, the stuffed animals, the birds' eggs in their glass-and-mahogany display cases, and the many trays of fossils had always held an undeniable fascination. This morning, out of the hazy memories of a less-than-ideal and often unreal-seeming childhood, he had remembered how the natural history museum had had its own sounds, and not merely those of dully echoing halls and hushed conversations. No, for added to those it had had the sounds of a certain isolated beach in Yorkshire. Those selfsame sounds, yes, or so close as to make no difference.

As to why places so disparate—so unalike—should have the same sympathetic vibrations... it was a mystery that Harry must solve.

So this morning he'd risen early and breakfasted, and left his home in Bonnyrig near Edinburgh for Sunderland, more than a hundred miles to the south. But being Harry, with access to his own special mobility . . . well, the trip hadn't taken much time, indeed none at all; so that upon his arrival the museum's doors were still closed to the public. And they would stay that way for at least another hour. Well, neither was that an insurmountable problem to the Necroscope; the museum's great arched-over oaken doors could stay barred all day for all Harry cared, for he had doors of his own . . .

Inside, the museum was exactly as he remembered it; which spurred him to further remember the coordinates of the shining, parquet-floored hall which was his goal. A Möbius jump took him there in a moment, and for all that Harry was unique (or almost so, for his lost infant son had inherited all of Harry's skills in spades), still he felt very small, indeed tiny, in the dead silence of that room of prehistoric relics.

"The dead silence," yes . . . except the dead weren't at all silent, not to the Necroscope, Harry Keogh. Neither man nor dog nor any creature which had once been a living, thinking entity, none of them were entirely silent. For to Harry they were still there: their thoughts and voices, and now apparently even their incorporeal auras. For those myriad members of the teeming dead who—*or rather which*—in their lifetimes had not been capable of "reasoned thought," certainly not as human beings understand and perform such acts of mental deliberation, even they had not passed on without trace.

And that trace was here: it was Harry's "sound."

It was—it could only be—the fossils, of course. It was their murmuring. It was what continued to go on in them following the lives that had fled them so many millions of years ago. Like an echo of their once-being, it was simply a reminder that they *had* been, that they *had* lived!

The whispers of a giant clam ancestor of today's tridacna, an ancient thing converted now to stone yet still "alive" with the wash of primal ocean. The sea-bottom scurryings of a creature as gray as the bed of slate into which time had welded it, a ten-inch trilobite of the Cambrian period, some half-billion years dead yet still brushing however indistinctly on the drum of the Necroscope's psychically sensitive inner ear. The eerie, haunting cry of archaeopteryx—but more truly "haunting" now—from a slab of Jurassic stone embossed with petrified wings and broken bones. All of these and a thousand more.

These forgotten "sounds" out of the past, revenant of the lives of myriad creatures...an inarticulate chorus whose primordial echoes only Harry Keogh could ever "hear" or experience, and then barely, as a hiss of background static from the stars but fainter far...

...Or perhaps not, or not in every case. For at least one exhibit—and a new one, for he had never seen its like before—had seemed to roar at him!

It had happened like this:

Moving from display case to display case, rapt upon their contents as never before, and stumbling suddenly, unexpectedly across a fearful relic—an almost complete raptor, or its complete skeleton at least, a thing as tall as himself fused half in and half out of a great slice of polished stone—the Necroscope's immediate, involuntary reaction had been to start violently and jump back a pace. It was only a harmless fossil, yes, the bony remains of an eons-dead predator, but in the light of Harry's weird talent it had seemed momentarily menacing...more especially so when he'd sensed a silent roar (or more likely a throbbing whistle) from those petrified, yawning jaws.

Moreover, the abrupt displacement of Harry's weight, his startled leap away from the exhibit, had set the sprung parquet floor shuddering under his feet, *and* under the mahogany base of the display cabinet. For a split second the great glass box had trembled, shivered...which had caused Harry to feel like some kind of vandal at what happened next.

For a stony tooth had come loose from the fossil's thrusting jaws—jaws which, if only for a frozen moment, had seemed to thrust more yet—to fall clattering to the sand and pebble-strewn floor of the exhibit case...

It was a coincidence, of course: an accidental fracture of ancient stone caused by the sudden movement of the cabinet, and nothing more. But to Harry Keogh, a man with the power to raise the dead up from their graves—

—Well, he couldn't help but wonder.

And it had been sufficiently unsettling to bring his visit to an end right there and then...

AND SO, in order to corroborate what now seemed an incontrovertible fact—that even the primordial dead, and the less-than-human dead, at that, were not without their revenants—Harry had come here: to this near-inaccessible Yorkshire beach where he believed he might put his discovery to the acid test.

Using Möbius coordinates established during those earlier visits, he had emerged from the Continuum at the sea's rim. And his luck was in: at high tide the small beach was deserted, and the sea lay still and leaden under unseasonal clouds. Moreover, now that he knew what he was looking for, the place was "alive" with those ethereal echoes from the distant past. Or perhaps it had always been this way, and it was simply that Harry's acceptance of his "sounds" had accentuated their reality.

The scalloped, crumbling cliffs were the main source, but Harry had neither equipped himself for a rock-hounding expedition—not with the usual tools: tough boots, hard hat, a hammer and cold chisel—nor did he intend to topple the shale stacks wholesale in order to satisfy his curiosity. No need when there were fallen slabs at the foot of the cliffs, not to mention an abundance of stony rubble on the beach and in the water itself.

And finally it was there—there at the ocean's rim, where he had crouched down to scoop at the damp shingle with his bare hands—that he'd found the belemnite . . . or it had found him. Less than a pace away from where he'd emerged from the Continuum, this small fragment of the prehistoric past, rolling on his palm like a bullet made of stone. And what was more, there were other relics close at hand: an ammonite buried in the core of a stony nodule just over there, and a tiny bony fish trapped in a shard of slate not nine inches from his left foot. Harry didn't have to see them to know that they were there.

And suddenly afraid—concerned that perhaps his newfound awareness was taking on permanency, becoming a runaway facet of his psychic skills, a mental tumult beyond his control—Harry shook his head to clear it as best possible, gritted his teeth, and tried to force the primal "voices" from his mind. They were gone instantly and silence reigned . . . the only exception being the plaintive cries of seagulls far off on the high ledges, and the wash of the smallest waves.

So then, he *was* the master of this thing—

—And to prove it he opened his mind again, tuning it in to that special wavelength . . . and all of those whispers out of time were back again.

He homed in on one, a hissing gasp, and moved to a boulder half-buried in the sand. Barely visible to any untrained eye—even to the eye of a practiced paleontologist—the faint outlines of the jaws, skull, and eye socket of an ichthyosaur were visible on the scarred surface. But only "visible" to the Necroscope by virtue of the fact that he *knew* they were there, could feel them under his trembling fingers, as if they'd been embossed on the stone.

In the next moment, however, he snatched his hands back as that lifeless boulder seemed to say to him:

Oh, my good Lord, Harry! But what wouldn't I have given for a talent like that!

II

It wasn't the boulder—no, of course not—but the voice of a dead man, one of the Great Majority, speaking to Harry from the void beyond life. It took only the briefest moment for the Necroscope to recognize the truth of the matter, but still he had to steady himself and take several deep breaths before he could answer:

"That makes two, no *three* times in the last half hour that dead things have caused me to start like that!" And immediately, realizing what he'd said—and trying hard not to bite his own tongue: "Er, I hope you'll forgive me for that. I mean, I'm not usually that blunt."

No, no! said the unseen other. *My fault entirely. But when I saw—or rather, when I felt—that it was you, then I simply had to make my presence known to you. So I just blurted out the first thing that came into my mind. It's not every day that one gets to speak to the Necroscope. And to be absolutely honest, I wasn't even sure I believed in you, or rather in it . . . I mean, in this—that I could speak to someone who was still alive—not until now, anyway.*

"Sometimes," said Harry, "in fact, quite a lot of the time, I don't believe in it—er, in *this*—either. But anyway, you have me at a disadvantage. What do I call you?"

Peter's the name, said the other, *or it was. Peter Carson.*

"You're sort of faint," said Harry, looking here and there at the stony rubble on the beach, finding himself drawn toward the foot of the cliffs. "What, did you fall or something?"

Or something, Peter Carson answered, with a sigh that only Harry could have detected. *These cliffs are pretty unsafe, it's true, but even more so if you choose the wrong climbing companion. As for my faintness: well, I suppose that's because I'm not all here. By that I mean this isn't exactly where I landed, and it certainly isn't where I ended up. I—my body—ended up out there* (the nod of an invisible head, to indicate the open sea). *But since I died when I hit, I sort of gravitate around here. I suppose you could say this place is my genius loci . . . or maybe that I'm its? Anyway, if I'm faint it's because the sea will do that to you, break you up and . . . move you around. You know?*

Harry nodded and shivered a very little. He would take the dead man's word for that last. "But you couldn't have been here very long," he said out loud, so that if anyone had seen him it would appear as if he were talking to himself. "Just a couple of years ago I used to come here myself, and I'm pretty sure you weren't around then."

It's been about a year, said the other. *I think that's why I can talk about it now. But at the time . . . well, I was pretty broken up about it.*

Literally, apparently, the Necroscope thought, having forgotten for a moment that the dead man—any dead person—could read his metaphysical mind as clearly as he read theirs. A sort of telepathy between the living and the dead.

But I'm over all that now, Carson told him hurriedly, nullifying the need for a second apology. *And I'm just, well, happy that you chanced along—especially since it seems you're here for the same reason I was. Originally, I mean.*

Now Harry frowned. Occasionally, like telepathy, the weird medium which he used to communicate with the dead conveyed more than was actually said. But this time he was confused. "I think . . . maybe we'd better start over," he said.

Oh! said the other. *How silly of me! I haven't made myself at all clear, have I? But it's the fossils, you see.*

"It is?" said Harry.

Yes! (And now the Necroscope sensed the nod of the other's incorporeal head.) *That's what I meant when I said I would have given anything for—*

"For a talent like mine?" Harry was getting it now. "But I thought you meant my being able to talk to the dead. While what you really meant was—"

The way you find fossils! Carson cut in. *Or is it just one and the same thing? I suppose it is, really. But to a paleontologist—even an amateur, as I am, or was—why, it would have been wonderful! I could even have been famous . . .*

And now it was all coming together. Or at least the Necroscope thought so. "You were searching for fossils when you fell from the cliffs?"

Well, I've had some time to think about that, the dead man answered, *and while in a way I'd like to tell you that's how it happened, I have to admit I'm not so sure.*

And now Harry remembered Carson's comment about a climbing companion: how maybe he'd chosen the wrong one. Also—now that the rapport between the two was established—the Necroscope's intuitive grasp of the other's meaning was strengthening and he began to understand more than was actually said. "You think you were pushed," he said, quietly.

Not pushed (the imagined shake of a head), *but simply allowed to fall. And I've also had time to figure out why. And you know, it's a shame really. Because while I've come to accept it now—the fact that I'm dead and there's no going back—it's much harder to accept what's going on right now in the world of the living. In your world, that is . . . I mean if it's going on.*

Carson's incorporeal voice, while it was still faint, had taken on a hard edge. Which was something Harry had experienced often enough in the past: the anger of men unjustly dead, their need to take revenge when they were no longer able, their frustration at the immobility of this final, ultimate incapacity.

"I know what you mean," he said, with a curt nod that the other couldn't see but could sense. "Myself, I try to live by a certain principle. It may seem cold to some but it's worked for me."

Oh, I've heard about that, Carson answered, his tone somewhat lighter now. *Heck, who among the teeming dead hasn't? Yes, I know the principle you've lived by. An eye for an eye, right?*

"You might find it hard to believe," said Harry, by way of an answer, "but there are worse things than death," (he thought of Dragosani, a necromancer he had known) "and worse places to be than dead." (And he thought of an East German secret policeman who had worked for the Soviets, a member of the GREPO, the Grenz Polizei, adrift now in the utter emptiness of the Möbius Continuum.)

Harry's thoughts were as good as pictures to the dead man, who said, *That last has to be horrible! Do you think he's still alive?*

"It's possible," the Necroscope answered. "If the Continuum hasn't ejected him somewhere. "But if he is still alive, and if he's still in there . . . well, he isn't sane, that's for sure. I've looked for him once or twice, not that I think I'd be able to do much for him. But that's not your problem . . ."

My problem? said the other, suddenly eager. *But that seems to suggest that you—*

"That I might be willing to look into it?" Harry finished it for him. "The Great Majority are my friends . . . the majority of them, anyway. I owe them—I owe them everything—so when I have the time I like to help out. Because there's no one else who can. So right now I'd like to know a little more about you, and about your problem."

You mean it? You'll look into it for me?

"If there's anything to look into, yes."

Harry had formed an opinion—he'd gauged something—of what the dead man must look like from his young "voice" (which sounded to him much as it would have sounded in life) and from Carson's warm, friendly attitude. But there was a way he could get to know him much better.

So now he said, "How did you used to think of yourself—I mean, how did you *see* yourself—er, before?"

When I was alive? Like, in the mirror?

"And in your mind. Can you remember your opinion of yourself?" An odd question, but not as strange as it seemed. Harry sometimes had difficulty remembering the way he himself—the original *him*self, before his reincarnation—had been.

The mere suggestion at once brought the dead man "alive" in the Necroscope's unique mind . . . Harry now "saw" Carson as Carson had once seen himself, not alone as a mirror image but also in his own imagination. Carson as *Carson* had known him:

A man in his late twenties or early thirties, green eyed and tousle haired, quick to laugh and slow to anger. He was—or had been—sturdily built and of medium height, and there was (still) an air of humility about him which reminded Harry quite a lot of himself as once he had been.

So now, having decided that he liked Peter Carson: "Tell me about it," he said. "The whole story right from square one. And then we'll see what's to be done about it, if anything."

And so the dead man told him about it . . .

IT WAS THE FOSSILS (CARSON BEGAN), with me it was always the fossils. An uncle gave me *The Observer's Book of Geology* in my preteens, and that did it for me. At first, I wasn't too interested in the rocks themselves; I just skimmed the pages. But when I got to the chapter on the fossil-bearing stuff . . . then my interest picked up.

There was a quarry close to where we lived, "we" being my family: my mother, my father, and myself—so I suppose I was some kind of spoiled only child. Anyway, they doted on me, and whenever they saw I was keen on something "educational" they'd go all out to help me explore my fascination.

Me and my father, we'd take our cold chisels, hammers, and collecting bags, go to the quarry on a weekend, and hammer away at any promising-looking rocks. At first it was just fun: a fun thing to do, a great hobby. But after my first few decent finds it developed into a lot more than that: it was exciting! And in the end it became my great passion. A pretty dull, dry-sounding sort of thing to most people, I suppose. But . . .

For me it stayed that way, a passion. But for the old man, my father . . . well, he *was* old. My parents had delayed having a child, me, until their last spark, as it were. And there came a time when Dad just couldn't face up to the quarry anymore.

But here I'd like to admit to something: I have never held down a job. Which is to say, I never once considered becoming a professional rock hound in order to earn my keep. You see, that would have taken all the pleasure out of it. And after my folks had passed away, well, I didn't need to work; they left me quite well-off. Better off, I think, than many a professional paleontologist. Certainly better off than Newton Loomis. But I'll get to him shortly . . .

By the time I was twenty-two I had opened a little shop in my home town a few miles inland from here, but it wasn't really what you'd call a business. I had a workshop at the back and my flat was upstairs . . . quite a nice little place, actually. What sort of shop? But that must be fairly obvious: I polished, displayed, and *occasionally* even sold fossils; some that I had bought, but mostly specimens I had collected on beaches and in various quarries. Yes, I admit to having sold this or that odd piece now and then (if the buyer was as keen and as fascinated as I myself), though as often as not I would have been just as happy to leave them in their showcases!

So you see, I was never a real "professional." No, not in any sense of the word. And it never dawned on me—not until it was much too late—that I was good enough to have ever *been* a real professional; though I've recently come to suspect that it might have dawned on someone else. A wrong someone, and a jealous one, at that . . .

Anyway, there was a young woman who loved my shop window; she rarely walked by without pausing to admire my specimens in their trays or against artistic backdrops of various paleogean relics, cycad forests and prehistoric oceans. I was very proud of the way I displayed those fossils, and I was certainly glad of the way they piqued her interest.

Eventually we got to know each other. Her name was Susan, and she was the younger daughter of a wealthy local landowner; which meant that despite her youth she was a girl of independent means. Only recently returned from studies in America, she hadn't yet decided on the course her life must take, and apart from family acquaintances no firm friendships had developed at that time—other than my own, that is.

I'll cut a long story short: we were engaged for fifteen months and then got married, a quiet affair in a local church. And because there were no children, and none planned, my small flat was ample to our needs. Of course we could have purchased a bigger place, but the romance of youth . . . the first blossoming . . . our little flat over the shop was like a nest which we would feather.

So we did just that, and I knew five years of bliss with Susan. She went with me on my field trips and seemed to enjoy them almost as much as I did. There are quarries and outcrops in the southwest that simply teem with fossils, while the so-called Jurassic Coast of Devon and Dorset was an absolute gold mine.

Our fossil collection grew, and with it the importance of some of our finds. Susan was something of a writer; she submitted articles to the scientific magazines; interested parties—mainly professional paleontologists—would arrive at our shop to view the more fascinating or as-yet unidentified specimens. We even got our name attached to a "new" (one-hundred-million-year-old) miniature Mosasauros. It was always exciting, and it cemented our love ever more firmly.

Then there was this beach . . .

We were on holiday—or was that simply another excuse to do a little rock-hounding? Anyway, it was summer; we did try to take time off and relax; we made a pact that this time when we visited the local beaches it would be for no other reason than to be alone together. A promise that we had somehow managed to keep, at least until we hit *this* beach.

We got here at around midday. The tide had turned and was coming in, but that didn't matter; toward the end of our break, we'd long since acquainted ourselves with the tide tables. The tidemark—like the forward edge of the battle area, where the ocean's advance had come to a halt, leaving a boundary line of stranded seaweed and shells etched on the sands—was clearly visible, reaching only halfway up the beach and well short of the towering cliffs. Besides which the sea was so calm that if by some freak of chance or nature we'd ended up in trouble, it wouldn't have been too hard to swim to safety.

And this was exactly what we'd desired: an opportunity to be completely alone together. For a further five or six hours, the sea would keep us apart from the rest of mankind . . .

MUCH LATER, after we picnicked and that dead calm sea had begun its gradual retreat, Susan walked off along the still-damp tidemark collecting shells. She loved how pretty and colorful they were when wet. And me—

—Well, I couldn't resist it. I'd pretended not to notice a few fossil fragments among the pebbles at the sea's rim, but as Susan got a little farther away I put on my shirt and walked up the beach, closer to the cliffs, examining some of the rocks as I went. And at the foot of the cliffs, among fallen pebbles and other debris, there I found the sickle claw of a dinosaur predator.

My eyes were drawn to it and fixed instantly upon it: that sharp, curving point sticking up from the loose sand and coarse scree rubble. And after carefully working the thing loose I saw that at some fourteen inches long it was a huge specimen of its sort. But what sort? What creature had worn something like this on its hind feet?

I at once suspected Utahraptor! Or if not him, then definitely a killer lizard of a similar era and like size, and possibly even larger. Probably a new, uncataloged species!

The find was one of a kind, something you could spend an entire lifetime searching for without finding it. And now when I least expected it, here it was. My feet scarcely touched the sand as I walked back down to the sea to wash the talon clean. And then, instead of calling out to Susan, I just sat there on my towel, finding it difficult to credit my good fortune while continuing to admire that wicked-looking instrument of prehistoric terror.

When Susan returned, I still couldn't speak. First of all she saw the look on my face, then the stony sickle shape in my hand. And as her eyes opened wide and her mouth fell open, the shells that she'd collected slowly slipped through her fingers and were soon forgotten . . .

BACK HOME, Susan wrote one of her articles. It went off in the post accompanied by photographs of the sickle taken alongside a twelve-inch ruler. And while we waited for publication, she and I searched our small library of fossil lore—from my dog-eared *Observer's Book of Geology*, to James Beerbower's *Search for the Past: An Introduction to Paleontology*—looking for clues as to the origin of the talon. For now, on studying the thing under a glass, there appeared a certain anomaly; which is to say, there was about the fossil this odd something which as far as we knew existed nowhere else in all the fossil record.

The claw had three shallow grooves on the perimeter of its outer curve, and the one at the thick end or root of the fossil formed the bed of a backward-leaning thorny extension which was still partly intact.

One day, after puzzling over this anomaly for hours, Susan had an idea and took a pair of secateurs into the walled garden behind the shop . . . and a minute or so later returned laughing, with a section cut from the stem of a blackberry vine. And as I watched her break off a thorn, it wasn't hard to guess what was on her mind. Then we made a comparison, and:

"Yes," I told Susan after accepting her theory. "It's most compelling—but thorns on a blackberry vine are very different things to hooks on the clawed feet of a dinosaur!" Nonetheless, except in size the shallow grooves on the talon were almost identical to the blemish where the thorn had been seated, so that the backward-leaning stump on the fossilized sickle might well have been the root of some huge thorn. Since animals don't have thorns, however, we now accepted that the talon of our unknown predator had borne barbs.

"Can't you just see it?" Susan said. "This great beast—this lizard—he attacked like a cat, but he was better equipped than a cat. He grabbed hold with his forelegs, toppled his victim, then fell on his side and gutted with his taloned feet while biting at the victim's head or throat. These huge talons would sink into the prey's belly smoothly enough . . . but coming out the barbs would excavate great chunks of flesh. After that the victim was finished; for even if he got away he would die, of loss of blood or his terrible injuries. What a monster this giant raptor-thing was!"

All that from this lovely girl-wife of mine, yes. And she said more or less the same thing to Newton Loomis when he came to visit . . .

III

Loomis was in the shop one day when I came back from town with some lapidary supplies; as I've said, I used to cut stones and polish my own rocks and fossils. And there was Susan with this smooth-looking character in the shop, talking to him about our talon. While he might have been trying to hide it, I could see that the thing fascinated him; he had that same greedy, sweaty sort of look on his face that many collectors get when they're handling something they very badly want.

He looked rather taken with Susan, too. But no complaints from me; I took great pride in the fact that other men admired her. I didn't mind them looking . . . as long as that was as far as it went.

Anyway, there he was and Susan was explaining to him her theory of this big raptorlike dinosaur with barbed hind claws. Well, he seemed suitably impressed, so after he introduced himself I gave him the benefit of the doubt; I thought that since Loomis was "obviously" an authority in his own right (for that was how he presented himself), perhaps the uneasiness I experienced in his presence was unjustified.

Loomis had "offices" in York; he'd taken degrees in archeology and paleontology, and gone on to teach both subjects at a London university. Now he merely "pottered about," lecturing and "loaning himself out professionally" to earn an occasional crust. He seemed awfully young to have gained such experience, no more than seven or eight years older than myself. But there again, what did I know? I was little more than an amateur with no professional qualifications whatsoever.

Tall and slim hipped, Newton Loomis was strong, athletically lithe, and handsome in what seemed to me a contrived sort of way; if anything he looked *too* well groomed. Which is probably to admit that I wasn't. It's possible that I saw him as a threat, a rival, right from our first meeting. But if so, then what sort of threat was he? And as for a rival, in what arena? For after all, he was the "authority."

His wavy hair was dark, with brushed-back streaks of premature gray at the temples which, along with dark blue eyes that he could focus almost unblinkingly, loaned him a sort of eager, wolfish attentiveness: like a dog waiting on his master's word of command. Or it could simply be that Loomis was a good listener, paying rapt attention in order to understand more surely... or perhaps in order to pick our brains?

Loomis' straight nose lay slightly flat to his face, his chin was angular under a wide mouth with sensual lips, and his teeth were very white and even. Yet as I've said, he contrived to be handsome, albeit in a way that's hard to explain.

And so much for a description.

If I've given him rather canine looks... well, that's in retrospect. Perhaps I'm prejudiced, trying to place him in the role of a dog that bites the hand that feeds him. But that, of course, remains to be seen...

SUSAN AND I had long ago agreed that we wouldn't advertise our search areas to the world in general, that we'd keep the locations of the quarries and beaches we visited to ourselves. Most of these places had in any case been well picked over by local rock hounds, and we weren't simply being greedy or jealous but saw ourselves as protecting the environment in however limited a fashion. Other collectors we'd met weren't nearly as concerned with the preservation of such sites as we were. Putting it plainly, many were simply despoilers; for every small specimen they collected, they left a pile of stony rubble behind them.

Thus in my conversations with Newton Loomis I was careful not to reveal too much, which was never easy, because he would find seemingly innocuous ways to slip his leading questions in almost without my noticing. And even during that first meeting I found myself in that awkward position: obliged to avoid saying too much to this persuasive stranger. Moreover, Susan told me later that her experience had been much the same.

Given enough time, however, a casual acquaintance may become a friend; and while familiarity can't always be said to breed contempt, it does tend to relax one's guardian instincts. Even if my wife and I were suspicious of Loomis at first, regular contact was bound to break down the barriers eventually.

And there was just such contact.

Loomis brought fossils for me to clean or cut and polish, and insisted on paying for the work; he invited us out to eat; he flattered us that "even as amateurs" we had discovered and identified a number of very obscure specimens. And eventually he began to accompany us on field trips to several well-known local sites. By which time, naturally enough, we'd started to trust him—well, within limits.

But you know, and now that I come to think of it, Loomis never once invited us to visit his "offices" in York. Perhaps we should have paid him a visit unannounced, as it were . . .

I think Susan trusted him the most. Certainly he paid her enough attention . . . but that was admiration rather than flirtation. Or so I allowed myself to believe.

Anyway, and despite this gradual relaxation of caution, I remained on my toes with Newton Loomis—especially after being approached by the paleontology department of Susan's university in America. She had stayed in contact with certain departmental heads, who through her articles had become aware of our discoveries. Chiefly they were interested in our barbed claw. Nothing quite like it had ever been found in any of the U.S.A.'s boneyards, and if I would divulge the location of the find, the university would be prepared to arrange, authorize, and fund an exploratory excavation in the hopes of finding other remnants of the claw's former owner. And in turn we had told them that we'd give their proposal our most serious consideration.

When first Loomis heard of this he seemed annoyed with us, and he explained his annoyance—or rather his "disappointment"—thus:

Here we were planning to team up with these American rock hounds—people who obviously thought they had every right to barge in on our work, make it their own, *and* probably take the lion's share of the credit in the event of any further discoveries—when for months now, despite that the three of us had grown close and had come to "trust and understand each other," Susan and I hadn't allowed *him* a hint—not even a sniff—at the locations of our most productive, secret sites. And as for the barbed talon: well, we'd been doubly secretive about that! What did we think? That *he* would exploit our knowledge or something?

And Susan and I felt bad about it because of course he was right. We'd stuck to our guns and hadn't given away anything of any real importance. As to why we ourselves hadn't gone back to the beach—this beach, that is—to search for more dinosaur relics in our own right: well, Susan's mother's health had been failing for some little time, so of course she hadn't wanted us to stray too far afield. And then out of nowhere the winter had been upon us, bad weather setting in, and plenty of work in the shop without requiring that we go off on any cold, damp, dreary expeditions. Ideally we'd be able to continue the search in the late spring or early summer, probably accompanied by a party of American experts.

But what amateurs we were, eh? To let the weather stop us. Or anything else for that matter . . .

AND THAT'S EXACTLY what Newton Loomis said to me the following March—that and a lot more—after Susan had gone off to America to show off the claw and liaise with our would-be sponsors.

"You know that this whole thing will fly right out of your hands," he said, the next time he turned up at the shop. "Don't you want to have your name associated with the talon? Don't you think you deserve some kind of recognition, you and Susan?"

"But we have it," I answered. "I found or 'discovered' it, Susan wrote it up, pictures have appeared in three science magazines . . . so you see, it's a done deal, Newton. No one can take it away from us."

He thought about that for a moment or two, then said, "But surely that's not all there is to it. Do you remember what you told me? About Susan, how she wasn't on the spot when you found the talon . . . how delighted she was when first you showed it to her? Well, just think: wouldn't it be great to be able to do it again? I mean, if you were to go there again, to the same site, and if you were to discover the rest or a part of this creature in the rocks, there'd be no way that anyone else could ever lay claim to it. It would be your discovery—yours and Susan's—but definitely. And where rocks and fossils, geology in general is concerned, why, you'd be established as the genuine article, not just a talented amateur but a professional with a real feel for the work."

"But I'm not a professional," I told him. "Oh, I'm fascinated by fossils—I will admit that much—but once you start talking about the classes and subclasses of species, and if you asked me to differentiate between various Devonian cephalopods, I'd simply be lost! And those are just a few things that spring immediately to mind. Oh, and something else. Perhaps I've never mentioned it but I'm not interested in being some sort of authority. There isn't a single academic atom in my whole body, and I don't want to spoil what I've already got—which is to say, a marvelous hobby."

And finally we got to it. "Then do it for me!" He blurted it out. "It *is* my life, it *is* my work and business to be expert in these things. To you a hobby—and nothing wrong with that, for you're right and it is fascinating—but it's a great deal more than that to me; it's my reason for being! You and Susan, you don't seem to know how lucky you've been in your discoveries. You almost take them for granted! Myself, I've never been half so fortunate, never found anything worth bothering about that any snotty kid with a pile of rocks and a hammer couldn't have found before me. Merely to have a connection with you and the specimens you've come across—that talon, for example—is more than I could ever have hoped for. And now there's this opportunity to go one step further, and you . . ."

"And I'm an obstinate fool," I finished it for him. "And a pretty poor friend at that—right?"

"Peter," he said, "I wouldn't take an ounce of credit. I would simply be an associate, an assistant in your work. What harm is there in that? Though of course I'd be of *real* assistance on site, knowing where to dig and which rocks and strata to explore. Now, what do you say? Why not go for it and see if we can't spring a surprise on Susan and these American people. For let's face it, we'll never have another chance like this."

So there it was, out in the open. And I honestly couldn't see my way round it; I didn't know how to turn him down. After all, what harm could it do? And it would be so easy to call it a "preliminary search" or some such (as an excuse or cover for my own weakness, of course).

But *was* I weak . . . or was I simply seeing sense? If he was all he professed to be—and I had no reason to suspect otherwise—Loomis could very well prove most useful; especially as a guide to the most likely fossil-bearing strata, the gradually eroding or weathering-out layers of rock in those crumbling sea cliffs which had contained the sickle talon and which might yet hold the stony bulk of its ancient bearer.

And without pausing to think it over, almost before I knew it, I'd said yes, okay, let's do it!

And that was that . . .

OF COURSE I REGRETTED IT ALMOST AT ONCE, but too late. Before I could even consider changing my mind, Loomis had asked me all of the relevant questions—location, terrain, distance, etc.—and I had answered him, told him almost everything, so there was no going back. I couldn't very well lie because if I did, then when Susan and the Americans got here he'd know it at once. So apart from the actual spot where I'd levered the barbed talon up from the sand and pebbles, Loomis knew everything.

And after that there was no stopping him.

We would go at once, he said, tomorrow or the day after at the latest. The weather had cleared up and it hadn't rained for a week or more; it was still blustery, but what were we, men or mice? Loomis had a van equipped with everything we'd need . . . I shouldn't concern myself with packing my tools . . . we could take our own food to eat on location . . . he'd pick me up at the shop at eight-thirty in the morning.

The one thing no one could deny about Newton Loomis: once he had his teeth into something, he wasted very little time in chewing it over! And from here on in I shall do the same; I'll try to cut a long story short . . .

WE ARRIVED AT THE BEACH AROUND TEN-THIRTY, him driving his van, and me in my old Ford. Loomis had advised me to bring the Ford in case his van broke down; he'd been having some trouble with it. But during the journey I had thought it through—thought about how Susan might react to my changing my mind with regard to Newton Loomis, and without reference to her—and had made up my mind to sidetrack him. I would still show him the little bay and beach, but not the actual spot where I'd picked up the talon. Instead I would play dumb, pretend I couldn't remember, choose a location well away from the actual site.

Which is what I did.

The bay was a crescent whose ocean-eroded cusps lay north and south. The place where I had found the toe sickle was central, at the foot of towering cliffs. But after we had scrambled down to the beach, I showed Loomis a place fifty paces south of the actual spot.

Scuffing at the sand and fallen debris with a booted foot, he backed off from the cliff well down the beach toward the incoming sea, and finally paused to take out a pair of binoculars and scan the cliff face high over the spot that I'd indicated.

"Of course, it could have been moved by the sea," he said.

"It's possible," I answered. "But the sea only comes right up to the cliffs during very high tides—like today. Also, the sickle showed little sign of having been tossed around. If such had been the case it almost certainly would have lost its sharp point and would be polished, which it isn't . . . but I would have thought all that was obvious."

"Er, quite right," he answered. "Stupid of me—but try to remember, I'm only recently acquainted with all of the facts. I haven't had much time to consider things. And even now I'm only thinking out loud." And again he put his binoculars to his eyes and scanned the cliffs.

"So what do you see?" I asked him.

"I can't be certain," he answered, "but those white layers above that ledge there could be mid-Cretaceous. And that's bang in the middle of raptor time, one hundred million years ago. In which case—"

And now he started back toward the cliffs, looking at the ground underfoot.

"—In which case we might expect to find other fossil evidence of that era?" I prompted him.

Loomis nodded, stooped, picked up a small polished trilobite fragment. "For example," he said, smiling.

"Yes, except you're four hundred million years too early!" I grinned. "For of course that's from the Cambrian."

"Eh?" Loomis looked startled, for a moment flustered. And: "Well, yes—certainly—I know *that*!" he finally replied. "I was simply making a point: the fact that this does appear to be one of those places where a variety of fossils may be found all in the one spot."

"Yes, of course you were!" I said, wondering why he was so upset. "Such as this one." For there on a half-buried boulder I had seen a much-rubbed imprint which couldn't be mistaken. "But this time it's from the right era."

Still smarting, from what I supposed was the embarrassment of his simple error—a snap assumption made on the spur of the moment, and immediately corrected—Loomis checked my new find. And: "Tree fern," he said abruptly. "A whole log of the stuff, and beautifully patterned."

"Yes," I agreed. "But badly eroded—washed by the sea—so that we know it fell from the cliffs a good many years ago."

"Well, there you go!" he snapped curtly. "Quite the little expert, aren't you?" And then, changing the subject: "Anyway, I think it's time we looked at the rocks over that ledge. And the ledge itself makes that an ideal proposition."

"What?" I looked at him and shook my head. "I can't see us climbing up there. In fact I'd say it's just about impossible!"

"Not up," he answered, "but down! I've got ropes in my van—or maybe you've no head for heights?" He seemed determined to get back at me for what he'd obviously considered several small professional slights.

In any case I shook my head. "No, heights don't especially bother me. I've done one or two quarries, as you know." In fact the idea of such a climb bothered me a fair bit, but Loomis had succeeded in needling me and I wasn't about to let him see it.

"Good!" he said, with a curt nod of his head.

And so we trekked up from the beach back to the van, first to eat from the food we'd brought with us, then to position his vehicle a little closer to the edge of the cliff...

IT WAS WELL AFTER MIDDAY when we climbed down to the ledge some twenty-five feet below the rim, and the sea was already foaming at the foot of the cliffs one hundred and more feet below that.

The ledge was maybe sixteen inches wide, more than sufficient for an expert climber, as safe a perch as one could desire—but I wasn't an expert. Loomis, on the other hand, seemed to be just that. And in fact on our way down he'd called across to me that this was scarcely a climb to test our mettle; this after I'd become mildly alarmed when a breeze came up out of nowhere.

"Eh, a breeze?" he'd called out sneeringly. "But they have real 'breezes' in the Swiss Alps, my friend! And in a good many other places where I've climbed, too. Yes, and snow to boot. No need to worry. We're well-anchored."

And we were at that, to anchor points on his van, which he had parked side-on to the edge. But no sooner were we down than Loomis snapped his fingers in disgust and said, "Damn! I've got the pitons here, but I've left the bridging rope up there. I'll go up for it."

"Bridging rope?" I said, probably a little nervously.

"A safety measure," he answered, already climbing. "We fix a piton in the cliff face on your side, another on my side, and string a rope between the two. Just a little something extra to hang on to. But it would be a complete waste of time and energy for you to come up too, so you'd be best employed having a look at this fossil-bearing stratum . . . which looks rather promising to me."

Standing there on that ledge, I glanced at the twelve-inch-deep layer he'd mentioned. Oddly, it didn't look at all promising to me! But after all, his was the professional eye.

When I looked up again, Loomis was already halfway to the top. So I made myself as comfortable as possible and waited—

—But not for long.

"Peter," he called down, his face appearing over the edge. "I'm afraid there's a bit of a problem."

"Eh?" I clung to the cliff face, craning my neck to stare up at him. "No bridging rope? But can't we use the extra length on our ropes for that?"

"No, it's not the bridging rope," he called back. "We have plenty of that. No, it's *your* rope. It's badly frayed. I saw it on my way up, just above that jutting knob of rock. There isn't that much life left in it. Worse, it's the same with my rope. I think that if I'd had anymore climbing to do it would have let me down. The stuff must have rotted through over the winter."

"But surely it's nylon, isn't it?" I could feel the breeze tugging at me again, and my alarm was mounting. Perhaps my fear showed in my voice.

"Now, don't panic!" Loomis cautioned me. "There's really no need. But you can't climb on that rope, and it appears we can't trust the rest of the stuff we brought with us because it's all from the same coil."

"But it's *nylon*!" I said again. "And from what I saw of it . . . well, it, looked okay to me."

"And to me," Loomis answered. "But even nylon can have its defects. What more can I say? This must be a bad batch from the factory. Now, look, the answer's obvious to me. We can't do anything more today, so we'll get hold of some new, superior rope and come back tomorrow or another time."

"Well, fine," I shouted. "But meanwhile I'm down here!"

"It's not a problem," he said, and his voice was very calm and controlled now. "I mean, you're safe enough right where you are—at least for the moment—aren't you?"

"For the moment, yes," I answered. "But—"

"Very well, then. So untie yourself and I'll haul your rope up, splice the good lengths together, then lower a double—or even a triple—length down to you. That way we can be certain it will take your weight. Believe me, you daren't risk climbing on what you've got there. I'm sure I only just made it myself."

And right there and then—like a light switched on inside my head—I suddenly realized that I was completely in Loomis' power. He was the difference between me and safety . . . probably between me and life itself. And nothing for it but to trust him to do what he'd proposed. But then, why shouldn't I trust him?

Before I untied myself, however, I hammered a piton into a crack in a suitable-looking slab of rock wedged in the cliff at the same height as my elbow; this simply in order to have something extra to hang on to in the event of . . . the event of what? Suddenly I wasn't at all sure . . .

But even stranded on this ledge, at least now I'd be safe enough for nine or ten minutes; sorting out the ropes shouldn't take Loomis too much longer than that. Then, provided my nerves hadn't got the better of me, I should still be strong enough to make the climb. And if I wasn't . . . then shame on me, he'd have to haul me up using the van!

Watching the end of my rope wriggling its way up the cliff and out of sight, I called these details out to him. And Loomis called back: "Yes, Peter, of course! So now stop worrying about it and just hang in there. I'll be as quick as I can."

Hang in? More like hang on! But nothing else for it.

Now, considering everything I've told you, you might think me a ridiculous, utterly naive idiot to have got myself in such a position; but I'll remind you that I had done a little climbing myself. As a sixteen-year-old on a school adventure scheme, I'd learned how to abseil. At eighteen I had owned a hang-glider, a gift from an uncle who had broken his leg flying the thing, and I in turn had flown it on the Yorkshire moors. Also, I'd done a little clambering around in those quarries that I've previously mentioned. So in fact the climb down this cliff hadn't seemed a very extraordinary thing to do. And while it now appears likely that I may have chosen a devious climbing companion, a man with some peculiar agenda of his own (and please note that I use *may* and *likely*, for even now there's no real evidence against him), there had been little or no indication of any major flaw in his makeup until that point.

Now that we had reached that point, however:

"Peter," he called down to me in a while, "more bad news, I'm afraid . . . these ropes are rotten right through. The moment I test my weight against them, they come apart! So I'm going to drive into the village and fetch help. I just want to make sure you'll be all right down there."

"No, I *won't* be all right!" I shouted back at him. "How long will you be?"

"Well," he said, "it's maybe twenty minutes to the nearest village and twenty back again. So I'll be forty-five minutes at the outside. I'm just a little concerned about the wind getting up, that's all."

"It's certainly getting up me!" I told him. "Anyway, we're wasting time and you'd better go." Then I had an idea: "Newton, wait! Why don't you telephone the coastguard? They can probably get here even quicker. And they have a rescue helicopter, don't they?"

"Good idea!" he answered. "I'll call them as soon as I get into the village. Just you hang on and keep yours eyes and ears open for them."

"Oh, I'll be listening for them, all right!" I told him. And I craned my neck again to look up at him.

He must have been flat on his belly, looking over the edge at me . . . and I shall never forget the look on his face. At the time I reckoned he must be afraid for me, and maybe he was. But on the other hand that look could have meant anything, or something else entirely.

His face was dead white, with eyes like coals in snow—a snowman's face, yes! But instead of a carrot nose, his nostrils were flared. His mouth was open, very nearly gaping or panting, and once again there was that lupine look about him—the look of a wolf crouched for the kill—a feral beast, gazing upon its trapped prey.

Too dramatic? Well, maybe. And even now I could be wrong. Anyway I didn't like it, and so to break the spell I once again said, "Newton, you'd better go."

"Well, then," he answered. "Yes, I suppose I better had. So I'll just say good-bye . . . well, for now."

HE WAS RIGHT ABOUT THE WIND: no longer a breeze but a gradually stengthening, occasionally gusting wind off the sea. Or perhaps it only felt that way to me in my predicament. But in any case, the longer I stood with my back pressed to that sheer rock wall—and not so much solid rock at that but more properly fragile slate or shale—the stronger the wind seemed to blow.

And perhaps that was why I hadn't heard Loomis starting up his van, because of the wind whistling in my ears. Odd, because I could hear the plaintive cries of the wheeling seagulls plain enough. Yes, and I could see where they'd been: their droppings on the ledge like crusts of chalk, dried out by the sun. Why, I could be standing on an inches-deep layer of the stuff; for all I knew the entire ledge might be made of it! Yet another terrifying thought: to be held in suspension here, and guano my only guard against gravity and certain death!

I thought to glance at my watch—which meant bringing my wrist up to my face, if only for a moment—which in turn meant releasing my hold on the piton. Loomis had been gone for twelve minutes. What, twelve minutes? Was that all? Incredible, for it had felt like half an hour at least!

Then, when I sent my hand back down again, groping for the piton, I could swear it moved when my fingers fastened upon it! Very well, so now I must try to hammer it more firmly home. But instead of clipping my climber's pick to my belt after using it, I had put it down on the ledge. At that time it hadn't seemed a problem; movement in general hadn't seemed a problem, not then. But now . . . ?

Inching the toe of my boot onto the pick's spiked head, I tried springing its metal haft into an upright position. That way I would be able to lean sideways and grasp it with my free hand. But my movements were stiff and jerky, and the tool went bounding from the ledge.

And the wind was now tugging at my hair, and blowing into the neck of my climbing jacket.

Do you understand my meaning when I say I froze? Have you ever been in such a funk that you couldn't move—couldn't even think—couldn't do anything except perhaps wet yourself? Well, that was me. I wasn't yet physically cold, but still I shivered like a leaf . . . and yet my legs were like warm rubber, warm from the sudden, spontaneous flow of urine. And no, I'm not ashamed to admit it.

I could no longer stare out over the sea—but I dared not look down! I had tried that and didn't like it. Down there, the marching waves were dashing against the foot of the cliffs, and I imagined I felt their impact even on my ledge. But the fallen rocks on the beach stuck up above the water in the wake of each wave, so that I knew that even as they struck there was no more than eighteen inches or so of ocean covering the sand and shingle. No way the sea would break my fall, but a certainty that I would break my neck!

I looked up—craning my neck to stare up at the rim—and prayed I might see a friendly face staring back down at me. But no such thing. I saw sky and clouds, and nothing else. Or maybe there was something else . . .

Loomis smoked a pipe, and as I stared up at the rim of the cliffs, so near and yet so far, I thought I saw a drift of blue-gray smoke. But no, surely not . . . It was only the tatters of a cloud dispersing in the wind.

My legs were no good now and I must sit down; I must lower myself until I sat down on the ledge. Oh, really? Well, just you try it. Even in your front room, with your back against a wall, it's not an entirely easy thing to do. Ah, but now try doing it on a ledge—up a hundred-foot cliff—in a wind off the sea!

But I made myself move, brought my leaden arm and wrist up to my face to check the time again. Twenty-seven minutes. I was only a little over halfway to when I could possibly hope to be rescued! And now I really *must* sit down. Indeed, my only choice was to sit or to fall.

Clinging to the piton, but at the same time trying not to strain it too much, I bent my left knee, stretched my right leg out sideways along the ledge, and so crouched down. All of this at a snail's pace—inch by inch—through what seemed like an eon of aching, trembling limbs, and my back feeling like it was on fire; until finally I could put my free hand down on the rim of the ledge . . . *which at once crumbled away!*

It was seagull shit! That's all it was!

My weight went onto the piton, which came away in my hand, turning me and toppling me forward!

My outstretched leg acted like a pivot, pushing me outward from the ledge. I tried to spring up in the air, turn about and perform some amazing aerobatic act. And don't ask me how but in fact I did somehow manage to land jarringly, with the left-hand side of my body on the ledge . . . while the rest of me succumbed to gravity as the soft rim gave way under my sudden weight! And I simply toppled lengthwise off the ledge, as easy as falling off a log.

Then it was all over—

—Everything was over.

The last thing I remember was the sheer cliff face sliding by me, and perhaps a bump or two on the way down. Then the wash of white-foaming waves, and a jut of black rocks hurtling up at me. And nothing else . . .

IV

And that's it, Peter Carson finished his story. *Since then I've sort of hung around this place. No easy matter because I'm kind of scattered, if you know what I mean. But don't ask me why I'm still here . . . maybe I was waiting for someone like you to come along. Except there is no one . . . no one like you. Just you.*

At the very last—with his last few words—emotion had caused Carson's dead voice to break up a little, and the Necroscope couldn't help thinking: *What a brave man this was. And he still is.*

But Harry's mind was wide open, unshielded, and Carson had "overheard" him. *Do you think so?* he said. *But you're wrong. In fact I didn't take to this at all well, not at first. A case of unfinished business, I suppose you'd call it. I would just have liked to know that . . . well, that everything I'd left behind me was* right! *That nothing was* wrong! *Then I think I wouldn't mind letting the sea do the rest. I mean, it's not really uncomfortable, being where I am. In fact most of the time I feel sort of lulled, you know? It's just that the way it all happened, well, it still bothers me. Oh, dear! I fear I haven't explained myself any too well.*

"You've done fine," said Harry. "And what you're trying to explain is called justice. Or maybe the need for justice, if we assume there is such a need."

And is there?

"It strikes me there very well could be."

An eye for an eye?

"That's something we'll have to see about."

Where will you begin?

"With Newton Loomis himself. I'm thinking that perhaps you took him too much on trust. So maybe it's time someone did what you failed to do. I'll check him out and see if his credentials fit his story."

His story?

"The one he told you and Susan: these authorities he loans himself out to, his qualifications, background, and his offices in York. Let's first see if he's all he professes to be. Then I might also get in touch with Susan—if that's okay with you."

Why with Susan? (An edge now in the dead man's voice.)

Harry had to be careful how he answered. "Peter, it's hard to find an easy way to say this, but if it turns out we're dealing with a murderer here—"

—There might be more than one motive? Not simply greed or professional jealousy but personal, too? Did you think I hadn't considered that, Harry? But surely I've even hinted at it: that Loomis might be more than just casually interested in Susan. So don't worry about offending my sensibilities, Necroscope. Go to it—and the sooner the better!

And so Harry went to it . . .

HE FIRST OF ALL CHECKED the telephone book. There was no office or business in York listed under Loomis' name. But there was a telephone number and an address under N. Loomis. Using the Möbius Continuum and traveling by night, Harry paid the address a visit and found himself on a dreary street in a fairly run-down district on the outskirts of the ancient city.

The house in question looked a bit dilapidated, hardly the sort of place befitting a person of Loomis' alleged qualifications . . . but there was a van parked on the short gravel driveway.

Harry thought about it and decided it meant nothing. A van is a van; there are hundreds of thousands of them; it was possible he didn't even have the right Loomis—but there might be a way to resolve that one way or the other.

And so, unusually impatient, the Necroscope found a phone booth and dialed Loomis' number. His call was answered almost at once: "Yes?"

In an assumed voice, Harry inquired: "Am I speaking to Mr. Loomis? That same bloke wot deals in fossils?"

And after a short silence: "Who is speaking?" A reasonably cultured voice, which was more or less what Harry had expected. But at the same time a seemingly cautious voice, too.

"I'm up from London," he answered. "Charlie James. And you was recommended."

"Are you a buyer?"

"I do a bit in the trade, yers," said Harry.

And following a second brief silence: "I'm afraid you have the wrong number, Mr. James. The gentleman you're after used to have this number but he moved. He's now at eight Longmore Street in the city—Ye Olde Fossil Shoppe—and his name is Mr. White. He opens at nine, I believe. You'll probably be able to see him there tomorrow."

"Funny," said Harry, sniffing. "It was your name they give me."

"Well," the other sighed, "it appears *they* got their wires crossed! Now you must excuse me." *Click!* And the receiver commenced its neutral buzzing . . .

THE NEXT MORNING Harry went to see Susan Carson. He couldn't be sure he'd find her at Carson's shop, the place that she and her late husband had made their home. In fact he was fairly sure that he *wouldn't* find her there, that she'd be back with her family; the place would hold too many memories, surely.

But he was wrong.

"A friend of Peter's?" She sounded surprised. "That's odd, because I don't recall Peter ever mentioning you. Oh!" Her hand flew to her mouth. "I hope that you'll forgive me, Mr. Keogh. I mean, that must have sounded so rude!"

"Call me Harry," he told her. "And no, I don't consider it at all rude. I know the accident was some time ago, but it must have come as a terrible shock to you. If I'd known of it sooner I would have contacted you. But even so it would have been as a stranger. And now I'm making a nonsense of everything. But I do understand. It takes a long time—and sometimes forever—to recover from certain things. And at times like that you can so easily say things without thinking. I've done it myself."

"You're very kind," she said. "But still, you didn't know Peter too well—did you? I mean, I'm sure he would have mentioned you—if he'd known you that well."

Susan Carson was small and beautiful. Her hair was glossy black, bouncing on her shoulders. Her dark eyes—looking very slightly bruised in their hollows (from lack of sleep, the Necroscope correctly supposed)—were huge under naturally curling lashes; her figure, still very young-girlish, was no less alluring for that. She and Peter had made a near-perfect pair . . .

But Harry must concentrate on his deception, for Susan had asked about his relationship with her late husband.

"We met just once or twice," he was obliged to lie. (But at least it was a white lie, and in fact he had "met" Carson once, and knew he would meet him again.) "You see, we both had an interest in fossils. Of course, Peter knew far more than me, and I was always too busy for our friendship to really get going. But after you two got together . . . I can understand well enough how Peter wouldn't have much time for anyone else! Besides, we were no more than casual acquaintances, and mostly out of touch when I was out of the country. Which was often."

"I see," she said, though she was obviously still a little puzzled. "And now?"

"Now? Oh, I see! Well, I was passing by this way, and—"

"—You came to look at the shop?"

"And mainly to pay my respects," Harry told her. "I mean, since there has been no closure, no burial, this shop is about the next best thing to . . . I mean, it's about as close as—"

"I know what you mean." She helped him out. "It's why I'm still here. Because so much of Peter is still here." And Harry believed he saw a tear forming in the corner of her eye. Turning away—ostensibly to admire the interior of the shop—he gave her the opportunity to hide the evidence of her overflowing emotions.

And in another moment he said, "The way you've got these fossils displayed is charming. Not so much a lesson in natural history or a museum as—oh, I don't know—a picture book for laymen?"

"Which is what Peter is . . . I mean was," she answered. "He never thought of himself as a professional, though I suspect he could have been one of the best in his field."

"You're probably right," Harry answered. "And the way he's got the window fixed up—or rather, the way it's fixed now—is a credit to him; to both of you, if you had a hand in it."

"No," she replied. "It's all his own work."

"I passed through York recently," Harry said then, determined to get on with his investigation. "There's a fossil store in the city that doesn't even compare with your little place." This despite the fact that he hadn't seen the other place.

"In York?" Susan glanced at him sharply, frowning now. "Do you mean Newton Loomis' place?"

Harry pretended surprise. "Loomis? No, I think the proprietor is a Mr. White." And he described "Mr. White" to her much as Peter Carson had described Loomis to him. "I didn't buy anything from him. In fact I didn't much like him."

Susan's face was looking pinched now, and the corners of her mouth had turned down. "Yes, that's him," she said. "White is Loomis' business name. It's the name he uses in his shop." Then, darting a glance at Harry: "You aren't here on behalf of Newton Loomis, are you?"

"What?" Again Harry feigned surprise. "Here on his behalf? But I don't even know the man! Is there something he's done?"

"Loomis is a bother and a pest!" she answered. "There was a time when we thought he was a friend—but he was more fraud than friend. After I came home from America . . . but you really don't want to know all that."

"If he's someone I should avoid I'd most certainly appreciate anything you can tell me about him," said Harry.

"Well, personally I would avoid him like the plague!" she answered.

"And he's been a pest, you say? Since Peter . . . er, since your bereavement?"

Susan sighed and said, "I was about to make a pot of tea. If you'll turn the sign in the doorway to Closed, and drop the latch, we'll go into the kitchen and I'll tell you what I know about Loomis."

WHEN THEY GOT SEATED in her small kitchen with their tea, she continued:

"They notified me about Peter while I was in America helping to organize a party of paleontologists. I put the American side of things on hold and flew home at once. Of course, after I'd learned the facts of the matter—how they'd found Peter's car with a rope attached, and the frayed end dangling over the sheer rim of the cliffs, so very close to the place where he'd discovered the talon—well, then I put the American thing on permanent hold. I believed I knew what had happened, and right then wasn't the best time to go digging for fossils. In fact I couldn't bear the sight of the things for, oh, quite a while."

"A talon?" said Harry, after Susan paused to sip her tea. Then he snapped his fingers. "Oh, yes! I think I may have read about that somewhere. In one of your articles, perhaps? It was a raptor claw, wasn't it?"

"Yes," she nodded. "Something like that. And I could only believe that Peter had gone back there in advance of the survey we'd planned in the hope of finding some more specimens, fossil pointers in the sea cliffs. But it was so unlike him to do such a thing without telling me—and with a rotten rope at that!"

"A rope, you say?" said Harry. "Not nylon?"

She nodded. "It puzzled me, too. And it still does. But at that time I was too stressed out to think straight. Since then, however, I've thought of little else. Peter was so *careful* with things like that, and I can't imagine what got into him to make him want to go climbing on his own. As for the rope: I had seen him using nylon lines while clambering about in the local quarries. But never *real* rope! He didn't trust the stuff."

"Maybe it was something he did on the spur of the moment." Harry shrugged. "You know, without thinking it through."

"I don't see it," she said. "To go climbing like that. And certainly not on his own."

"Perhaps it was to be a surprise for you," said Harry. "He was hoping to find something new." And to bring her more surely on track: "Could it be that he wanted to ensure he got his fair share of the limelight as the talon's original discoverer?"

"That's just what Newton Loomis said," Susan replied, favoring the Necroscope with her frown again. "But Peter wasn't a glory hound. He was a *rock* hound! Anyway, we're back to Loomis, and that's who you were inquiring about—though I'm still not quite sure why."

"Simply to know to avoid him," said Harry. "That's if he's the fraud you say he is. But tell me: why do you say that?"

"Because he was supposed to be the big know-it-all paleontologist, that's why. When all he really is is a rogue dealer—like someone who robs eggs out of birds' nests, and the rarer the species the better. Or an antique dealer, lying about the value of some old ladies' furniture, then selling it for ten times the price he paid to her. Loomis' 'offices' in York? Just a grubby little shop full of expensive and probably fake fossils! *Huh!*"

"He lied to you?"

"Oh, he did far worse than that. Out of respect for Peter, I had made up my mind not to divulge the site of his claw find. He and I had kept it to ourselves, and I decided it should stay that way. It would remain Peter's secret—and mine—so that no one else would go searching the area where he'd fallen. That would have been too much to bear. Of course my American friends respected my wishes: they might have been disappointed but they didn't press me to reveal the location . . ."

Susan paused and took a deep breath, her dark eyes narrowing a little before she continued. "In fact, everyone respected my wishes—except

Newton Loomis! I hadn't been back in England a week; I was still upside down, so full of grief; and there he was, mooching around the shop, pretending to be my friend while offering to buy me out—cheaply, of course—with his grubby hands on Peter's things, *and* wanting to have his hands on me! I could feel it: how eager he was to . . . to . . . 'comfort' me. And he even dared to ask me to show him the site—the *actual* site, I remember him saying—of my husband's find, so that he could 'continue Peter's work.' In the end I had to order him from the shop and told him never to return."

Harry nodded and said, "Well, he seems a really unpleasant character, and I shall have nothing to do with him. But what do you think he meant by asking about the 'actual' site? I thought you had kept that a secret?"

"I can only believe," she answered, "that Peter might have relented while I was away and told him it wasn't far from here, a little bay on the coast. It must be so, for I've learned that Loomis has been seen there, on the beach, searching the shingle and looking at the cliff face through his binoculars."

"Or he simply worked it out for himself," said Harry. "For he would know the spot from the police and newspaper reports—the place where they'd found Peter's car, with that rotten rope attached."

"I suppose so," Susan replied. "But whatever it was, there was something very shifty about Loomis. And the really horrible thing is that in those first few months—at a time when I was still hoping it was all a dreadful mistake and my husband would suddenly turn up out of nowhere—I honestly believe that awful man had already written him off! Every time he mentioned him it was in the past tense. Until I'd had all I could stand and told him to go."

"I don't blame you at all," said Harry. "And now it's time I should go, too. But I'm very glad to have met and spoken with you. There's just one more thing."

"Oh?"

"If it's at all possible," Harry said then, "I would very much like to see the talon—but I'll certainly understand if I can't. It's the connection with Peter, mainly. But of course it's also the sheer fantasy of it, or maybe the reality? To be able to touch a thing as fabulous and as tragic as that."

She stood up and answered, "It'll soon be gone from here, but until it's collected by the museum I keep it in the safe in the workshop. Wait here."

In less than a minute she was back, handing him the barbed claw. "There it is, and to be honest I'll be glad to get rid of it. There are far too many memories, and but for this talon . . . if Peter hadn't found it . . ." She offered a sad, helpless shrug.

Harry understood. And he also understood—far better than any other living man could ever hope to understand—the *power* of this relic of Earth's past. For as he held it and opened his metaphysical mind to it, it was as if the thing spoke to him:

It spoke of vast cycad forests, of murky lakes where giant reptiles and plated fishes swam, of a moon more smooth than the one we know, lighting the hunter's night. It spoke of the chase and of the fleeing prey, the ripping of soft flesh and grinding of bones. And Harry heard, as if from a million miles away, the triumphant bellows of a killer born, echoing in tree-fern woods that had long since turned to coal . . .

It reminded him of something, a thing forgotten until this very moment: a dream he had dreamed on the selfsame beach where the fossil was discovered. But like the dream itself the memory came and went—even as fleeting as that— and Susan Carson was saying:

"Is something wrong?"

"Eh?" Harry started, but quickly recovered, and said, "Oh, no, nothing—I was daydreaming, that's all." Then, handing the talon back to her, he said, "Now I really must be going. But if I've caused you any trouble—if I've in any way disturbed you—then please accept my apologies."

"No," she said, smiling at last. "Actually, I can see why Peter would have liked you. It's almost as if he were close by, listening to us talking." And then, before the Necroscope could say anything more: "But don't worry, Harry, for I know now that he'll never be close again. And it *is* closure, of a sort."

Then, as Harry left the shop and went out into the street:

Thanks, Harry, said Peter Carson, his voice drifting in off the distant sea. And:

"Don't mention it," said the Necroscope gruffly . . .

———

293

AS FAR AS HARRY WAS CONCERNED, the case against Loomis had been proved beyond any reasonable doubt; Carson's fears—his worst fears—were realized. The only relief lay in the fact of Susan Carson's total rejection of the man; not only his lustful intentions (always assuming that she and her husband had interpreted them correctly) but also his avaricious pursuit of the rare and presumably valuable giant raptor remains.

So now all that remained was to prepare a suitable lure—indeed, an irresistible lure—and then to spring the trap...

V

Harry spent the next weekend boning up on geology, fossils, and paleontology in general. It could do no harm to learn something of his subject, the basics at least, before attempting to beard Loomis in his lair, as it were...or rather, to draw him *out* of his lair.

With that in mind, Monday morning he traveled to York via the Möbius Continuum, and a minute or so after 9:30 A.M. called in at Ye Olde Fossil Shoppe.

The place was styled after an antique shop, which in a way it was. But these were antiques out of prehistoric time. Loomis was unmistakable behind a partitioned glass counter with an old-fashioned till, from where he could keep watch on his potential customers as they moved in the aisles between display cabinets.

The Necroscope wasn't in a hurry; for some thirty minutes, with his hands behind his back and leaning slightly forward, he moved from cabinet to cabinet, apparently admiring the exhibits in their lined boxes or on their marble plinths. Every so often he would pause before this or that fossil, nod knowingly to himself, and study the specimen minutely before finally moving on. Until eventually he was alone in the shop with its proprietor.

And at last Newton Loomis came out from behind the counter to approach him. "Can I perhaps, er, interest you in something? Is there anything special I can show you?"

"Special?" said Harry, straightening up. "Hmm! But they're all quite special to me."

"Ah!" said Loomis. "Then you're a student—of paleontology, that is."

"No, not really." Harry shook his head. "I just find these fossils fascinating, that's all. Their variety—their stories, written in stone—the fact that they were here, alive, before we came down from the trees."

"Before we even went up into them!" Loomis laughed.

"Is that so?" said Harry. And with a shrug: "Well, yes, I suppose so. And so, as you see, I'm little more than a novice."

"But a clever novice," said Loomis. "With a discerning eye for the nicer, rarer specimens? I can see that much, at least!"

"Rarer specimens?" Harry raised an eyebrow. "What, here? I mean, there are some decent ammonites in that display case over there, and a very nice trilobite right here . . . but rare? A few bony fishes might liven things up—perhaps the odd pterodactyl fragment? But I have to say I've seen nothing of the Dinosauria at all. I would have thought a small ichthyosaur at least, or a raptor claw at the *very* least! I've heard there are plenty such in the cliffs nearby. But if not the real thing, then why not a plaster model or two? Er, not that I would ever think to criticize, you understand."

Loomis' false smile had started to fall away before Harry mentioned those magic words "raptor claw," but from that moment on his attitude visibly changed. Now narrow eyed and deadly serious, he said, "Fossils of that sort do of course exist—they are found from time to time in England—but they're extremely rare. I can't imagine where you might have picked up the notion that any of the nearby cliffs are full of them. Which cliffs do you mean, exactly?"

Harry waved an airy hand. "The sea cliffs west of here. To my knowledge there are dinosaur remains in those cliffs. Indeed it's not so very long ago, on one of your local beaches, that I was fortunate enough to witness the discovery of a raptor claw. A toe claw, huge and sickle shaped."

Loomis had paled a very little. "Really?" he said, cocking his head on one side inquiringly, and falling back a pace. "And this on a local beach, you say?" And then, inhaling sharply and with his eyebrows shooting up, as if he'd just remembered something: "Ah, yes! You're quite right. It had slipped my mind but I do recall just such a find. It caused quite a stir in certain magazines . . . a young woman wrote an article on the thing, yes. But a talon's a talon, and one fossil does not an ossuary make. I have to protest your statement that there are *plenty* of these things. If that were so there'd be paleontologists all over the place!"

"Well, I was there," Harry insisted. "I saw the thing discovered, simply picked up from the shingle near the foot of the cliffs. And in fact I was hunting for fossils myself—well, in my entirely haphazard, amateurish way, you understand. *Huh!* The nicest thing *I* ever found was a beautifully preserved bony fish on the beach at Lyme Regis. But a raptor talon—that was something! And the young man and woman who found it, well, they were delighted. As for the man himself—I can't remember his name, but he seemed something of an authority—he was just bubbling over with it, full of himself; so excited that he didn't at all mind talking to me about the fossil, even though I could barely follow his drift . . ."

The Necroscope paused, shrugged and said, "But there, I've probably bored you to death, Mr. er—?"

"White," said Loomis. "David White. And no, not at all. In fact, I wish you'd go on. This beach of yours sounds a fascinating place." He was staring directly into Harry's eyes now, and there was that certain something about his rapt gaze that Peter Carson had mentioned; he was like an eager—perhaps an *overly* eager—undecided or suspicious wolf, "But first you must tell me what you're doing here in York. You're not local, are you? I think I detect something of a northeastern accent. Also, there seem to be several odd coincidences here."

"Coincidences?" Harry played the innocent.

"Well, yes," said Loomis. "Quite a few of them. You see, I frequently visit the local beaches myself; one never knows what one might find. Also, once you'd mentioned it, I remembered the toe claw to which you referred. But perhaps more importantly, I too knew the young man who found the claw . . . or rather, I knew him by reputation, because we had the same business interests."

Then, with a glance aside at a nearby display case, Loomis tut-tutted and said: "Hmm! Look at this, some visitor must have bumped into the case." He made a slight adjustment to the position of one of the specimens, and said, "There. These asteroids are rather pretty, don't you think?"

"I beg your pardon?" said Harry, staring hard at a display of fossils half-buried in white sand. "I mean, surely those are echinoids, sand dollars or sea urchins. Asteroids, on the other hand, are more properly fossil starfish! Their very name gives them away."

"Ah! A slip of the tongue," said Loomis. "Well, let's not quibble about it. But it does prove your credentials: that you may be a novice, but not quite the novice you pretend, eh?"

"Your credentials, too," said Harry. "Well, in a way. For of course the asteroids *are* a class of echinoderm. And so despite your 'slip of the tongue,' still you were half-right. It's easy to confuse the various species—or so I would suppose."

"Well, well, *well!*" said Loomis, wearing a painted smile, which caused Harry to recall how this man had hated being corrected by Peter Carson. "So then, I'm at least *half*-right, am I? It seems you have a fairly extensive knowledge of your subject, and of course it's always a pleasure to meet and talk to someone on more or less equal terms."

"Hardly that!" Harry shrugged. "I read books, that's all. And as for why I'm here in York for a few days: my great-aunt, Edith Millifer, was buried Saturday morning." (He had done his homework. Ms. Millifer's obituary had appeared in a local newspaper; only an hour or so ago the Necroscope had spoken to her "in person," first to introduce himself, as was his wont, then to ask her permission to use her in his subterfuge—to which she'd readily agreed.)

"Oh, dear!" said Loomis. "My dear fellow. You have my sincere—"

"There's really no need," Harry cut him off. "For the fact is Edith was something of an old fossil herself!" (He hoped she would forgive him for that.) "But she was after all family, and so I've done my duty."

Whatever suspicions Loomis had harbored, they now seemed to have been assuaged. "Listen," he said. "I've really enjoyed our talk. We seem to have so much in common, and I find it fascinating that you were in on the discovery of that talon on the beach. Yes, and I'd be very interested to learn more about your conversation with the chap who found it." He paused, glanced at his watch, and continued: "Look, it's much too early for lunch, but I often have brunch about this time. There's a little café just across the street, and since at the moment I've no customers, I'd be delighted if you'd join me for a coffee and a sandwich, Mr.—?"

"It's Keogh," said Harry. "Harry Keogh. And thanks for the invitation. My pleasure, I assure you . . ."

"SO, YOU SAW THE TOE claw collected, as it were?" Loomis looked across the tiny table at Harry, who looked right back at him.

"Yes, and I know precisely where it was picked up. She—the young woman, I think her name was Susan?—believed it must have weathered out and fallen from the cliff, and her companion agreed. He said he must think about contacting a museum here in Yorkshire, to see if they'd maybe organize and finance a search. But his wife—I take it she was his wife—didn't think that would be necessary; she knew people in America who were certain to be far more interested. As for yours truly . . . well, I'll let you into a secret: I even contemplated doing it myself! I mean, can you imagine it? A rank amateur like me, finding a raptor on a beach in Yorkshire? What a wonderful thing!"

"Indeed," said Loomis, nodding. "So why didn't you, er, do it yourself?" And once again he was wearing that wolfish look.

"Well, first of all the expense," said Harry. "And I could hardly claim the *right* to it, now could I? I hadn't 'discovered' the talon, and I certainly wasn't a professional. I mean, there are such things as ethics—aren't there?"

"To hell with ethics!" said Loomis. "Ethics? Just think of the boon to paleontology, to science. Anyway, neither were they professionals. Why, they never did do anything about it—not a thing! No search, no Americans, nothing. And that cliff remains unexplored. As for that young man—his name was Peter Carson, by the way—he . . ." But there Loomis paused. Perhaps he'd seen something in the Necroscope's eyes. And so Harry preempted him:

"But he did try to do *something* about it, surely? A rather stupid something, that cost him dearly?"

"You...know about that?" (Loomis's wolfish gaze was very intense now.) "You know that he fell from those cliffs?"

"It was in the papers." Harry shrugged. "Even on the television. I heard about it when I was home briefly from the south of France, where I'd been helping my parents do up an old farmhouse. So now that I'm back for good I've researched everything I could find on it. Yes, I know he fell; also that there's been no further mention of a search. It appears Susan Carson doesn't want to reveal the location; which in the circumstances is perfectly understandable, I suppose. The only thing I *don't* understand is how her husband came to fall there."

"There?" Loomis was now leaning forward in his chair, his coffee long since gone cold. "Where, there?"

"Eh?" said Harry. "Oh! Why, so far away from the real site—the actual spot where he'd found the fossil—of course!"

"Not the actual spot," said Loomis, his words a mere whisper. "You're saying that we—I mean he—that he was climbing in the wrong place?"

Harry shook his head, apparently in defeat. "How might one explain it? Yet that's how it appears."

Loomis flopped back in his seat—and at once straightened up again. "How can you be sure he was in the wrong place?"

"I told you I had researched the whole thing," said Harry. "That includes the police report, which is on file at the local coroner's office. There are some good photographs, too. And the place where they found Carson's car and that frayed rope is nowhere near where he took the talon from the shingle."

"But you...you could find your way back there?"

"Oh, yes," said Harry. "Absolutely. I've already told you: I know the exact spot."

"Well, then," said Loomis. "And now we get to it. Isn't it a clear, obvious fact, Mr. Keogh, that our coming together like this is a lot more than sheer happenstance? It's anything but a coincidence—am I right?"

Harry smiled and said, "Have I tried to hide that fact?"

"Well, if you did, then you failed miserably," Loomis answered, frowning. "Very well, so why have you come to me?"

"Because I may need your advice, your expert's eye," Harry replied.

"Yes, fossils fascinate me. And yes, I've read all the books, walked the beaches, and have a small insignificant collection. But those cliffs we've been talking about, they contain something else entirely. And I'd be perfectly happy to share my knowledge with the right person. And when you said 'to hell with ethics' a minute ago, I knew I'd found the right person!"

Loomis leaned closer yet. "A joint effort?"

"And joint rewards," said Harry. "For me the pleasure, and a little something to remember it by? And for you the fame."

Loomis narrowed his eyes. "You *could* have gone it alone."

Harry shook his head. "I don't have the expertise. Knowing the difference between an asteroid and a sea urchin won't do me any good if I can't tell a piece of dinosaur's vertebrae from a chunk of rock, now, will it? It's not as if the creature will be glaring at me out of that sheer cliff face. It'll be there, but hidden in the strata. And besides, I don't think I'd care to go climbing those cliffs on my own. You might say I've learned the error of Carson's ways."

Now Loomis sat up straight again. "You can climb?"

"I've climbed in Scotland," said Harry. And that was true, but he couldn't remember where, when, or why. Just another part of his lost period, he supposed. "I think I could manage those cliffs all right. There's a ledge near the top and, incidentally, that's where Susan reckoned the rest of our beast might be. Her husband agreed with her. That's as much as was said in my presence; perhaps they realized they were giving too much away."

Loomis was staring hard at Harry again, but eventually he said, "I find your proposition most appealing. And it couldn't have come at a better time: the weather's ideal, and a respectable period of time has passed since Carson's accident. Someone was bound to follow this trail sooner or later, and it might as well be us. How are you fixed for a date? My business can wait. I could be ready tomorrow, at least for a preliminary investigation. But the way I see it, if we were to climb down the cliff face directly above the spot where Carson found the talon—"

Harry nodded and finished it for him: "—It shouldn't take you too long to determine whether or not the rest of the creature is still there in the rocks, right? Well, I'm all for it."

"Tomorrow," said Loomis. "Nine o'clock, at my shop. We can use my van, and I'll fix us up with climbing gear and something to eat and drink. How does that suit you?"

"The sooner the better," said the Necroscope. "It suits me down to the ground—or down the cliff face, anyway!" He rubbed his hands. "So then, that's decided and I'll see you at nine in the morning."

Loomis called for the waiter to freshen their coffees. But while Harry made a brief note in a small black notebook, he was aware of the other's intense, penetrating, wolfish gaze. Averting his eyes, he pretended not to notice . . .

AT 10:15 A.M. THE NEXT DAY, the Necroscope and Loomis were down on the beach looking up at the cliffs.

"You are quite sure that this is it?" Loomis was frowning, occasionally biting his bottom lip in frustration . . . and Harry believed he knew why. The man saw how badly he'd fallen prey to a red herring, Peter Carson's ploy to put him off the scent. He knew that Carson had had a change of heart, and that he, Newton Loomis, had been shown the wrong location. His only consolation must be that falling prey to a ruse wasn't nearly as serious—or as fatal—as falling off a cliff!

"Yes," Harry replied, "this is the spot, and the talon was right there." He kicked at the sand and shingle with the toe of his shoe. "Apart from being black, the claw looked like new, as if its owner had lost it just a moment ago. It must have fallen recently else the sea would have touched it. And Carson . . . well, he wasn't stupid: he licked the claw and said he couldn't taste any salt."

"He licked it?" Loomis' eyes opened wider. "A nice touch, that. Not many would have thought of it."

"Oh, he was a smart one," Harry answered. "No doubt about that. Academically smart, that is, but not much horse sense. Or else he was too much of an eager beaver."

"Oh?" said Loomis.

"What, to go climbing up there?" Harry shifted his gaze to the sheer cliff face. "Alone, on a rotten rope? It doesn't make too much sense, now, does it?"

Loomis shrugged it off, albeit awkwardly. "The blind passion of a dedicated but hopeless amateur—no offense intended, I assure you—ignoring the danger and taking chances in order to pursue his obsession."

Harry nodded. "I suppose you're right," he said. And then, more to the point: "Have you marked the spot?"

Loomis indicated a piece of driftwood—the gnarled white sea-sculptured branch of a tree, half-buried in the sand—and said, "It's in an almost direct line. And on high, right on the rim, there's that big gorse bush. If we drop our lines to flank that bush, there's no way we can miss our target."

"Then let's go," said Harry. "And if there's a dinosaur up there in that cliff—"

"—Then he's all ours," said Loomis . . .

TWENTY-FIVE MINUTES LATER, checking the ropes as Loomis lowered them over the cliff edge, Harry said, "Nylon. And good quality. Each one of these would take three men. They could be cut halfway through and they'd still take the strain."

Loomis stopped short and said, "Not necessarily. Sometimes a line is faulty but the fault is in the core; you can't always see it from the outside. Still, I'm pretty sure these lines are okay, else I wouldn't be using them."

"No, of course not," said Harry. But then, as Loomis made ready to lower himself over the edge: "Aren't we taking a bridging rope? You know, as extra security when we've got down onto that ledge?"

Loomis stopped what he was doing to stare long and hard at the Necroscope. And after a moment: "We've got more than enough length in our ropes to cover that," he said. "But listen, don't tell me you're getting cold feet or something. I mean, you have mentioned some previous climbing experience—in Scotland?"

"Cold feet?" said Harry. "No, nothing of the sort. And I'm quite sure you know exactly what you're doing. It's just that I don't want to end up another eager beaver, if you know what I'm saying."

This time Loomis merely glanced at Harry, half smiling his wolfish smile before starting down the rope. "Do you know something?" he said, as he disappeared from view. "I'm beginning to worry about you. I know that I can rely on *myself*, but it seems to me that you're . . . well, not too reliable: a very changeable sort of fellow. Your heart's not really in this, now is it?"

Harry looked down over the rim at him. "It's just that I'm the cautious type," he said. "And this is—you know—a very lonely spot. There'll be no one around to help us out if we get in trouble. A passing thought, that's all. So don't worry about it. I should be okay."

Loomis paused to look up, narrowed his eyes, and answered, "Well, I'm not so very sure about that." And then, as if coming to a decision: "Now, don't you concern yourself. It isn't everyone who has the nerves to manage stuff like this. So if there's a problem—any problem at all—you stay right where you are. I shall be perfectly fine on my own, and I certainly won't hold it against you . . ." But the look in the man's eyes was scathing, taunting.

Pretending to take the bait, the Necroscope made a show of gulping and rapid eye-blinking, before angrily replying, "There *isn't* a problem, I assure you! And I'll be right behind you."

"Good!" Loomis grinned up at him, and carried on down past the gorse bush . . .

TAKING A LITTLE LESS than two minutes, the climb was easy. When Harry reached the ledge Loomis was already studying the face of the cliff. His excitement was plain as he brushed away dirt and chalky seagull detritus. And with a glance in Harry's direction he said, "You know, this is looking very, *very* promising!"

For once Loomis knew what he was talking about. And as for the Necroscope, he was absolutely certain it was promising. For as he opened that special receiver in his metaphysical mind, he could actually *feel* the prehistoric world. It was right here in these rocks, in this cliff face, in the strata laid down all of those millions of years ago.

And it reminded him of something.

There it was again:

The thundering of giant reptiles, the snaky floundering of primordial plated fishes, and the whup-whup-whupping *wings of leathery, anvil-headed bat-things. The cycad forests and soupy, steaming lakes, under a moon with fewer craters than the one we know today. And the bellowing in the gloomy tree-fern woods. It was Harry's beach dream all over again. His dream of—*

"Pterosaur!" Loomis whispered. "Look, *look!* This monstrous great display crest on its beautifully preserved head! It's got to be Tapejara—I cannot be mistaken—and almost full-grown. But man, from the size of the skull the wingspan must be all of twelve or thirteen feet! And here are the wing stems all folded back. An almost complete specimen! But what an incredible find! A once-in-a-lifetime discovery which has to be worth a fortune. And it's all—"

"Ours," said Harry. "Or yours? But it should be—it would be—Peter Carson's, if he was still alive. But he isn't, is he, Mr. White? Or should I call you Mr. Loomis?"

"Eh, what's that?" Loomis looked at him, cocked his head a little on one side and smiled his wolfish smile. He didn't seem at all surprised. "By all means, Mr. Keogh. Call me Newton Loomis; call me anything you please—but don't forget to call me persistent! Persistent, oh, *yes!* And I've been looking for something like this all my life."

Loomis stopped speaking, sidestepped along the ledge a few paces away from the Necroscope, unclasped a knife and commenced scraping at the slaty rock at what might be the location of the pterosaur's hindquarters. In another moment, however, matching the change in his demeanor, his strokes became a lot more savage.

Noting Loomis' suddenly wild appearance, Harry made ready for whatever trouble might be brewing, and said, "Well, then, now that your so-called 'persistence' has paid off and you've found what you were looking for, causing so many problems and so much pain to so many people, what's next?"

"Ah, but now it's your turn!" said Loomis, at once pausing in his digging, his face damp and red where he turned it in the Necroscope's direction. "Now you tell me, Mr. Keogh—Mr. Harry bloody Keogh—what exactly have *you* been looking for? For you see, it's been fairly obvious for some time now that you aren't much interested in hunting for fossils . . . but you've certainly been doing more than a little *digging around*, now haven't you?" And then, without waiting for a reply, but glaring at Harry out of the corner of his eye, he continued his attack on the cliff.

The way Loomis was hacking at the cliff was hardly an example of ideal paleontology; large scabs of shale, fused together with an eternity of seagull guano, were shearing from the sheer cliff face and tumbling into space. But neither Loomis' sudden frenzy nor the Necroscope's apparently perilous situation bothered the latter too much. His plan was already laid—had been in place even before he met Newton Loomis—and he believed it to be infallible. It was simply this:

If Loomis tried to deal with him as he'd dealt with Carson, Harry would conjure and enter a Möbius door, exiting on the rim of the cliff. Then he would have a choice: either to wait there for Loomis to climb up, or cut the ropes and leave the murderer to the same fate suffered by Peter Carson. An eye for an eye.

At least, that was his plan . . .

But right now—

In his own unique way Harry was aware of a lot more going on here than Loomis' wild attack on the cliff. All of that was in the physical world, the world of here and now, while Harry's awareness was metaphysical and currently concerned with the far distant past . . . while *yet* being of the present! A paradox, but by no means a contradiction of terms.

For Harry *was* the Necroscope, with a talent which was frequently a two-edged sword. In precisely the same way as he felt the presence of the dead, so the dead sensed him. But there are dead and there are dead, and not all of them are people . . . and not all of *them* are friendly.

"*Ah!*" exclaimed Loomis, a gasp of astonishment rather than a spoken word, breaking in on Harry's amazing temporal perceptions, his rapport with . . . with something other. "Look!" Loomis went on, his tone hoarse with excitement. "Do you see it, or am I totally insane?"

And Harry thought, *Quite likely, the last!* But he already knew what Loomis had unearthed. It was the thing in the Necroscope's mind, or one of them: his contact with the dead past.

"It's the raptor-thing," he said, before Loomis could even draw breath. "The beast whose claw weathered out first and fell to the sand and shingle down below. Your persistence really has paid off now. But was it worth it? To kill a man for a chunk of rock?"

Loomis wasn't listening, or if he was he wasn't paying any attention. "My God, it's here!" he whispered. "This whole black mass beneath the loose shale. I've never in my life seen a more perfect specimen. It's . . . it's *huge!*"

As he spoke he dislodged another great sheet of shale that went clattering down to the beach, and his bottom jaw fell open more yet at what was revealed: a skull some thirty inches long, with all of its wicked teeth intact.

"It was hunting the pterosaur," said Harry with certainty, as he sidestepped along the ledge toward Loomis to get a better look (this despite that he was putting himself in danger . . . or perhaps in order to put himself in danger?). "It had just caught up with its prey when the cliff avalanched down on them, trapping them under tons of rock just as you see them here."

"Oh?" Loomis cried, his voice shrill now. "Really? And you know that for a fact, do you? Well then, you must be another of these oh-so-clever bastard amateurs like dear old Peter Carson. Him and his oh-so-precious Susan, sitting tight on their little secret so that no one else in the world might ever find it. But I *have* found it, and it's all mine. Not yours, Mr. Keogh—not even the smallest part of it—but *all* mine!"

"You poor demented bastard," said the Necroscope, *aware in his way of a bestial sniffing, of great nostrils sucking at the air, tasting a strange, hitherto unknown scent: the sweet smell of Man which—courtesy of Harry's weird talent—the prehistoric creature had detected from beyond the grave and across all the ages.*

"Demented?" Loomis turned swiftly on Harry (whose concentration was momentarily elsewhere, distracted by emotions—more properly instincts—out of time, which were suddenly impinging on his present). "Why, yes, you're probably right," Loomis continued. "Indeed, I've suspected it for quite some time. It's my obsessive nature, you see. Well, that and the fact that I *can't stand* you bloody know-it-alls!"

He turned on his rope like a spider on a thread, continued to gouge at the cliff with his jagged-edged knife, and followed the curve of the pterosaur's broken spine with an arcing, sweeping slash of arm and hand. And just a moment too late, the Necroscope saw what Loomis was about.

The knife left the cliff face and slashed at Harry's rope. Stretched taut, the rope offered no resistance. But in the selfsame instant of time Harry had adjusted his balance, flattening himself to the naked rock.

Loomis' knife had a guard and heavy bone handle. Having cut Harry's line he continued the downward sweep of his hand, crashing the handle into his intended victim's right temple. And the lights almost went out—but not quite.

Harry fell to the ledge and clung for dear life. Too dazed to conjure a door to the Möbius Continuum, he felt the thin wet trail of blood on his cheek and jaw, tasting it where it leaked into the corner of his mouth. He tasted it . . . and so did something else.

All of its life, spent by the lakes and water holes in the steamy cycad forests, the raptor-thing had been a great hunter. And as in life, so in death. Dinosaur dreams had been buried in these rocks for all those many millions of years: terror of the pterosaur and savage triumph of the predator both, cut short by a rockfall in an age before the first ape swung in the trees.

But the mind goes on—even the minds of monsters—and in their dreams the hunters hunt as before, with skills more terrible yet. The Necroscope was the lure, his blood the scent, his weird talent the trigger. He might even have become the victim, but that was not to be.

Aware of Newton Loomis bending over him—his treacherous wolf smile a snarl now—Harry mumbled, "Well, why not? Come on if you can. Come and get me!"

But he wasn't speaking to Loomis.

The madman heard the gunshot *crack!* of splitting rock, but Harry was the only one who heard the bellowing out of time, the triumphant trumpeting of the beast. The ledge shuddered; a skeletal pterosaur wing broke loose and flapped one last time, fragmenting as it fell; Loomis glanced over his shoulder, barely in time to see . . . an utterly impossible thing: those great raptor jaws snapping open as the cliff face split asunder!

Then, caught up in the teeth, he screamed. Screamed as the ledge and the cliff, the stony monsters and all, leaned outward and toppled over into the abyss, snapping his line like so much thread and taking him with them to a well-deserved end.

As for the Necroscope: Falling from the ledge through a Möbius door, Harry exited the Continuum at the ocean's rim in time to witness all of that awesome tonnage crashing down at the foot of the cliffs, and to feel the shuddering of the sand under his feet . . .

LATER.

Finding himself a flat-topped boulder, Harry sat for a few minutes laving his wound with a handkerchief soaked in the sea. He knew the bruise would disappear quickly enough, and the salt would help heal the cut. *His* wounds would heal, yes, but as for Susan Carson, hers would take a lot longer.

"Your wounds, too," the Necroscope told Peter Carson, sensing him there. But:

No, came the answer, a whisper from far, far away. *I think I'll be okay, think I'll be able to let go now. You see, things stopped hurting the moment that mad bastard hit the ground, and so at last I'm able to stop worrying about it. Newton Loomis is gone for good, buried in as much fossil debris as even he could have lusted after.*

"He was a murderer," said Harry. "You should rest easy now in the certain knowledge that the Great Majority won't have any truck with him. There'll be no helping Loomis where he is now."

Ah, no, said the other. *I think I'll be best avenged after I talk to him— which I must while I've still got it together, and when he's accepted what's happened—and explain to him who* you *are, and who put you onto him. That will be the best time.*

But Harry shook his head. "You don't want to go there," he said. "I've already been there and I didn't like it."

Oh?

Harry nodded. "He's under a hundred tons of rock, piled up against the foot of the cliff. He's buried with a creature that dreams of the hunt, with all of its memories made fresh. And he is the prey. He's running even as we speak—by steamy pools in tree-fern forests—pursued by a hunter who can't catch him but who won't give in for another hundred million years. That's the grand irony of it: that all his life, by hook or by crook, Newton Loomis has hunted for fossils—"

—And now, by hook and by crook, a fossil is hunting him?

"Exactly," said Harry. "He's the exception that proves the rule. He won't continue to do, but will be done to. And really, you don't want to go there. I think you'd feel sorry for him."

And after a moment: *You're right, of course,* said Carson, his voice gradually fading away . . .

AN HOUR LATER the Necroscope abandoned Loomis' van on the outskirts of a small village some ten miles inland, then took the Möbius route home to Edinburgh . . .

RESURRECTION

Harry Keogh had dreamed a monstrous dream, indeed a nightmare, but one so real it had seemed like life. It had been *his* life, lived in the space of a single night, but such an *amazing* life! In the dream he had been gifted with astounding, even frightening, talents; they came from genes passed down from his Russian grandmother, through his beloved mother, to Harry. He was like a faith healer or a layer-on of hands, but instead of hands he used his metaphysical mind. And his cures—mental rather than physical—were not for the living but the dead. He befriended and gave succor, like a life after life, to the teeming dead, the so-called Great Majority. (Moreover, he gave the gift of death to the undead . . . which some of them even appreciated.)

And in Harry's dream there were victims, innocent victims of life and of undeath. And no one to comfort or avenge them—no one to talk to them and ease their troubled minds—except Harry, the man they called the Necroscope.

He dreamed of Mary Keogh, his beloved Ma, and of how she'd been murdered by his stepfather, drowned beneath the ice in the river that flowed past their home. And that was the real nightmare, the worst imaginable nightmare, because Harry blamed himself that he'd ever let such a tragedy happen. But how could it have been otherwise, since he himself had been little more than an infant at the time? Which is to say that *in his dream* he had been an infant. And in that same dream all he could do was wait until he was big enough, powerful enough, to wreak vengeance on the madman who had taken—stolen away from him, and away from life itself—the one he'd loved the most.

And so Harry's dream continued, an interminable nightmare, but so detailed, so real—so filled with fears and fantasies, with men and monsters, weird worlds and alien adventures, loves and losses—that however briefly, the waking world was forgotten entirely as the dream became reality.

Reality . . . all bar that greatest loss of all, whose truth *he could not bear*: the loss of his dear Ma, her life's aura extinguished, snuffed like a candle, leaving only her memory like a thin spiral of scented smoke, and the empty shell of her poor cold body drifting under the ice . . .

HARRY STARTED AWAKE wanting it, *needing* it to have been a nightmare. His Ma wasn't dead—*she* couldn't possibly be dead—not that golden, glowing, smiling face leaning over him, her warmth bathing him, her soft flesh and sweet smell cradling his infant form—not gone forever! It was the *way* of it that he couldn't accept: murdered, drowned, destroyed by a madman; the knowledge that he could never visit her grave, not if it had happened the way of his dream. What? To sit on a riverbank and converse with a poor, tormented creature—his dear Ma—who had lived only one third of her appointed time, whose fleshless corpse now lay entangled in the slime and rotting vegetation of a riverbed in Scotland? What was that for a grave? No, it *couldn't* have happened like that! It must be something that he'd dreamed! Nothing but a monstrous nightmare!

And because the Necroscope refused to accept it, it simply wasn't so. It *hadn't* happened like that. Not at all . . .

Then, coming more fully awake, Harry's terror ebbed and he knew that he'd been nightmaring, and that things weren't really as bad as he had dreamed them. They were certainly bad—though how or why, he couldn't say precisely—but not nearly as bad as all that.

His mother was dead, yes, and she had died when he was yet an infant, true—but not at the hands of a madman, no. It had been . . . an *accident*! Yes, of course! She and Harry's stepfather both, in a car crash, and her grave was in that little cemetery in Bonnyrig. He would go there today— this morning, as soon as he was up—to pay his respects and let her know how things had worked out: how at last he'd found his wife and son, not in the alien world of his nightmares but here on Earth, in Harden, the village of his youth, where he and Brenda had come up together. Indeed, he might even take Brenda and the child with him to see his mother . . . except in that case he must refrain from talking to her, because his wife and son wouldn't understand . . .

HARRY WENT THERE, to the cemetery; he went alone for the afore-said reason, and because he so desperately desired to talk with his Ma. He went to her grave—which, oddly enough, he experienced some difficulty in locating, because he couldn't remember having buried her there—and he sat in the morning chill, with his coat buttoned tightly about him against a wind that swirled parched brown leaves over silent plots. But the strang-est thing of all: his Ma's plot was silent, too!

Harry knew she was there—he sensed her presence as only the Nec-roscope could—but she wasn't answering him. It was as if he had called her on the telephone, and his Ma had picked it up. But while he knew she could hear him as clear as day, still she refused to reply.

For the first time in Harry's life, his mother didn't want to talk to him.

Worse still, when he probed the psychic aether with all of his meta-physical might, she resisted him! And then, if only for a single fleeting moment, he sensed her cringing there; his own Ma, shrinking down into herself in a place beyond life—as if she feared him and what he might do next.

And for all that he sat there on her cold slab that lacked an inscription, calling and calling, Mary Keogh kept her peace. She made no answer, leaving her son alone with only the keening wind and skittering leaves to keep him company.

And the Great Majority were silent too, so that the Necroscope could only wonder what he'd done—or what they, like his mother, *suspected* he might do—that so frightened them . . .

LATER:

Harry wondered why he hadn't thought of it before. He felt astonished that the idea hadn't dawned on him until now. It was because she was his mother, of course. And he supposed he'd put it to the back of his mind because the idea was so very frightful, indeed *terrible* in its conception and perhaps even blasphemous . . . yet it could well mean absolution for the Necroscope, so torn by his great loss.

Yes, she was his mother, so very long dead and buried that by now she might even be satisfied to lie still in her grave—or afraid to move—like a man so long imprisoned that the very thought of freedom is a terror in itself.

Ah, but if suddenly, without warning, she should find herself alive . . . what then?

The idea grew on him, and he had the power. He had brought back Trevor Jordan; Penny, the poor innocent; Bodrogk the Thracian warlord, dead for two thousand years; even Paddy, a mongrel dog! Yes, even a dog, because he couldn't bear the tears of its young owner. And yet his own mother lay still in her lonely grave. His Ma and all her dust—all of the *materia medica,* the essential salts of her very being—with her!

HARRY COULDN'T ANY LONGER resist it. Shielding his mind so that the Great Majority wouldn't know what he was about, he returned to the graveyard in the dead of night and exhumed his mother in her coffin. He was strong beyond reason, beyond belief, and the work scarcely taxed him at all. So that when Mary Keogh's oaken casket lay exposed, it was a relatively simple task to stand in the grave, conjure a Möbius door, and drag the long box through after him to the coordinates of the old house of his childhood.

The location he'd chosen seemed a strange thing in itself, because from somewhere in the Necroscope's mind came a repetitive but obviously false memory: a picture of the house on fire, of its seeming destruction in an inferno! And perhaps it was so . . . there was so much confusion in Harry's mind, such a lack of clarity in his thoughts, that he couldn't be certain . . . but in any case the cellar remained intact, and that was where he kept the last few handfuls of Janos Ferenczy's catalyst powders . . .

NOW HARRY LAID his Ma's box over twin trestles and brushed away any last remaining traces of dust and dirt, and wondered at the durability of the good oak. Despite that the coffin's nails had rusted, the grain of the wood was still very fresh; the marvelous pattern had lost its polish but very little of its natural beauty, and the wood as a whole was showing only a few signs of rottenness, and only then in the more susceptible joints of its paneling.

As for the lid: that came away quite easily when Harry cut through the rusted nails with a sharp chisel and prised the box open. But for all that he had seen in his weird life—for all that he was the Necroscope to whom death and the ravages of the grave were commonplace things—still he couldn't bear to look upon his own mother, not while she was like that.

And so with the coffin lid askew, averting his face, Harry poured all that was left of Janos Ferenczy's chemical catalysts into his Ma's box and, praying it was sufficient, stood back for a moment to recover from a sudden dizzy spell—

—Or was it?

A whirring in his brain—or the whirring of mental wings as the teeming dead tried to enter his shielded mind? What? The Great Majority all astir? But why were they so frantic? And why try to engage him now, when it must be obvious that he was occupied as never before?

Harry steadied himself, reinforced his shields, sensed the mental scrabbling fade away, and for the last time gave thought to what he was about to do. But no; if he considered it for too long he might decide against it; he couldn't delay now for fear of never again finding the courage. And as for his Ma: what had she to lose? On the contrary, she had everything to gain—life itself.

Throwing caution to the wind, he pointed at the coffin and uttered the rune of resurrection:

"Y'AI 'NG'NGAH, YOG-SOTHOTH,
H'EE-L'GEB, F'AI THRODOG,
UAAH!"

Then, thrust back immediately as by some howling wind (one sensed but neither heard nor felt in any sort of injurious way, except as a force of utterly alien expansion), Harry came to an abrupt, jarring halt backed up against the nitre-spotted cellar wall. And from there, with his mouth agape, he watched his Ma's coffin shrivel down into itself until it imploded in a seething cloud of purple smoke and chemical stench.

In a moment the center of the room—containing the trestles, casket and all—was lost in that mushrooming nebulosity of fusing *materia* and necromantic chemicals, but Harry had seen as much before and believed he knew what was coming next.

At least, he *believed* he knew.

That massive volume of smoke pouring outward from such a relatively small source; the acrid stench that stung his eyes, causing him to blink away the tears; and that sudden movement, the formation of a vague outline within the cloud. All of this was as it should be. All of *this*—

But not the high-pitched screeching!

At first Harry didn't know what to make of it. Was it perhaps the residual keening of that initially silent vortex which had thrust him against the wall? Or maybe the disintegration of old oak whose outer appearance had belied the fact of its inner rottenness? Or, as a last resort, evidence of an alchemical interaction between physical and metaphysical spheres? Or—

Or wasn't it so much a screeching sound . . . as a screaming sound?

Screaming? But never a voice. Never his Ma's voice. Surely not sounding like this: like the vastly amplified creaking of a great door, or the squeal of tight floorboards under foot, or a splintering of green wood bent across one's knee, or a chalk on a blackboard, or a shovel in the cold ashes of a fireplace. All of these things, but all in one.

The purple smoke was clearing faster now, and that unknown sound slackening off, becoming an exhausted gasping; a definite voice, yes, but utterly alien or, if not of this Earth, at best non-human or -animal.

But if not entirely animal, then what?

The smoke dispersed in rapidly diminishing tendrils, as if siphoned off into some other place, some other time. And in its place the Necroscope saw what he had achieved. For several long moments he couldn't believe it; his eyes refused to accept what they were seeing. But then the thing moved—or tried to move.

It was a tree, part of a tree, something of a tree. But it was also Harry's

Ma, part of her, something of her. And he knew why. Like a deafening clap of thunder—like a lightning bolt, crashing down upon him, upon his consciousness—he knew why.

On every previous occasion when he had used the Ferenczy's necromantic art, he'd called his subjects up from dead, inanimate sources, notably out of ancient lekythoi or from a concrete floor, where their long dead *materia* had been separate from any organic or formerly living creature or thing. On every *previous* occasion, yes . . . but not this time.

This time his subject had been one with an oaken box—her casket—and the casket too was once alive. *As it was now!*

The thing could only be likened to a tottering, lightning-blasted oak, a half or quarter tree with withered roots sprawling across the floor . . . but some of those roots had toes! The bark of its bole was peeling in places, and from one such place a wriggling human upper arm protruded to the knobbed elbow. And at a height of some five feet from the floor, there embedded in the bark, a human face—the face of Harry's Ma—but staring out with an expression of such horror and agony that it set her son swaying from side to side, immobilized at the sight of this atrocity.

Its "trunk" was entirely grotesque: seven or eight feet of gnarled, shattered oak on the one side, and on the other—separate except for where human flesh met with lumber at the thigh—a woman's leg, its free foot stepping blindly here and there, going nowhere, unable to pull away from its vegetable bondage.

With his tongue glued to the roof of his mouth—almost as incapable of thought as he was of action—Harry felt as rooted to the spot as the thing he'd called up to this mockery of life. But only for a while, until that screeching of commingled human and vegetable voice came again, matching its single discernible word or *sound* to that shape formed by his mother's oak-bordered face and mouth:

"Haaaaaa-rrrrrrrr-*yyyyyyyyyy!*" A cry of pain, horror, accusation and outrage—but mainly of horror.

At which the Necroscope regained his senses, somehow summoned up enough spittle to moisten his parched mouth and throat, pointed his trembling hand and called out the runes of devolution:

"OGTHROD AI'F, GEB'L-EE'H,
YOG-SOTHOTH, 'NGAH'NG AI'Y,
ZHRO!"

Harry's Ma's relief was obvious. Her eyes rolled up in her trapped face as she sighed her last, and in the next moment the cellar filled with stench and rushing smoke as the hybrid thing disintegrated in a cloud of gray-green chemicals, obscuring the Necroscope's view.

Then everything turned to darkness . . .

. . . AND THEN TO LIGHT, or at least starlight. But this time when Harry woke up it was real—no longer a dream within a dream of events that had never happened—yet still in an alien, nightmarish world of sorts. Indeed of the very worst sort. A vampire world on the other side of creation.

At first he didn't understand; he thought he was still in the cellar of his old house; he babbled prayers of forgiveness and brokenhearted apologies to the heaped chemical *materia* of his poor devolved Ma and her oaken casket. And finally, uttering a last desperate cry, he started yet more surely awake . . . to find himself cradled in the Lady Karen's arms on Starside!

And as he gasped and fought against her, she said, "Harry, oh, Harry! It's a dream, that's all. A nightmare."

"What?" he panted. "What? A . . . a nightmare?"

"Just an evil dream," she insisted. And then, holding him still: "Strange, isn't it, that such as we still suffer them?"

He sucked gratefully at the night air, gazed on the floating ice-chip stars burning blue over barren boulder plains, and knew that it was so. Just a dream, a nightmare. And in a little while—after gathering his wits and wiping the cold sweat from his brow, and gulping to make sure he could speak—he was able to answer Karen's question:

"Not so strange really. Our dreams are governed by what we were, by the fears we knew, and not by what we've become."

Beautiful, deadly Lady of the Wamphyri that she was, Karen touched

Harry's face and smiled a sad smile. "You are right, of course," she said. "But what we were is over and done with, and how we are become . . . is our lot." And then she shrugged. "Anyway, there are far worse nightmares still to come. And they are on their way. I sense them even now—their flyers and warrior creatures, crossing Starside from the Icelands."

But Harry shook his head. "My dream was worse."

Now she laughed, albeit humorlessly. "No, I can't believe that, Harry Hell-lander."

"Believe it," he told her, shuddering inside.

And there and then the Necroscope made himself a vow: that come what may and however the future turned out, he would nevermore play the necromancer. Necroscope, yes. Necromancer, never!

Alas, but while he couldn't know it, that vow was entirely unnecessary . . .